RICHARD KURTI

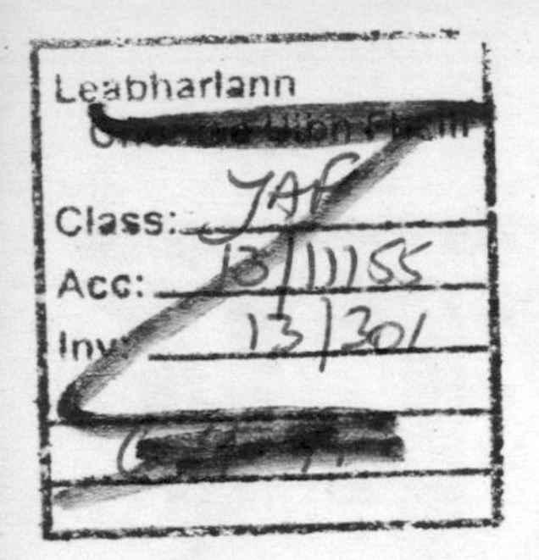

This is a work of fiction. Names, characters, places and incidents are either the product of the author's imagination or, if real, used fictitiously. All statements, activities, stunts, descriptions, information and material of any other kind contained herein are included for entertainment purposes only and should not be relied on for accuracy or replicated as they may result in injury.

First published 2013 by Walker Books Ltd
87 Vauxhall Walk, London SE11 5HJ

2 4 6 8 10 9 7 5 3 1

This book has been typeset in Cambria

Printed and bound in Great Britain by Clays Ltd, St Ives plc

British Library Cataloguing in Publication Data:
a catalogue record for this book is
available from the British Library

ISBN 978-1-4063-4610-7

www.walker.co.uk
www.monkeywars.co.uk

To
K and H
with love

In memory of
A and J

PART ONE

THE OTHERS

The people to fear are not the Strong,
but the Weak. It's the Weak who'll buckle
when you're least expecting it, the Weak
who'll betray you without warning, the Weak
who will stop at nothing to save themselves.

MARK SACKS, PHILOSOPHER

BASED ON A TRUE STORY

NEW DELHI TIMES, 21 OCTOBER, 2007

WILD MONKEY ATTACK KILLS MAN

Delhi's citizens are becoming increasingly alarmed by the hordes of wild street monkeys who roam public buildings, temples and street markets, assaulting and stealing at will.

In a sinister development, the Deputy Mayor of Delhi, S. S. Bajwa, died this morning after being attacked by a gang of Rhesus Macaques.

According to eye witnesses, Bajwa was reading a newspaper on the terrace of his house when he was surrounded by the Rhesus monkeys. As he struggled to fight them off, Bajwa fell from the balcony, sustaining multiple injuries.

Despite being rushed to hospital, the Deputy Mayor died this morning from severe internal bleeding.

City authorities are now coming under renewed pressure to find a solution to the monkey scourge, but are unable to take direct action because devout Hindus believe that all monkeys are manifestations of the Monkey-God, Hanuman.

In recent months the authorities have tried using Langurs, a larger and fiercer breed of monkey, to scare away the Rhesus, but the attacks show no signs of abating.

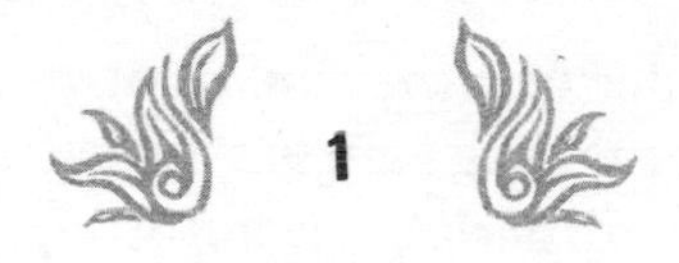

1

SURVIVE

They struck at noon.

Monkeys shrieked in confusion as Langur fighters sprung down from the Cemetery walls, howling in an attacking frenzy. As they stormed through the tombs, fear and panic flashed everywhere. And with the screams came the smell of blood.

It was so terrifyingly fast Papina barely had time to think.

One moment she was relaxing in the sun-dappled tranquillity, the next her mother was scooping her up and leaping into the banyan trees, abandoning everything in a frantic scramble for survival.

Swooping through the canopy, clinging to her mother, Papina glanced down and saw an unstoppable wave of Langur monkeys thundering through the Cemetery. They pounced on their Rhesus victims with howls of bloodlust and dragged them into the shadows to finish them off, Langur claws savaging Rhesus flesh.

Papina closed her eyes, desperate to shut out the horror, and suddenly her mind jerked to save the one thing she could still understand—

"My carving!"

"WHAT?!" Willow screamed, incredulous.

"I have to get it!" Papina shouted, as if somehow clutching it would make everything all right.

"NO!"

"PLEASE!"

Suddenly the branches in front of them snapped apart as two forbidding Langurs lunged towards them.

Willow let go of the branch and dropped – two breaths in free fall – then reached out, grabbed a vine and swung.

With claws scratching across stone, Papina and Willow grasped for the perimeter wall and dropped down on the far side, outside the Cemetery for the first time in their lives.

All they could do now was run.

Chaat had been out scavenging, and had no idea anything was wrong as he casually made his way back through the streets carrying some pilfered pomegranates ... when suddenly he stumbled on a group of trembling monkeys huddled in the shadows. They looked so distraught Chaat assumed they were just Slum-Monkeys. Then Willow called his name and he realized with a shock they were his own family.

The words tumbled out of Willow's mouth – "ambush ... blood ... slaughter ... attacked by Langurs".

But it didn't make sense to Chaat – everyone knew the Rhesus lived in the derelict Cemetery; they'd *always* lived there, ever since the Humans had abandoned it generations ago.

He tore open a pomegranate, squeezed some white pith onto his fingers and rubbed it on his forehead, making the Universal Sign of Peace. But as he turned to run back to the Cemetery, Willow grabbed his arm.

"No!"

"I have to."

"You mustn't go back!"

"They can't just drive us out of our home!"

Then he felt another pair of hands clamp around his leg – it was Papina, emphatically refusing to let him leave.

Softening his tone, Chaat put his arm around his daughter. "Don't worry. Before you know it, we'll all be safe at home again." He lifted Papina's head to look into her frightened eyes. "Tell you what, while I'm there, I'll even check your carving is in its usual place, make sure it's safe. How's that?"

Papina gave a mute nod. Chaat hugged her one last time then turned and scampered away over the rooftops, determined to set everything right.

Now Papina sat silently on top of the Public Library, her heart slowly breaking. Why had they been attacked with such hatred? she wondered. Just because they looked different? Because they had brown fur, not grey, and pink faces not black? But Rhesus or Langur, they were all monkeys and they all needed somewhere to live.

Papina looked from the distant Cemetery to the handful of shattered survivors huddled further along the roof, her young mind struggling to make sense of what had just happened.

Underneath all her confusion lay the darkest fear of all – even though they had waited the whole afternoon, still her father hadn't returned. As the sun sank towards the horizon, Papina was gripped by the dreadful foreboding that she would never see him again. It felt as if a hole was opening up inside her, a yawning emptiness that nothing would ever be able to fill.

"We have to go." The voice cut hard across her grief.

Papina looked up and saw her mother beckoning.

"No."

Willow scrambled over the roof tiles and grabbed her hand. "Move. Now!"

Papina pulled back defiantly. "Not without Dad!"

"We have to get away before the Langur hunt us down."

Papina didn't want to hear it; she clamped her hands over her ears.

"Listen to me!" urged Willow. "We have to survive. It's what Chaat wanted."

With that she took hold of Papina, dragged her across the roof and bundled her down the stepped walls.

Furtively, fearfully, the Rhesus survivors made their way into the Kolkata streets.

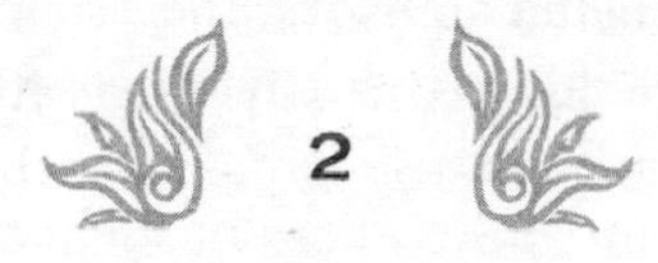

2

SHADOWS

For Mico it was like entering Paradise – one moment he was clinging to his mother, surrounded by all the frantic noise of the City, the next he was in the cool, green tranquillity of the Cemetery. Whatever the Humans had meant this strange place to be, for monkeys it was perfect. High walls kept out the chaos of the City, there were row upon row of small stone buildings to scramble over, and a thick canopy of banyan trees was just begging to be explored.

Dropping down from his mother's back, Mico scampered excitedly up the Central Pathway, following the rest of the Langur Troop as they processed in.

"Mico, wait!" Kima called after him, but it was too late.

Hopping onto a fallen tombstone, he reached up, grabbed a low hanging branch, swung himself round the corner ... and skidded to an astonished stop.

Towering in front of him was an imposing mausoleum. The walls were lined with carved pillars, and each corner of the long, rectangular building was adorned with a magnificent stone tiger. On the roof of this Great Vault, all the Langur leaders were lined up.

In the centre stood the Lord Ruler Gospodar, large and handsome with a coat of pure grey and a striking flash of white fur crowning the top of his head. Crouched next to him were his trusted advisors, the Troop Deputies; and ranged on either side of them in two long, brooding lines, were Gospodar's Elites.

Mico gazed up at the Elites in silent awe; he'd never seen the fighting monkeys all gathered together like this. Powerfully built, with long limbs and even longer tails, many of them had tramlines in their grey fur, the marks of battle, which they wore with pride. But to Mico's young eyes, the scarred faces and ragged ears made the Elites look grotesque.

Instinctively he edged backwards, and suddenly felt a hand grab him.

"How many times do I have to tell you about running off?" said Kima as she slung him onto her back, and for once, Mico was grateful to have been caught by his mother.

By now the last of the Troop had arrived, and spontaneously the monkeys started expressing their elation by thumping the ground with their fists. It sent a wave of excitement surging across the crowd. A huge smile spread across Lord Gospodar's face as he bathed in the euphoria, until finally he raised his arms to speak.

"My fellow monkeys, this is a day when right conquers wrong!" he boomed. "A day when courage is rewarded!"

A huge cheer went up from the monkeys.

"As we admire our magnificent new home," Gospodar opened his arms, embracing the Cemetery, "there should be one thought in our minds: WE DESERVE THIS!"

The howls of approval were deafening. Enthralled by the sheer energy of the spectacle, Mico started to laugh. As he gazed up at Lord Gospodar standing on the mausoleum, so full of conviction, suddenly he understood why everyone loved the Leader, why they trusted him.

Encouraged by the adulation, Gospodar started to reminisce. "Those of us who are older will remember it was just three Monsoons ago that we were Slum-Monkeys, scavenging around in the filth of the City. I spent my youth not playing or laughing, but trying to fight off the pangs of hunger..."

With dismay, Mico realized that the speech was going to go on and on. "Can we go now?" he whispered in his mother's ear.

"Shhh!"

Which left a simple choice: boredom or escape.

Mico's eyes gazed up at the tangled tree canopy – so many tempting runs to be tried out; he looked across at the maze of strangely shaped miniature buildings surrounding them, and made up his mind.

Gently letting go of Kima's ears, he slid down her back and edged his way through the mass of monkeys until he stood at the very edge of the crowd. He surveyed the network of shady paths leading off into the Cemetery, gave a final backward glance to check he wasn't being watched, then slipped away.

Other young monkeys would have found the damp, decaying structures in the Cemetery unnerving, but to Mico they were fascinating.

He wondered why there were strange markings on all the stones, why the Humans had made buildings that were too small for them to live in, and why the whole place had been abandoned. For Mico there were always questions to be asked. Intrigued, he scrambled up the side of a miniature pyramid, launched himself onto a dome, dropped down between some stone columns—

And instantly froze.

Up ahead something was moving in the shadows. Quickly Mico darted behind a tombstone, then very cautiously peeped out. At the end of the pathway he could see a group of Langur Footsoldiers working in the shadows. They seemed to be dragging something through the dirt.

Suddenly a gruff voice boomed angrily at them, "Kill like the thunder; clean like the rain!"

The Footsoldiers snapped to attention as General Pogo emerged from the shadows. "*Monsoon rain*. Not a spring shower," he said, glaring darkly at them.

"Understood, sir. Won't happen again."

They had good reason to be nervous. Pogo was a warrior with a fearsome reputation, backed up with an admirable scar that slashed across his face, right over the empty socket that had once contained an eyeball.

"Next time I say clean everything up, I mean *everything*," he said, rolling his eye sternly from one soldier to the next. "We have rules for a reason."

"We think he may have come back, sir."

"Come back?" Pogo seemed puzzled.

"We caught him hiding, sir."

"More fool him." The General's solitary eye rolled down in its socket, scrutinizing the lump on the ground. "Well," he shrugged, "better get rid of it before it starts to rot."

"Yes, sir."

And with that the General launched himself into the tree canopy and was gone.

Part of Mico wanted to run too, but his feet didn't move. He peered into the gloom and watched as two of the Footsoldiers scrambled up the perimeter wall and perched themselves on top.

"Come on then, let's have it."

The others picked up the lump they'd been dragging and Mico's blood suddenly ran cold as he saw the flailing limbs, the limp tail, the head lolling lifelessly. They were carrying a dead monkey.

Mico dropped onto his haunches, unable to tear his eyes away from the gruesome sight, his stomach knotting. As the soldiers hauled the corpse up the wall, Mico saw that it had suffered horrendous injuries – there was a gaping wound in its chest, one of its ears had been bitten off, the limbs were slashed – blood still dripped from the torn flesh.

Trying to recognize the scent of the victim, Mico drew a deep breath and realized the corpse wasn't a Langur at all. He blinked, looked again – brown fur, short tail ... it was a Rhesus.

Indifferent to the horror, the Footsoldiers on top of the wall started swinging the corpse by its feet.

"And here's what we think of peace," one of the others sneered, and he threw a stone at the corpse, hitting a white pomegranate smear that had been made on its forehead.

The others laughed, then with one great heave tossed the dead monkey over the wall as casually as if they were disposing of an unwanted tree branch.

Suddenly Mico lost all his curiosity.

With pounding heart he darted back across the tombs, swerving past mossy statues and sliding between headstones, until he reached the main path. He scrambled across the cobbles and snuggled into the safety of the crowd, worming his way through a tangle of legs until he found his mother standing near the front, listening with rapt attention to Lord Gospodar.

Mico clambered up onto her back, gripped her fur and tried to blot the ghastly images from his mind. Perhaps if he listened to the speech, joined in with the cheering, everything would be all right.

"... because we, the Langur, are the only Troop that has the courage to fight for peace..." Gospodar was still in full flow, and his grand words were stirring Langur hearts.

All hearts except Mico's. Didn't Gospodar know what was happening just a short swing away?

Then Mico's confusion turned to fear as he saw General Pogo drop down from the tree canopy and silently take his place on the roof of the Great Vault. Lord Gospodar threw a questioning look at the General, who gave a silent, reassuring nod.

They were both in on it.

Which is when the guilt gripped Mico. He had witnessed a disturbing secret, and even though he was clinging to his mother, surrounded by all the members of the Langur Troop, suddenly Mico felt very alone.

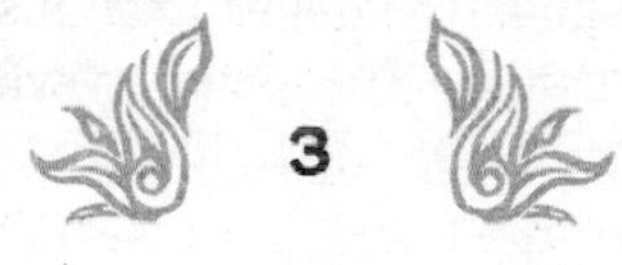

3

LOST

As they staggered, bewildered, through the streets, the Rhesus survivors realized with shame that they were strangers in their own City.

Food gathering had always been the responsibility of the Rhesus males, and as the generations passed, the females had become increasingly detached from the hurly-burly of City life; many of them had never even ventured outside the Cemetery walls. But the males had been the first to die in the slaughter, all their knowledge dying with them, leaving the females to rue their seclusion.

Out here everything was chaos: crumbling buildings jostled for space, piles of rotting garbage lay in the streets as if deposited by some monstrous tidal wave, and the noise was everywhere – hawkers haranguing passers-by, couples arguing in shabby apartments, cars blasting their horns.

The Rhesus wandered, dazed, through street after confusing street, searching for somewhere to shelter, until finally, wretched and exhausted, they arrived at the banks of the Hooghly River.

Papina had never seen such a large body of water. "Look how it ripples!" she exclaimed, mesmerized by the river's dark, quivering energy.

None of the other monkeys shared her fascination.

Cappa, one of the mothers, gave a resigned shrug. "Well, this is the end. It's every monkey for herself now."

"You can't break the Troop up!" said Fig, alarmed. Fig was younger than the others, still with two small infants clinging to her back.

"What Troop?" scoffed Cappa. "We've no leaders, no males. Just infants. We're nothing."

"Then let's choose a new leader," said Rowna, the oldest of the females. Although neither the quickest nor the sharpest, she had a confidence that most of the others responded to.

"Who? *You?*" Cappa rounded on Rowna. "Are *you* going to lead us out of this?"

Rowna hesitated. The responsibility of leadership was beyond her; she knew it and Cappa knew it. That was Cappa's great talent: knowing everyone's weakness.

There was silence – Cappa waited for someone to suggest that *she* should become the new leader; but when Willow finally spoke it was with a different idea altogether.

"Why do we even need a leader?"

Everyone looked at her as if she was mad.

"We're monkeys. And monkey troops have leaders!" snorted Cappa.

"Did our last leader protect us when the Langur rampaged into our homes?" Willow asked. "Maybe we need to find new ways of doing things now."

"With no leader, who would make the decisions?" Rowna persisted.

"We could all make the decisions," ventured Willow.

"All?!" Cappa sneered indignantly, baring her teeth.

"But we all have different ideas!" exclaimed Rowna.

"When we were protected by the Cemetery walls we could afford to have different ideas. Now the only thing that matters is survival." Willow looked at the monkeys as the cold truth of her words struck home. "We have to take responsibility. All of us."

There was silence as the monkeys' minds grappled with the idea.

"So how exactly would it work?" asked Fig.

"We talk problems through. Share ideas. Agree what to do. Consensus. Like the ants."

Cappa snorted. "You really think we can learn from the ants?!"

"Oh how funny!" Fig smiled as she started to understand. "I think I like it."

And once the first monkey had endorsed the idea, some of the others felt bold enough to nod their agreement, until the weight of opinion swung behind Willow.

"So, which way do we turn now?" asked Fig with disarming innocence. "What do we all think?"

The monkeys looked at one another. They looked across the river. And no one said anything.

"And *that* is what happens when monkeys have no leader," pronounced a voice from the shadows. "They starve by the riverbank."

The Rhesus immediately huddled, shielding their young, peering into the darkness to see who had spoken. All of them shared the same terrifying thought: the Langur had returned to finish them off.

Cappa snarled defiantly, "You want to taste your own blood? Step closer!"

"If you insist." The reply came loaded with dark intent, as a patrol of Bonnet Macaques emerged from the shadows.

Papina stared at them wide-eyed. A fluffy mop of hair on top of their heads made it look as if they were wearing caps, and several of them walked on their hind legs, giving them a distinctive, imperious air.

Although she'd never seen one before, Willow knew that the Bonnets were the oldest monkeys in the City, and demanded obedience. Aware that an aggressive response would only get them into more trouble, Willow hurriedly stepped forward. "Our Troop has been attacked. We're looking for a new home."

"So, you're all alone?" the Bonnet leader mused as he strode over to Willow. "No males?"

Papina slid closer to her mother, gripping her hand tightly as the Bonnet paced around them.

"Well, staying here is out of the question, old girl," he finally pronounced. "These are our streets." As much a warning as a statement of fact.

"We meant no harm," Willow said hastily. "Only we don't really know the City at all."

The Bonnet scoffed. "Word of advice: start learning your way around, or you won't last two moons. Every corner of this City is bagged. Every monkey Troop has its own patch. And this is ours."

The Bonnet turned his back on the Rhesus – as far as he was concerned, the matter was closed – but Willow scampered around to block his path. "There must be room for us somewhere?" she pleaded.

"Still here?" The Bonnet's patience was wearing thin.

"Please. We have infants. They're hungry and cold. They can't walk much further. Please."

The Bonnet cast his arrogant gaze over the fidgeting young Rhesus. "I believe there's still some room in the Slums," he said loftily, evoking wry chuckles from his comrades.

"We're not Slum-Monkeys!" protested Rowna.

The Bonnet turned and glared down his snout at her. "It looks to me as if you don't have a choice."

"But that's not fair," said Willow. "You're monkeys just like us and—"

"Fair?!" Aggression flared across the Bonnet's face. "Did you care about fairness when you were lording it inside the Cemetery walls? Did you ever think about what it was like outside?! We won these streets, over many moons. We fought for them. We earned them. If you were careless enough to lose your home—" he shrugged indifferently—"that's no concern of mine."

"So you're just going to abandon us?" Willow retorted.

The Bonnet paused, exchanged a dark glance with the patrol, then pointed at Fig. "We'll take her ... and her." He had picked out the youngest, most comely females.

A malevolent smirk spread across the faces of the Bonnet patrol. Papina glimpsed it, but didn't know what it meant.

Willow drew her monkeys into a huddle and whispered urgently. "It smells of danger."

"But maybe it's our best chance," said Fig. "How long will our infants last out here?"

"They have plenty of females," Cappa warned darkly. "You'd never make it back to their Troop."

"If they were going to hurt us, they'd have already done it, wouldn't they?" said Fig.

Willow could see how torn she was. "Look, if you want to go, go. Do what you think is best."

Fig looked at Willow searchingly. "Would *you* go?"

Willow turned and studied the Bonnets – for all their airs and graces, she knew what lurked in their hearts. "No. I wouldn't."

It was enough for Fig. “Then that’s settled,” she said and, turning to the Bonnets, announced with a breezy smile, “Sorry, we’ve had a better offer.”

Her friends stifled a laugh. For a timid monkey, Fig really picked her moments to be cheeky. But none of the Bonnets smiled. They were irritated that these strays showed so little respect.

The leader paced over, stood on his hind legs and looked down at them darkly. “If you’re still here when we come back, we won’t be nearly as civil.” Then he gestured to his patrol and in an instant they were gone.

Papina looked up at her mother, at Fig and the others, and felt a swell of pride. So *that* was how consensus worked.

Then, with a guilty jolt, Papina realized that for the first time that night she’d stopped pining for her father. Maybe the only way to cope with this strange new world was to tackle it head-on.

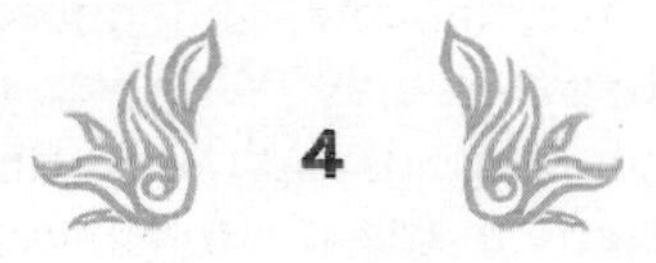

4

CHOSEN

"Mine!" declared Breri.

"Why?" protested Mico.

"Because I'm the eldest."

"What's that got to do with anything?"

Just a short while ago Mico and his brother had been delighted when they'd set eyes on their new home. It was a small mausoleum with matching triangular walls, a flat roof for lounging on and a ledge running all the way round, ideal for ripening fallen fruit. But the moment they dashed inside and saw four large stone blocks arranged in the cool, dark space, the trouble started. Both young monkeys wanted the same tomb for their bed.

Breri bared his teeth. "You want it?" he sneered. "Fight me for it!"

Mico hesitated – he longed to lash out at that smug, domineering face, but he didn't want to deal with the consequences. Breri was a big, muscular Cadet, with a reputation for being able to wrestle three friends at a time; while the one thing everyone knew about Mico was that he was small.

Mico was ashamed of his size. He had always been smaller than other monkeys his age, and his mother continually made excuses for him. "Every monkey grows at their own pace," Kima would say, or "He's been a little ill recently."

But the truth was simple: Mico was small, and in the Langur Troop, physical strength was everything.

"So that's settled then," Breri announced, as he stretched out on the tomb, gloating. "The lesser monkey loses."

Infuriated, Mico leapt at Breri, landed on his back and knocked him to the ground.

"You want some?!" sneered Breri. He swung round, but Mico clung on tightly, staying just out of reach. Relishing the fight, Breri thrust backwards. "Take this!" And he slammed Mico into the wall.

Mico grunted as the air was knocked out of him, but still he held tight, digging his claws into his brother's fur. Breri had no option but to grab Mico's tail and yank it as hard as he could.

Mico screeched, loosened his grip and, before he knew it, Breri had pinned him painfully to the ground.

"Pathetic!" Breri smirked. Then he grabbed Mico and lifted him off the floor, holding him above his head like a trophy.

"I am the master!" he trumpeted.

It was a humiliating end to the fight; Mico tried, unsuccessfully, to wriggle free.

"Say it!" ordered Breri.

"No!"

"I am the master!"

"NO!"

Suddenly another voice boomed across the room.

"*I* am the master!"

Still holding Mico above his head, Breri spun round and saw their father, Trumble, standing at the entrance.

"Put. Him. Down." Trumble spoke with utter self-assurance.

For a moment Breri hesitated. It was a brief flash of rebellion, but Trumble saw it and knew that his eldest son was already starting to break away. Soon Breri would be his own monkey.

But for now Trumble was still the head of this family, and he still had a few tricks up his sleeve. "Put him down before I swap this for a poky little crack in the Cemetery wall. Then there'll be no arguments."

Mico and Breri knew their father well enough to understand that this wasn't a bluff. Reluctantly, Breri dropped Mico to the ground and skulked off.

"Are you hurt?" Trumble asked gently.

Mico shook his head. His father swung over and put his arms around him. Neither said anything; they didn't need to. Trumble had lost count of the number of fights he'd broken up over the years; a vindictive streak ran deep in Breri and there was no doubting the pleasure he derived from bullying Mico.

Just then, from outside, they heard Kima call, "Fresh mangoes! Nice and juicy!" Which made Mico and Trumble feel suddenly hungry.

As the moon rose, bright and clear, Kima chased everyone out so that she could lay some fresh palm leaves on the floor. Breri scampered off to be with his Cadet friends, who were discovering new swings up in the tree canopy. Left on his own, Mico decided to check out the views from the roof.

When he scrambled up the pediment, though, he found his father already sitting there in a pool of cool moonlight, surrounded by carefully arranged piles of stones.

In his youth Trumble had fought in the Elites until a bad injury cut short his career. Desperate to still serve, he had become a quartermaster, responsible for Troop supplies. Trumble's logical mind was well suited to the job, but the key to his success was the Stones.

Over many seasons Trumble had carefully scoured Kolkata's streets and collected a mass of small stones; some contained flashes of colour, others were deep black, while a few were transparent like glass. Having carefully polished them all, Trumble set about devising a complex system of accounting. Some stones represented different types of food, others stood for weapons, that much Mico knew, but the clever part was how these stones were distributed across a set of empty coconut shells. This told Trumble exactly which provisions were running low, what had to be acquired today and what could wait.

Only Trumble fully understood how the system worked, but the whole Troop knew that it *did* work. Shortages were something the Langur didn't have to worry about.

Mico watched Trumble carefully moving the Stones from pile to pile, from coconut to coconut. Not wanting to disturb the air of studied concentration, Mico remained silent, and instead started running his finger along the scar that stretched across his father's back.

Even though it was now an old wound, the fur stubbornly refused to grow back, leaving a bumpy pink ridge that was curiously insensitive to touch. Ever since he could remember, Mico had enjoyed running his finger along the scar, pressing harder and harder until his father noticed with a start.

Tonight, though, Trumble quickly sensed that

something was troubling Mico. He put the Stones down and peered over his shoulder.

"Not playing with the others?"

Mico shrugged. "Did it hurt? When it happened, I mean?" he asked, stroking the scar again.

"Not at the time. It was in the heat of battle. But afterwards, when it was being patched up..." Trumble grimaced, remembering the pain.

"Was there a lot of blood?"

"Oh yes. It was a real mess."

Mico nodded. Now they were getting to the heart of the problem. "So ... when you were in the Elites ... were there things you did that ... did you ever have to... "

"Did I have to kill?"

Mico looked at his father, amazed that he could read his mind.

"Your brother asked the same thing when he was your age." Trumble smiled at Mico's astonishment. "Every young monkey asks – it's natural."

"Well?" persisted Mico.

"The Elites protect the whole Troop," Trumble replied gently. "Sometimes that means doing things that are ... difficult."

"So that's yes?"

Trumble nodded – Mico might be small but he was sharp. "Does it worry you?"

Mico hesitated; he remembered the mutilated, lifeless monkey being dragged up the wall, the gaping wounds, the lolling head, the fur matted with blood. "Was your fighting ... brave?"

"It was dangerous, if that's what you mean."

But that wasn't what Mico meant. "Were you..." he tried again. "Were you heroic? Did it matter *how* you killed?"

Trumble felt out of his depth. He'd never been questioned so closely about this. The Langur were a fighting Troop; it was what they did.

"What's upsetting you?" he asked.

Mico hesitated. He couldn't tell the truth without revealing the terrible secret he had witnessed. "I think I'd be frightened," he said finally.

"That's what training is for. It teaches you to put your fears aside."

"But when monkeys get horribly wounded or killed… How can that ever be right?"

Trumble sighed. "It all comes down to trust. We don't have to question everything, because we trust Lord Gospodar."

"But asking questions is…" Mico frowned. "It's what monkeys do. Monkeys question."

"The Langur Troop aren't like other monkeys. We were chosen," Trumble replied solemnly. "Chosen to fight for peace. The Langur keep the streets safe from the hordes of wild monkeys out there. If we questioned every decision Lord Gospodar made—" Trumble broke off to look around the Cemetery—"we wouldn't have all this."

Mico looked up at the trees, where swarms of midges were darting back and forth in a frenzied dance. The Cemetery certainly was a perfect place to live, but still, no matter how hard he tried, Mico couldn't shake off the memory of the monkey corpse.

Sensing his son's doubts, Trumble put a firm hand on Mico's shoulders. "The City needs us. And it needs us to be strong."

5

SNAKE

Papina lay trembling in the cold dawn light. It wasn't the damp that made her shiver; it was the fear.

She had urged her mother not to rest here, but everyone was so exhausted they were beyond reason. All night they had been roaming the streets searching for a place to sleep, and all night they had been chased away. Rival monkey Troops, packs of street dogs and scurrying rat colonies had all spurned them; once they had even been hustled along by a family of wild pigs.

So Willow, Cappa, Fig and Rowna had led Papina and the others, zigzagging across the City until they were too exhausted to carry on. They had stopped here, in a sprawling garbage dump on the edge of the Slums, and when they found to their relief that no one had pounced to move them along, they all slept.

All except Papina.

She had a dreadful sense that there was a compelling reason why no one else wanted this spot, and she lay awake the rest of the night trying to work out what it was.

They were in a small hollow in the middle of the dump where three open sewers met, so the smell was appalling. But out here in the City there were all manner of offensive smells; that alone would not stop animals moving in.

Papina gazed at the multi-coloured piles of garbage that formed a rolling mountain range – it might not be pretty, but it offered rich pickings. Rats should have been thriving here – they had no scruples about where they lived – but even they had abandoned this place.

Then a murmur.

Papina sat bolt upright. She held her breath, muscles tensed, then glimpsed movement out of the corner of her eye. She spun round – a solitary tin can rolled lazily down a garbage hill.

Everything was still again, but Papina knew in her bones that something was very wrong.

She stood on her hind legs, ears straining to unravel the medley of sounds bobbing in the air: the bark of dogs marauding for their breakfast, the wail of Slum babies, the bubbling gurgle of the sewers. The sinister rustle of something sliding through the trash.

Papina's heart raced as she craned her head, tracking the sound. Another tin can tumbled down a slope, this time triggering a mini-avalanche of ripped packaging. As she gazed across the winding valleys of debris, Papina had an awful hunch that something was moving underneath the mounds.

She reached a hand out towards her mother, but Willow was so exhausted she just turned over, brushing her daughter away.

Papina was torn – if there was danger out there, it was her duty to raise the alarm; but if it was nothing but the wind and her own fearful imagination, she'd be in big trouble for waking everyone so early.

As silently as she could, Papina picked her way across the dump, following the slow, undulating movement of the trash, through a valley, under a hill.

Suddenly the movement stopped.

Whatever was down there had sensed her presence. Papina peered into the dark cracks between the garbage and saw a strange texture inching its way along.

Snake.

As she staggered backwards, the monster started to surface, effortlessly shrugging off its shroud of trash to reveal a body of enormous proportions, a massive, rippling tube of muscle. The python's head, grotesquely small compared to its body, twisted round to inspect its prey.

Mesmerized, Papina looked at the cold, black eyes that promised nothing but death; she saw the snake's neck muscles flex and knew the strike was only a heartbeat away.

Adrenalin surged through her body. She turned and leapt just as the python's head lunged past her and smashed into the debris like an explosion. Papina dodged in the opposite direction, scarcely able to believe that it had missed its first strike.

"SNAKE!!!" she howled.

The word was like a bolt of lightning flashing through the monkeys' brains, galvanizing their bodies. Rowna led a terrified scramble up some pipes running along a crumbling wall; Fig, hysterical with fear, dragged her sleepy infants towards the pipes, but in their panic one of them tripped and tumbled, screeching down an escarpment of trash.

Fig froze, for a terrible moment torn between saving the youngster in her arms and turning back to save the other.

Cappa saw what was happening and sprang down from the wall yelling, "I've got him!" as she grabbed the baby monkey and hurled it back up to Fig. But the impact of her landing trigged a landslip of trash that made it impossible for Cappa to find a foothold and she was washed away from the wall.

Papina saw the landslip tumbling towards her. Hoping to outrun it, she turned, tried to wade through the trash, but was so blinded by panic she didn't concentrate on her footing, and found herself sinking into the debris.

She opened her mouth to scream for help when suddenly a hand grabbed her arm and hauled her back to the surface.

"It's all right! I've got you!" It was her mother. Paying no heed to her own safety, Willow had bounded across the dump to rescue Papina, her darting eyes picking out firm footings with incredible speed.

"Follow my feet!"

Willow started to charge back towards the wall, when suddenly a mound of trash rose up in front of them as a huge length of python body broke the surface. Papina and Willow spun round to scramble the other way only to see another section of python slither into view – it had encircled them, cutting off their escape route in one calculated sweep.

"The head! Where's its head?!" Willow yelled.

Papina looked left and right but couldn't see it. How could they know which way to run if they didn't know where the head was?

Too late. The loop of the python's body was already tightening on them.

"Do exactly as I do!" shouted Willow, then she ran straight at the loop of muscle surrounding them, reached out and put one hand on the python's hideous body just long enough to use it as a springboard to leap clean over.

Papina gritted her teeth and ran, stretched out her hands, shuddering as she felt the dry, rough skin, then her legs pushed hard and she sprang over the beast.

Just in time – a split second later the python's ugly head drove up from below at the exact spot where they had been standing.

The python hesitated. If it went for another strike too quickly it risked tying itself in a knot. The momentary pause was all Willow and Papina needed to dive across the dump and scramble up the wall to where the other monkeys were waiting.

Willow hugged her daughter tightly as her eyes scanned the faces, checking everyone was safe.

And then she realized. "Where's Cappa?!"

The monkeys spun round and peered down, but all they could see were disjointed bits of the python's body as it slithered, half-submerged, through the garbage. Suddenly with an enormous clatter, a pile of tin cans exploded as a great length of the snake emerged – and trapped in its coils was Cappa.

"He–help ... meeee..."

She was already gasping for breath as the snake tightened its relentless grip.

The monkeys on the wall started shrieking, hysterical with fear, as with majestic elegance the snake's head emerged from the trash and inspected Cappa with a cold gaze.

Irritated by the noise of the spectators, it turned its black eyes on the howling monkeys, who immediately fell silent. The python's head rocked from side to side, taking its time, enjoying its total power.

The monkeys could only look on helplessly as Cappa wrestled with death – but the more she struggled, the more she gasped, and each time she exhaled the python tightened its grip around her body. Terror engulfed her as she looked into its eyes, knowing that death was imminent and inevitable.

Cappa's last utterance was not a word, but a dreadful howl that cut through the morning air.

Then a strange creaking sound echoed across the dump – the snake distended its mouth, the skin stretching to disgusting proportions as it dislocated its jaw and engulfed Cappa's head.

"NO!" Willow screamed, as horror flared into fury. She picked up a rock and hurled it at the python.

"NO!!!"

Her defiance ignited Rowna, who took up the angry protest, throwing anything that came to hand.

"NO! NO! NO!!!"

Stunned by the fight-back, the python stopped swallowing and stared at the monkeys, Cappa's legs still protruding from its mouth in a grotesquely comic fashion. For a few moments the Rhesus believed that somehow they could defeat this gargantuan snake.

As the python hesitated, it loosened its vice-like grip on Cappa. She was able to draw in just enough air to keep her alive a little longer, and her legs started writhing in a desperate attempt to escape. The snake leaned towards the wall, almost gloating, then with a final suck of its muscles drew the remainder of the monkey into its gullet.

Willow and the others staggered back, dropping their missiles, stunned and appalled by the thought that Cappa may still be alive inside the snake.

The python swayed left then right, then slipped its huge, dark body back under the piles of trash.

The monkeys crouched in shocked silence on top of the narrow wall; Papina clung to her mother; Fig whimpered, trying to console her young. None of them dared move.

And then a voice called out, "Well, there's nothing you can do for her now."

The monkeys huddled together. Only Willow and Papina had the courage to peer down to see who had spoken, as a male Rhesus monkey clambered out of a hidden niche in the brickwork below them.

"It's all right. I won't harm you." His voice was sympathetic, gentle. He scrambled up the pipes and perched next to them. Willow and the others edged away, but he extended his hands in a gesture of friendship.

"Perhaps it's best you follow me."

The monkeys looked at him suspiciously. As he smiled, the stranger twitched his ears – a quirky mannerism that gave him an endearing appeal.

"Let's face it," he said, looking down at the mountains of trash that now hid the python, "I can't be any worse than him, can I?"

6

TRIBUTE

Mico woke early, his nostrils twitching. The sweet smell of mangoes and banyan leaf had bowled into the room in the night, and he lay there for a few moments savouring the damp scents. It was all so different to life outside the Cemetery; there you awoke to a cacophony of smells all wrestling with one another – drains and cooking and people and smoke and the pungent oil of engines.

He swung down from his stone perch – none of his family were stirring, but it was out of the question that he should go back to sleep on such a beautiful morning, so he scampered out of the doorway and climbed up onto the roof to discover that the whole Troop seemed to have been lulled into a deep slumber.

The solitude was so enticing; it was as if Mico was the only monkey in the world and laid out all around him was his own personal playground. He just had to explore.

He clambered and swung his way from tomb to tomb, examining everything closely, studying the strange engravings. On some tombs he found pictures, a pointed star or a cross; on others there were solid shapes – a marble peacock, frozen mid-strut, an upturned stone hat that collected rainwater and now served as a bird bath.

But most common of all were the marble depictions of Human babies with wings on their backs that seemed to smile down at him from all directions. Mico wondered why he had never seen these flying babies darting around the skies above the City; they looked so mischievous and full of energy he couldn't imagine why they kept themselves hidden.

And it was just as he was running his fingers over the delicate features of one of these cherubs that he heard the footsteps.

Swiftly he scurried inside a hollow tomb and peered out through the ventilation holes, just as some Elites appeared. Mico held his breath, fearful that the soldiers were on another brutal mission.

Two columns of soldiers marched on either side of the Central Pathway, and between them strode the leaders of the Langur Troop – General Pogo, Deputies Tyrell and Hani, and, most important of all, Lord Gospodar.

They processed with great solemnity towards the huge Cemetery gates, but something about the way the Elites' eyes constantly scanned the shadows gave the whole thing a clandestine air. Mico felt certain that if they knew he was watching he would be in big trouble, but now it was too risky to make a dash for home; he'd never make it without being spotted. So instead he made himself as comfortable as he could and watched in silence.

The Elites formed a ceremonial line on either side of the path as General Pogo slid the heavy bolt back and swung the gates open, then Lord Gospodar strode out of the Cemetery followed at a respectful distance by Tyrell and Hani.

The Lord Ruler paused and gazed out proudly across the City. He had led his monkeys out of the desperate scramble for survival on Kolkata's streets below up to this, the fortress of their Cemetery. How many monkeys could look back on their lives and say they had made such a difference? Gospodar knew in his heart that he had done well.

And then, irritatingly, Tyrell stepped forward and punctured the moment. "Sometimes I worry that the Humans take us for granted."

Gospodar sighed. Tyrell was small for a Langur, but he had a sharp, agile mind that never missed a trick, and this, rather than martial prowess, had won him influence. His habit of over-analysing could be annoying, but Tyrell was a vital part of the Langur success story, so Gospodar was patient and smiled indulgently.

"Your worrying is what makes you a good Deputy, but it's turning your fur white."

Tyrell was not going to let the point drop. "We must remember—" he peered down the dusty road—"the Humans will betray us in the end."

"Why the bleak mood?" asked Gospodar. "It's a beautiful morning. We have a wonderful new home. Can't you just relax?"

Tyrell smiled politely. "I feel most relaxed, my Lord, but the pleasantness of the morning cannot change the fact that everyone betrays you in the end."

"Not the Humans," smiled Gospodar, and as if timed to perfection, a group of people appeared at the bottom of the hill. "As you can see for yourself."

All eyes focussed on the colourful procession of Humans making its way up the street. Two monks dressed in flowing orange robes led a column of women adorned with ceremonial jewellery; on their head, each woman carried a large wooden platter piled high with the most succulent fruits, and accompanying the whole group were two boys who tapped out some enchanting rhythms with finger cymbals.

With every step the procession took towards the Cemetery gates, Gospodar felt his authority grow. He loved to see the rewards for his achievements delivered with such reverence.

From his hiding place, Mico watched, wide-eyed, as the Humans paid tribute to the monkeys. One by one, each placed their platter before Lord Gospodar and bowed respectfully, until a sea of fruit surrounded the monkeys.

The Holy Men paused to chant a prayer, then, as they turned and led the procession back down to the City, the Elites started ferrying the fruit inside the Cemetery walls and back to the Great Vault.

So *that* was the secret of the banquets, thought Mico, astonished. There was a long-standing tradition in the Langur Troop of Fruit Feasts, hosted by the Leadership. Everyone was told that Lord Gospodar and his Deputies spent all night gathering the fruit as a tribute to the rank and file, but now Mico had stumbled on the truth: the fruit was a gift from the Humans. This must be what his father was talking about when he said the Langur were chosen.

But why the deception?

Mico came to his senses. With the sun climbing higher, the heat was starting to build, which meant his family would be waking up soon, and if he wasn't there they'd start asking questions.

The quickest way home was straight down the Central Pathway, but that was the route the soldiers were using, so instead Mico took a path that led the long way round, in the shadow of the Cemetery wall.

Too late did Mico realize that this took him right past the fateful spot where he'd seen the dead monkey being dragged away.

As he drew closer, he looked the other way and tried to just keep running, but his legs had other ideas. Moments later, he found himself standing silently by the wall, staring at the stones.

At one stone in particular...

There at the base of the wall was a single bloody handprint, confronting Mico with the stark question: who was the poor Rhesus that had left this terrible mark?

The question plagued him all through the magnificent Fruit Feast that morning. While the other monkeys laughed and chatted as they stuffed themselves, Mico sat quietly, his mind bombarded with doubts.

He looked over to Gospodar, the General and the Deputies, desperately wanting them to stand up and make a speech explaining that this lavish banquet had all been provided by Humans. But they didn't.

First the dead monkey, now the Feast. How many more secrets were there?

7

TO BE A GOD

The recent horrors had left the Rhesus survivors utterly exhausted. Despite the agreement that there would be no leaders, they all looked to Willow for a decision about whether to go with Twitcher (his distinctive ear movements had apparently earned him the nickname many seasons ago).

Willow agreed to follow him mainly because she liked his easy charm; it soothed her jangled nerves. But, underneath the nonchalance, she sensed Twitcher was razor-sharp – he obviously knew the City streets intimately, and darted through shortcuts with urbane ease.

He also understood that although the monkeys were numb with shock, there was no point dwelling on what had happened; a lot of wailing and hysteria helped no one.

So he led them to a roof that overhung one of the street markets and announced, "Now this little place is *the* business for breakfast on the move." He twitched his ears excitedly. "Anyone care for a bite?"

The Rhesus nodded hungrily.

Twitcher cracked his knuckles. "Excellent."

The market had an array of large canvas sheets strung chaotically across it, offering shade from the burning sun. Underneath, traders were already setting up their stalls, selling everything from sweet pastries to cheap jewellery and gaudy make-up.

Papina leaned over the parapet, watching Twitcher as he navigated his way through the rigging until he emerged by a fruit stall where the owner was busy unloading boxes of apples and bananas from his hand-cart. Audaciously, Twitcher sat himself down on the stall and looked directly at the owner with an unashamedly cute expression.

Papina couldn't believe he was hoping to charm his way to breakfast, but she had underestimated Twitcher.

The owner spun round to dump a box of fruit on the table and suddenly saw the monkey. Impatiently he barked a rebuke but Twitcher stayed put, made his eyes bigger and sadder, and then slowly started to waggle his ears back and forth.

Despite himself, the owner gave a gruff laugh, picked up a bruised apple and tossed it to Twitcher, who caught it and started eating hungrily. This, however, was all cunning misdirection, for the instant the owner's back was turned, Twitcher stole two bananas and quick as a flash hurled them up onto the canvas stretched above the stall. Just as the owner turned back, Twitcher changed his expression again, his big honest eyes earning another affectionate smile.

Getting into the spirit, Papina started to clamber over the roof ledge.

Willow grabbed her. "Stay here!"

"He needs a hand."

"He said to stay here! We don't know how things work yet!"

But Papina disentangled herself from her mother's grip. "I think breakfast is served," she said defiantly, then she swung down the side of the building, made her way across the canvas until she was next to the growing pile of fruit, and began tossing it up to the roof so that the others could eat.

By the time the monkeys had finished, the heat of the day was starting to build. Willow knew they still needed to find shelter, but at least none of them would starve today. She looked over to Twitcher, who was licking a few last bits of mango from his fingers.

"Thank you," she said quietly.

"No worries."

"You're the first good thing that's happened to us," Willow replied, and all the other monkeys murmured their agreement.

Twitcher gave a stoical sigh. "You'd be surprised how many monkeys are in trouble these days."

It was not what Willow wanted to hear and it didn't bode well for their chances, but it prompted Papina to spring over to Twitcher and clasp his hand.

"Could we live with you?" she asked.

"Don't be rude," scolded Willow, but Papina had only articulated what all of them were thinking.

Twitcher looked down at Papina and smiled. "Well, that depends," he said, "on whether you're ready to be Gods."

By mid-morning they had arrived. Twitcher led them along a quiet backstreet which unexpectedly opened up on to a lush, circular park, in the centre of which was the biggest statue Papina had ever seen.

It was a huge figure, as big as a building, and incredibly it had a Human body but the head and tail of a monkey. Its legs and arms had powerful, carved muscles; perched on its head was an ornate crown; and its right arm clutched some kind of golden sceptre.

Even more remarkably, there were hundreds of real monkeys, all of them Rhesus, lounging in the dappled sunlight of the small park. Some had found resting places in the nooks and crannies of the statue itself, others lay stretched out on the grass, while many preferred the shade of the trees. The only Humans Papina could see were two bald monks dressed in orange robes who seemed to be carrying out some kind of strange ritual at the statue's feet.

"Well, what do you think of the big fella?" Twitcher asked casually, fully aware of how overawed they were.

"What is it?" exclaimed Papina.

"It's a Monkey-God – conveniently for us," Twitcher smiled. "Apparently, the Humans know him as Lord Hanuman, but to me he's just a stroke of luck."

"You mean Humans worship monkeys?" asked Willow, struggling to take it all in.

"Took me a while to get used to the idea," Twitcher chuckled, "but looking back, becoming a God was the best thing I ever did."

"That's a statue to *you*?" Rowna didn't even try to conceal her incredulity.

"Well, not just me. All of us monkeys. But it's important to get into the spirit of the thing," he said, leading them into the park. "Now, where do you fancy pitching camp?"

Willow scampered after him. "No! This isn't right—"

"Relax!" Twitcher gave her one of his disarming smiles. "You'll be safe here."

"But we're not Gods! We're just monkeys! They'll find us out!"

"Not necessarily," replied Twitcher. "You see, we know we're not Gods, and the Humans know we're not Gods. But they think he's a God." Twitcher gestured to the statue. "And he looks after *all* monkeys. So if the Humans harm us, the big fella harms them." He looked up at the giant stone Hanuman. "And no one fancies their chances there."

Willow and the others glanced from Twitcher to the giant statue, wondering if this was all some kind of elaborate joke, but there was a multitude of Rhesus monkeys here, and they all seemed happy and relaxed.

Papina put her hand up. "Now we're Gods, do we have to behave ... differently?"

"Well, let's see... Don't harass the Holy Men," Twitcher said, pointing to the monks. "They keep everything clean. Don't screech at night – it upsets the neighbours. Oh, and try to keep your fingers out of your bum. Doesn't look very God-like."

He said it with such aplomb, Fig burst into a fit of the giggles. That started Papina off and soon they were all laughing.

By the time the sun was setting, Willow's Troop had found a nice spot in some shrubs near the foot of the statue. Being so close to Hanuman, it stayed in the shade for most of the day, which explained why the other monkeys hadn't already taken the spot. But Willow and the others felt that the closer to the Monkey-God they were, the safer they'd be.

Having explored Temple Gardens, as they were called, Papina returned carrying an armful of food to share.

"Well?" Rowna looked at her expectantly.

"The monkeys here all seem very friendly," said Papina. "There's plenty of food and plenty of room."

"Seems Twitcher was telling the truth," said Rowna.

Willow nodded sceptically. "Maybe."

But Papina was impatient with her mother. "Of course he was! Why would he lie to us?"

Willow gave a rueful smile – her daughter had a lot to learn.

As the light faded, so did all optimism, and by the time the moon was up, the monkeys' thoughts had turned inwards as they remembered everything they had lost.

Papina huddled closer to her mother to try and find some comfort. "It's going to be all right, isn't it?" she whispered, hoping for reassurance. But none came.

"Why did your father have to go back?" Willow said, her sorrow tinged with bitterness. "He could have been here with us..." Her words tailed off. She was frightened that if she said any more she would break down, so she remained silent and just clung to her daughter.

8

THE CARVING

The mango hit the stone baby on the nose and exploded in an orange stain all over its innocent face.

Breri and his friends howled with delight and slapped one another's hands, then the next monkey picked up a kiwi and took aim. He hurled the fruit and watched with bated breath, but this time it clipped the top of the statue's wing and ricocheted off down one of the paths.

Disappointed "oohing" from the monkeys, then, much to their amusement, Breri shouted, "Fetch, boy!" to Mico, who had to scamper down the path after the fruit, the sound of his brother's mocking laughter in his ears.

How Mico hated all this. Breri and his friends were practising throwing skills they'd been learning in the Cadets, but Mico had been made the "Collector", which meant he had none of the fun of hurling fruit and all the work of scurrying around restocking the ammunition dump.

He found the kiwi, scooped it up and while he was there combed through the long grass looking for any other fruit that could be used. But as he made his way back, he heard his brother shout, "Too slow! Too slow!", urging his friends to take up the chant. Mico braced himself – Breri loved playing rough, and when he and his friends started whipping one another up, trouble was never far behind.

Sure enough, when Mico emerged from the undergrowth he was bombarded.

"No! Leave off!" Mico protested, as the fruit splattered around him, but his indignation just encouraged Breri, who howled with delight.

Fed up with the stupid joke, Mico turned and scampered off just as an orange winged his right ear.

"Come back! We were only messing around!" he heard Breri call after him.

"Find your own fruit!" Mico retorted angrily, and he kept going until he reached the safety of the main Cemetery cross path, where some females were busy sorting and grading a pile of cashew nuts.

Mico stopped by a tree to break off a chunk of bark rich in sticky gum, but just as he started chewing, a stray orange from the throwing game rattled out of the undergrowth and bounced manically down the path. Intrigued, Mico chased after the orange and picked it up; it was heavy with juice, but surprisingly hard. Was this what made it so lively? Mico wondered.

He started experimenting, bouncing the orange, throwing it, rolling it down the sides of sloping tombs to see how far it would travel; he scrambled up the tallest pyramid he could find and unleashed the fruit.

It picked up speed until it was hurtling down the tomb, then as it hit the plinth at the bottom it bounced off, flew through the air and plopped into the dense undergrowth at the base of the Cemetery wall.

"Nice one!" Mico laughed and chased after the orange.

Finding it, though, was not so easy – the tangle of shrubs made it hard to move, forcing Mico to lie on his belly, his hand flailing around. Finally, his fingers brushed against the smooth waxy skin. He plucked the orange to safety and checked there was no damage. Then, just as he was about to slither back out of the shrubs, Mico noticed a neat hollow in the base of the perimeter wall ... something had been placed inside it.

He crawled closer and saw a small bundle, carefully wrapped in bamboo fibre. Someone must have stashed a delicacy here, perhaps a succulent piece of honeycomb. With his stomach rumbling in anticipation, he reached out and took the bundle, but when he unwrapped it, Mico was astonished to find a small carving painted in beautiful colours.

Three monkeys were perched side by side on a branch – the first covered its eyes with its hands, the second covered its ears, and the third clamped its hands over its mouth.

Strange. It had obviously been made by Humans – Mico knew how much they loved their gaudy, intricate objects – but what was it doing here, hidden in the base of the Cemetery wall?

One thing was sure, if it had been stolen from one of the street markets the thief couldn't have been anyone from Mico's Troop, because the carved monkeys weren't Langur – they were Rhesus. Someone had gone to a lot of trouble to make the carving, carefully painting the brown fur, the pink faces, just like...

Mico felt his guts tighten as he remembered. Just like the bleeding, mutilated monkey he'd seen being dragged over the wall yesterday, barely a stone's throw from here. Did the carving have anything to do with that corpse?

A shudder ran down Mico's spine. He knew he was straying into forbidden territory, but his restless mind was urging him to investigate this dark mystery.

Carefully, he wrapped the carving up in the bamboo

fibre and placed it back in the wall, just as he'd found it. Then he clambered out of the shrubs, steeled himself and made his way down the gloomy path that ran along the perimeter wall.

It wasn't long before he found himself standing at the front of the wall gazing at the handprint stamped in blood. Already it was starting to fade; one big rainstorm and it would vanish altogether. Slowly he reached out his hand to the bloody print, as if hoping somehow to unravel its mystery through touch—

"Oi! You!"

Mico spun round to see two burly Elites striding towards him.

"What you doing here?"

"I–I…" Mico stuttered.

"You–you…" the Elites mocked.

"I think someone's been hurt. Look!" And he pointed at the handprint.

The lead Elite bent down to sniff the handprint, and then Mico saw him exchange a fleeting, shifty look with his subordinate. They knew something.

The lead Elite stood up and waved Mico aside dismissively. "There's nothing for you here. Run along."

But Mico wasn't running anywhere. Pandering to their vanity, he looked up at the Elites with awestruck eyes and asked, "Was it one of our enemies?"

A dark smirk flashed between the Elites.

"Did you deal with them?" persisted Mico.

"As it happens, we did," said the lead Elite.

Mico gasped, "What happened?"

And the one thing no Elite could resist was telling a good battle yarn.

"We were so pumped, they never stood a chance,"

the lead Elite began. "A few lucky ones escaped. The rest..." he snapped his fangs, hinting at the brutality of their demise. "So we'd just finished cleaning up, when this Rhesus bolts out of the shadows. Don't know whether we missed him first time, or if he'd come back—"

"Not that it mattered much," smirked the junior Elite.

Even though he felt cold dread rising in his guts, Mico needed to know the truth. "So what did you do?"

"We took him down." The lead Elite pointed to the bloody stone. "Right there."

Said with such malevolence, it jarred Mico's imagination, which started painting the horror in vivid colours – in his mind he saw the Rhesus scrambling through the undergrowth, desperately trying to escape.

"He was fast, but we were faster..."

Mico imagined the Rhesus hurtling down the path, glancing back as the menacing Langurs surged towards him.

"He was going for the wall. No way could we let him escape."

"No way," the other Elite chuckled.

"We circled round and slammed him."

"BOOM!" The junior Elite leapt across the path to demonstrate.

"Heard his bones crunch, we did."

The impression was so vivid, Mico felt himself reeling from the impact.

"Oh, then he started begging for his life."

"Begging!"

Mico shuddered as he pictured the helpless Rhesus surrounded by Langurs, violence burning in their eyes.

"Please! I have a family," the Elites mocked as they recalled their victim's pleas for mercy.

"That's what you think!"

The lead Elite slammed his club down in the dirt next to Mico.

"Right across his legs."

Mico could almost feel the spasm of pain shooting through his body.

"Mind you, he was stubborn."

"Very stubborn. Tried to crawl away." The junior Elite pointed to the wall. "As you can see."

Mico looked at the bloody handprint, heart pounding as he shared the fear of the dying Rhesus.

"That's when I dropped him," the lead Elite boasted. "With a rock."

Mico closed his eyes, feeling the horror as the rock came smashing down.

"Epic kill!" said the lead Elite.

"Epic!" echoed his subordinate.

They both looked at Mico, who was desperately trying to hide his nausea. For one dreadful moment, he thought he had betrayed his doubts.

"You got a problem with that?" the lead Elite said darkly, looming towards Mico.

"Epic," mimicked Mico, snapping to his senses. "Epic."

It was enough to assuage their pride. The lead Elite bent down and patted Mico on the head. "Now run along and eat your fruit. One day, if you grow big enough, you can be just like us."

Mico nodded obediently, then turned and hurried away.

He had his answers all right, but they had only made everything worse.

Now Mico knew for sure that what he'd witnessed was murder. Cold-blooded murder. And somewhere a Rhesus family had been left without a father.

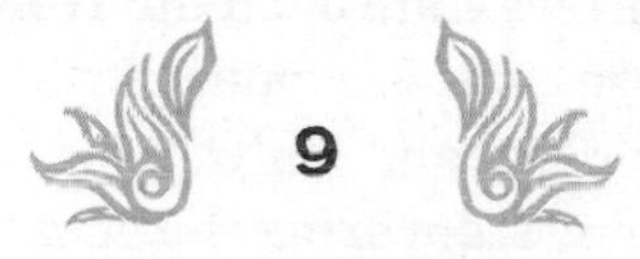

9

THE POOL

Built around a long, formal pool, the Great Vault was the largest and most luxurious mausoleum in the Cemetery. As soon as the sun climbed over the walls and the shadows of the tamarind branches retreated, the waters warmed to the perfect temperature for bathing.

Several seasons had passed since the Langur had occupied the Cemetery, and in that time the Great Vault had become not just Gospodar's personal residence, but also the heart of his Empire. Monkeys came here to receive orders and to volunteer for service; they gathered to celebrate births and to honour retiring soldiers; sometimes they simply came to share gossip. Gospodar had even instructed Trumble to draw up a rota so that twice a moon, every monkey in the Troop could bathe in the soothing waters.

At certain times, however, the pool was set aside for the exclusive use of the Ruling Council. They were meant to discuss "big strategy", but in practice the leaders were quickly seduced by the relaxing waters and wonderful fruits from Gospodar's private store.

The Ruling Council was small but powerful, comprising of Lord Gospodar, the Deputies Tyrell and Hani, General Pogo, plus one ordinary monkey whose job was to voice the concerns of the common Langurs. Between them, these monkeys controlled the Troop.

General Pogo was responsible for the Military (Cadets, Footsoldiers and Elites). Deputy Hani looked after Internal Affairs, ensuring the efficient organization of the Troop's resources and the quick resolution of disputes, while Deputy Tyrell was in charge of External Affairs. It was his job to find out what was going on in the world outside the Cemetery, and he seemed to have eyes and ears everywhere.

Tyrell was good at his job, but there was a personal price to pay. He was not a popular monkey, which explained why he now found himself alone in the shady waters of the pool. While Gospodar, Hani and General Pogo laughed and joked as they were served fruit by two pretty young monkeys, Tyrell sat silent and tense, watching.

There was something disconcerting about the way Tyrell observed his fellow Council members. He looked at them the way the street chess players looked at their pieces, assessing which could be sacrificed and which had to be protected, endlessly running through the permutations of power.

It was an intellectual killer-instinct that Tyrell had honed in his infancy. Because he had been born small, other youngsters spurned him – even his parents were disappointed in him. But scorn was fuel for the young Tyrell, powering a ruthless determination to prove everyone wrong. By skilfully wielding his sharp mind, he had been able to outmanoeuvre rivals, win the trust of those in power and make himself indispensable, until the day came when Gospodar promoted him to Deputy.

It had been a long, tricky climb to get a seat in this pool, and Tyrell was determined to hang on to it.

Summoning one of the young females, he took a papaya from her and waded over to where Gospodar sat bathing in the sunshine.

"Ripened to perfection, my Lord," he said as he offered Gospodar the fruit. The Lord Ruler smiled and started eating.

"Mmmm. As always, your analysis is perfect." Gospodar took a few more mouthfuls then turned his steady eye on Tyrell. "But you didn't just want to talk about fruit, did you?"

Tyrell smiled dutifully. "You know me too well, my Lord."

"So what's worrying you?"

"We've gained so much as a Troop – this fine, walled home, thriving numbers," began Tyrell, frowning. "But only yesterday, I overheard two young monkeys talking as if Langur life had always been like this, as if there was no time before the Cemetery."

Gospodar chewed the papaya pensively. "Good," he said. "What we went through should be forgotten. Today is all that matters."

Tyrell nodded, but his troubled expression belied his real feelings.

Gospodar tried to put him at ease. "Tyrell, just because we suffered doesn't mean the young must have it thrust down their throats. Let the new generation grow up as kings, not Slum-Monkeys made good."

"But, my Lord, if the young aren't reminded of the past, how will they know what you've done for them? Your great achievements in lifting this Troop will be forgotten."

Gospodar's vanity was immediately tweaked. Tyrell knew each monkey's weakness, and for Gospodar it was vanity. He wanted to be remembered after he was gone.

"Discipline, courage and determination have achieved all this," Tyrell declared as he waved his arm expansively around the Great Vault. "And it is *you*, my Lord, who have taught us these virtues."

Gospodar smiled; he never tired of hearing his praises sung. "So what do you suggest?"

"An education programme for the Cadets, my Lord. History must be passed down, lest we forget. Young monkeys must understand *why* we are the Chosen Troop."

Gospodar looked over to General Pogo and Deputy Hani. "What do you two think about an education programme?"

Pogo and Hani's first thought was that they didn't want to get lumbered with the job. More responsibility would steal precious time that could be used for bathing and feasting. But, of course, neither would admit to this.

"It's a good idea," Hani volunteered instead. "If we could find someone to take on the task."

"Not really a military matter, though, is it?" said General Pogo quickly.

Gospodar nodded. No resistance, but not much enthusiasm either, he thought to himself.

"Perhaps some retired Instructor could be persuaded to take on the task," Hani suggested. But Tyrell quickly short-circuited the discussion.

"*I* would be honoured to take on the whole burden, my Lord. The task is too important to be left to any of the lower ranks."

Gospodar looked at Tyrell with genuine concern.

"But you barely get time to rest as it is," he said, putting a solicitous arm on Tyrell's shoulder. "We don't want you collapsing on us."

"I'm happy to work harder, my Lord. The time spent bathing could be reallocated to the task." And to underline the point, Tyrell clambered out of the pool and shook himself dry. "I was never much of a water monkey anyway."

Gospodar could see that Tyrell had already made up his mind.

"Very well. You shall be in charge of this special education programme."

Tyrell bowed his head appreciatively. "I am honoured." And with that he strode away from the pool.

As soon as he was out of sight he stopped and just for a moment hid behind a doorway, straining his ears to listen. He heard Pogo and Hani chuckle, relieved that they had dodged the extra burden.

"He's such an obsessive," he heard Hani mutter. "Work, work, work."

"That's what happens when you're small," quipped General Pogo, and the two shared a laugh.

Tyrell smiled to himself. Comments behind his back had long since failed to upset him. If anything, it was he who should be laughing, because he had realized what the others had failed to grasp, that the monkey who controls the past, controls the future.

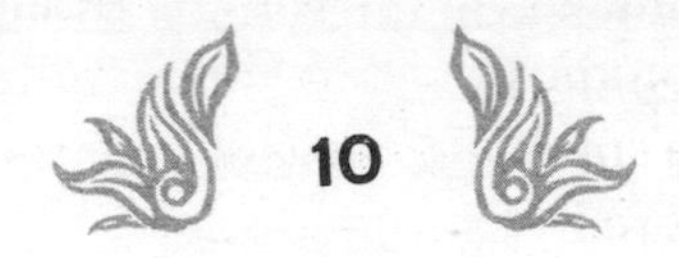

10

MUSCLE

"Forget everything!" Drill Instructor Gu-Nah declared as he inspected the row of new Cadets. "Whatever you've heard about Basic Training, however tough or strong you think you are, forget it!"

Mico glanced along the line of new Cadets. There were big ones from military families who just knew they were going to breeze through training, and aggressive ones with too much attitude and too little brain. Mico, sick with nerves, was convinced he was going to fail miserably because he was so small.

But the Drill Instructor's voice rang out again. "Today, you are all equal. Yes, sir. Equal," Gu-Nah mused. "By the time training is done, some of you will be better warriors than others." He paced along the line of new Cadets. "Some will become Footsoldiers. The really good ones will end up in the Elites. All of you will be more than you are today. Much more. I will make monkeys of you. That's my promise. But you're going to have to work for it. Yes, sir. Day and night. Follow orders, face your fears, graft until you drop. You do that for me and I won't let you down. Every Cadet has a chance to prove himself." His eyes rested on Mico and he lowered his voice as if for that moment Gu-Nah was speaking just to him. "Everyone."

The Instructor stood up and strode back down the line. "What would hurt more? This?" he picked up a melon that was lying on the floor. "Or this?" Gu-Nah opened his palm to reveal a small chickpea. One of the bigger Cadets, Mudpaw, sniggered at the question.

"Easy, eh?" smiled Gu-Nah. Then suddenly he hurled the melon at Mudpaw, who instinctively dodged, letting it splatter against the wall.

"Good reactions," said Gu-Nah, eliciting a proud smile. Then without warning he flicked the chickpea hard at Mudpaw, stinging him painfully in the face.

"OWW!" howled the big Cadet.

Gu-Nah smiled. "Just not good enough."

The Instructor pointed dramatically to the Cemetery gates. "The dangers out there aren't always obvious. The rock python can crush, but the baby cobra can poison. There are many different types of strength. I believe what makes the Langur a great fighting force is not just the size of our muscles, but the fact that every monkey can contribute to the fight. No exceptions."

For Mico, it was an alluring promise; he longed to take his place in Langur life, to understand what it really meant to be one of the "Chosen", and make sense of all the mysteries and deceptions that had worried him these past moons. Above all, he wanted to understand why you needed to kill to keep the peace.

Hoping that all his doubts and questions would finally be resolved, Mico threw himself into Cadet training with a vengeance.

Building stamina and strength were top priorities, so gruelling physical exercises started the moment the Cadets woke up; lifting piles of watermelons, endless swinging through the tree canopy and relentess pull-ups became a way of life. Interspersed with these sessions were exercises in speed and agility, where the Cadets had to scamper around the narrow perimeter wall. At first they moved slowly, fearful of the drop, but day by day, spurred on by Gu-Nah's barrage of instructions, their speed improved.

In the heat of the day the Cadets often ventured out of the Cemetery and clambered into the branches of a large mahogany tree. Here, with a panoramic view across the City, Instructors would teach them about the weather, how to read clouds and predict storms.

Even when darkness came the Cadets couldn't bank on having a quiet night, as Gu-Nah liked to organize "stealth exercises". The Cadets would be sent to the furthest corners of the Cemetery to hunt for objects that had been hidden among the tombs, while being stalked by their Instructors. The idea was to train the Cadets to keep a steady nerve no matter what.

Mico liked the throwing lessons best of all. They learned the art of the long throw – solid stance, arm pulled back, balancing arm out front, lock the target with your eyes, then let the power uncoil. To practise, the Cadets would spend whole afternoons hurling oranges and kiwis against targets that had been daubed on the Cemetery wall.

Mico knew that once he could reliably hit a target, he would finally be able to take on Breri and his friends, which would be deeply satisfying.

In fact, one of the surprises of Cadet training was the way it improved his relationship with his brother. Whereas before Breri had always dismissed Mico, now they could talk about training and tactics, share jokes about the Instructors. Most importantly, Mico could now defend himself. If his brother cuffed him or tried to steal something, Mico would retaliate and Breri relished the tussle that followed.

The more Cadet training progressed and the more they learned about fighting techniques, the more Mico realized that most Langurs were like Breri – they loved to fight, and they lived for the rush of conflict. Aggression fulfilled them.

It was a realization that worried Mico, because there was a part of him that was sickened by violence, horrified at the thought of actually killing another monkey. This wasn't something he could talk about with anyone else, least of all his parents. Now that he was finally getting muscle and starting to prove himself, Trumble and Kima were showing real pride in him. Not wanting to disappoint, Mico kept his anxieties to himself.

As the Monsoon approached, the Cadets were due to start learning advanced hand-to-hand wrestling. But when Mico entered the special training mausoleum one day, he was surprised to see that instead of limbering up, the Cadets were sat in rows ready to listen to a lecture.

"What's going on?" he whispered to Nappo, a wiry Cadet with whom he'd become quite friendly.

"It's jaw-jaw, not war-war today," sighed Nappo, who always found the more theoretical aspects of Cadet training challenging, and he shuffled up to make room. A few moments later, when all the Cadets had arrived, Gu-Nah swung down through a hole in the roof and landed dramatically in front of the class.

"So, what have I been teaching you?" Gu-Nah boomed.

"FIGHTING!" the Cadets shouted back in their well-drilled chant.

"Fighting. Yes, sir. Fighting. But, how do you know what you should be fighting for?"

Silence. This was way beyond anything most Cadets had ever thought about.

"Exactly," said Gu-Nah. "That is a trickier problem. Much trickier. Which is why the Ruling Council has put a new lesson into your training, to be taught by Deputy Tyrell himself."

With perfect timing, Tyrell strode into the room, setting off an excited murmur.

"So pin your ears back," Gu-Nah boomed, "put your tails down and listen up."

The Cadets thumped the ground in appreciation as Tyrell took centre stage. He looked out at the faces of the Cadets, young and open, ready to receive his wisdom.

"Don't worry, this won't be the boring recollections of an old soldier." Tyrell smiled, earning a relieved chuckle from the Cadets. "In fact, it's old soldiers that are part of the problem, with their exaggerated stories of heroic battles," he continued. "Their big talk makes it very hard for a young monkey to know why all this fighting is necessary. So, today I'm going to tell you the truth, pure and simple."

Tyrell paused, cleared his throat, then nodded thoughtfully. "There was a time, many seasons ago, when the streets of this City belonged to Rhesus monkeys. They occupied all the best rooftops and the greenest parks. They were insolent and thieving, but strangely, it was these very qualities that endeared them to the Humans, who fed them, allowed them to breed.

"These were dark times for us Langur. We've always been a proud Troop, unwilling to demean ourselves by sitting on the shoulders of Human children, or performing tricks on a leash. The Langur are fighters, and we needed to be strong just to survive. Because back then we lived a harsh existence in a derelict button factory by the railway shunting yards.

"But our time was coming. As the City grew, the green spaces were swallowed up, and the Rhesus were pushed off their lands. True to form, they turned nasty.

"They started to attack Humans. Marauding bands of Rhesus monkeys would roam the streets, biting and scratching. Some specialized in attacking eating places – they would gather on the rooftops and swoop down on a café, overwhelming the Humans with teeth and claws, defecating on the tables, stealing as much food as they could carry.

"The Humans started to live in fear of the Rhesus. But they couldn't lift a finger to stop them. Why? Because among the many gods the Humans worship is a Monkey-God."

Tyrell could see the surprise on the Cadets' faces. He smiled indulgently. "I know, it seems incredible. To be honest this God is an abomination – half Human, half monkey," he laughed patronizingly. "It's nonsense. But it's nonsense that Humans take very seriously. And because of this Monkey-God, they couldn't strike back at the thugs.

"So the Rhesus grew even bolder, until one day a wild gang of them descended on the home of a Human leader. Hordes of them streamed out of the trees and ransacked his house. Terrified, the man staggered onto his balcony to call for help, but the Rhesus rampaged after him. They started biting, gouging their fingers into his eyes..."

Tyrell paused for dramatic effect as he recalled the horror of the attack. "The poor Human never stood a chance – blinded and mauled, he fell from the balcony ... smashing down onto the street below.

"The Humans wanted revenge, but their Holy Men warned, 'The great Monkey-God will get angry if Humans harm the Rhesus!'

"So they turned to us, the Langur, as there is nothing in their religion that forbids monkey from punishing monkey. The Humans had always ignored us because we were war-like and aggressive, but now those very qualities were what they needed.

"And so one morning the Holy Men arrived with their tribute – plates of the most delicious fruit. And when we'd eaten, they took us to the home of the Human leader. It was overrun by the Rhesus savages. The smell of them was everywhere, their raucous screeches filled the air, their vile little bodies scurried over the house like vermin. The Holy Men led us into the grounds and shut the gates. We were on our own, monkey against monkey. Langur against Rhesus..."

Tyrell paused, savouring the anticipation on the Cadets' faces. "The Battle of the Palace has passed into Troop legend. Each hero has his own story, so you don't need me to add another. But let me just say this: not only were we heavily outnumbered, but we occupied the inferior ground. The Rhesus held the roof; we had to fight from the gardens, which put us at a grave disadvantage. But Lord Gospodar held his nerve, drew on Langur discipline.

"We deployed the Troop's best throwers to the front of the house, from where they mounted a bombardment with rocks. The Rhesus replied with a barrage of objects pilfered from the house, but we held our positions, refusing to retreat.

"With the Rhesus distracted by the missile attack, a squad of Langur volunteers climbed a bank of trees and dropped onto the roof. Arming themselves with makeshift clubs, they started to fight their way down through the house.

"Those heroes had to endure bitter fighting, but for every one of ours that fell, three of theirs were killed. With the Rhesus now fighting on two fronts, Lord Gospodar himself drove the final, decisive move.

"He led the Elites across the gardens, then, pretending to be wounded, we collapsed on the lawns. The Rhesus were in such a murderous frenzy, they stormed out of the house to tear us apart with their teeth.

"Imagine their surprise when we leapt up, clubs in hands, and started lashing out. Skulls were smashed, limbs broken, eyes gouged! The Rhesus tried to retreat, but we had encircled them. While some of the Elites finished them off, the rest of us surged through the open doors and drove our way up through the house.

"By the time the sun set, the grounds were strewn with the bodies of dead monkeys. The Langur had triumphed."

A spontaneous cheer went up from the Cadets, who had clung on to Tyrell's words with rapt attention.

"This was just the beginning!" the Deputy boomed, silencing the Cadets. "Rhesus scum were attacking Humans right across the City, stealing from shops, biting children, terrorizing the elderly in their own homes. The Humans had a whole City to clear, and they looked to us, the Langur, to do it.

"Battle after battle we fought, and gradually the Rhesus savages were driven back. The more they lost, the more violent and desperate they became. In their bloodlust, they even turned to butchering their own kind – time and again we found evidence of cannibalism everywhere we cleared.

"Thanks to the courage of Langur forces, and the wisdom of our Leadership, that first phase of the Rhesus clearance has been completed. They are now contained within strict limits, seeking refuge in a handful of Monkey-God temples, or subsisting in the forgotten Slums. But we must be vigilant or the Rhesus will rise up and terrorize the City again. And that is why *you* are so important." Tyrell gestured expansively to his audience.

"The Langur have been chosen to bring peace to this City. A peace that it is your duty to defend, with your lives if necessary. And I for one can think of no finer cause."

As Tyrell sat down, the Cadets immediately started cheering and thumping the ground in rapturous approval.

Gu-Nah smiled at their enthusiasm, leaned across to Tyrell and shouted above the racket, "Makes you proud to be a Langur, sir!"

Tyrell nodded. "It's important to keep our story alive."

"There were things even I didn't know," laughed Gu-Nah. "And I lived through it."

"In the hurly-burly, you can't always see the bigger picture," Tyrell said with a smile.

He looked across the room and basked in the applause, unquestioning pride written on every face.

Except one.

The smallest Cadet in the room was looking worried. He applauded like the rest, but Tyrell could see confusion in his eyes. What was it that the young monkey had failed to grasp? He waved his arms to restore quiet, then pointed at Mico.

"You seem worried, Cadet." All eyes turned to Mico, who suddenly felt very awkward.

"N–no. Not at all, sir," he stammered.

But Tyrell wasn't going to let it go. "Please, feel free to ask questions. After all, that's what monkeys do." The words were sympathetic, but there was something chilling in his tone.

Mico hesitated, remembering how the Footsoldiers had sneered at peace as they disposed of the dead Rhesus. Sneered at the very thing they were supposed to be protecting.

"Cadet Mico, tell the Deputy what's troubling you," barked Gu-Nah.

So now it was an order, thought Mico, he had to say something. Drawing a deep breath, he looked up at Tyrell. "I was just wondering, sir, if the Rhesus lived here in the Cemetery, before us?"

"They certainly did. We had to fight our way in and drive them out. But what about it?"

Mico hesitated. "It's just that ... there were no signs of cannibalism when we arrived."

Tyrell nodded thoughtfully. "Do you really think we would have let our females and our young witness the true horror of the Rhesus? We took great care to clean up all evidence of their barbarity before we opened the gates."

Mico made a big show of smiling as if his worries had been allayed. But Tyrell looked at him sternly, as if memorizing every hair on his face.

"Satisfied?" asked Tyrell.

"Yes, sir," lied Mico. "Sorry to have—"

"No, no. It was a good question," replied Tyrell with a polite edge that suggested it was anything but a good question.

Gu-Nah quickly stepped in to draw the lesson to a close – he didn't want any more awkward questions being posed on his shift – and as the Cadets filed out of the room, Mico was careful to avoid eye contact with Tyrell.

Had he glanced over, he would have seen Tyrell draw Gu-Nah to one side and quietly ask, "What sort of a Cadet is Mico? Troublesome?"

And if he had heard the dark tone in Tyrell's voice, Mico would have known for sure that he had been marked out as a monkey to be watched.

Later that night Mico lay on the roof of his home, silently running through the events of the day. He was struggling to come to terms with history according to Tyrell. Certainly it was logical and heroic; it made you feel proud.

But was it true?

How could soldiers sworn to preserve peace take such delight in killing?

He sat up, checked that no one was around, then leapt down from the roof and hurried away down the dark paths.

A few moments later he was crouching in the shrubs by the perimeter wall, taking out the small bundle that had been hidden there, unwrapping the carving of the three monkeys in their distinctive poses.

Mico ran his finger gently over the carved figures; they had been looked after with such loving care. Surely this was not how savages and cannibals behaved.

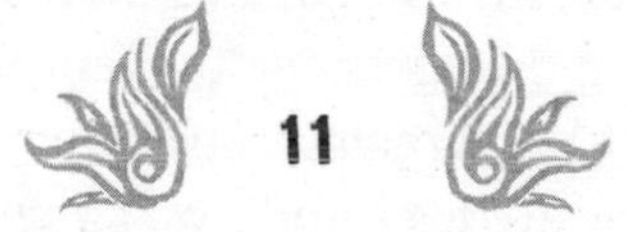

11

UNFINISHED BUSINESS

Temple Gardens proved to be a welcoming home for Papina and the remnants of her troop. The rough encampment they had made at the foot of the Hanuman statue when they first arrived had now grown into an established part of the Gardens. Various new monkeys had joined their group, and while Rowna had become involved with a handsome male monkey called Titan, Fig was being courted by at least a dozen monkeys who she played off against one another with an easy charm and plenty of flirtatious laughter.

Twitcher ran a class every morning to teach the young monkeys about the layout of the City, and this had been a great way for Papina to make new friends, but the main reason she was starting to feel settled was that they were no longer the newest monkeys in the Gardens. In the early days her troop was always the one asking questions and looking lost, whereas now they were regarded as established residents. Newcomers would turn to them for advice about the routines of the Temple, which helped Papina feel as if she belonged somewhere again.

But the influx of new monkeys also meant that she had to face up to the grim realization that a darker story was unfolding across the City.

Twitcher and other volunteers did an amazing job scouring the streets for Rhesus monkeys in need of sanctuary, and guiding them to Temple Gardens, but each new batch of arrivals had harrowing accounts of violent abuse at the hands of Langur troops. They spoke of dawn raids, of males butchered as they slept, of females running for their lives with infants clinging to their backs, of being driven from streets they had inhabited for generations.

What puzzled and frustrated Papina, though, was that no one asked the question, Why? Why was all this happening? Neither did anyone ask what would happen when space at Temple Gardens ran out. It was as if everyone feared the answers, so no one asked the questions.

Although Papina's own grief had dulled into a background ache, every time they sat huddled in a group listening to the latest accounts of Langur attacks, her mind floated back to the last time she saw her father, and the longing to find out what had become of him grew stronger.

She tried to talk to her mother about it, but Willow seemed to have closed that part of her life down. Willow was pragmatic; she knew they had narrowly dodged death on that fateful night; she knew they had been given another chance and she was determined to build a better life here in Temple Gardens. Thinking about the past would only be a torment.

But Papina's young mind didn't understand this. She wanted answers, and if her mother wouldn't help, then she'd find someone who would.

It was halfway through one of the lessons that the idea first occurred to Papina. Twitcher had been teaching the monkeys to play a game where they imagined they were birds flying high above the City.

"Close your eyes and picture what it would look like ... the river flowing up and down ... the great streets running in lines next to it ... the smaller ones crossing them to make little boxes ... the railway lines sprouting out the side of the river like the stalk of a giant fruit.

"Now pretend that you're a dot moving around the City. Got it? Well, the trick of navigation is to always have one eye in the sky looking down. So when you turn left, you have to move that little dot left; if you turn round and go back the way you came, that little dot has to bounce back as well."

Papina concentrated hard – it was certainly true that from the top of a tall tree everything looked different, but what happened if you went even higher? She tried to imagine the City as a pattern of lines and boxes; the image fluttered across her mind, but just as she was starting to pull it into focus it slipped away again, eluding her.

Suddenly she heard fits of giggles. Papina snapped open her eyes to see everyone laughing at Honeydew, the youngest monkey in the class, who had closed her eyes and promptly fallen fast asleep.

"Honeydew, you really should learn to relax more," Twitcher said with a wry smile.

Everyone laughed, and the noise woke Honeydew with a start. "What? Is it lunchtime?" she said in a dazed voice.

Now that food had been mentioned, Twitcher knew it would be impossible to regain the youngsters' concentration, so he dismissed the class. As the monkeys rushed out, though, Papina hung back.

Twitcher smiled at her. "Do you think it was too

difficult for them? Some monkeys just can't get above street level."

"It was starting to make sense," Papina said thoughtfully, "but it's going to take a bit of practice."

"Once you get it, there's no turning back. You just do it all the time, without thinking."

"Twitcher, I was wondering ... from the bird's eye, looking down, where would the old Cemetery be?"

Twitcher hesitated. He knew from long experience that answering these questions was like stirring up a bees' nest of trouble.

"You don't need to know that, Papina. It was from another life."

"But I *want* to know," she insisted.

"Have you spoken to your mother about this?"

"She won't talk about the Cemetery."

"She's got good reasons."

"I have to know what really happened to my father. I was too young to remember much, but if I go back, maybe..."

Twitcher shook his head. "You can't go back. Not ever. It's too dangerous. The Langur have taken the Cemetery for themselves."

"Well that's too bad. I've already made up my mind," she replied defiantly. Then, softening it with a charming smile, she added, "I just need your help to tell me how to get there."

Twitcher studied Papina. He'd always had a soft spot for her, ever since he first saw her in the dump in the Slums, dodging the jaws of the python. Many young monkeys would have fallen to pieces, but she had steeled herself and outwitted death. Twitcher thought she had real courage, not something many monkeys had, and he did not want to be the one to crush her spirit.

"Well ..." he said finally, "I suppose it wouldn't be very responsible of me to let you go roaming the streets on your own now, would it?"

Papina's face lit up with joy and she threw her arms around him. "Thank you, Twitcher! I knew you'd help."

Three nights later they put their plan into action. During the day Papina collected chamomile pollen from a herb garden on a nearby balcony; she took it back and secretly mixed it with her group's food, careful to avoid eating any herself because chamomile was a sedative. As the moon rose, she watched her mother and the others all drift off into a deep, drugged sleep, then she crept away to meet Twitcher and they set off into the tangle of City streets.

It was the first time Papina had strayed far from Temple Gardens since arriving as a nervous refugee, and she immediately felt her stomach knotting with anxiety. But she had huge faith in Twitcher – he was not one of those loud boastful monkeys who went strangely silent when things got difficult; his self-deprecating manner belied a real strength of character. Papina felt that she could trust him no matter what.

His knowledge of the City was exhaustive – he seemed to have the entire street network lodged in his mind, and it wasn't long before they found themselves running stealthily up the road towards the old Cemetery. At the crest of the hill, Twitcher dived into the shadows under a mobile tea stall and pointed to the main gate – they could see silhouettes moving in front of it in the shadows.

"The entrance is guarded. This is as far as we go," he said, trying to hide his relief.

"You didn't really think we were just going to walk in?" Papina smiled. "As if. There's a secret entrance. We used it all the time when we played hide-and-seek. I bet they haven't found it yet."

"That's really not a good idea," Twitcher warned, trying to think of a reason that would stop her.

"Why don't I lead from here?" Papina cut in.

"Do I have a choice?"

"No."

Twitcher gave a resigned sigh. "After you, then, I suppose." And he followed Papina as she darted down an alley that skirted the Cemetery.

Even though it had been many moons since she'd last played here, the memories flooded back, and soon they arrived at a stone pool built into the outside of the Cemetery wall which collected water from a nearby rising well. Papina looked down at the fresh, clear water gurgling gently, and the sound transported her back.

Twitcher watched her silently. He'd seen that air of loss so many times on the faces of refugee monkeys, but to see Papina in the grip of it stirred something within him that he'd never felt before, a longing to make things better, to somehow heal her life.

Being Twitcher, of course, he wouldn't dream of telling her, so as usual he made a quip. "Ah, so we're going to swim in?"

"How did you know?" Papina's earnest expression wiped the smile from Twitcher's face.

"You what?!"

"This is how the fresh water gets into the bathing

pool. There's a hole in the bottom of the wall. All you've got to do is dive down and feel for it."

Twitcher peered nervously into the bubbling water. "Fine," he said, trying to put on a brave face. But Papina knew that monkeys who hadn't been brought up as swimmers could be frightened of water.

"Look," she said gently, "why don't you stay out here and keep a lookout for Langur patrols?"

"I can't let you go in there on your own!"

"And I can't have you splashing about like a bird in a bath." Papina smiled. "It'll be safer this way—"

"No."

"I'll be fine!"

Twitcher realized he was trying to persuade an immoveable will. He nodded reluctantly. "Just don't get caught. Whatever you do, don't get caught."

Papina smiled. "Don't worry, I know this Cemetery like the back of my hand."

And with that she dived into the pool and was gone.

12

STRANGER IN THE NIGHT

Mico had come to really enjoy the night exercises.

Once he'd learned to conquer his fear of the dark, he found that in many ways night was the soldier's friend. Although it was harder to see the enemy, it was easier to find hiding places, and because there was much less noise, it was possible to use each sound to read the darkness.

Tonight's exercise was a solo mission, "Going to Ground". Mico had to dig himself into the undergrowth and stay there until dawn. At some point the Instructors would come looking for him, and he had to try and avoid detection.

Judging by the position of the moon, Mico reckoned he was about halfway through. He'd made a shelter in a secluded corner between a collapsed headstone and the gully that ducted fresh water into the Great Vault. It had all gone pretty smoothly apart from the group of cockroaches that had tried to invade his camp, but after he'd eaten a few, they got the message and retreated. Now he was just sitting and waiting for any sign of the Instructors.

It was a subtle splash, but Mico's ears immediately pricked up. He had listened to the steady babble of the water in the gully long enough to detect even the slightest change in sound.

He spun round and pulled back into the shadows, ears straining to track every movement.

Someone seemed to be wading down the gully towards him; their approach was cautious, as if they were checking every shadow.

Mico had expected the Instructors to approach through the trees, as he'd assumed they wouldn't want to get their fur wet, but he'd obviously misjudged them. Quickly he worked out a plan: he'd wait until they were nearly on him then he'd slip out, double back and hide under a tomb they'd already checked. Whatever happened, he was determined not to get caught.

The splashing got closer and closer; they weren't changing their course – this was going to be easy.

Mico picked up a palm leaf and bored a small hole in it, then, lifting the leaf to his face, he leaned forward and peered down the gully. The leaf trick was something they'd just learned; it meant the whites of his eyes couldn't be seen and it was surprisingly effective.

He inched forward without a sound until he could see along the entire length of the stream...

Then he froze in shock.

Wading towards him was a small Rhesus monkey up to her chest in water.

Cold dread seized Mico, the fur on his back bristled, he felt his heart start to pound ... the enemy was *here*!

If this was an attack, he should raise the alarm. But if he moved they'd surely pounce on him.

They?

Mico looked again. The Rhesus was alone. And far from being savage and dangerous, she looked rather vulnerable.

Suddenly she stopped, looked around cautiously, then climbed out of the stream and darted into the undergrowth.

Mico immediately followed. He had to track her, find out exactly what kind of sabotage she was planning. The Rhesus was quick, and she seemed to know exactly where she was going. Dodging from shadow to shadow, she made her way to the perimeter wall, where she disappeared into the bushes.

Mico crept down the path. He could hear the rustling of leaves as she clambered through the dense shrubs. She obviously hadn't been taught the art of silent approach, unlike Mico, who slipped into the bushes and picked his way through the tangle of vegetation…

Creeping up on the Rhesus, undetected…

Closer and closer…

Until he glimpsed her fur in the moonlight. Incredibly, she was crouched by the same niche in the wall Mico had discovered, and she was slowly unwrapping the little bamboo bundle, until she held the monkey carving in her hand.

Mico watched as she gazed at the three little monkeys longingly, running her fingers gently over the carved figures.

Instinctively he knew she wouldn't harm him.

Despite his oath of allegiance to Lord Gospodar, despite the punishments he risked, Mico couldn't help feeling that he wanted to help this Rhesus. She was not a savage barbarian, but a frightened and lonely young monkey.

"So it was yours?" he whispered.

Papina spun round, fear pulsing through her body.

Mico pulled a branch aside, revealing his face. "I've been looking after it for you."

Panic and confusion gripped Papina. She stumbled back, then turned and bolted towards the path.

"Wait!" Mico urged. But it was no use, he could hear her feet scampering away. He had to stop her or she'd run right into one of the night patrols, and then she'd be in real trouble.

Darting out of the shrubs, he leapt over a row of tombs and landed on the path in front of her.

"Are you trying to get yourself killed?!" he hissed.

Papina lashed out with her fists, trying to knock him out of the way, but Mico grabbed her arms.

"I won't harm you! But you have to be quiet!"

She stopped struggling and looked at him, her eyes searching his face for a clue to his intentions.

"You used to live here, didn't you?" Mico asked. "This was your home."

"Until you destroyed it!" Papina retorted angrily.

Mico shook his head. "Not me."

Papina looked him up and down. She knew he was too young to have been involved, but in her mind all Langurs were guilty.

Mico pointed to the carving that she clasped in her hand. "What does it mean?"

The simple directness of the question caught Papina off guard. "Nothing. It doesn't mean anything. It's just a toy."

She surrendered it to Mico as if handing over contraband, but he shook his head. "It's yours. Keep it."

Kindness was the last thing Papina was expecting. She scrutinized Mico, noticing his soft eyes, not the eyes of the killers she'd been warned about.

Too proud to say thank you, Papina went instead for an explanation. "My father gave it to me. He stole it from a market stall. He said it was our family."

Suddenly there was a deep sadness in Papina's eyes.

"Are they with you?" asked Mico.

"My mother's alive. My father..." She didn't need to finish the sentence. "I came back to see it one last time ... where we lived."

Mico shook his head. "It's impossible. Guards patrol all the main runs. If they found a Rhesus..." Now it was his turn to leave the words unsaid.

But Papina had come too far to give up. "I miss him so much. I thought maybe I could find out what happened to him after he came back."

A dreadful foreboding stirred in Mico's guts. "He came back after the battle?"

"Yes," Papina said, daring to hope. "To try and set things right. He put the Universal Sign of Peace on his forehead."

Mico hesitated as he remembered the male Rhesus being butchered by the Cemetery wall.

"Tell me," Papina urged. "Please."

"Your father was killed." Mico said the words as gently as he could, but he saw Papina's face tense with pain.

"How?"

"Does it matter?

She felt sick, but if she didn't find out the truth, she'd be condemned to spend the rest of her life wondering. "I need to know what happened."

They made a strange sight creeping through the Cemetery from shadow to shadow. Papina trusted Mico enough to follow his every move, freeze when he did, dart when he darted, yet she maintained a cautious distance between them, as if she suspected he might turn on her at any moment.

Finally they emerged by the section of the wall where Mico had found the bloody handprint.

The rain had long since washed the stain from the stones, but it would take more than the weather to erase the disturbing memories.

"This is where your father died."

"How? How did it happen?"

"They chased him, from down there." Mico pointed along the path. "They ambushed him."

He saw a numbing wave of despair overwhelm Papina, but still she pressed on. "Did it last long?"

Mico shook his head. "He tried to talk to them; he said he had a family."

Papina slumped onto her haunches.

"I'm sure his last thoughts were of you."

In the silence of the night, Papina felt something inside her break, something that would never fully heal. She stared up at Mico; she should hate him, but as she looked into his eyes she realized that he shared her pain, that he felt the horror as keenly as she did.

Suddenly Mico tensed – he could hear movement down one of the paths. The night patrol.

"You have to go!" he whispered urgently, pulling her back into the shadows.

As they retraced their steps, all Mico's training kicked in; he circled around the guards, double backing, darting for the places they'd just checked. It was as if he was still on the night exercise, only this time his hand clasped his enemy's in a strange bond of trust – two monkeys betraying their own sides for something they didn't yet understand.

Eventually they made it back to the gully where Mico helped Papina slip into the water.

"Thank you," she said quietly.

"I'm sorry ... for everything," Mico whispered.

But both knew the guilt and the blame lay elsewhere.

Then as Papina turned to go, Mico blurted out, "Tomorrow there won't be as many patrols."

Papina looked at him uncertainly.

"They've finished the night exercises for a while. Perhaps ... perhaps you could tell me what life used to be like in the Cemetery?"

Papina knew that Twitcher would be furious, but she couldn't let go of this last remaining thread that connected her to her father.

Sensing her confusion, Mico reached out and touched her hand gently. "I'll protect you. I promise."

Despite everything she'd been told about the Langur, Papina believed him. "All right, tomorrow."

Then she turned and waded along the gully into the darkness.

13

SHADES OF GREY

"It's madness! You can't go back!"

For once Twitcher didn't hide behind a wry comment; he told Papina exactly what he thought. But she had already made up her mind; seeing the tree-lined avenues in the Cemetery, rich with the distinctive sweet mosses that grew on the tombs, was like paying tribute to her father, and that felt good.

In any case, she told Twitcher the monkey she'd met was nothing like the Langur thugs that everyone described; Mico could easily have betrayed her, but he hadn't.

"Exactly!" admonished Twitcher. "That's how cunning they are. He's probably trying to lure us *all* back so he and his pals can finish us off!"

Papina shook her head. "Spare me the hysterics. It wasn't like that."

Twitcher growled impatiently and darted down an alley behind the trolleybus depot. They were nearly back at Temple Gardens now and he was starting to regret ever helping Papina. She was just the sort of monkey to have memorized the route from one outing, just the sort of wilful character to attempt the journey on her own.

And that was exactly what happened.

* * *

The following night, Papina steeled her nerves and set off on the lonely journey across the restless City that was struggling to sleep under a blanket of humid air. Her courage was rewarded – before long she found herself by the feeder pool in the Cemetery wall.

This time there was no hesitation – she dived straight into the water, swam through the submerged hole and emerged into the gully ... to find Mico already waiting for her.

He was determined that Papina should come to no harm, and had secretly found out from his father's Counting Stones about the rostering of the guards and the new schedule for the night exercises, so he knew exactly which areas of the Cemetery to avoid.

As Papina shook the water from her fur, she tossed Mico a glistening pebble. "We used to hide them at the bottom of the pool. I thought you might like it."

Mico turned the pebble over in his hand, admiring the flecks of colour that glinted in the moonlight.

"My father would really love you!" he smiled.

And so began a secret friendship.

Mico and Papina started to meet every night, and she told him all about how life used to be when the Cemetery had been home to the Rhesus. As they stole around the dark paths she showed him the tomb where she grew up, and the trees where her father taught her to climb; she recounted how the Great Vault used to be a huge adventure playground, and she smiled wistfully as she remembered the long afternoons spent playing there, chasing shadows and digging up ants just for fun.

At other times, unable to roam for fear of running into the night patrol, Mico and Papina would stick close to the gully, which is when she told him all about the carved monkeys.

"The one covering its eyes is my father," she explained. "So that he doesn't see where I'm going when we play hide-and-seek. The monkey covering its ears is me, stopping anyone from grooming my ears because I'm so ticklish. And this one is my mother." She pointed to the monkey with its hands over its mouth. "She can do this trick where she blows through her fingers to make it sound like my name is floating on the breeze. She'd do that to wake me gently when I'd dozed off in the afternoon."

The world Papina described was a far cry from the Cemetery that Mico inhabited, and the more she saw of Langur life, the more she understood why the Troop was so successful. But success wasn't the same as happiness, and she wanted to show Mico a different way of life.

She waited until they were busy hunting for frogs one night, then nonchalantly asked, "Just for a change, why don't you come and see where I live?"

Mico blinked nervously. She pretended not to notice his anxiety and added, "After all, why is it always me who has to make the journey?"

Wild thoughts rushed into Mico's mind: Papina had been sent as a spy and had identified him as a weak link. She was feeding back valuable intelligence about guard patrols and defences. Even as they spoke Rhesus attack squads were massing, ready to launch a devastating strike on the Cemetery, and it would all be his fault—

"Are you all right?"

Mico jumped with a start as Papina touched his hand. "You suddenly looked a bit queasy."

Mico looked into her open face. No spy could be this good – a traitor's gaze wouldn't be so steady, her hand so cool and dry.

"I'm sorry. It's just..." But how could he explain without insulting her?

"What have they told you? That we're all monsters?" she quipped. But Mico looked at her earnestly.

"They really told you *that*?!" she exclaimed.

Mico nodded. For a moment Papina didn't know what to say, then she just burst out laughing at the absurdity of it. Mico tried to hush her up, but Papina couldn't stop. He leapt over to her and put his hand across her mouth, trying to suppress the noise.

"Tell me the truth!" he demanded.

"Come and see for yourself!" Papina retorted, pulling away, not wanting to make this any easier for him. "I trusted you. I put my life in your hands. Are you willing to do the same for me?"

The challenge had been laid down – Mico knew that if he didn't agree to go, it would be the end of their friendship.

"So you're not ... I mean, you've never ... they told us about cannibalism."

Papina's eyes went wide. "Do I look like a cannibal?"

Even though he'd never met a cannibal, Mico had to admit he'd be surprised if they were as pretty as Papina. He shook his head.

"Good," she said decisively. "We're all set. Tomorrow night I'll take you home." Then she added under her breath, "Should keep the family fed for a few days."

"What?!" exclaimed Mico.

"Sorry, couldn't resist," said Papina as she dissolved into another fit of the giggles.

* * *

The next day passed nervously. Mico practised his military drills, hoping to prepare for whatever dangers lay out in the City, but one of the sternest tests of his courage came before he'd even left the Cemetery. He had very little experience of bathing, let alone diving underwater, and he couldn't hide his anxiety about plunging into the pool.

"Just hold your breath, keep your eyes open and head for the hole in the wall," instructed Papina when she met him by the gully.

"Just?" thought Mico ruefully. Why do they always put "just" before the really difficult things in life? But he was not a quitter and, steeling his nerves, he took the deepest breath he could muster and plunged into the water.

Immediately he felt himself getting pushed back by the current; he tried to open his eyes, but the water stung and all he could see was a blurry confusion. Suddenly water was rushing up his nose and he started to panic. Just as he thought he wasn't going to make it, a hand grabbed his fur and hauled him up. Next thing he knew he was bursting to the surface in the pool outside the Cemetery.

"Don't worry, first time's always the worst," Papina smiled.

Mico coughed the water from his airways. *The first time?* How often did she think he was going to do this? But the one thing Mico was starting to learn about Papina was that she was very determined.

As they made their way through the City streets, Mico's eyes darted about nervously, checking every shadow.

Trying to make him relax, Papina started pointing out various landmarks across Kolkata, and even though she was just repeating things that Twitcher had told her, she liked playing the role of a worldly-wise monkey. When they were halfway there, she darted through an archway and down an alley that opened onto a small piece of scrub ground dotted with beekeepers' sheds.

"Fancy a treat?" she asked, and without waiting for an answer, scrambled over the fencing and headed towards the hives.

The bees were silent in their hives, but it still made Mico nervous to be near such deadly insects. Anxiously he crept closer, until he found Papina sitting under one of the hives that had a long dribble of honey running down its front leg. She dipped her finger into the honey and offered it to Mico.

"Here... Try some."

The taste exploded in his mouth, sending waves of pleasure through his body; it was so much more powerful than the sweetness of fruit.

"How do the Humans do it?" he asked. "Why don't the bees sting them?"

"They've got special clothes." She pointed to the netted hats hanging on the side of the shed. "But they look pretty stupid when they wear them."

Mico swung over to have a closer look, then plucked one of the hats down and plonked it over his body, vanishing completely under the nets. Papina started giggling, which set Mico off as well – this honey was pretty strong stuff.

Buzzing from the sugar, they set off again, and by the time dawn was glimmering in the sky they were just a couple of streets away from Temple Gardens.

Instinctively Mico hung back. "Maybe this is far enough."

"Oh no. You're not backing out now," Papina said as she reached under a market stall to retrieve a squashed pomegranate.

Mico knew he must be out of his mind to be doing this – time and again dire warnings of Rhesus barbarity had been drilled into him, yet here he was, about to walk right into the heart of their territory.

Papina squeezed the pith between her fingers and started to make a white mark on Mico's forehead – the Universal Sign of Peace.

"That won't help," Mico said. The Sign hadn't saved Papina's father; why would it save him?

"Trust me." But Papina could feel the tension under his fur. "When I came to the Cemetery, you promised to protect me." She clasped his hand and whispered, "The promise works both ways."

A few moments later, they were standing on the edge of Temple Gardens, Mico gazing up in wonder at the enormous statue of the Monkey-God. But if Papina was expecting his first question to be about Hanuman, she was wrong.

"Where's the wall?" he asked.

"What wall?"

"To protect you, to keep other monkeys out?"

"But we don't want to keep monkeys out," Papina replied with disarming simplicity.

She waved her arm across the tranquil Gardens. "So, do they look like monsters?"

Mico remained silent; everywhere he looked, he saw Rhesus monkeys fast asleep, in the trees, under the shrubs, in the nooks and crannies of the statue.

"Do savages sleep so peacefully?" Papina wanted an admission from Mico that he'd been wrong.

Mico wasn't convinced – they might be peaceful now, but when they woke and found a Langur in their midst it could turn very ugly. He looked up at the sky where the light streaks were getting broader by the heartbeat.

"I have to go back."

"No! Not yet."

"There's no time—"

"How do you know we're not cannibals unless you stay for breakfast?" Papina demanded.

"But my parents will think I've gone missing!"

"So? Just make up an excuse. Say you went foraging for food."

Mico shook his head. Didn't she understand anything? "All foraging parties have to be sanctioned by Deputy Hani."

"Then just say you couldn't sleep. You went for a walk."

"You need permission to leave the Cemetery!"

"How can you live like that?!" It was a devastatingly simple question, and Mico had no answer.

Papina grasped his hand and led him into the Gardens. "You have to see the way we do things here."

By now, the energetic youngsters were starting to wake, cajoling their parents into action, their rumbling stomachs demanding food.

Papina had hoped everyone would be too distracted to make a fuss; there were so many strangers arriving every day that one new monkey would normally have blended into the crowd.

But Mico was a Langur, and immediately he provoked fearful and suspicious glares; with every step he took, the adults edged nervously away as if he was diseased and the young shrank behind their parents' legs.

"I really think I'd better go now," he whispered, but Papina gripped his arm firmly. Ignoring the wave of hostility, she pulled him towards the Temple statue, determined that he should meet her mother.

Willow was scratching between her toes with a twig when she heard Papina's voice.

"This is Mico."

Willow looked up and felt her stomach jolt as she saw the Langur. Immediately she sprang over, pulled her daughter away and bared her teeth, ready to attack.

"What is *he* doing here?" Willow demanded, her voice loaded with contempt.

"He's my friend," urged Papina.

Nervously Mico stretched out his hand, offering Willow a bright yellow lemon. "P–Papina said you liked these," he stuttered.

Willow looked at the lemon in disbelief. Did he really think the violations and abuse could all be atoned for with a lemon?

"He's been very kind to me," Papina said with a firmness that warned her mother to tread carefully. "I know he's a Langur, but they're not all the same. He's taken a big risk coming here – the least we can do is offer him some breakfast."

"I'll eat anything. Really, I'm not fussy," said Mico, trying to please.

It didn't work.

Willow glared at him with a thunderous scowl, as more females gathered round to show their solidarity.

Papina moved closer to Mico, trying to protect him. "You know what the Langur teach their young? That Rhesus monkeys are wild savages! Cannibals!" she scoffed at the absurdity of the idea. "What better way to prove them wrong than to share some fruit with him?"

Even though Willow was furious with her daughter for showing such disloyalty, she hesitated, trying to understand what was going on in Papina's confused mind, when suddenly another voice, hard and uncompromising, answered for her.

"Give him nothing."

The monkeys spun round and saw Twitcher standing in the shadows. "He is the enemy of all monkeys; he is the destroyer of your homes and the killer of your families." Twitcher paced closer as he spoke. "He is the one who has spread misery to monkeys across the City. He's not welcome here."

None of them had seen this side to Twitcher before – gone was the easy-going charm. He turned to Willow and scowled at her in disbelief. "You should be ashamed to be standing next to him. You of all monkeys should know better."

"*I* brought him," said Papina, stepping forward to defend her mother.

It was not the answer Twitcher wanted to hear. He looked from Papina to Mico, sensing the connection between the two monkeys. It ignited a smouldering anger in his belly.

"Please, I meant no harm coming here," offered Mico. "Now I can see with my own eyes there's been a terrible misunderstanding. You're monkeys just like us. Whatever happened in the past, things can be different. Thanks to Papina, I can take that message back."

"You want to take a message back?" said Twitcher, looming forward in a gesture of dominance. "Take this: remind them that it was us, the Rhesus, who roamed this City freely when the Langur were still a savage and forgotten Troop. The Humans loved *us*, talked to *us*—"

"Then why did you turn on them?" Mico retorted.

"We didn't."

"But it was you who killed the Human leader."

"Was it?" Twitcher looked at Mico with a penetrating gaze. "The Human fell. He died. That much is true. There was evidence of monkeys, but no one actually saw what happened. No one. We were mischievous; we still are. But to kill?" Twitcher shook his head. "The idea that a Rhesus would kill a Human is an abomination. But the Humans panicked. They turned monkey against monkey. They encouraged the Langur to vent their jealous rage on us. We were driven from rooftops where we had lived peacefully for generations. Wherever we settled, the Langur waged war on us. Now we're reduced to this..." Twitcher's arms swept around the Gardens. "Refugees huddled in the shadow of a statue."

Twitcher glared at Mico with grim foreboding. "The Humans don't understand what they've unleashed. But one day ... one day the Langur will overreach themselves. When they fall, their enemies will be waiting to pounce – and we'll be the first to remind them of the suffering they've meted out." He looked at Mico with hatred and contempt. "Go tell your Troop that."

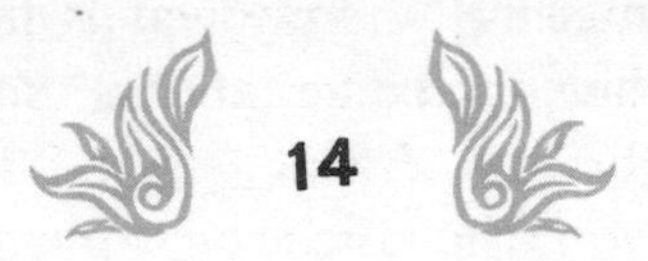

14

THE CONFORMIST

It was a long, lonely walk back across the City; as Papina had been forbidden to accompany him, a hurriedly explained route and some quickly memorized landmarks were all Mico had to go on.

Getting home, though, was the least of his problems; Mico was lost in a much more profound way, his mind reeling from Twitcher's version of history.

He tried to reassure himself that the Langur were the Chosen Troop who had brought peace and restored order. Surely if what Twitcher said was true, Mico's mother and father would have known what was going on. His father was well connected and played an important role in the Troop; no way would he have stood quietly by while innocent monkeys were persecuted.

On the other hand, if the Langur version of events was true, and the Rhesus really were debased barbarians, he couldn't understand why Papina was the way she was.

Which history should he believe?

The question swirled round and round in Mico's mind until before he knew it, he was standing outside the Cemetery walls. Quickly he dived in through the pool and made his way home, pretending that it had been so hot in the night he'd slept out under the stars.

No one believed him. Worse still, this wasn't just any day he'd gone missing – today was Warrior Day, when gifted Cadets who showed a real talent for fighting were inducted straight into the Elites, and Breri would be among them.

Not surprisingly, his parents were fussing around Breri like flies, grooming him again and again until his fur shone, and as soon as Mico showed his face, they all rounded on him.

"Where have you been!"

"You know today is your brother's special day!"

"They've sent three patrols out looking for you!"

Faced with the barrage of hostility, Mico retreated and scampered over to Cadet School, where Gu-Nah was too busy drilling the guard of honour to waste much energy bawling Mico out. Instead he ordered him to remove every leaf and twig from the parade area until it was pristine.

Mico accepted his punishment silently; considering how many rules he'd broken that night, he was relieved that everyone was too preoccupied to ask more searching questions.

The ceremony was held in great esteem by the Langur. It began with every family in the Troop bringing a coconut shell filled with fresh water to the steps of the Great Vault. Lord Gospodar had to take a sip from the shells, then select a certain number which were put on the top step. He would then take each of these coconuts in turn and approach one of the Cadets to be inducted.

"From all the monkeys before me, you stand out as one of the Troop's very finest," Gospodar would say with great solemnity.

"I am honoured, my Lord," the soldier would reply.

"Will you dedicate your entire being, tooth and tail, to the service of the Langur Troop?"

"I will."

Gospodar would then drink from the shell and offer it to the soldier, who would drink the remaining water; when it was finished, the Cadet had become an Elite.

Mico watched intently as Gospodar moved down the line, getting closer and closer to Breri. He could see the haughty pride written on every line of his brother's face, the total belief in his own superiority; he was born for the Elites and he knew it. When Mico looked over to his parents, he could see that they shared this conviction.

Finally it was Breri's turn.

"From all the monkeys before me, you, Breri, stand out as one of the Troop's very finest," Gospodar pronounced. It was a small gesture, but one that everyone had noticed – Lord Gospodar had broken protocol and mentioned Breri by name, surely a sign of great favour. Mico glanced over to his parents, who were trembling with excitement.

"I am honoured, my Lord," Breri replied.

"Will you dedicate your entire being, tooth and tail, to the service of the Langur Troop?"

"I will."

Lord Gospodar smiled and drank from the shell, offered the remainder to Breri, who finished the water, and the moment was complete.

Mico shuddered as he realized the enormity of the gulf between him and his brother. If he was going to persist in his search for the truth he would never be able to talk about it with anyone, not even his own family, *especially* his own family.

From now on Mico would be walking a lonely path.

As usual, the Warrior Day Feast was held in the Great Vault. The Instructors chatted casually with the new Elites, treating them as equals; parents crowed over their offspring, basking in the reflected glory; and a group of pretty young female monkeys were busy charming the Troop's rising stars.

It was a magic circle of exclusivity, and Mico wasn't part of it. Instead he helped himself to a couple of oranges and found a quiet spot by the pool. But just as he was squeezing the first orange into his mouth, a voice spoke to him.

"You're looking very worried, Cadet Mico."

He looked up and saw Deputy Tyrell standing over him.

"I'm sorry, sir. I was just..." he said, springing to his feet, but Tyrell waved the formalities aside with a nonchalant sweep of his arm, and he sat down next to Mico.

"Try bathing your feet. It's most refreshing. When your feet are cool, your whole body is comfortable," he said with avuncular charm, and dipped his toes into the water to demonstrate.

Mico hesitated; it seemed wrong to behave so casually with such a high-ranking official. Tyrell turned and looked at him with his penetrating gaze.

"No need to be afraid. I know you're not like the other monkeys."

There was a dark ambiguity to Tyrell's words, and Mico felt sure he would only antagonize the Deputy if he rejected his advice, so he dutifully let his feet dangle in the water.

"So," Tyrell went on, "what's on your mind?"

Mico scrambled to think of a convincing lie to explain why he was so gloomy when his family was so happy.

"Worried you won't be able to live up to your brother's achievements?" Tyrell suggested.

Mico nodded. "Yes, sir."

A sly smile crossed Tyrell's face. "You're not a very good liar yet."

Mico felt the sweat break on his brow; it was as if Tyrell could read his mind, look straight into his wavering heart.

"Now tell me," Tyrell said with chilling calm, "what *is* on your mind?"

Mico knew he wouldn't get away with another lie, but the truth was out of the question.

"It's just that—" he glanced over at the new Elites—"the battle's been won – the Rhesus have been defeated – but still all we talk about is fighting. Shouldn't we be thinking about what happens next, sir?"

Tyrell scrutinized Mico for a few agonizing moments. Then slowly a smile broke across the Deputy's face. "That's why you are destined for greater things, Mico. Far greater than them," he said, throwing a derisive glance at the Elites. "They just obey, but you ... you dare to question."

Mico was stunned; it was the first time he'd heard anyone speak dismissively of the Elites.

"The fact is," Tyrell continued, "the battle is never over. The Rhesus have been defeated, but not eliminated." He chose the word carefully and uttered it with cold precision. "Sooner or later they are going to rise up, thirsty for vengeance. In fact we already have intelligence reports that a Rhesus Resistance is forming, determined to stir up trouble."

This was news to Mico; he'd never heard Papina talk about a Resistance.

"A Troop should know when it's beaten," Tyrell continued. "Sadly the Rhesus have not learned their lesson. So we'll just have to press them harder."

But when Tyrell looked at Mico, he saw hesitation. "You are with us on this, Mico?"

"Yes. Of course, sir."

"The Langur must take responsibility for the City's monkeys, no matter how heavy the burden. We are the Chosen Troop."

"The City is looking to us, sir," Mico said, dutifully quoting the Troop's mantra.

But Tyrell sensed his doubts. "Why do you hesitate? Perhaps you don't relish the fight because you're small." He looked Mico up and down, perfectly aware of how the accusation would hurt.

"I've proved myself in Cadets, sir. Ask my Instructors."

Tyrell smiled indulgently. "You know, I hated being small when I was your age. I tried everything – dangling from trees to stretch my arms, overeating till I was sick, trying to bulk myself up."

Mico felt a sudden kinship with the Deputy. He too had tried every imaginable trick to grow taller, and not one of them had worked.

"Then I realized," Tyrell went on, "not all monkeys fight in the same way."

"I don't quite follow, sir."

Tyrell studied Mico with a burning intensity. "When I look at you I see a kindred spirit. We are not like the others, Mico. Our minds are what give us strength. But turning that strength into power is not so easy. I could help you there. If I knew that you were loyal, truly loyal ... to me."

He let the words hang in the air between them. Mico sensed that just for a moment he had glimpsed a dark secret. *"Me,"* Tyrell had said. "*Loyal to me*". Not "the Troop".

"Such loyalty could be rewarded with untold power," Tyrell whispered. It was the voice of pure temptation. Mico looked at him in silence, trying to work out exactly what was being offered, when suddenly a breathless Footsoldier pushed through the crowd.

"Forgive the interruption, sir! But there's trouble!"

Tyrell quickly led the Footsoldier to one side where no one could hear them talk. Mico watched closely – judging by the alarmed gestures and the growing concern on the Deputy's face, this was serious.

Moments later Tyrell made his way over to Gospodar for more urgent briefings, and now the other monkeys were starting to sense the electric atmosphere. Speculation started to run wild, until finally Lord Gospodar swung up onto a plinth.

"My fellow Langur!" he boomed in sombre tones. "Today we celebrated the achievement of our most courageous young monkeys; would that they never had to shed a drop of blood." Gospodar looked across the sea of attentive faces. "But Deputy Tyrell has just informed me of a terrible atrocity. The Bonnet Macaques have stolen a Human baby!"

A ripple of shock pulsed through the Troop.

"The Rhesus anarchy that we have battled against for so long has now spread to the Bonnets!"

The newly promoted Elites bristled with anticipation as they realized another war was imminent; mothers who were so proud of their martial sons only moments before now instinctively reached out to cling on to them.

"The City is looking to us," Gospodar declared. "It needs us to eradicate the scourge of savage monkeys!

The Ruling Council and I are of one mind: in the name of peace, we must mobilize for war!"

A roll of ground-thumping broke out, everyone was talking at once, fired up with a sense of purpose. Even Mico was caught up, now he could confront Twitcher with proof – the Bonnet Macaques had crossed the line between Humans and monkeys, they had violated the natural order, and only the Langur had the courage and strength to set things straight.

Immediately the whole Troop went onto war footing. Trumble was assigned three assistants to help with the complex task of setting up a supply chain for the soldiers; female monkeys were instructed to set aside their domestic chores and report for special duties gathering stones for ammunition and sorting branches to be used for fighting sticks; throughout the Cemetery, monkeys old and young psyched themselves up for battle.

Breri's Elite squad was to be part of the main attack force and they were moved into advanced positions near the Bonnets' territory. Mico's Cadet squad was deployed to an old railway signal box that had long since fallen into disuse. From here they could see both ways: forward to the bridge that marked the start of Bonnet territory, and back to the Cemetery perched on the hill. The Cadets' job was to ferry food and weapons forward, and carry any wounded Langurs safely back.

The preparations were arduous, and as daylight faded so did the Cadets' initial excitement; the sense of imminent danger became palpable.

As Mico looked around the gloomy signal box, he couldn't help thinking that by this time tomorrow it could be strewn with the bloodied bodies of wounded fighters. Suddenly warfare wasn't something that happened to others; it would be his friends – his own brother – who would be right in the thick of it.

And there was another worry.

It made Mico feel guilty even to be thinking about it at a time like this, but he couldn't help it: Papina.

He looked up at the moon – it was just reaching its highest point, which meant he should have been secretly meeting her. Defying her mother, she'd still agreed to meet him and hiding in the shadows outside the Cemetery wall, she would have no way of knowing that there'd been a sudden mobilization. Most likely she would assume that Twitcher's harsh words had made Mico change his mind about her, that he wanted to end their friendship.

Nothing could be further from the truth, but Mico had no chance of explaining that to her now. And if the battle turned ugly, who knew when, or if, he'd ever have a chance.

15

BATTLE STATIONS

Soames snorted with laughter.

"I get it! Good one ... very good." And still chuckling, he popped a couple more juniper berries into his mouth.

His friend, Morton, looked up quizzically. He'd told Soames the joke yesterday, and he'd only just got it? Morton shook his head. Good job they weren't in a hurry. But then the Bonnet Macaques were never in a hurry, especially in the afternoons.

For as long as any of them could remember it had been their custom to gather when the shadows of the trees reached the crumbling walls, and take juniper berries on the Great Lawn. It was one of those traditions that made the Troop feel calmly in control of its destiny.

Morton and Soames were the leaders of the Bonnets. Getting on in years, they weren't particularly bright or agile, but they had an aristocratic bearing that commanded respect.

"Hot one today," mumbled Soames as he chewed.

"Blistering," replied Morton.

"Maybe it'll be cooler tomorrow."

"Maybe."

Not the thrusting talk of dynamic leaders, but Morton and Soames didn't need to be. They were really only guardians of tradition.

Many generations ago the Bonnets had stumbled into the City as refugees and battled their way up the pecking order. Being courageous fighters, it wasn't long before they controlled a very desirable patch – the old Ambassador's Palace, which had fallen into dilapidation.

"Fancy a stroll after Berries?" suggested Soames.

"Why not?" agreed Morton. "Be nice to have a shufti of the old spread."

They said that every afternoon, but they never actually got round to doing it – too much effort in the heat. Which was a pity, because it was a lovely area – the Bonnets had free run of the gardens from the Hooghly River in the west to Market Junction in the east, encircled by a wall that added an air of exclusivity. At the centre of the gardens was the old residence, which had been the Bonnets' main dwelling until a series of harsh Monsoons brought the roof down and the monkeys decamped to the Summer-house in the middle of the Great Lawn.

The name "Summer-house" implied an unassuming, building but there was nothing modest about it. Two long wooden halls were laid out in a large "V"; where they met a tower rose up, affording the Bonnets grand views of Kolkata. Punched into the walls were a set of openings that allowed a steady draught through the building; each one had a shutter that could be swung down for security if necessary.

But it never was necessary. No one had challenged the Bonnets' control of this part of the City for a long, long time.

Of course, the Troop still sent out patrols to make sure that everyone respected their borders, but deep down, none of the Bonnets ever expected to have to fight to keep what was theirs.

It was this invulnerability that was celebrated every afternoon in the sharing of juniper berries.

Morton and Soames chewed in silence while they thought of what to say next ... when suddenly they heard a voice shouting across the lawns.

"Give us a berry, mate!"

The Bonnets turned and peered at the far wall, on top of which was perched a single Langur monkey, grinning at them.

"Bugger off!" bellowed Soames, expecting the Langur to scamper away.

But he didn't.

"There's always one, isn't there?" Morton sighed. Soames, however, was feeling irritated that some urchin had defied his authority. "Where's the patrol? The rascal needs to be taught a lesson."

"Patrol's not due back till sunset," replied Morton, scratching his buttock thoughtfully.

He didn't know that the patrol was lying dead in a ditch, having been ambushed by a Langur kill squad.

"Ignore the blighter," counselled Morton. "He'll soon get bored."

But the Langur monkey didn't get bored. Instead he crouched on his hind legs and started to defecate down the garden wall.

"Good grief!" exclaimed Morton in disgust.

Soames stood up, trying to impose his authority, aware that everyone was watching. "Now look here," he boomed, "this is Bonnet land! I suggest you get your ragged, flea-infested hide off it before I come over there and give you a good thrashing!"

But the Langur just grinned back. "You and whose army?"

"That's it!" growled Soames. "Let's break him in two!"

"Pleasure," said Morton, cracking his knuckles.

But just as the Bonnet leaders started striding across the lawn, they heard a strange massed scurrying sound.

The Bonnets hesitated. "What was that?"

Then suddenly a whole army of Langur monkeys appeared, a menacing presence perched along the entire length of the garden wall like birds of prey.

Apprehension gripped the Bonnets.

"Stall them," Morton whispered. "Play for time."

But there was no time left. A couple of terse commands were shouted down the Langur line, and the entire army dropped from the wall and started to advance across the lawns in a single, unbroken line.

Panic tore through the Bonnets – females started smacking their lips in their distinctive alarm call; males ran in circles, trying to grab their young; Morton and Soames started thumping their chests furiously, hoping to intimidate the attacking army.

But still the Langur line approached, unstoppable, unswerving. It caught up with an elderly monkey and engulfed him – there was a flurry of fists and stones, then a painful, howling scream as the Bonnet fell and the Langurs swarmed over him, biting off his fingers, tearing out his eyeballs.

The horror jolted Soames into action. Deep down, buried under years of an easy life, he had a military training, and faced with these brutal killers, the old disciplines clawed their way to the surface.

"SIEGE!!!" he roared.

The word boomed across the lawns. "SIEGE! Siege! siege..."

It echoed off the walls and drilled into the Bonnets' minds – as one they turned and bolted for the Summer-house.

Immediately a roar went up from the Langurs and they surged forward, determined to catch their prey before they reached cover.

Some of the Bonnets stumbled in the panic and were quickly set upon and consumed in a frenzy; others were just too slow and made pitifully easy targets for the Elites, who leapt onto their backs and dragged them to the ground, sinking teeth into their necks.

Soames reached the Summer-house and spun round, desperately looking for Morton, only to see his old comrade encircled by a group of screeching Langurs.

"MORTON!" He wanted to run back and help his friend, but so many Langurs were now streaming across the lawns it would have been suicidal. All Soames could do was watch in horror as they started beating Morton with their clubs, spearing his flesh with fighting sticks.

Morton roared his defiance, spun this way and that, flailing with his fists ... but it was no use. The flurry of blows rained down on him mercilessly, until he crumpled to the ground.

Soames felt physically sick.

"Get up! Get up!" he urged, waiting for the moment when Morton would rise onto his legs, flinging his assailants aside ... but the moment didn't come.

His oldest friend would never get up again.

That was when the fear gripped Soames like a claw in the back of his throat.

"IN! IN! IN!" he started thundering at his Troop as they reached the porch of the Summer-house. "Shutters down! Siege positions!"

It was all starting to come back to him now – the Bonnets had a plan for this sort of thing; he'd show those upstart Langurs that they were still a force to be reckoned with.

As the last Bonnet tumbled into the Summer-house Soames ran inside, heaved the door shut and slid a large beam of wood across the hooks, sealing it. He stormed down the length of the halls helping the others release the catches on the shutters which slammed down to block the open windows. As Soames glanced out across the lawns he saw groups of Langurs gathered round the bodies of fallen Bonnets, beating the last signs of life from them.

What made the savagery more terrifying was the Langur discipline – after each kill, soldiers would rejoin the line which was now starting to encircle the Summer-house. They were preparing for a mass attack and Soames knew it would come soon.

Slamming the last shutter down, he turned to face the throng of frightened Bonnet eyes that stared at him expectantly. *Concentrate.* He had to push his own grief to one side; he could deal with that later – when this was all over.

"These barbarians will never steal our lands!" Soames boomed. "Look around! Look at the walls that protect us, the Tower that commands the landscape. This is our fortress now! If we have the will to defend this, no one can take it from us!"

A wave of relief swept through the Bonnets as they realized their leader knew what he was doing.

"They wanted a lightning strike and a quick victory. We'll give them a long and bloody siege!"

A chorus of defiant roars erupted from the Bonnet Macaques. Shock was behind them now, thoughts of defeat driven from every mind. They were ready for war.

Soames pulled up the trapdoor in the floor, revealing secret supplies that had lain undisturbed for generations. Many seasons ago, as a young officer, he had been taught about the emergency plans for surviving a siege and now his training was paying off. No matter that the nuts and leaves had all rotted and crumbled, food was the last thing on the Bonnets' minds. What mattered was weaponry: there were piles of sharp throwing stones, rows of long sticks with lethal points, coils of thornbush bristling with barbs, all stacked in the cellar, ready and waiting.

This was an arsenal for warriors. Faded warriors maybe, but Soames knew he could draw on heritage and breeding to win this battle.

"The perimeter is secure, the grounds are in our possession, sir," panted Commander Leaf as he delivered his report to General Pogo. "The enemy defences have been wiped out, Elite squads have surrounded the Summerhouse ready to finish them off. Congratulations on another victory, sir."

General Pogo didn't even bother to turn his solitary eye in the Commander's direction; he just wiped the sweat from his brow and stared across the battlefield. All around him he saw the cocky swagger of his troops enjoying their apparent victory; Pogo was alone in discerning the truth; they had failed.

The General had wanted to fight the whole battle on the large open lawns where superior Langur discipline would prove decisive; that was why he had given orders that the Bonnets should be cut off from any retreat. But frenzied with bloodlust, the Elites had become distracted by the easy pickings, and half the enemy Troop had escaped into the Summer-house.

Pogo couldn't complain too much; it was precisely this aggression that made his forces so dangerous, but today it had cost them the strategic advantage. Now they had to deal with a siege, and that was always tricky.

Adding to the General's unease was his suspicion that Lord Gospodar had underestimated the Bonnet Macaques. Certainly they were out of condition, but the Bonnets had been a formidable force in the City for as long as Pogo could remember and he knew they would never surrender; they would have to be defeated one monkey at a time. It was going to be an ugly battle of attrition.

"Is everything all right, sir?" asked Leaf.

Pogo ignored the question and let his mind run through the battle options. He could storm the two wings of the Summer-house with a mass attack – there would be bloody hand-to-hand fighting, which favoured the Langur, but some of the Bonnets would hole up in the Tower and this would give the Langur real problems. From the Tower the Bonnets would be able to see every attack being prepared, know exactly when and where the next strike was coming.

"Give me a squad with six of our best Climbers," Pogo ordered. "We're starting at the top."

Breri had been in the second wave over the wall and, having missed the main action, had to content himself with some minor skirmishes. He was desperate to make his first kill, as he knew blood was the best way to glory. When the call for volunteers went out, he was the first to step forward.

He was assigned to the Diversion Troop; their job was to move into open ground in front of the Summer-house, find any moveable objects they could (fallen branches, bits of roof timber) and build barricades which would act as a shelter for the main attack force.

It was a tricky mission, as working without cover made them vulnerable to attack, but that was the whole point. Because while all Bonnet eyes were on Breri's squad, a group of Langur Climbers was stealthily making its way up the Tower.

Once on the roof, they examined the wooden tiles – they were laid in neat rows but the weather had taken its toll and the Climbers silently started lifting them off.

It wasn't long before all the tiles were stripped and the monkeys were standing on the woven laths. Gently the lead Climber bounced up and down, testing the laths with his weight. By the way they flexed he knew they had no strength; a few good smashes and his soldiers would be through.

The Climbers exchanged glances, making sure that everyone was ready, when suddenly they heard a shuffling movement beneath their feet. They froze, their eyes swivelled down trying to peer through the gaps in the laths.

Something stirred in the shadows ... then it was gone.

The lead Climber crouched down and pressed his face to the slats. By the time he saw what was coming, it was too late. A sharp, spear-like branch thrust up through the laths, drove clean into the Langur's eye and smashed through his skull. He didn't even have time to scream; he just lay there on the roof, twitching.

The other Climbers staggered backwards, stunned by the speed and lethal force of the attack, but their shock quickly turned to fear as more spears thrust up through the slats – four, five, six moving spikes driving up blindly, impaling whatever they could.

Two of the Climbers tried to scramble back down the Tower, but before they had gone any distance at all the spears starting driving out through the Tower walls – one monkey was impaled and died splayed out, defying gravity; another lost his grip and tumbled through the air, plunging to his death on the granite patio stones below.

Watching from his command post, General Pogo thumped the ground in disgust. "By my beating heart!" he shouted, furious with frustration; the Bonnets had anticipated his play and lured his forces into a trap. Pogo needed a counter-attack fast.

Breri's heart leapt as the orders came through: his squad was no longer just a diversion; they were going in.

Troops from all across the gardens were marshalled and armed with sticks. The plan was simple: smash through the base of the Tower and establish a beachhead. Because of its limited size, only a small number of Bonnets would be able to defend the Tower base, but the Langur could attack from three sides with overwhelming force. Once they had seized the Tower, they could surge out into both wings of the Summer-house.

That was the theory. On the ground it felt more like a frenzied ruck, and Breri was right in the thick of it.

He and the huge mass of Langurs charged the Summer-house and started beating their clubs against the walls, sending a menacing noise reverberating through the whole building.

The pounding grew louder and louder, planks started to splinter, Breri screeched with excitement, swirling his club above his head, battering the wooden walls with violent, intoxicated glee.

And then he heard a strange, eerie whistling sound.

He thought it was a battlefield command, but quickly realized that the sound was coming from above. He looked up and saw a strange black swarm descending. A swarm of stones, lethal sharp flints.

No one had a chance to run. Moments later the flints tore through the Elites, slashing flesh and embedding in skulls.

Breri covered his face with his hands and by some miracle avoided the first cloud, but through the cracks in his fingers he saw the shutters at the top of the Tower swing open as another swarm of flints was unleashed.

This time Breri wasn't so lucky.

Instinctively he curled up into a ball, trying to make himself as small as possible. The whistling crescendoed then turned into a deadly pitter-patter as the flints struck home. Breri felt a warm jab in the side of his head – there was no pain, it was more of a jolt.

Then he realized his hands were sticky. He looked at his fur – it was dark. He lifted his hand to his mouth and licked it. Blood. He was wounded.

Breri had got his wish; he'd tasted blood. But it wasn't the enemy's blood, it was his own.

16

A SIMPLE PLAN

Perched on top of the signal box, Mico had been watching the supply lines all afternoon, but as yet no word had come back from the battlefield.

With no requests for reinforcements or more weapons, the Cadets were starting to think that General Pogo must have won a lightning victory, and anticipation was running high as they talked excitedly about the rewards that would flow from being part of a successful campaign.

Which made the sight of blood-stained monkeys staggering back twice as bitter.

Scouts immediately rushed out to help them, messengers were sent scampering back to the Cemetery to raise the alarm, and Mico was assigned the task of preparing the medical supplies. Urgently he laid out various herbs and plants – aloe vera to aid the healing of bruises, dried palm leaves to wrap around gashes, a collection of barbed thorns for scraping wounds clean.

But when he picked up the hemlock root, Mico hesitated. Although no one liked to talk about it, every medical kit contained hemlock, a desperate medicine for use when a soldier was in agony from wounds that would never heal. Swallowing a single dose didn't just relieve the pain; it put the victim into a deep sleep from which he'd never wake.

No, not this time. Mico put the hemlock down, refusing to accept that any of the injuries would be that grave.

As the wounded fighters were brought in, the well-organized supply post quickly descended into a chaos of injured monkeys sprawled wherever they could find a space. Most of the victims had deep lacerations where the sharp flints had rained down on them, and the top priority was to stop the bleeding. But as Mico dashed around the signal box ferrying medicine, he discovered that there was something far more serious than the physical wounds: shock.

Knitted into the fabric of Langur life was the expectation of victory, the assumption of dominance; now faced with defeat, the monkeys couldn't make sense of what was happening. Mico saw this most clearly of all in Breri when he limped into the signal box and slumped down on the floor.

"Breri!" Mico cried out as he ran over. "You're safe!"

Breri clasped Mico tightly; it had been a long time since he'd shown any affection to his little brother and there was something desperate about his grip, as if he was clinging on to the only thing that he understood.

"What happened?" Mico asked. "What went wrong?" But when he looked into his brother's eyes he saw an expression of utter bewilderment.

"The Bonnets ... they're insane," Breri whispered. "We've taken their land ... they've nothing left to fight for ... still they fight."

"But General Pogo will have a plan?" said Mico, hoping for reassurance.

Breri looked around uneasily, as if he didn't want anyone to hear, then whispered, "The General's never met an enemy like this before."

It was the first time Mico had heard Breri express anything other than admiration for the Leadership, and it frightened him.

Suddenly the whole Langur world was threatened. Everything Mico had ever known was hanging in the balance – the security of his friends and family, the familiarity of the Cadets, the reassuring beat of Langur ways and habits. He tried to imagine what life would be like if all that vanished, if the Troop was defeated and scattered. Twitcher's ominous warning still rang in Mico's ears: *when the Langur fall, their enemies will be waiting to pounce.*

He couldn't let that happen. Whatever doubts Mico had about the Langur, they were still his monkeys, and he had a duty to protect them.

As he dressed Breri's wounds, he found out about the geography of the siege and understood why General Pogo was so worried. Using conventional Langur tactics it would be a long, bloody seige, but Mico's unconventional mind could see another way.

He hurried out of the signal box to try and find a senior military commander – they were all huddled round a very grave Deputy Tyrell, briefing him about the scale of the casualties. Already the bodyguards were making preparations to escort Tyrell forward to the front line. Mico had to make his move now.

"Excuse me, sir. We spoke at the Warrior Day Feast."

Tyrell spun round and glared at Mico, his mind so preoccupied it took a few moments for him to register who this Cadet was. "Not now," he snapped.

"Not all monkeys fight in the same way!"

The Deputy's bodyguards had just lunged forward to bundle the troublesome Cadet away when Tyrell raised his hand.

"Wait."

The bodyguards stopped in their tracks as Tyrell scrutinized Mico.

"What did you say?"

"You once told me the only way to win is by remembering that not all monkeys fight in the same way."

"Well, well..." muttered Tyrell. He drew Mico to one side, taking him into his confidence. "So tell me, how does that help us now?"

"A siege is no good, sir. Our troops are just going to get wounded, or worse. Instead we need to make the Bonnets' fortress their prison."

"How do you mean?" asked Tyrell curiously.

"If we throw a bees' nest into the Summer-house, they'll either get stung to death or they'll be forced out into the open."

Tyrell nodded indulgently. "It's a good idea. Not a new idea, of course. We've tried bees in previous campaigns, but the problem is that all monkeys look the same to bees – they sting us just as readily as they sting our enemies."

And with a patronizing smile he turned and started to walk away.

"That wasn't the idea, sir," Mico persisted, chasing after him. "There's a place in the City where men live with the bees. They use nets so that they can get close without getting stung."

Tyrell glared at Mico. "Where is this place?"

Mico ignored the question. "If we steal the nets and wrap them round the hives, we would control when they fly, where they swarm, who they sting."

Tyrell's eyes narrowed; he liked the way Mico had sidestepped the question, but most of all he liked the idea.

He glanced sideways, checking that no one had overheard their conversation. Then, with a dark smile, he whispered to Mico, "Wait here. Say nothing."

Even though he was secretly brimming with confidence, Tyrell kept a grim countenance as General Pogo showed him round the battlefield and explained the complexities of the siege.

"Any attempt to storm the building leaves us open to attack from above," Pogo lowered his voice to avoid alarming his own troops. "And even if we accept the high casualty rate there's only one way up the Tower. Our forces could go in no more than two at a time – they'd be picked off before they reached to the first level."

Tyrell frowned and rubbed his chin; it was important to give the impression that he was thinking on his feet. Then after a credible pause, he smiled as if an idea had just occurred to him.

"Forgive my simplicity, General, but it seems to me that getting the Bonnets *out* is the only solution?"

"If we had them in the open, we could deal with them easily," growled Pogo impatiently.

"And if I gave you a swarm of bees, could you get it into the main building?"

General Pogo stared at Tyrell blankly. "But bees—"

"Could you get them inside?"

The General looked over to the Summer-house, his mind testing out the various options. "Yes. We could get them inside."

Tyrell smiled at the thought of the massacre that would follow. "Just the answer I was looking for."

* * *

The moon was up by the time the raid on the beekeeper's yard swung into action. Tyrell took personal command of the mission as it was of the utmost importance that everyone should see this was all *his* idea.

Mico went along in an ostensibly minor capacity, but in fact he was the only one who knew the location of the beehives. Tyrell had demanded to be told everything, but Mico explained that he couldn't actually describe the location; he could only find it again by smell, by literally nosing his way from one street to the next.

Tyrell didn't believe him for an instant, but he played along. Mico obviously had secrets, and powerful ones at that, which made him a monkey to keep on side.

"There..." Mico whispered as they emerged into the scrub ground dotted with hives. "The ones hanging from the trees." He pointed to a large banyan tree that wove between the sheds – from its lowest branches hung a cluster of clay beehives.

"And the nets?" Tyrell demanded.

"On the side of the sheds. The Humans put them on their heads, but we can wrap them round the hives."

"Remind me," asked Tyrell innocently, "how did you come by these again?"

Mico hesitated. His mind flashed back to the night he had come here with Papina...

And the thought of her name suddenly reminded Mico of all the suffering the Langur had inflicted on the Rhesus. For one terrible moment he felt doubt pulling at his fur. Could he really trust Tyrell with a weapon as deadly as the bees?

Mico gripped his fists, forcing the nails into his palm,

reminding himself that he was doing this to *save* lives … his own brother's life.

Looking up at Tyrell, he shrugged. "I got lost one day. Sense of direction was never my strong point."

Tyrell scoffed. "I don't believe that for a moment."

But Mico was not going to be drawn any further.

Tyrell watched as the troops unhooked the beekeeper's veils then cautiously approached the banyan tree. The hives were silent; nothing stirred. Stealthily the monkeys climbed the tree, then very slowly, working in pairs, they stretched the veils around the clay hives, gently tightening them, trying not to cause any vibrations.

The monkeys paused, checking that each hive was secure; Tyrell gave the signal, and in one sweeping move the monkeys dropped from the branch, yanking the hives as they fell.

They crashed to the ground in a chaotic flurry, the terrifying jolt sending thousands of bees into a frenzy, But the monkeys held tight, gripping the nets in place, so that when the bees tried to swarm from the hive, they slammed straight into the nets. Trapped.

Tyrell crouched down and listened to the enraged buzzing of the bees, now rendered powerless by his cunning. Such a simple trick and the deadly insects were utterly at his mercy.

17

BLOOD ON THE GRASS

It was a strange thing, but in the midst of all the death, Soames had never felt more alive.

The Langur attack, swift and savage, had torn through his Troop with devastating cruelty. He had seen families executed, old friends cut down...

And yet...

In the darkness of the carnage, a rush of adrenalin had surged through Soames, galvanizing him, and that had brought a strange thrill, the kind of thrill you never got sucking juniper berries on the lawn.

From his perch high up in the Summer-house Tower, he gazed out across the moonlit lawns with grim satisfaction – he'd shown those arrogant Langurs what true strength was. They'd attacked with such conceit, and now they were cowering behind the trees.

Soames knew the Bonnets had the mettle to withstand this siege; their grief had hardened into anger, and they had enough ammunition to turn anger into bloody vengeance. They could cut down an entire army if it came to it, but Soames knew it wouldn't. In war morale was everything, and once the bodies started piling up outside the Tower, the Langur leaders would be forced to retreat.

It was true the Bonnets didn't have that much in the way of food, but they could all do with losing a bit of weight. As for water, the skies looked heavy with rain, which would come straight into the Tower now that it had lost its roof tiles; all the Bonnets had to do was sit under the leaks with their mouths open.

Soames rolled backwards off his perch and started to make his way down the Tower, offering a reassuring nod here and a friendly word there. The Spear Monkeys were poised and ready with their sharp sticks, the Flint Monkeys were surrounded by piles of cutting stones, and two younger monkeys were busy ferrying fresh ammunition up from the basement.

When he got to the bottom of the Tower, Soames swung into the main body of the Summer-house, where the large monkeys wielding fighting sticks were ranged. As he looked at them, Soames felt a swell of pride. Just yesterday these monkeys had been lazing on the lawns; today everything about them declared "warrior". It would be a brave Langur who would take on these Bonnets. Brave, or foolish.

Even though the Langur attacks had ceased as the sun set, Soames kept his forces on high alert, just in case. But it had been quiet for a while now, and as the strong moon made it impossible for anything to move on the lawns without being spotted, Soames gave the order to rest. The lookouts could work in shifts; everyone else was to sleep by their weapons.

Confident that the momentum of the battle had swung the Bonnets' way, Soames snuggled down between two wooden pillars and dozed off.

The Langurs spent the night perfecting their plan. They had left the beehives, still wrapped in netting, in a quiet corner of the gardens, trying to calm the swarms down, while General Pogo worked with his troops on a method of levering open the shutters of the Summer-house.

There was no room for mistakes – if the Langur were beaten here, it would send a signal to monkey troops right across the City, advertising their weakness. The Bonnets didn't just need to be defeated; they needed to be annihilated for daring to resist.

As the rising sun stained the grey sky with ominous red streaks, General Pogo put everyone onto high alert; he was waiting for the perfect moment, when it was light enough for the bees to navigate, yet dark enough for the Bonnets to still be asleep.

All eyes were on the General.

All thoughts on the imminent carnage.

All hopes pinned on the beehives.

Until finally Pogo gave the order.

"Go."

Immediately a dozen Langur Elites scurried across the lawns, hugging the damp shadows. When they got near the Summer-house they split into three groups, each taking a beehive. They scurried to the windows and, in a carefully synchronized move, jammed their sticks into the shutters and heaved.

The shutters split open and the Elites hurled the beehives into the building, ripping away the netting, then raced back across the lawns to the waiting lines of Langur troops.

A drone in the darkness, that's all it was. Not angry; if anything, rather soothing, almost hypnotic. But different enough to wake Soames, who sat up, peering into the gloom.

It was beginning to get light but there was a shadow swirling like a fast-moving black mist. It didn't make sense to him.

Soames shook his head, trying to cast off fatigue, trying to understand...

And with a shock he realized. The drone. The cloud. *Bees!*

Soames leapt up, senses jangling, when the first one hit him, like a hard berry, bouncing off his face. He lashed out with his arms, turned away ... and saw the cloud swarming towards him.

"BEEES!!!"

It was the only warning he had time to scream before the insects engulfed him, followed by a storm of searing stings.

Desperately Soames clawed at his eyes, trying to protect them, but it was no use – the bees crawled over his hands, between his fingers. No matter how furiously he shook, still they overwhelmed him.

Suddenly a new sound of terror echoed through the Summer-house as the bees found other sleeping monkeys. Screams of agony and confusion as the Bonnets cannoned into one another, trying to escape the swirling cloud of death.

Even as he stumbled to the door, Soames knew the massed ranks of Langurs were waiting to pounce, but in here death was inevitable, maybe out there he could still fight.

With a desperate lunge, Soames hurled himself at the door, bursting it open, and started dragging his comrades out into the open.

"Weapons ready!"

He heard the cry echo up and down the Langur ranks, but it was too late to turn back now. Following his lead, other Bonnets were tumbling out of the shutters, desperate to escape the bees.

A blood-thirsty war-cry erupted in the morning gloom as the Langurs charged, falling on their victims in a frenzy. They attacked with primal savagery, biting off fingers and ears as if trying to devour the Bonnets.

Soames had gone beyond agony. As he hauled himself to his knees, numb to the stings that still lashed his body, he could only look on, helpless, as the Langurs carved a bloody swathe across the lawns. It was like watching a ruthless killing machine, pitilessly cutting down everything in its path, sparing no one.

Round and round the Langurs swirled, destroying everything Soames had ever known or cared about. He had fought with every last drop of courage, but still it was not enough. He had failed his Troop. On *his* watch, the proud and ancient Bonnet Macaques had fallen.

There was a sharp jolt in his back – Soames looked down and saw his stomach distend as a fighting stick punctured his fur and burst out through his gut. He stood there, swaying gently, looking down at the spear that impaled him.

Finally, death was coming, relief from the torment of his catastrophic failure.

A force welled up inside Soames like a huge bubble trying to escape, as the old leader opened his mouth and let out one last primal scream.

It wasn't a scream of pain or fear or even sorrow; it was a scream of shame.

Then silence.

As the strength ebbed from his body Soames felt dizzy. Gently he toppled forward, and the Great Lawn caught his fall.

The grass felt soft on his cheek, which he found strangely comforting. The magnificent expanse of the lawns had so long been a symbol of the Bonnets' status that, even now, the fact that it was lush and green gave Soames a melancholy twinge of pride.

He watched as green turned dark red with his own blood until, with relief, Soames closed his eyes and died.

The clean-up squads had their work cut out for them. Their orders were to remove the dead bodies, Bonnet and Langur alike, drag them out of the walled gardens and dump them in storm gullies, where wild dogs and other scavengers would finish the unpleasant task of disposal. Because of the scale of the task, all the Cadets had been seconded to help.

As he stared at the brutal aftermath of the battle, Mico discovered with dread that it was one thing to talk about victory, quite another to see the reality of torn flesh and spilled entrails. There was no heroism here, no glory.

He felt numb with guilt as he wandered across the body-strewn lawns. His handprints were all over this horror. But what else could he have done?

Faced with a stark choice – help the Langur or watch them die in battle – Mico had tried to do the right thing. But there was nothing right about this gruesome vista.

He closed his eyes, but the darkness only intensified the smell of blood.

"Cadet Mico, what's come over you?"

Mico opened his eyes to find Deputy Tyrell standing in front of him.

"I–I ... my squad has been ordered..." Mico stuttered, but Tyrell just reached out and started to lead him away from the carnage.

"These degrading duties are not for monkeys of your calibre. You should be proud; this is a great day, and I appreciate your contribution to its success." Tyrell turned and looked at Mico; strangely, one eye seemed to be smiling, the other warning. "Although it was *my* idea that won the day, your role as an advisor was most appreciated. You'll be handsomely rewarded."

Despite himself, Mico felt a swell of gratitude – it was as if Tyrell was taking the whole burden onto his own shoulders. All the guilt in Mico's heart could vanish under Tyrell's guiding hand; it could all be so easy.

Too easy.

There was a part of Mico that refused to walk away, because there was one question that needed to be answered. A question that had been forgotten in the heat of battle and the rush to avoid defeat, but which refused to go away.

"Where's the Human baby?" Mico asked with disarming frankness.

Tyrell looked at him and blinked, momentarily lost for words.

"Where is the baby the Bonnet Macaques kidnapped?" Mico repeated. "The baby we went to war for?"

Tyrell nodded silently as his slippery mind wound its way around an answer. "Whatever the Bonnets did with it, they won't get a chance to repeat their crimes," he said gravely.

Not good enough.

"I've asked some of the troops who were on the front line—"

"It really doesn't matter now," scoffed Tyrell.

"And none of them have seen anything—"

"Mico, enough!" The sharp tone silenced him. "War is an ugly thing, a shocking thing. The reasons for it are complex, the truth too difficult for ordinary monkeys to understand. They need the comfort of simple solutions."

Tyrell put his hand on Mico's shoulder. "But you *do* understand. You've shown today that you're not like the others. You have a gift that marks you out for great things. I could help you climb to where you really belong."

Tyrell studied him closely – he could feel the young monkey's resistance, but that was good; it showed spirit.

"Take some well-earned leave," said Tyrell. "Forget about all this," he waved a dismissive hand across the battlefield. "Enjoy a break from Cadet duties. Think about what we've discussed. Then come and see me."

But Mico didn't want to forget the battlefield. He felt a primal need to face the sea of corpses, to get their blood on his hands. He was not innocent; he should not stay clean.

"If it's all the same to you, Deputy Tyrell, I'd rather return to my unit," Mico said curtly.

Tyrell shrugged; no point forcing the issue. Give the young Cadet time to understand what was in his best interests.

Give him time.

18

VICTORY

The Langur had never seen a celebration like it; close encounter with defeat made their eventual victory that much sweeter, and the Troop was determined to savour the moment.

Flowers had been gathered from all over the neighbourhood to create a colourful carpet of blossom for the returning soldiers. The females, elders and young all lined the Central Pathway, and as General Pogo led the Elites in through the Cemetery gates, a huge roar went up and the waiting monkeys started throwing armfuls of petals.

Mico's Cadet squad was right at the back of the victory procession and secretly he'd been hoping that by the time they entered the Cemetery the euphoria would have died down; no one should be cheered for slaughter.

He was out of luck. The adoring monkeys waited until every last fighter had returned, welcoming each like a hero, forcing Mico to celebrate just like all the others, even though inside he was desolate.

The procession doubled back and came to a halt outside the Great Vault, where Lord Gospodar stood, flanked by Deputies Tyrell and Hani, greeting each squad as it arrived.

As ever, Gospodar read the crowd perfectly. He knew the monkeys didn't want to listen to speeches, so, carried along by the magnanimity of victory, he simply reached across, grasped Tyrell's hand and raised it high in the air, publicly acknowledging the Deputy's decisive role in the battle.

A huge roar went up; Tyrell looked surprised and modestly tried to back away. It was all an act – secretly he had made sure that word of his brilliant beehive ploy had spread to all corners of the Troop, but he knew that humility would win hearts in a way that arrogance never could.

From his place in the throng, squeezed and jostled by the other Cadets, Mico watched with a growing sense of dread. His idea had not only devoured the Bonnets; it had turned Tyrell into a war hero.

As the doors to the Great Vault were thrown open the troops surged into the victory feast, but Mico pulled back. He had to get things straight, work out who he could trust.

And there was only one monkey who could help him do that.

The moment he swung round the corner and saw the Hanuman statue, Mico knew the world had changed. The last time he'd been here Rhesus monkeys came and went as they pleased, chaotically spilling into the surrounding streets; now everyone had been marshalled inside Temple Gardens, and a group of large monkeys patrolled back and forth.

Mico drew a deep breath and started towards the Gardens, when suddenly there was a shout: "No further!" and a figure leapt down from one of the overhanging trees and landed right in front of him, blocking his path. It was Twitcher, bristling with aggression.

"I just want to see Papina," Mico said quietly.

"What makes you think she'd want to talk to a thug like you?"

"You don't understand—"

"The Bonnets are lying dead in a ditch!" Twitcher couldn't contain his outrage. "All of them! And for what?!"

Mico didn't want to get into another fight. "We were told they'd stolen a Human baby. We were only trying to keep the peace—"

"How can you say that?!" Twitcher snarled furiously. "The Bonnets kept themselves apart from Humans!"

"I didn't know! I thought it was true. It's what they told us."

But Twitcher wasn't interested. He started pacing round Mico like an animal stalking its prey. "The truth is, *you* are warmongers! The Langur are the cause of all the misery in the monkey world."

The words cut into Mico, hard and uncompromising. It was painful to hear it said so clearly, painful because in his heart he feared it was true.

"No one's more sorry than me." Mico's voice was thick with emotion.

"It's too late for sorry! They're all dead!"

"I know! I saw it!" Mico rounded on Twitcher. "But it doesn't make me proud. It makes me sick."

"Why should I believe a word you say?"

"Because I came back! I came here to find out what's really going on!" The two monkeys were nose to nose, glaring at each other.

"I could have led a troop here," Mico pointed at Temple Gardens, "and cleared you out myself! But I didn't."

He hadn't meant it to sound like a threat, but it silenced Twitcher, who edged backwards. So that was how it worked – when you were feared, you were listened to.

"Now, please," Mico said, regaining his composure, "I'd like to see Papina."

Twitcher said nothing; he just stared at Mico.

It was another voice that broke the deadlock:

"Wait over there."

Mico spun round and saw Willow pointing to the far side of the road. He had no idea how long she'd been standing there or how much she'd heard.

"I just want to talk to her."

"I thought I'd raised her to have more sense," Willow replied curtly, and pointed again to the far side of the road. "Wait."

Mico felt like an outcast. With every passing moment he became more anxious. Maybe Twitcher had double-crossed him; maybe right now he was rounding up a gang to come and attack him, throw him in the gully with all the other dead monkeys. Why else would it be taking so long?

But just as Mico was about to turn and run, abandoning all hope of seeing Papina, she emerged from the horde of monkeys in the Gardens and walked slowly towards him. Her gait was cold and steady, and she resolutely avoided his gaze until she was standing in front of him.

"Papina—" He stepped towards her, but she backed away.

"So you finally decided to show yourself?"

"Can we go somewhere else to talk?"

Papina shook her head.

"I was mobilized. I had no choice."

"So you were there," she said accusingly, determined not to make this easy.

"Papina, I swear, if I could have been somewhere else, anywhere—"

"Spare me the sob story," she scoffed.

"I had to follow orders."

"You were *there*! You were part of the massacre!"

Mico fell silent. Her indignation was like a spotlight shining on his own guilt.

"There are some good Langurs," he said quietly. "My friends, my parents. If you could only meet my father—"

"If you could've met *my* father!" Papina cut him off sharply. "He was gentle and kind; he harmed no one. But he was killed by Langurs. And all for what? Because you wanted to live in the old Cemetery. And now you want the land that belonged to the Bonnets. And after that, it'll be somewhere else. You'll never stop."

Mico shook his head, desperately trying to distance himself from the bloodshed. "I was too young when we moved to the Cemetery. I didn't know any better."

"But you're not too young now, Mico." It was the first time that morning she'd used his name; perhaps it offered a glimmer of hope that she was reaching out to him.

Mico hung his head low. "If I could change the past, undo what happened..." His voice was heavy with regret. "But it's too late."

"Then change the future," Papina said. "Choose which Troop you'll stand with, and fight with them."

Mico was taken aback by the bluntness of her ultimatum. "I can't just turn my back on the Langur."

"Why not?"

"They're my home, my family ... everything." Mico looked at her earnestly, hoping for some form of reprieve.

It didn't come.

"Then we can never see each other again."

"Papina, please! I need you to believe me!"

Mico looked at her, his eyes pleading with hers, and just for a moment he glimpsed sadness behind her coldness.

"You need to choose, Mico. You can't be a bystander any longer. That's what it means to grow up."

And she turned and walked back into Temple Gardens, leaving Mico utterly alone.

19

EMPIRE

Two days later, Lord Gospodar made the proclamation: "Following our successful clearance of the derelict Ambassador's Palace and Gardens, a Langur colony will be *re*-established there." His words were met with rapturous enthusiasm – a new colony was exactly what the Langur needed.

Thanks to plentiful food supplies, birth rates were up, and the younger families longed for space to make homes of their own. This was their chance, and what homes they would be – everyone knew the old Bonnet lands were among the best in the City.

All Cadets were assigned to help the new settlers move into the Eastern Province, as it was now to be called, and as the excited column gathered at the Cemetery gates ready to move out, the leaders swung up onto the perimeter wall to make the inevitable speeches.

Mico groaned inwardly; the very last thing he wanted to hear was Tyrell's rhetoric. At one point the Deputy even went so far as to claim he wished he could go with the settlers.

And then something strange happened – an anonymous voice in the crowd called out, "There's always room for one more!" Which provoked a laugh.

Even Tyrell chuckled, before humbly declaring that he was too old for such an adventure, and he really didn't have the energy or stamina.

A chorus of "No! Not true!" mingled with more cries of "Join us! Join us!"

Mico looked from Tyrell to Gospodar and saw rivalry bristle between the two senior monkeys.

Ever since the Battle of the Summer-house there had been tensions at the top of the Troop. Gospodar had been generous in his praise of Tyrell's role in the victory, but rather than showing humility, the Deputy had subtly kept reminding everyone that it was his actions that had averted disaster.

It made Gospodar very wary. Had Tyrell now set his eyes on higher things? Did he see himself as Lord Ruler of the Langur?

If that was true, the very last thing Gospodar wanted was for Tyrell to move to the Eastern Province and establish a power base of his own.

Now, however, with this clamour from the settlers, Gospodar had been publicly backed into a corner: if he refused to let Tyrell go he would be seen as mean-spirited.

Tyrell could see Gospodar's discomfort and deliberately let him swing in the uncertainty for a few moments, before finally coming to his rescue. "I'd be honoured to play a small part in helping you get started, just for the first few days. If Lord Gospodar agrees..."

The settlers immediately thumped their approval; Gospodar had little choice but to go along with it and hope that his Deputy meant what he said.

Which is how Tyrell came to take his place at the head of the column of settlers, leading his monkeys to a bright new future.

* * *

General Pogo and a squad of Elites were waiting in the Eastern Province when the gates creaked open. Deputy Tyrell strode majestically in and looked around, his nose twitching as it caught the last remaining scents of blood. He smiled as he gazed across the beautiful lawns that stretched around the Summer-house.

"Good work, General. Excellent. You'd never know. Line your troops up to welcome the settlers. Let them know who they have to thank for all this."

In a well-rehearsed ritual, two rows of Elites lined up on either side of the entrance to form a guard of honour, then the Cadets escorted the settlers into their new home. For most it was a moment of pure excitement, of hope, of pride; but for Mico it was eerily reminiscent of his own family's arrival in the old Cemetery all those seasons ago.

With one big difference: now he knew the bloody price that had been paid.

As he watched young monkeys squabble innocently over who would sleep where, without even a passing thought for the Bonnets who had lived here for so long, Mico realized that Papina's dark warning was coming true: this was nothing more than a land grab.

Who would be next?

Suddenly Mico sensed a presence behind him – he spun round and saw two large Elites looming over him.

"You're to come with us."

"Why? What have I done?" Mico said defensively.

"Deputy Tyrell wants you."

It was clear from their tone that he had no choice.

As they approached the Summer-house Mico's mind was racing; you never knew which way it would go with Tyrell. By rights the Deputy should be grateful, keen to reward Mico for his loyalty and discretion, but he could equally feel threatened that Mico knew the truth behind the defeat of the Bonnets, and there was always a risk that a monkey under threat would lash out.

Mico tried to steady his nerves as he was taken up the Tower staircase; even if he wanted to run there was no way he could evade the Elites. All he could do was keep calm and hope.

As they emerged into the room at the top of the Tower, Mico was stunned: the whole space had been transformed into luxurious living quarters. The last time he'd been here was just after the battle, when the roof was smashed through and broken weapons littered the bloody floor. Now all traces of violence had been erased, the roof had been repaired with a mat of leaves, windows had been opened up in each wall to give spectacular views across the City, and the whole room was stuffed with fruit and sweet-scented herbs. There was even a water trough at the far side filled directly from the guttering on the roof.

And at the centre of it all stood Tyrell.

"Impressed?" he asked with a smile.

Mico could only nod, wide-eyed. But he wasn't just marvelling at the room; he was marvelling at the Deputy's cunning. Tyrell had given the impression that his decision to accompany the settlers had been made on the spur of the moment. But all this? It seemed to have been prepared ahead, for a leader, for Tyrell. What he said and what he did were clearly two very different things.

Tyrell put his arm around Mico and drew him to one of the windows. "What do you see?"

Mico squinted in the bright light and started to pick out familiar Kolkata buildings, but Tyrell chuckled indulgently – he wasn't interested in geography.

"Opportunity, Mico. That's what I see. Opportunities are opening faster than at any other time in Langur history. Fruit? Or bugs?"

He offered Mico two coconut shells, one containing some juicy berries, the other a collection of freshly killed insects; Mico went for fruit.

"But change brings upheaval," Tyrell continued. "New allegiances are being formed; old loyalties are being tested. If you listen carefully—" Tyrell cupped his ear—"you can almost hear the footsteps of power on the move."

He gave a wry chuckle. "The question is, Mico, are you ready to take advantage of these opportunities, to play your part in the new world?"

"Once I've finished my Cadet training I hope to follow in my brother's footsteps—"

"No, no, no. Forget the Elites. Use this." Tyrell put his finger right in the middle of Mico's forehead. "Your mind," he continued. "Your mind is the key to power."

Tyrell lounged back against the wall and made himself comfortable. "You know, when I was a Cadet, times were harsh for the Langur. We lived in the shunting yards, every scrap of food had to be fought for, every sliver of territory defended. "I knew I had a lot to offer, but just because I was small, I was ignored. None of the Instructors would take me seriously because I couldn't win those puerile hand to hand wrestling matches. So I fought back with *my* weapon of choice." Tyrell tapped his fingers on his head.

"One night, I crept out of the shunting yards and made my way along the tracks. It was lonely and frightening. Trains rumbled everywhere; one slip and I'd have been killed. But I found what I was looking for: a boxcar stacked with kiwi fruit.

"I hid in the shadows until the labourers arrived to unload the train, then furtively I swung down and stole a sackful of fruit.

"Next morning, the Cadets woke to find piles of fresh kiwis waiting for them. Too hungry to care, they just tucked in. But after breakfast, their stomachs were unsteady, their minds cloudy and sickly. So when it came to training, they struggled. Especially in hand-to-hand combat. Imagine their astonishment when they were beaten by the weakling Tyrell."

"You poisoned them?!" exclaimed Mico.

"It was just a little effluent from the railway latrines. They were queasy for a couple of days, no harm done," Tyrell said dismissively. "But it taught me a valuable lesson: if your will is strong enough, an enemy can always be beaten. I started applying that lesson every day, climbing the ranks, outsmarting my rivals, until I became what I am today. Now the whole Langur Troop benefits from my wisdom."

He leaned forward, fixing Mico with his intense gaze. "The monkey who can out-think his enemies can achieve anything. Like this magnificent home." He waved an arm extravagantly around the Tower room. "Don't you want to live like this, Mico? Perhaps even be the commander of a province of your own?"

Mico couldn't hide his astonishment. "You really think..."

"With a mind like yours, why not?"

The Cadet's stomach tightened with anticipation. Suddenly the allure of power filled the room.

"Of course, you're very raw. There's much you need to learn," Tyrell said casually, showing how easily he could slam the secret door shut again. "Perhaps I could make arrangements for you to join my Intelligence Division."

Mico frowned. "I've never heard of an Intelligence Division."

"Which just proves how good we are. Only a few ... *chosen* monkeys ever get a chance to serve in Intelligence. Those who understand the importance of absolute loyalty ... to *me*."

The way Tyrell said the words filled Mico with unease – there were dark undercurrents to this proposition. He needed time to think it through, to understand what he was getting himself into.

"My parents ... they'll be disappointed if I don't go for the Elites," Mico said, trying to extricate himself.

"Make no mistake about what's on offer here, Mico. The Intelligence Division is a fast track to the top of the Troop. The *very* top. You will be looking *down* on the Elites, and I can't tell you how good that feels." He gave a sharp laugh, then leaned forward and whispered, "Intelligence is where leaders are made."

Tyrell reached out, put a conspiratorial hand on Mico's shoulder, and just for an instant felt the Cadet bridle under his touch. In that moment he knew Mico's conscience was still wrestling with the realities of power.

"Ruling a Troop is a difficult calling," Tyrell said. "To innocent eyes, it may look at times as if the line between right and wrong has been forgotten. But once you've seen the vision behind everything, then you will understand."

Mico looked at Tyrell, trying to read the deep, calculating eyes. "I thought we were the Chosen Troop because we kept the peace," he ventured. "Isn't that the vision?"

Tyrell nodded thoughtfully. “That’s true. But it’s not the whole truth.”

He fell silent; clearly nothing more would be revealed until Mico had made his choice.

“Look, if you want your parents’ blessing, talk to them,” Tyrell said with affable ease. “It’s rather touching that you respect them so much. But be careful what you tell them. Secrecy is the great weapon of the Intelligence Division.”

Mico nodded. “I understand.”

“Tell them you’ve been offered a chance to come and work on my personal staff. See what they say then.”

And with the offer left dangling tantalizingly in mid-air, Tyrell pointed to the door. The interview was over.

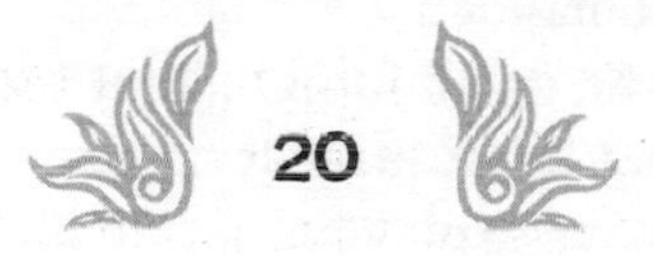

20

CROSSROADS

The last Supply Monkeys were just entering the Eastern Province as Mico made his way out into the street. He stopped and looked back as the gates were swung shut. Across the City, guards would be closing the Cemetery gates as well, securing everything for the night.

There was a time when Mico would have felt anxious to be alone in the City without the secure embrace of Langur walls around him, but right now he needed to be alone; he needed to think.

At this time of day the City streets were crowded with Humans, so Mico scrambled up the tangle of drainpipes that clung to an apartment block, skittered across the roof and leapt onto a railway embankment that carved through Kolkata in a lazy arc. He could follow this to the disused signal box, then branch off back to the Cemetery.

It was turning into a beautiful evening, the sky was filling with great flocks of swallows wheeling above the buildings, the ramshackle markets were buzzing with the banter of a thousand hagglers, but all Mico could see was the huge decision looming in front of him.

If he accepted Tyrell's offer and threw himself into the Langur cause, maybe he would come to understand why the war on the Rhesus and the destruction of the Bonnets were necessary. Tyrell had spoken of a secret master plan; perhaps that would explain the morality behind the trail of blood.

But even if he could forget about the violence of the past, what about the future? If he became Tyrell's creature he would have to play his part in bloody deeds yet to come. Mico shuddered at the thought of being implicated in more slaughter.

And there was another, more personal, fear gnawing away at Mico's heart: if he followed Tyrell, he would never be able to see Papina again.

The sense of loss cut sharply across Mico as he imagined what that would mean. From the moment he first glimpsed her in the Cemetery, he had felt a special connection to Papina; it was as if a part of him had always known her, always trusted her. Without understanding why, he felt deep down that if he lost Papina, he would lose his way altogether.

Which meant he could not take Tyrell's offer.

Except that wouldn't be so easy.

Tyrell had made it quite clear: if you weren't for him, you were against him; and Mico feared the Deputy would make a very bad enemy. It was a harsh reality of the Langur Troop – upsetting powerful monkeys meant you were denied any chance of moving up the hierarchy.

The repercussions might not even stop with Mico; his parents might suddenly find themselves spurned; maybe his father would be stripped of his duties controlling Troop supplies, which would break his heart.

And it would all be Mico's fault.

To accept, or not to accept? The conflicting thoughts bumped relentlessly into each other as Mico made his way back, until before he knew it, he could see the outline of the Cemetery walls in the twilight. He paused and looked at the guards perched on top of the gate pillars, proud servants of a triumphant Troop. How he envied those monkeys who never questioned anything, who lived their entire lives accepting the world as it was given to them. How easy that must be.

Instinctively he went round to the drinking pool in the back wall. There was no particular reason to avoid the guards; after all, he was returning from vital work establishing the Eastern Province. But this evening Mico didn't want to deal with anyone.

He plunged into the cool water and stretched out his hands, feeling for the hole in the wall, but instead of pulling himself through, he paused, holding himself in the currents, enjoying the sensation of weightlessness.

The water tickled as it flowed through his fur, brushed past his face... There was something deeply comforting about its cool caress; it made him think of the happy, secret times he'd shared with Papina before everything became so complicated.

Maybe Papina was the answer – get everything back to simpler times. She had urged him to choose sides – what if he chose the Rhesus?

If he was living in Temple Gardens, surrounded by hundreds of Rhesus, he wouldn't have to fear Tyrell's anger. He and Papina could be together, playing in the trees and lounging in the sun without a care in the world.

But as Mico tried to imagine that life, the vision started to crumble before his eyes, because it meant he would never see his parents or friends again; he would be turning his back on everything he'd ever known. And for all the sacrifice, he could never become a Rhesus, never truly be like them. When the Langur went to war again, maybe the Rhesus would turn against him, drive him out of the Gardens to live as a lone monkey.

Suddenly Mico felt suffocated. He pulled himself through the hole and lunged to the surface, filling his lungs with air.

A lone monkey.

There were rumours about exiles who survived like that, but "survive" was the word, not "live". No one to play with or laugh with, no one to share your food or look after you when you were sick. And at the end of it all, to die alone and forgotten.

Mico shuddered as the dampness of the night crept up on him. He scrambled to the top of the wall and perched himself on the smooth coping stones.

On one side of him was the Cemetery, on the other the City stretching out into the distance. He was perched between two worlds in more ways than one. Whichever decision he made seemed to lead to unhappiness. Maybe he should just spend the rest of his life sitting up here on this wall...

Suddenly his mind did a somersault as a whole plan effortlessly revealed itself. Perhaps there was a way he could straddle two worlds, be all things to all monkeys.

Mico leapt to his feet, a huge smile dancing across his face. It was beautiful, the perfect answer to an impossible problem.

The last person Papina was expecting to wake her was Mico. She sat up groggily and looked around – it was horribly early, her mother and all the others were still fast asleep, and yet here was Mico, standing over her alert and breathless, having just run across the City.

"What's going on?" she said tetchily.

" Shhh." Mico gently put his fingers on her lips. "How do you fancy breakfast?"

"It's too early."

"It's never too early for chocolate," Mico smiled. "The night watchman at the bakery forgot to lock the back window again."

Papina couldn't resist.

She sat and ate the pilfered chocolate in silence as Mico paced back and forth, exhilarated by his plan.

"So I accept Tyrell's offer. I play the loyal monkey. But all the time, I'll be secretly feeding information to you. Everything you need to keep you safe: the routes of Langur patrols, which targets are going to be hit next, who's safe and who's in danger. I'll belong to the Langur, but secretly I'll be helping the Rhesus!"

His enthusiasm was met with a sceptical silence. Papina pressed her fingers into the chocolate crumbs then licked them clean, as she tried to articulate what her guts were screaming at her: that this was a terrible idea.

"No one can work for two masters," she said finally.

"It'll be difficult, but it's got to be worth trying," Mico replied, undaunted. "And if I can please Tyrell, rise up the hierarchy, maybe I can change the master plan so that the different Troops can live in peace, right across the City."

His optimism was so laudable, but so naive. "The other Langurs don't think like you, Mico. They're not interested in peace."

"Which is why I need to work from the *inside*. Where I can change things."

He had an answer for everything, but what really worried Papina was that this whole plan was just a way for Mico to avoid the brutal reality.

"If something is wrong, you have to fight it," she said.

"But there are many ways to fight. The tiny cobra is as deadly as the giant python," Mico replied. "Why can't my weapon be deception?"

Papina shook her head pensively. She wanted to tell him the truth, but Mico was so fired up with hope, she didn't have the heart to cut him down.

He took her hand and clasped it tightly, willing her to believe that this could work. "Anyone can run away, but to stay and fight for change, maybe that's the courageous thing to do."

"But you'll be lying to everyone. You'll be so alone."

"Not if *you* believe in me." He looked into her eyes, desperately needing her approval. "I once promised to keep you safe, no matter what. I meant it then, and I mean it now. But to keep that promise, I need to change the world."

He looked at her as the sun crept above the roof of the bakery, waiting for the reply that would determine the rest of his life. Until finally, Papina gave a hesitant smile ... and nodded.

Mico had gone up onto the roof to talk with his father, who was using the Stones to organize supplies for the Eastern Province, but he had barely uttered the words "Tyrell wants me to work for him", when Trumble dropped everything and stared at his son in astonishment.

"*Deputy* Tyrell?"

"Yes. But it's—"

He didn't get a chance to finish the sentence – Trumble leapt over and hugged his son. "Everyone was so quick to judge you, Mico. Just because you were small." He cradled his son's face in his hands and looked at him with such love. "But now you can hold your tail high!"

Kima's reaction was just as effusive – she gripped his hand, refusing to let go. "I can't wait to tell—"

"No!" exclaimed Mico. "You can't tell anyone. It's secret work."

Which made Kima even prouder. "They'll know when they see you living in the finest quarters, moving in the highest circles. They'll all know that my son is important."

It was the first time in Mico's life that he'd felt so unhesitatingly loved by his parents.

But what surprised him most of all was Breri's reaction. At first he was incredulous, then jealousy crept into his heart; but as Breri worked out that having a younger brother high up in the echelons of power could help his own career, jealousy gave way to respect.

"I'm glad they found a place for your talents," he said, patting Mico on the back. "That's what makes the Langur great: we all do our bit in the fight."

So this was what success felt like – an intoxicating mix of flattery and respect. Suddenly Mico no longer felt small or vulnerable; he felt as if he had power.

Mico strode into Tyrell's room at the top of the Tower and was puzzled to find the Deputy scratching a squiggle of random, intersecting lines across an entire wall.

"Impressive, isn't it?" Tyrell said without even turning round. Mico tilted his head left and right, trying to make sense of it.

"It's the City," said Tyrell proudly, pointing from the lines to the panoramic view through the window. "The lines represent the streets below."

Mico half closed his eyes and looked from the lines to the streets and back again ... and suddenly he understood.

It was a beautiful, brilliantly simple idea; for all his darkness, Tyrell was touched by genius.

"Your parents were suitably impressed by my offer, I take it?" the Deputy said, scratching another line.

"They were. Very."

"You were discreet, of course – about the nature of your new life."

"Yes, sir. Very discreet."

"And?"

Mico drew a deep breath. There would be no turning back from this moment.

"And?" Tyrell repeated.

"And I would be honoured to serve in the Intelligence Division ... to pledge my loyalty to you, Deputy Tyrell."

A genuinely warm smile broke across Tyrell's face. "Then welcome to my world, Mico. This is the start of your new life. Great things await."

"I won't let you down," Mico said, surprised how easy it was to tell a blatant lie.

A thrill of excitement ran down Mico's spine. His double life had started, a life of secrets and lies, of plotting and duplicity, of diverting the course of power.

All in the name of peace.

PART TWO

THE ASCENT OF MONKEY

For this is the true strength of guilty kings,
When they corrupt the souls of those they rule.

MATTHEW ARNOLD, "MEROPE"

21

POWER SHIFT

He was dead.

The news ran through the Cemetery like a shock wave. Gospodar, Lord Ruler of the Langur had been found dead at dawn.

In the seasons since the conquest of the Eastern Province the Langur had been confidently sweeping all opposition aside. Now suddenly their beloved Leader, the monkey who had guided them from outcasts to conquerors, had been snatched from them by death.

Mico first heard the news as he enjoyed a leisurely breakfast in his private rooms. One of the immediate benefits of joining Tyrell's secretive Intelligence Division had been the provision of exclusive quarters close to the Great Vault. They were spacious and light, and had a carefully concealed door that enabled Mico to come and go at any time of the day or night without attracting attention. Best of all, a Cadet had been assigned to look after all his domestic needs, from keeping the rooms clean to delivering fresh meals and running errands.

Tyrell had set this system up to sharpen the sense of obligation among his Intelligence operatives, and the psychology seemed to be working – Mico was proving to be an assiduous officer, learning all about the many secret sources of information that kept the Langur safe.

His star was rising fast.

But that was yesterday. Gospodar's sudden demise could change everything.

"He's dead! He's dead!" was all the Cadet messenger could blurt out. "It can't be true! It can't!"

He was too overwhelmed to make much sense, so Mico forced him to sit still and drink some water.

"Deputy Hani went to wake Lord Gospodar ... to give him the report just like normal. But he was ... he was lying on the floor ... cold..." The Cadet slumped forward, clasping his head in his hands.

Mico felt his entire world reel and judder as if it was about to collapse. Turning his back on the grieving Cadet, he left his rooms and hurried out into the Cemetery.

Had this happened a year earlier, Mico would have rushed straight to the Great Vault, but one of the first lessons Tyrell had taught him was never to do the obvious; a monkey that was hard to predict was hard to outwit. So, instead, Mico headed for the tree-lined avenues of the Cemetery, mingling with the Troop, tuning into the monkey on the branch.

Everywhere he looked, monkeys were milling around aimlessly, all sense of routine erased. They clung to one another for comfort, they spoke in subdued tones, each compelled to explain exactly what they were doing when they heard the news, as if their actions were in some strange way linked to their Leader's sudden death. Mothers weren't bustling their youngsters off to Cadet School; patrols weren't setting off in every direction; the normal buzz of morning activity had dissipated into a cloud of shock and grief.

It was as if the very future of the Langur was hanging in the balance.

A large, forlorn throng of monkeys had gathered outside the Great Vault, desperate for news. All eyes gazed at the main doors which were shut tight and guarded by a squad of Elites. As Mico edged his way through the crowd he caught sight of his own parents standing silently with all the other monkeys. Kima was trembling fearfully while Trumble held her tightly, trying to calm her down.

As Mico emerged from the crowd, the Elites immediately stepped forward. "Stay back!"

Calmly Mico opened the palm of his left hand to reveal a strange, intricate mark of swirling black lines – the mark of the Intelligence Division.

Once Mico had sworn loyalty to Tyrell, they had retired to the privacy of his rooms in the Tower, where Tyrell spent an entire afternoon creating the pattern using the dye from crushed berries. Dot by dot, he'd used a cactus thorn to inject the dye under the skin of Mico's palm; it had been painful, and Mico's hand was swollen for several days, but Tyrell had promised that the Insignia would open doors that were closed to other monkeys.

He hadn't exaggerated. Whether it was going out after curfew or gaining entry to restricted weapons stores, the Insignia always got Mico in, and today was no exception.

Seeing the mark, the Elites hurriedly swung the doors open. Mico heard anticipation ripple through the crowd; everyone else had been kept waiting outside, and now he alone was being ushered into the Troop's inner sanctum. As he strode through, Mico glanced over his shoulder and just for a moment caught the look on his parents' faces, impressed that their son wielded this kind of power. Despite the gravity of the situation, Mico couldn't help feeling a swell of pride.

His sense of empowerment didn't last long – as Mico entered Gospodar's private rooms the true horror of the situation struck home.

The two Deputies, Tyrell and Hani, sat on opposite sides of the room, silently staring at Gospodar's corpse – the Lord Ruler looked as if he had died in appalling agony. His body lay contorted on the stone floor, hands gripping some invisible enemy, mouth twisted open, legs splayed at an awkward angle. It was as if life had been physically ripped from his body.

Deputy Hani turned slowly to Mico.

"Get out."

His voice wavered with fear and incomprehension.

Mico bowed and turned to go when Tyrell's hard voice cut through the gloom.

"He stays."

Mico froze, looking from one Deputy to the other.

"I need time to think!" growled Hani, angry to have been contradicted.

"Right now we need to manage what the monkeys out there are thinking." Tyrell pointed to the Cemetery. "Which is *my* job. Now." He glanced at Mico. "And *he* is with me."

The air was brittle with tension. Mico hardly dared breathe as Tyrell and Hani tried to glare each other down, until the heavy-footed General Pogo thundered into the room. His solitary eye gazed at the twisted body.

"By my beating heart!"

Even though the General had seen plenty of death in battle, the image of his Leader splayed on the floor still shocked him.

"What happened?"

Hani shook his head slowly. "I came in, as usual,

to give him the plans for the day. I knocked, waited for a reply. When none came I entered..." Hani looked down at the silent corpse. "And found him like this."

The General scowled; monkeys didn't just die for no reason.

Sensing Pogo's unease, Tyrell stepped towards the body and turned it over.

"No signs of violence; nothing to suggest a struggle." Tyrell ran his hands through the cold fur. "He's not been murdered."

"Then why did he die?" Pogo shook his head, bewildered. "He wasn't old; he wasn't sick!"

"I don't know why, General. All I know is that the Troop must never know Lord Gospodar was found like *this*." Tyrell pointed at the grisly corpse. "Our great Leader does not deserve such a demeaning end. We owe him everything; the least we can do is give him a death worthy of his life."

Seeing Tyrell move back into the political arena jolted Hani to his senses. He drew himself up to his full height.

"I'll organize a fitting ceremony. And I expect your full co-operation," Hani commanded. "I want the transition of power into my hands to be as smooth as possible."

"The arrogance of the monkey!" Tyrell bellowed when they were back in the privacy of his rooms in the Summer-house Tower. "The presumption that *he* will be Gospodar's successor! The Troop deserves better than that plodding oaf." He turned and looked out of the window, gazing across the City.

In the silence, Mico glanced at the two other members of the Intelligence Division who had been summoned – Castro and Rani. Handpicked from Cadet School many seasons ago, they had a talent for remaining unobtrusive, while always being by Tyrell's side when he needed them. They were trusted, hard-working and loyal, but right now they were out of their depth – neither had ever seen Tyrell so rattled.

Mico's agile mind quickly ran through the options; this ability to grasp new situations was what had earned him a special place in Tyrell's heart.

"Hani is considerably larger than you, sir. And he still believes that's enough."

Tyrell turned his sharp eyes on Mico, insulted at the rudeness of the comparison.

Aware that he had to underline where his loyalties lay, Mico hastily added, "He doesn't understand that times have changed."

"He's not the only one," Tyrell mused as he gazed down at the Langur families on the lawns. "I dare say many of *them* are still dazzled by bodyweight. Such a pity that in Hani's case his intellect is out of all proportion to his size."

Castro and Rani exchanged an uncomfortable glance; Tyrell was now criticizing the Lord Ruler-in-Waiting, and that amounted to sedition, but Tyrell was quick to reposition his thinking.

"Don't get me wrong, I like Hani. He makes a fine Deputy, and in another time he would have made a competent Leader. But these are ... complicated days for our Troop. We've won so much, but we've made enemies along the way. If we're not careful, we could lose everything."

Tyrell scrutinized Mico, Castro and Rani; they had taken an oath to him personally, but you couldn't always rely on that. He needed these three to really believe that, for the sake of the Troop, they shouldn't back Hani.

"Was it strength that won us all this?" Tyrell pointed out of the window. "If I remember rightly, it was a small monkey with a big brain." A fleeting glance between Tyrell and Mico, for a moment acknowledging the truth before burying it.

"It was *me* who devised the strategy that won the day, not Hani," said Tyrell firmly. "What the Langur Troop needs is a Leader with intelligence." He turned to face his monkeys. "And it is your job to make them realize it."

So now it was clear: Tyrell's ambition was to be the next Lord Ruler.

There was a critical moment of silence between the wavering monkeys. Tyrell locked eyes with Mico. "I'm counting on your full support in this."

Mico's mind raced through the implications. What Tyrell was proposing was treason, the Leadership should pass to Hani; not only was he older, but he had twice the size and strength.

But Mico wasn't here just to serve the Langur – he had his own secret agenda, and that cause would surely be helped if Tyrell became the Lord Ruler, as it would put Mico right at the centre of power.

Which is why he lowered his head and with great solemnity announced, "I am the rock for you to build on."

A compliance which instantly robbed Castro and Rani of any lingering doubts.

They had two days. Two days to subtly infiltrate the mind of the Troop. Two days until Lord Gospodar's funeral and the anointing of the new Leader. It was a fine art, shifting opinion, but Tyrell had taught them well.

Mico, Castro and Rani started by dividing the Troop into sections, and identifying the monkeys in each section whose voices could sway others, the so-called "rainmakers". Then they created a set of political messages that they could inject into casual conversation in such a way that these rainmakers would pick up on them.

The shock of Gospodar's death had made the Langur Troop a hotbed of speculation – ordinary monkeys struggled to understand why he had died. Was it the work of Rhesus monkeys? Was it the dead Bonnets somehow exacting revenge? Would the Humans still favour the Langur as the Chosen Monkey without Gospodar as Leader?

Into these fevered speculations, Mico, Castro and Rani planted their carefully worded suggestions, that "the problems facing the Troop were complex", that "the wind of change is in the air", and that "Gospodar would have wanted the Troop to be bold in this crisis".

The trick was timing – they couldn't just blurt out the messages; they had to listen to the conversation and drop them into the flow, subtly steering thoughts this way and that.

A good sense of humour helped – a couple of witty remarks always made the monkey on the branch more receptive.

Rumours and speculation swirled around the Troop, and by the time of Gospodar's funeral, Langur minds were hungry for change.

22

SERVANT OF THE MONKEY

The Langur Troop had never seen so much honour lavished on the dead.

It was their tradition that any monkey who could feel the grip of death in sickness would share a final meal with their loved ones, then quietly crawl away in the night never to be seen again. A monkey who fell in battle was disposed of as quickly as possible in the nearest ditch. But for Lord Gospodar it was different. Gospodar had been the architect of the Langur's rise to greatness and he needed a final resting place that would keep him at the heart of the Troop.

Which is why, as the black Monsoon clouds loomed threateningly in the sky, the Langur lined the avenues of the Cemetery clutching fistfuls of flower petals. They stood, silent and solemn, as Deputy Hani emerged from the Great Vault followed by four Elites who carried a long flat stone on their shoulders. Lying on the stone was the body of their dead Leader, wrapped in a silk shroud.

The shroud had been Hani's idea, a very practical solution to a rather sordid problem. Because the monkeys had no experience of storing corpses, they had been caught unawares when, in the heat, Gospodar had started to rot. To counteract the stench, aromatic herbs had been stuffed around him, and to conceal the damage the maggots had done, Hani ordered the theft of a silk sheet from one of the nearby street markets. But it had been Tyrell's idea to present the shroud as a gift from the Humans, celebrating the unique bond Gospodar had forged between monkey and Man, transforming a practical solution into a potent symbol.

As the body came into view, tightly wrapped apart from the head, a wave of raw emotion swept over the monkeys. A plaintive wail erupted as they threw petals in the air and watched them drift down onto the passing body.

Tyrell was waiting at the foot of the Great Banyan Tree, next to a hole that had been dug between its jutting roots – this was to be Gospodar's final resting place, for ever protected by the huge tree.

As the Elites gently placed the stone on the ground, Tyrell studied the crowd, fascinated by the baying of their collective grief.

Hani crouched down and with great solemnity touched Gospodar's cold face, as if the gift of leadership was being passed from the dead to the living. Then he stood up, letting all see the size and power of his body.

"I have chosen this tree for Gospodar's resting place," Hani's voice boomed across the Cemetery, "because it towers over us just as he did. This tree has weathered storms and droughts, just as Lord Gospodar guided us through good times and bad." He looked up respectfully at the huge canopy of the banyan, then gave a signal to the Elites, who lowered the body into the hole.

Tyrell watched impassively, considering the merits of Hani's oration. Simple, short, sincere, but not very inspiring. An easy act to follow.

The Elites stepped back – Gospodar's body had been placed feet first in the grave, its head a little below ground level. But just as they were about to start filling the hole, there was an emotive shout:

"NO! Let the final honour be mine!"

All eyes searched for the monkey who had interrupted the funeral ... and found Tyrell.

"Let it be my hands that serve our Leader for the last time," he cried, his voice bursting with emotion. "It's the least I can do for the monkey who gave me everything, taught me everything ... like a father."

The Troop watched, astonished, as Deputy Tyrell threw all rank and dignity aside and scooped the sticky mud into his arms.

"Wisdom, hope, ambition – it all flowed from him," Tyrell declared, as with great reverence he placed an armful of mud around the corpse then dramatically held up his stained palms. "These hands bury Gospodar, but remember that it was *his* hands that guided us to greatness. His was the mind that had the vision."

A low moan of assent echoed through the Cemetery. Tyrell had captured the drama and the grief of the moment.

"But," Tyrell declared, "the lands we rule, the power we wield, these are just trifles. Gospodar's real gift was in here." Tyrell put his hands on his head, letting the damp soil mark his face as if anointing himself.

"He taught us that we can *choose* who we are. We can choose to be oppressed or we can choose to be free; we can choose to follow, or choose to lead. If you want to honour Gospodar, never forget, monkeys can choose their own fate. Don't meekly accept what you are given; strive for what you desire!"

As he spoke, Tyrell could feel the mood of the monkeys lifting.

And then a lone voice spoke from the depth of the crowd: "Lead us, Tyrell."

Was it Mico, or Castro, or Rani? Or was it some anonymous monkey who had been genuinely moved by Tyrell's words? Whoever it was, the voice articulated what many of the Troop were feeling.

"Lead us, lead us!" The cry was taken up by others.

Tyrell shook his head, modestly. "I'm not your Leader. *This* is your Leader." Tyrell turned and bowed respectfully to Hani. "Hani, Lord Ruler of the Langur." Without a hint of irony, Tyrell started to thump the ground in a show of loyalty.

The Elites immediately took up the rhythmic beating, their loyalty beyond question. But the dissenting chorus in the crowd would not be silenced.

"Tyrell! Lead us!"

"We choose *you*!"

"Lead us!"

Hani looked at the crowd anxiously as the chanting escalated.

"Monkeys! My monkeys!" he boomed. "Tyrell has spoken wisely. Which is why he is our most valued and trusted advisor. I swear, everything he spoke of is safe in my hands!"

Pathetic, thought Tyrell; he can't even articulate his vision without referring to me.

Many in the crowd sensed this same weakness and joined in the pro-Tyrell chanting, but others rallied behind Hani, preferring to stick to the time-honoured rules of succession.

The Troop split in two, and the solemnity of the funeral was all but forgotten as each faction chanted for their chosen Leader.

Then out of the chaos, a new refrain started to grow, one that unified the Troop: "Let us choose! Let us choose!"

Hani could feel his authority slipping away. Suddenly he was facing a crisis in the first moments of his reign.

"Show them strength, my Lord!" advised Tyrell, shouting above the noise. "They *must* listen to you!"

Hani looked at the restless surge of monkeys, wondering what Gospodar would have done. The crowd seemed evenly divided, but when it came to it, surely no one really wanted Tyrell as Leader; he was too small and weak, and he had no charm. Perhaps in a straight contest everything would sort itself out.

"Very well!" Hani boomed above the chanting. "If that is your wish, *you* shall choose the Leader!"

A huge cheer went up and the ground started to tremble with the deafening thump of fists pounding the dirt in a show of support.

A smile spread across Hani's face; he'd made the right decision. The first of many, no doubt.

23

DATES

No one knew why, but the trees in Temple Gardens had enjoyed a spectacular growth spurt that year, enabling the bravest monkeys to clamber to the ends of the topmost branches and swing down onto the head of the giant Hanuman statue. Not many were brave enough, though, which is why this had become the perfect rendezvous for Mico and Papina.

Perched on the statue's shoulder, tucked discreetly in the shadows of his flowing stone hair, Mico had commanding views of the surrounding streets, enabling him to make covert visits to Papina while keeping a lookout for Langur patrols.

The system worked well – their clandestine meetings took place every other day, allowing Mico to pass vital information about attacks all across the City. Although he couldn't stop the land grabs, his espionage had prevented any more massacres.

So far.

But there had been some close calls. Only a few days earlier a patrol had targeted some Rhesus families living on the roof of a new shopping centre, allegedly scavenging from the cafés. By the time Mico had got word to Papina, the Langur Elites were already storming across the City and the families only just escaped.

No matter how dangerous it became, though, Mico wasn't going to give up. Beyond the Rhesus lives that he was saving was a more powerful reason: every time he delivered secret information, he got to see Papina.

The danger of getting embroiled in the struggle between the warring Troops had forged a new intensity in their relationship, and their meetings were so absorbing, there was never any time for the excitement and longing to fade.

From the top of the statue he could see Papina now, scampering through the crowds of monkeys, clutching a sprig of fresh dates for them to share. He recognized so many of the monkeys she passed that, even though Mico's visits were covert, in a strange way he felt part of the Rhesus Troop, especially as Papina always found time to update him on the latest gossip.

He knew that Rowna was now on her third mate – the previous one had found her overbearing manner too much to handle, and one night he simply ran away. But far from mellowing Rowna, this had made her even more outspoken. She wanted a male to boss around, and she found one in a chubby monkey called Uzi who spent much of the time teasing her, but was careful to do exactly what she said.

Fig didn't have to do any of the pursuing. As she was still young and pretty, there was no shortage of males trying to woo her. In the old days she would have been swayed by a muscular body, but the trauma of exile had taught her that real strength came from knowledge and connections, which is why Fig chose Twitcher as her new mate.

Observing all this pairing-up from a distance was entertaining enough, but it also made Mico feel anxious, because the pressure on Papina to choose a mate had started to grow. Strong as their feelings were for each other, the fact remained: she was Rhesus; he was Langur – and neither knew how that would end.

There was a sudden rustle of leaves and Papina swung across from the top branch and landed right next to him on Hanuman's shoulder.

"So, who grabbed the Leadership?" she asked, offering him a date, then popping one into her own mouth.

"There's going to be a ballot."

"A what?"

"It's a new thing. Every monkey has a say in choosing the Leader. It was Tyrell's idea, but I think it's a good one."

Papina chewed thoughtfully. "I don't trust him. How can the whole Troop speak at once?"

"That bit was my idea," said Mico proudly. "Each monkey will be given one of my father's pebbles. They have to place it at the feet of the monkey they'd like to be Leader. Whoever gets the most pebbles wins."

Mico spat out his date stone; they watched as it drifted down ... and just missed the pool.

"Hah!" Papina smiled triumphantly, then demonstrated how it should be done, sending a stone plopping right into the water.

"Tyrell's a cunning operator," Mico admitted, "but this ballot, it could be a whole new way of doing things. It makes the Leader answerable to the Troop."

"Nothing good ever came from cunning," replied Papina.

"Give things a chance to settle down," urged Mico. "Tyrell trusts me – I'm his closest advisor. If we time it right, I know I can swing his thinking, make him stop this war between the Troops."

Papina gave Mico a wan smile. "I want to believe you, Mico, I really do." She reached out and took his hand, gazing darkly at the tattoo that marked him as one of Tyrell's creatures. "But I have a bad feeling about Tyrell. Very bad."

24

THE DEATH OF CHOICE

"You and I make a fine team," Tyrell said with an approving smile, as Mico led him into the room where all the polished pebbles were stored.

For as long as anyone could remember, Trumble's Stone accounting system had been a vital part of keeping the Langur running smoothly; now it was to determine the very Leadership itself ... one pebble for each member of the Troop.

Tyrell stepped forward and ran his fingers delicately over the Stones.

"Beautiful," he muttered to himself. "And so simple."

Commandeering a squad of Cadets for the afternoon, Mico set about distributing the Stones; by the time the sun set, there was a line of eager monkeys – each clasping a pebble – stretching from the Great Vault back through the Cemetery paths.

The air buzzed with chatter and restless energy; the monkeys couldn't contain their excitement at this new way of making decisions and were eager to get started. Finally the two candidates emerged from the heavy doors of the Great Vault to a rousing cheer.

Hani made sure he walked at his full height, confident that when it came to the crunch, the Troop would never choose an undersized monkey as Leader. Tyrell didn't bother with such theatrics; he believed that physical bulk paled into insignificance next to his sharp intellect.

The two Deputies took their places, then Hani drew a deep breath and made his proclamation:

"By the authority vested in me from the hand of Lord Gospodar, I call on each monkey to step forward and place his Stone at the feet of the one who shall be his Leader."

Thrill galvanized the Troop as Hani beckoned the first monkey in line to come forward. It was Nappo, now a young Footsoldier. But he sprang forward with such excitement he tripped and went flying headlong in the dirt, sending his Stone skittering across the ground.

The whole line of monkeys burst into laughter as poor Nappo scrambled to his feet and tried to make light of the accident, but when he looked for his voting Stone, he saw that it had landed at Hani's feet.

"Good choice," smiled Hani indulgently. But Nappo shifted uneasily from foot to foot. Then he quickly darted over, retrieved the Stone and placed it at Tyrell's feet instead.

"Better choice," smiled Tyrell.

Trying to hide his embarrassment, Hani gruffly ordered the next monkey to step forward; fortunately for Hani the next Stone did go to him, and by the time the first few dozen votes had been cast the piles were pretty even.

But as twilight crept up on the monkeys, the balance started to shift – slowly Tyrell's pile grew larger as the weight of support eased his way.

It was not completely one-sided; Hani came from a big family and they all voted for him, but many others seemed to be in the mood for change.

And then Mico noticed something sinister: Tyrell was scrutinizing each monkey as they stepped forward, as if he was taking a mental note of everyone who voted against him and filing the information away for future use.

A shudder ran down Mico's back as he realized the terrible flaw in this ballot: there was no anonymity. Monkeys were forced to declare their loyalties in front of the whole Troop. So once it started to become clear that Tyrell was in the lead, those Hani supporters who had not yet cast their vote worked out that they would only harm their prospects by voting with their hearts. Better to hide their true beliefs and place their Stones at Tyrell's feet instead.

Inexorably, Tyrell's lead gathered momentum, until every single monkey that stepped forward voted for him.

It was painful to see Hani standing in silent humiliation, desperately hoping for a few Stones to go his way. It was no longer about winning; now he just wanted someone to acknowledge his existence.

But no one did.

Collective cowardice had taken control. Just hours before, Hani had been the Lord Ruler of the Troop; now it was as if a curse had descended on him.

By the time the last Stone was cast, dusk filled the Cemetery. For Hani the gloom brought some relief – at least his shame was partially hidden by the darkness.

Tyrell turned to him and with surprising gentleness said, "The Troop has spoken."

Hani nodded. It had been agreed before the ballot that the winner would take up his duties at dawn the following day, which meant that Hani had the right to sleep in the Great Vault for one last night. In a final act of defiance, he stubbornly insisted on sticking to the terms.

"That's all for tonight, Deputy Tyrell," said Hani, desperately trying to sound authoritative. "You may go."

"Until dawn?" Tyrell replied sharply.

"Until dawn." Then Hani turned and disappeared into the Great Vault, a broken monkey, his brief reign over before it had begun.

Failure has no friends; it is the loneliest solitude of all. Hani sat in his rooms in utter silence, trying to comprehend the speed of his downfall. In just a few short hours his world had crumbled to dust, all his hopes and plans shattered.

The more he brooded, the more Hani felt he had been dealt a mortal blow. All the achievements of his life, his loyal service under Gospodar, the high rank he had enjoyed for so long, all that would be forgotten. From now on, he would only be remembered for the crushing defeat that had snatched the Leadership from him. Behind their false smiles, the Troop would be laughing at Hani's humiliation; his voice would never be taken seriously again.

In the dark stillness, Hani came to believe that his only hope of peace would be to run away and wander the City alone. Life as a lone monkey, with all its dangers, was surely better than the daily ignominy that would eat away at him in the Cemetery.

It was perhaps the most courageous decision Hani had ever taken. And, like so many courageous decisions, it was born out of desperation.

The next morning it was as if Deputy Hani had never existed. Mico, Castro, Rani and General Pogo were summoned to the Leader's quarters to receive their briefing, and when they arrived they found Tyrell perched on the raised plinth at the far end of the Vault, from where he could look down on all who entered.

"Good morning, monkeys," Tyrell began. "I suggest we get straight to work."

And then the bombshell:

"Deputy Hani has gone." He spoke as casually as if he was talking about a mislaid coconut.

"Gone where?" exclaimed Pogo.

Tyrell just shrugged.

"Is he unwell? Does he need help?" Pogo asked, genuinely concerned for his old friend.

"There are more pressing matters to engage us than the fate of Hani," Tyrell said tersely.

"But—"

"He was rejected by the Troop," interrupted Tyrell, as if he had merely been an innocent bystander in the whole affair. "The burden of Leadership can be heavy; the duty to serve exacts a high price."

Tyrell hesitated as he looked Pogo up and down, like a fighter sizing up his opponent. "Which is why I feel it would be unfair – cruel even – to impose that burden on another," he continued. "For this reason, I have decided to shoulder the full responsibility of Leadership on my own."

Tyrell waited to see if anyone was going to howl in protest, but they all just stared at him in stunned silence.

"It was in my name that the Troop demanded a ballot," Tyrell explained. "It is *me* who the monkeys are looking to for Leadership. The Troop has asked *me* to bear the responsibility for their prosperity and safety. It would be a dereliction of duty if I was to delegate that to others.

"Henceforth, I shall lead *without* Deputies or a Ruling Council. And in recognition of this new role I shall be called Lord Tyrell, Supreme Leader of the Langur Troop, Overlord and Protector of the Provinces."

Tyrell looked at the four monkeys, his eyes searching for any trace of doubt. "I will of course be looking to you, my most trusted advisors, to support me in this great task."

Still trying to absorb the enormity of what had just happened, Mico and the others could only nod silently.

"Good," said Tyrell with a smile. "Then your task for today is to make sure the Troop understands the huge sacrifice I am making by taking on this duty of office."

With a curt wave of his hand, Tyrell dismissed the monkeys. "That will be all."

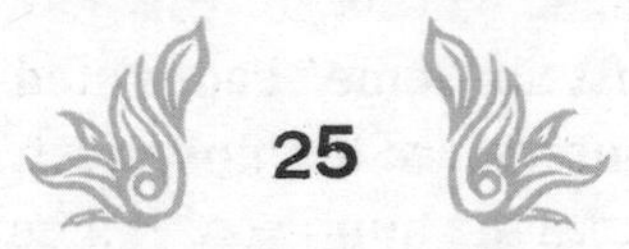

25

INSURGENCY

Mico was stunned.

Without the slightest compunction, Tyrell had dashed all hope of a more enlightened future. As casually as if he was gathering fruit, he had plucked total power into his hands.

Mico paused in the shadows between two buildings to get his bearings – he wasn't too familiar with this part of Kolkata, but had been forced to abandon his normal route because Tyrell's first proclamation had been to double Langur patrols across the City.

With eyes darting left and right, he sprinted across the street and slid down a side alley; these covert visits to Temple Gardens were going to get more and more dangerous.

The one thing Mico couldn't do, though, was share his concerns with the Rhesus. If they sensed things were slipping out of his control, it would only spread panic.

Papina knew him too well to be deceived. As Mico dropped down onto Hanuman's shoulder, she took one look into his eyes and knew things had gone wrong.

"I warned you," she said.

"It's all right. I still have sway over him."

Papina shook her head anxiously. "Not any more."

Doubts roared up in Mico's mind, but he wrestled them back down.

"Tyrell still listens to me," he insisted.

"You're supposed to be his most trusted advisor – look how he just ran rings around you! It'll only get worse."

Papina hadn't meant it to sound so harsh, and a pang of guilt stung her as she saw Mico wilt under her judgement. She shuffled next to him and with soothing fingers started to groom his fur, gently stroking the back of his neck and scratching his ears.

"You have to get out," Papina said quietly. "Before it's too late."

"It's not that easy."

"I can help."

Papina clasped his hand and squeezed it – a simple gesture, but for a few moments it made Mico believe that he could find a way through the complex tangle.

A sudden rustle of leaves, the branches bowed and Twitcher dropped onto the statue, startling Mico and Papina, who quickly pulled apart.

Twitcher looked warily from one to the other. "What's going on?"

There was an awkward silence. How long had Twitcher been there? How much had he heard?

"Tyrell's grabbed power. All of it," Mico said finally, trying to keep things business-like.

"Not good," said Twitcher pensively.

"And things may well get worse before they get better." It was the only spin Mico could think of to explain the wave of renewed Langur aggression that was coming.

Twitcher looked down at the hordes of monkeys crowded into the Gardens; they occupied every nook and cranny, playing, grooming, idling in the sun, digging for grubs in the shadows.

"It's going to give us a big problem," Twitcher said grimly. "These Gardens are the only safe place for Rhesus now. But every day more arrive, from all corners of the City. I don't know how many more we can take."

"You'll have to find room somehow," said Mico.

Twitcher examined him closely. "If Tyrell keeps pushing for expansion, sooner or later he's going to find it hard to keep control."

"Don't underestimate him."

"Nevertheless, you can't patrol the entire City."

"Tyrell knows all other monkeys are frightened of the Langur. No one dares raise a fist against them."

"He knows that, does he?" Twitcher nodded. "He knows that..."

Mico and Papina looked at him, waiting for an explanation, but Twitcher just turned and leapt across to the low hanging branch, then vanished into the tree canopy.

A few days later, Breri was on a routine patrol in the City. The Langur Elites were in good spirits, heading home after an uneventful shift, when suddenly they heard monkey shrieks close by, then the shatter of glass.

Stoneball, the Patrol Commander, immediately went to battle stations. Homing in on the violent racket, the Langurs stalked towards the mouth of a narrow passage. They peered into the gloom, but dusk had cloaked the alley with impenetrable shadows.

"Breri, guard the entrance with Nappo and Mudpaw. The rest, with me, in there," Stoneball said, pointing into the blackness. "If they get past us, make damn sure they don't get past you," he said to Breri with a grim smile.

Deploying his monkeys into two files, Stoneball advanced into the alley; Breri watched as they were swallowed by the gloom, then he and the two remaining monkeys spread out and braced themselves.

Suddenly the howling and smashing stopped, leaving an eerie silence. Whoever was down there knew they'd been cornered.

"Those Rhesus thugs don't sound so cocky now," smirked Breri. He strained his ears, trying to pick up a clue about what was happening ... and then he heard a weird, shuffling sound, like feet being dragged across cobbles.

Silence again.

Then, without warning, something came flying out of the darkness towards them, a weirdly familiar shape tumbling through the air like a huge rag doll. Breri squinted. It was a monkey. Before he could dodge, the monkey landed at Breri's feet with a breathless slap.

It took him a few moments to recognize Stoneball's face peering through a curtain of blood that streamed from a gash across the top of his head.

"Sir!" Breri gasped as he dropped to his knees to help. He could smell the fear on Stoneball's breath; he wasn't dead yet, but his eyes were rolling in his head.

"Save us..." Stoneball gasped as his head lolled back.

Anger flared up inside Breri. Who had dared ambush an Elite patrol?! Quickly laying Stoneball on a doorstep, he ordered Nappo and Mudpaw to follow him into the darkness of the alley.

They advanced slowly, ears alert to every creak and rustle, eyes straining to adjust to the gloom, clubs raised high, ready to lash out.

"Uurrrrrghh..."

It was more of a gasp than a cry for help. And really close by. Breri froze and signalled to the others to stop. In the silence they heard it again, like air bubbling through liquid. Breri looked down and saw shapes on the ground. He raised his club, but something made him hesitate. One of the shapes reached up, and Breri realized that these weren't the enemy, they were Langurs. His own patrol were lying battered and bloody, sprawled in the filth of the alley.

"L-look..." one of them gasped, struggling to breathe through the blood dribbling from his mouth.

"It's all right," gasped Breri. "We're here now."

But the trooper gripped Breri tightly, forcing him to listen.

"Look ... up... "

Breri gazed up into the grim shadows ... and froze as he saw the whites of dozens of monkey eyes staring at him. A shudder of dread ran down his spine, then a guttural shriek tore through the darkness.

"Eeeaaarrrrugggggghhhhhh!!!"

It was the sound of malice, bent on destruction.

"GO!" screamed Breri to his troops. "Get them out of here!"

They grabbed their fallen comrades and desperately started to drag them to the mouth of the alley. But it was too late – rocks and debris started raining down on them, glass bottles smashing onto the cobbles all around.

"Don't stop!" yelled Breri to his troops, as with each step he felt the attack intensify – missiles were thumping into his body, bruising and lacerating.

Don't stop! Don't stop! Breri knew if he paused even for a moment he would be overwhelmed. He tightened his grip on the blood-sticky arm of the trooper as he dragged him along the ground ... trying to blank out the chaos around him, ignoring the pain, focussing only on the light at the end of the alley ... desperate to escape.

The verbal report was stripped of all grisly details.

"One of our patrols was ambushed. We sustained some casualties," was how General Pogo explained the incident to Lord Tyrell.

"Rhesus!" growled Tyrell darkly.

"They hid in the shadows. Our patrol couldn't see for sure, but who else would attack us?"

"This won't do," said Tyrell coldly. "It won't do at all."

"Our soldiers displayed great courage under fire," said the General, trying to offer up some good news.

"Of course. I expect no less. Make sure they're well rewarded."

Rewards were important, especially as Tyrell sensed that the coming days would test Langur nerves to the limit.

And so it proved.

The following night, three beehives were thrown over the walls of the Eastern Province in an attack mimicking the techniques used to seize the land in the first place. It was a taunt designed to provoke. Someone out there wasn't afraid of the Langur and they were determined to show it.

Dawn brought even worse news. An early morning patrol came across a grocery store that had been ransacked in the middle of the night. It clearly wasn't the work of Human thieves as money had been scattered all over the floor and ignored. This was an attack done for the joy of destruction ... and to lay down a challenge.

As soon as the alarm was raised, Tyrell hurried to the scene. He wanted to see exactly what had happened, before the Humans arrived. Accompanied by General Pogo and Mico, surrounded by Elite bodyguards, Tyrell picked his way through the debris with statesmanlike gravity.

Mico was shocked by the level of wanton destruction. The shop windows had been smashed, spraying a carpet of glass over the ground; shelves had been toppled over, tins hurled across the street; the raiders had even paused to defecate on the counters.

"Sir! You should see this," said one of the Elites.

Tyrell, Mico and Pogo followed as the trooper led them to the back of the store, where they found a display case that once held religious trinkets. Now the front was smashed, and lying on the floor among the broken glass was the twisted body of a Rhesus monkey.

Mico recoiled at the sight. The corpse lay in a large and still-growing pool of dark blood. He edged around it to get a better look at the face; it wasn't anyone he recognized from Temple Gardens, but that wasn't the point. If the Rhesus were going to fight back like this it would ramp up tensions between the warring Troops, and any chance he had of restraining Tyrell would vanish.

"Something wrong?"

Mico glanced up and saw Tyrell studying him. "You seem distracted."

"Angry, my Lord," replied Mico, recovering his composure. "The Humans look to us to stop all this. We've failed them."

"Anger's not enough," said Tyrell with quiet venom. "This scum is the cause of all our woes! The Rhesus are trying to destroy everything we've built. Peace and stability mean nothing to them. They are savages!"

He cast his eye around the wreckage, making sure every monkey present felt his indignation.

"But they will rue the day they challenged the authority of the Langur Troop. Our response is coming. And it will be ... uncompromising."

The hatred in Tyrell's words was blistering. "The Rhesus should be very afraid."

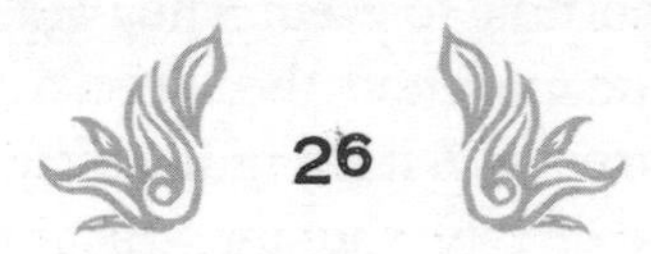

26

A NEW ORDER

"Someone must know!" demanded Mico. "Who's behind the Resistance?"

He glared at the Rhesus Elders crouched in the shadow of a low wall that ran along the north side of Temple Gardens. Normally Mico only passed information to Papina and Twitcher, but this was so serious he'd insisted on talking to the leaders face to face. Yet even though time and again Mico's information had saved Rhesus lives, the Elders remained defiantly silent. Many of them harboured misgivings about the duplicitous role he was playing and they were in no mood to open up.

Mico drew a deep breath, trying to calm down; he knew confrontation would only antagonize them further.

"I understand the hatred you feel towards the Langur. But I promised to keep you ahead, and I've kept my word. And now I'm telling you, if you want to live in peace, these Resistance attacks have to stop."

"When you're attacked, you strike back," one of the Elders muttered.

"I listen to Langur opinion," countered Mico. "I pick up what's being said on the branch. And I know for a fact, with every attack, hatred towards the Rhesus is inflamed."

One of the Elders leapt up to confront Mico. "You're a great one for words, but I like actions!"

"I don't care what you like," Mico snapped back. "You need to be patient! If we wait for the right moment, I can soften Langur policy."

"But I *like* seeing the Langur suffer," the Elder said defiantly. "It's about time someone hit back!"

A chorus of support welled up – finally someone had said what they were all thinking.

"I'm putting my life on the line for you!" Mico cried with sudden ferocity. "Day after day! And all I get from you is blind stupidity?!"

Twitcher stepped between Mico and the Elders, trying to calm things down. "Passions are running high—"

"Passions are for infants!" Mico said angrily. "Passions are for brawling idiots! You have no idea about Tyrell's cold-hearted brutality."

"All the more reason for us not to trust you," muttered one of the Elders.

"A trigger, that's all he needs," Mico warned. "And the attacks by the Resistance are exactly that. If you turn this into all-out war, you'll lose."

Finally he could see that his words were getting through. Except perhaps to Twitcher, who allowed a muted smile to play across his lips.

It made Mico wonder if Twitcher was the weak link. He always gave the impression of holding something back. Perhaps he was the one who knew about the Resistance, or even commanded them. Mico would have to keep a close eye on him in future.

"Search your souls. Ask around," Mico said tersely. "Someone must know who's behind the Resistance. Those are the monkeys I need to talk to before it's too late."

With that, he jumped down from the wall and started to make the lonely journey back.

"Whose side are you really on?"

Mico spun round and saw Papina emerge from the shadows.

"I'd hoped you'd be there to back me up." But as he moved towards Papina she backed away, gazing at him warily.

"I heard enough," she said.

"All I'm trying to do is stop things spinning out of control—"

"Are you?"

Mico could hear the accusation in her question. "Papina, please—"

"You *talk* about peace, but what have you actually *done*?" She looked back at the Gardens, heaving with refugees. "Every day things get worse. It's so crowded the water's gone rank; there's the filth and stench everywhere, and all the while the Langur strut around the City, taking what they please." She looked at him with such disappointment in her eyes. "And every day you go back to the home that was mine."

She said it with such a yearning sense of injustice, Mico could find no answer. His silence was confession enough. Papina turned her back on him and swung up into the trees. She didn't even glance back, and Mico realized with a heavy sadness that he was losing her.

"Check this out," Tyrell said as he slid a stone aside, revealing a neatly made hole in the wall of his Tower room. "Now I don't even have to leave the building to relieve myself."

Eager to demonstrate, he thrust his buttocks into the hole and waited. Mico saw his face tense, then relax into an easy smile.

"Come and see," urged Tyrell.

Mico dutifully hurried over. They looked through the hole and saw a small pile on the grass at the bottom of the Tower.

"Every morning the Cadets come and clean it up. They feel honoured to do it." Tyrell laughed and slid the stone back in place. "There's nothing they wouldn't do for me."

It was unnerving to see Tyrell in such a flippant mood. Only that morning he had been issuing dark, vengeful warnings; now it seemed as if all that had been forgotten.

"My Lord, about the Resistance," Mico ventured, trying to flush out Tyrell's true position. "How serious a threat do you think it really is?"

"Opportunism," Tyrell replied casually. "The Rhesus are trying to exploit Gospodar's death. And you can't blame them for having a go, can you?"

What a change in the monkey. Mico wondered if this good mood could be tipped into a change of policy.

"Perhaps if the Rhesus had more living space they wouldn't be so desperate," he ventured. "Then the Resistance would fade away."

"Undoubtedly."

"So, should I instruct the patrols—"

"But I *want* the Rhesus to be desperate," Tyrell interrupted. "That's the whole point."

Darkness clouded his face as all the good humour vanished. "I want them to goad us, prod us, flaunt their barbarous ways in our faces. Then we can show them just how strong we really are."

Tyrell waved his hand dismissively, indicating that the audience was over.

Mico clambered slowly down the Tower steps and emerged from the gloom into the burning sunlight, but the brightness just made his own loneliness more intense. His mind was so congested with deception, his heart a tangle of conflicting loyalties, and there was not one monkey in the entire City he could talk to, not one kindred spirit to ease the burden by listening.

He'd always known covert operations would be lonely; but he hadn't understood until now that loneliness could be so painful.

The Resistance attacks created a climate of paranoia in the Langur Troop, which Tyrell lost no time in exploiting, pushing through a series of initiatives, dubbed Central Command, that only a few moons previously would have been unthinkable.

The first concerned the Great Vault. It had always been the civic heart of the Troop, but now it was announced that for security reasons access to the Vault would be restricted to "key personnel" only.

When the news first broke there was much grumbling in the leafy avenues of the Cemetery, so Mico, Castro and Rani were dispatched to help ordinary monkeys understand "the truth": the Great Vault was where Tyrell and his military commanders worked tirelessly to combat the wave of Rhesus violence that was sweeping across the City; for obvious reasons, it was vital that these plans were formulated in the utmost secrecy.

The Intelligence Division pushed the message home with dogged determination and some judiciously placed fruit bribes, until the Troop all agreed that the closure of the Great Vault was necessary.

Tyrell instinctively understood the theatre of leadership. One day he started rumours of a Rhesus plot to assassinate him, then having unnerved the Troop, he announced new security measures, doubling his personal bodyguard and drastically cutting down his public appearances.

While Tyrell became more elusive, his uncanny knack of appearing when least expected created the impression that he was everywhere, constantly guarding over his monkeys.

The more power Tyrell appropriated, the more the Langur loved him; they felt grateful to have a Leader who was prepared to take on the weighty burden of responsibility.

It wasn't just Tyrell who was cloaked in the mysterious aura of power; it was everything that was close to him – as Mico found out when his old Drill Instructor asked for an audience.

In Mico's mind, Gu-Nah was a towering presence, but the monkey that entered Mico's rooms did so with surprising humility.

"Thank you for agreeing to see me, Colonel Mico," he said, bowing his head deferentially. (Colonel was a newly created rank, reserved for members of the Intelligence Division.)

"Come in, come in! Good to see you again," said Mico, genuinely pleased to see his old Instructor.

"I know you're busy, so I'll keep it short." Gu-Nah looked anxiously at Mico. "The thing is ... I'm only speaking up because I want the best for the Troop. Your intelligence stood out as a Cadet, sir. And that's what we need now."

Mico could barely believe that this self-effacing monkey was the same one who had screamed orders at him all through Basic Training.

"Make yourself comfortable. Something to eat?" Mico gestured to a pile of fruit in the corner, but Gu-Nah respectfully declined.

"Here, take this." Mico offered him an orange.

"Thank you, sir." Obediently Gu-Nah reached out to take the fruit, but at the last moment Mico pulled back. "No. This one instead." And he switched the orange for a mango.

Gu-Nah nodded obediently. "As you wish." He took the fruit and ate in silence.

Mico suddenly understood how much his world had changed. Part of him was embarrassed to see Gu-Nah squirming before him but, worse than that, part of him was amused.

"So, how can I help?" Mico said brusquely, trying to get back to business.

"Of course, it's right that we have security measures, but this new Central Command, it's..." Gu-Nah hesitated and looked at Mico, trying to judge how much dissent would be tolerated.

"It's...?" prompted Mico.

"It's my job to train the next generation of fighters. Fact is, the skills they need aren't the skills you, or even Lord Tyrell, were taught."

Mico frowned. Was Gu-Nah implying that the Leadership was out of touch? *Dangerous territory*.

Gu-Nah quickly justified himself. "Look at the ambush your own brother got caught in. His patrol wasn't trained for that kind of warfare."

"It was a cowardly attack—"

"That patrol could've turned the tables. If they'd only known *how.* If they'd had a different type of training."

Mico leaned forward, his eyes locked on Gu-Nah, using a mannerism he had learned from Tyrell that never failed to subtly intimidate. "If you know how to do this, Gu-Nah, why aren't you teaching it?"

"That's the problem, sir. Under the new rules I'm not allowed to change the training without permission from Lord Tyrell. Everything has to be approved from above. I've been asking to see him for days, but it's impossible..." The frustration in Gu-Nah's voice was obvious.

"I see," said Mico.

"You have his ear. Everyone knows how much he trusts you. If you could explain, I'm sure he'd understand."

Mico said nothing; he felt his stomach knot, because Gu-Nah's proposition had just made his life impossibly complicated.

If he wanted to protect the Langur, Mico simply had to talk to Tyrell and get the new training approved. Gu-Nah knew his stuff and would no doubt deliver more effective fighters. But better Langur fighters would mean more Rhesus blood on the streets, and an escalation of hatred.

On the other hand, if he didn't help Gu-Nah, Langur patrols would carry on using outmoded tactics, suffer more defeats; and defeats meant death. Breri had had a lucky escape. How many more ambushes could he survive?

This was a side of espionage that Mico hadn't bargained on. He had imagined it would simply be about passing information to save lives. Now he was being forced to make a hard choice: Langur blood or Rhesus blood?

Whatever Mico did next, someone was going to die.

27

MATES

Trumble and Kima were delighted to have their family together again, even if it was just for a short time. Kima fussed as she piled up a fantastic mound of fruit, while Trumble took great pleasure in grooming his sons as he caught up with all the latest news. Everything had to be just right for Breri's special day – he had chosen a mate, Bandha, and today was her introduction to the family group.

For Mico, being back in his old home came as a welcome relief from the complications of life at the top of the Troop. For one precious afternoon, he could immerse himself in the innocence of his childhood. Just the smell of the place brought back memories of a time when he didn't have to analyse every decision.

"She's here! She's here!" Kima's excited voice called out, as Breri ushered in his mate.

Bandha was a small monkey with a pleasant, open face, but there was a steeliness about her eyes that reminded Mico of his mother.

As they started to eat, Kima could barely contain her excitement at having a new female in the family; she had spent so much time managing the competing egos of three males that she now reached out to Bandha like a lifeline, and it wasn't long before the two of them started to manoeuvre. Everyone knew how much Breri loved being in the Elites and it was unthinkable that he would voluntarily step away from the sharp end of battle, but the two females had other plans.

"He's already been wounded twice, you know," said Kima. "No one can say you haven't done your duty, Breri, but perhaps it's time to let others do their bit."

Bandha proudly stroked his face. "There never was a braver Elite."

"Oh, I'm just warming up," Breri boasted.

"But you need to think of Bandha now," Kima reminded him.

"I hear there are great opportunities in Central Command," Bandha added seamlessly.

"Exactly!" smiled Kima.

Breri blinked, trying to take everything in. His mind turned over this new idea that he was a distinguished veteran who deserved great rewards. Both females could see him considering it; perhaps just a little help was needed.

"What do you think, Mico? Could it be arranged?" asked Kima.

All eyes turned to Mico.

"Well ... I could put in a word," he said evasively.

"There you are!" cried Kima. "Anything's possible. If Mico says so, it's as good as done!"

Mico marvelled at the wilfulness of Kima and Bandha; in their own quiet way, they were as forceful as the roots of a banyan tree, slowly drilling into the hard earth until they had a tight grip on the soil.

Breri puffed himself up, relishing their admiration, accepting their praise. "I suppose I do have a lot to offer," he pronounced.

"And with such a beautiful mate it won't be long

before there are little mouths to feed," said Kima, unable to resist, and everyone laughed.

Bandha turned to Mico with genuine gratitude. "Thank you. It would mean so much."

"It's nothing." Mico smiled and tucked into an orange. Despite all the family politics, there was no doubting the love these monkeys felt towards him. They needed him; they respected him. Mico looked at his mother and father; they were so proud to be nurturing their sons – it made sense of their lives.

And then came the ugly stab of guilt – at the very time his family were looking to him to keep them safe, Mico was aiding the enemy. An enemy that didn't even appreciate what he was trying to do. Mico's fur bristled as he remembered the hostility and suspicion the Rhesus had heaped on him at their last encounter.

And in that instant, sitting on the floor of his old family home, Mico made up his mind – he did not want Langur blood on his hands, least of all his brother's. He had warned the Rhesus to rein in their Resistance. If they wouldn't listen, that was their lookout.

The last thing Gu-Nah was expecting in the middle of the night was a visit from the Colonel.

"I've been thinking about your proposal," Mico said as he entered Gu-Nah's modest quarters.

"And?"

"And I want to know more."

A relieved smile broke across Gu-Nah's face and all thoughts of sleep vanished as the two monkeys made themselves comfortable around a mound of pine nuts.

By the time dawn broke, Gu-Nah had explained not just the details of his new fighting techniques, but the whole philosophy behind them. The more Mico heard, the more he was impressed.

The tricky thing would be convincing Tyrell.

"Discipline and courage are all that's needed," said Tyrell dismissively.

"I understand, my Lord, but these new tactics the Resistance are using force our hand," countered Mico as diplomatically as he could. "If we have to fight them in dark alleys, we have to train in dark alleys, so the first thing we need to do is create a dedicated practice area."

Tyrell nodded, reluctantly acknowledging the point.

"The Resistance lie in wait for us. It's as if they know the routes of our street patrols." Guilt welled up inside Mico as he spoke, knowing that it was *he* who had passed this very information to the Rhesus.

Steeling his will, Mico pressed on. "But if each Patrol Commander was allowed to *alter* his route, the enemy wouldn't know when or where to ambush us."

Tyrell shook his head. "You see, this is precisely what I don't like. Orders come from Central Command. I don't want street patrols making decisions. Give them power, you get chaos."

"You wouldn't be giving them power; you'd be giving them tools." Mico was determined to get to the end of his speech. "The Resistance fighters hide in the shadows, luring us into their traps, so we need to come at them from unexpected directions."

He tossed a coil of vine on the floor.

"If each patrol was equipped with vines, they could attack from above, even when there are no trees."

Tyrell picked up the vine rope and examined it. "This I like."

"That's just the start. Gu-Nah has found a stall in the City where we can acquire pots of fire."

Tyrell instinctively drew back – no animal played with fire – but Mico had anticipated this. "Fire can do to the Resistance what bees did to the Bonnets."

"Fire is death."

"Not if we train with it. Learn from it."

"Do you want the whole City to burn?!"

"We just need the smoke, my Lord."

Tyrell hesitated. "You can't have one without the other."

"But the pots that Gu-Nah has found hold the fire safely. If you feed the pot with green leaves, you get clouds of smoke. With smoke, we can flush our enemies from their hiding places."

Mico could see Tyrell's mind working, calculating the risks and weighing them against the glory that success would bring.

"Very well. I'll allow Gu-Nah to start his new training regime. But—" a hardness flashed into his eyes—"I'm holding *you* to account. If you lose control of the fire, if you bring disaster to us..."

He didn't need to finish the sentence. Mico understood perfectly – if things went wrong he would take the blame; but if they went right, Tyrell would take the credit.

Isn't that what it meant to serve a master?

Mico and Gu-Nah wasted no time putting their plans into action. A derelict street near the Eastern Province was found and the Elites cleared it of all the rats and feral dogs. This would be the Langur's special training ground for street warfare. A few days later a fire pot was stolen and a special unit assigned to guard it and keep it fed with leaves.

The moment they started field trials, though, things became difficult.

Langurs lived and breathed battle, but it was combat of the massed army. Footsoldiers showed total obedience to their commanding officers, and in battle after battle this discipline had given them the crucial advantage. Now Mico and Gu-Nah were trying to get their soldiers to unlearn all this. Faced with an ambush, they needed individual soldiers to make their own judgements without waiting for orders.

Gu-Nah and Mico staged exercises, each one designed to teach the soldiers to think for themselves, assess a situation, react to it quickly. But time and again the soldiers – whose instinct to obey orders was deeply ingrained – were outwitted.

Hoping to expand the soldiers' minds, Mico and Gu-Nah started working with the smoke pot. They positioned it in one of the dilapidated buildings and ordered the troops to creep in, overcome the enemy guards and steal the pot. Once the attack squad was inside the building, though, Mico added masses of damp, green palm shoots to the fire, making it belch out thick clouds of white smoke.

In no time a pungent fug filled the whole building, engulfing everything, including the attack squad.

Mico had hoped the troops would turn the poor visibility to their advantage, using it as extra cover. But instead, as soon as the soldiers lost visual contact with their commanding officer, they all froze. It was as if someone had just turned them off.

When the smoke cleared, Mico found the soldiers crouched silently on the floor, waiting for orders.

* * *

Strangely, Lord Tyrell seemed unconcerned at the slow progress of the new training. In secret, he took perverse pleasure from the fact that his monkeys were unable to think for themselves, but he was impressed by Mico's initiative and hard work.

That they were both small monkeys who had used their brains to climb to power, only strengthened the feeling of kinship. Tyrell now saw himself as a kind of father figure to Mico, protecting and guiding his protégé.

Trusting anyone was a strange experience for Tyrell. Whereas in the past he had always believed that his strength came from self-reliance, now he discovered a whole new sense of empowerment through trust in Mico. He started to feel that between them, they could conquer the world, and to show his appreciation, he heaped rewards on the Colonel.

"As you can see, things have moved on a bit," Tyrell said as he ushered Mico into the long room at the heart of the Great Vault to reveal an amazing transformation. All the tombs that lined the pool had been emptied to create a series of private booths. At the far end, masses of stones had been stacked into a platform like a dais, and around it sat four pretty young female monkeys arranging fruit.

"I thought you'd closed the Vault on security grounds," said Mico, slowly taking it all in.

"In this magnificent room, I draw my inner circle close," said Tyrell, ushering Mico deeper into the chamber. "There's no greater virtue than loyalty."

He looked at Mico with genuine appreciation. "Here I can reward my friends with the finest gifts ... starting with you."

"There's really nothing I need," said Mico, trying to sound nonchalant. "Thanks to you, I have the best quarters, the finest food—"

"But no mate," said Tyrell.

Mico's first reaction was inner panic. The very last thing he needed was a female living with him, watching his every move, asking endless questions. And, in his heart, he still longed to find a way of bridging the gulf that had opened up between him and Papina.

"There's plenty of time for that," Mico said, trying to brush the idea aside with an easy laugh. "Right now the important thing is to retrain our soldiers."

But Tyrell pointed to the far end of the pool. "Look closely ... then tell me you're not interested."

Mico's gaze followed Tyrell's outstretched arm.

"She's a rare beauty," said Tyrell invitingly. "Her name's Hister."

Hearing her name, one of the females looked up and smiled; she was the epitome of youth and beauty and it caught Mico totally off guard.

"You don't have to be coy. I've been keeping her specially for you." Tyrell beckoned to Hister, who strolled over.

"With Hister as your mate, you will be the envy of the Troop," Tyrell said as he gently stroked the side of her face.

Confusion whipped up around Mico like a dust storm. He didn't know anything about this female; he'd never even set eyes on her before. For all Mico knew, Tyrell was using Hister to spy on him. But how could he refuse? Everything about her was alluring; it was impossible to be close to her and not feel a surge of desire, and it would be impossible for Mico to reject her without arousing Tyrell's suspicions.

"Enjoy," Tyrell said with a salacious grin, then he turned and scampered away.

"I ... er ... perhaps..." said Mico awkwardly.

"Shhh." Hister smiled and took his hand.

She looked at him with such uncomplicated desire, it was like a drug dulling Mico's senses to anything other than the here and now.

As she turned and walked to one of the booths that lined the pool, Mico felt his willpower crumble. He followed her, and found comfort for his confused mind in pure, sensual pleasure.

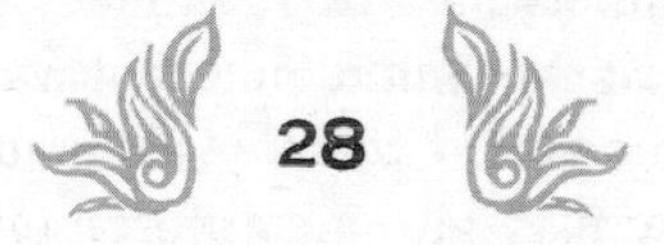

28

THE UNDERCROFT

It was quite a shock for Mico to suddenly find himself with a mate. Being single had made his life of deception safer, but it also meant that every waking moment had become dominated by his Intelligence work.

Living with Hister started to change all that.

Her demands were simple, but she wasn't prepared to give them up – she wanted to be the perfect mate, she wanted to run a well-ordered home and, most of all, she wanted to become a mother. Although this was the last thing on his mind, Mico found Hister's beauty and easy compliance hard to resist.

He hadn't seen Papina since their angry exchange at Temple Gardens, and lately he hadn't even thought about passing on secret information. The flow of domestic ease had picked Mico up and was gently carrying him away from his idealistic purpose.

"We've got to take the training onto the streets," pronounced Gu-Nah one morning, and Mico knew he was right. There were only so many times you could practise fighting an enemy; not until you faced real danger did the lessons hit home. It was agreed that Mico would go along as an observer to monitor how well the tactics were working.

As it turned out, the six-monkey patrol was under Breri's command with an extra monkey, Nappo, detailed to carry and tend the smoke pot. If everything went well the plan was to make the pot part of standard equipment.

For Mico it was an uncomfortable eye-opener to stride through the City as part of a feared Langur patrol. The moment they entered a street, the animals living there scurried away fearfully because, although the official objective was to root out Rhesus monkeys, in practice any animal that the Patrol Leader took a dislike to was at risk.

Stray dogs, rat colonies, wild pigs, even the odd donkey had found themselves surrounded by screeching Langurs. Only the snakes were left alone, eyeing the monkeys with wary disdain from the unreachable shadows in the roof eaves.

As always, Breri was happy to toe the party line on this persecution. "Who knows what alliances the Rhesus have made? You see a stray dog; I see an informer."

"On what evidence?" challenged Mico.

Breri shrugged. "We've got a saying on the patrols: the animal that's not at your feet is at your throat. And I know which I prefer."

All attacks by the Resistance were marked on the great map in Tyrell's rooms, which showed a recent upsurge of violent activity in the area surrounding Park Circus railway station. As ever, there had been no actual sightings of Rhesus fighters – they seemed to vanish into the shadows. Gu-Nah reasoned that they must have a well-concealed base in the heart of the area, and the railway station was a good candidate for closer investigation.

And so the patrol gathered in the street that ran opposite the target; it all looked quite normal, with a throng of

Human passengers coming and going. Some mobile food stands were dotted around the station selling honey-covered nuts and fried bananas ... and yet there was not a monkey in sight.

This was the clue. The food should have attracted opportunists, waiting for a vendor's turned back; but, despite the delicious smells wafting from the stalls, there were no monkeys lurking near by.

Mico's eyes scanned the buildings, then he noticed a small opening underneath the railway platform and scampered across the street to take a closer look. Poking his head cautiously into the doorway, he waited for his eyes to adjust to the gloom ... and knew he was onto something. The entire area under the platform was a honeycomb of small chambers – a perfect hiding place.

Mico hurried back to the patrol. "You need to see if the Resistance are holed up in the Undercroft."

"You want us to attack?" Breri asked.

"Investigate? Attack? Capture? You decide."

Mico could see the confusion on Breri's face.

"What's the mission objective?" he insisted, desperate for clarity.

"Gain a strategic advantage over the Resistance," Mico replied with equal stubbornness. He was not going to get sucked into giving orders – this was what it meant to pass power down the chain of command.

Breri's discomfort was palpable, but he was damned if he was going to let his younger brother embarrass him with fancy talk.

"All right," Breri said, drawing himself up. "Let's assume the Resistance *are* holed up under the platform. First thing is to identify all the exits and entrances."

Breri dispatched his number two, Sweto, to do a reconnaissance, which quickly established that there was one other entrance at the far end of the platform.

Trying to get into the collaborative spirit, Breri turned to his troops. "Any thoughts on how to tackle this?"

A moment of uncomfortable silence, before one of them ventured, "Send for reinforcements. Storm the Undercroft from both sides."

It sounded like a sensible plan – overwhelm the enemy and win the day; the soldiers all nodded as if they'd thought of the idea first.

"What if you do that and nothing's hiding in there?" asked Mico sceptically. "All those monkeys just to trap a few lizards. Then next time, when you really do need reinforcements, they'll be reluctant to send any."

Frowns and mumbled assent from the soldiers, now anxious to distance themselves from the foolish idea.

More awkward silence; no one wanted to risk saying the wrong thing. Until finally Nappo ventured, "Why don't we use the pot to smoke them out?"

Sensing this was the sort of thing Mico wanted to hear, Breri pounced on the idea. "Very good. We'll split into two groups. Sweto, you take Nappo and three others and get into the Undercroft from the far end. Once they smell smoke, the Resistance will come scurrying out this side," he gave a malicious laugh, "where we'll be waiting."

A good plan.

Moments later, Sweto and Nappo were leading their group into the labyrinth under the station platform.

As the monkeys' eyes adapted to the gloom they became aware of tiny pencils of light punching through the blackness, where bits of mortar in the platform above had worked loose. These became beacons for Sweto and his troop as they darted nervously from one beam of light to the next.

The first few chambers contained nothing but brick dust and a scattering of rubble left over from when the station had been built. But as they went deeper, Sweto started to notice evidence of monkey habitation – fruit stones piled in a corner, spaces neatly cleared where you could sit or sleep. He beckoned for Nappo to come to the front – if they were going to encounter the Resistance, they wanted to strike quickly with the smoke.

Nappo started blowing into the pot to generate some dense billows, which wafted into the dark chambers ahead. But as they watched the smoke swirl, the monkeys were suddenly gripped by a ghastly sense of dread.

"Stand firm!" Sweto hissed, but he too could feel the ominous rumble in his guts – something was coming and it was going to overwhelm them.

The ground under their feet started to tremble, small showers of stone dust rained down on them. Moments later the rumble broke into a deafening metallic clatter, and suddenly Sweto started to laugh.

"Train!" he shouted over the roar. "It's just a train!"

And as the squeal of the brakes tore through the Undercroft, the soldiers realized that Sweto was right. They were underneath the platform, which meant that the thundering train was just on the other side of the brick wall. No matter what it sounded like, the train couldn't actually harm them in here.

A few moments later it was gone. Silence returned to the Undercroft, but just as they resumed their search, Nappo grabbed Sweto's arm.

"Look!"

Sweto followed the direction of his gaze and saw a

cloud of smoke from the pot waft through a hole in one of the foundation walls and disappear upwards.

"If the smoke can escape, maybe there's another way out, up there," Nappo whispered.

Sweto studied the pattern of smoke; he wasn't really sure what it meant. He didn't really understand the pot, and the whole idea of working with fire unnerved him, but he wasn't going to admit that to anyone, least of all Nappo.

"It's just a crack. Like those," Sweto said, pointing to the pinpricks of light all around them.

Nappo wasn't convinced. Over the past days he'd spent a lot of time tending the smoke pot, studying the gentle pulse of the embers and the restless energy of the white billows. The smoke was like an old friend now, whose changing moods he instinctively understood, and he knew that it was being sucked out of the Undercroft through something much bigger than a crack in the brickwork.

"Shouldn't we investigate, sir," he ventured.

"What you should do is shut up and follow orders!" Sweto snapped. "We're to flush the enemy out through there." He pointed to the far end of the Undercroft. "Understood?"

Nappo hesitated. He was only trying to put the new training into practice. "But if there's a third exit, sir—"

"What if we change the plan and it all goes wrong? What if one of us gets killed? Will *you* take responsibility?"

But Nappo was now looking beyond Sweto. The way the smoke was swirling in the shafts of light made it seem as if something was approaching.

"It's all very well thinking you can make decisions, but who's going to take the blame?" ranted Sweto.

Nappo wasn't imagining it; something was definitely out there, circling round them.

"If everyone follows orders, everyone knows where they stand."

Closer and closer.

"No monkey was ever punished for following orders. Even if the orders are wrong."

And then it happened...

A screech followed by a sickening crack as one of the soldiers was plucked from their side and swallowed into the darkness.

The monkeys spun round, frozen with fear, smoke swirling between them, stunned at the speed of the strike.

"Close formation!" barked Sweto, and the monkeys clustered together, back to back, desperately looking in all directions at once.

"Sightings?"

"Nothing, sir."

Their ears strained to get a fix on the enemy, but all they could hear was the gentle patter of Human footfall on the platform above, which masked all other sounds.

"If we stay here, they'll pick us off, one by one," Sweto whispered. "We have to storm our way out. Brace yourselves."

Nappo piled all the remaining leaves into the pot and blew through the holes until great billows of pungent smoke enveloped them.

"NOW!" screamed Sweto, and they charged towards the exit at the far end of the Undercroft, lashing out blindly in the darkness, screeching and yelling, tripping and stumbling, leaping over half-hidden obstacles, until finally they burst through the doorway at the far end, tumbling out into the blinding sun.

And heard Breri's blood-curdling scream.

"NO!" yelled Sweto, cowering in the dust. "It's us! It's us!"

Just in time Breri realized who it was. He lowered the club and looked down at Sweto panting on the floor.

"You had them cornered and you let them escape?" Mico's voice trembled with frustration.

Just when he had a chance to come face to face with the Resistance, to identify who they really were, Sweto had bungled it.

"We'll get reinforcements, attack again," said Breri, trying to placate his brother.

"They'll be long gone by now!" snapped Mico. "They'll have vanished the way they always do."

And so it proved.

Stoneball's mid-town patrol swung across to join forces, and together they combed through the Undercroft, discovering supplies of food and a collection of fighting sticks ... but no monkeys. Not even the body of the hapless Footsoldier who'd been seized; the grisly death he must have endured didn't bear thinking about.

Mico wandered through the empty chambers taking it all in – this was a well-resourced operation; someone in the Rhesus Troop *must* know who was behind it.

"Sir, over here!"

Mico swung across the chamber to where Nappo was crouched by a recess in one of the foundation walls.

"I think I've found how they escaped," Nappo said, holding up the smoke pot to the recess and watching the plume get sucked into the darkness of a chimney shaft.

Mico stuck his head into the shaft and felt the draw of air across his face. "Three exits. Not two," he muttered. "Cunning. Very cunning."

He pulled his head back and bumped into Sweto, who was watching the smoke waft upwards.

"If we'd known there was another exit, we would've changed tactics, sir." Sweto spoke with such conviction that Nappo could only look at him in stunned silence.

"We had no idea the Resistance had a third way out," Sweto continued, peering up into the shaft. "Such a shame we didn't see this when we came through first time."

He looked sternly at Nappo, silently demanding he go along with the lie. Nappo was too shocked to say anything.

Sensing his unease, Sweto clapped an arm around his shoulder. "Excellent work! Observation beyond the call of duty. You'll be rewarded for this."

Nappo nodded obediently, but Mico could see that something wasn't right between the two monkeys.

The patrols finished their search and withdrew from the Undercroft, leaving Mico alone in the darkness.

Identifying the Resistance was crucial to Mico's plans, and he had been so tantalizingly close... If only he could find that vital clue.

He put his head into the cool shaft one last time and peered up at the patch of light far above, then from the corner of his eye he saw something glinting. He reached across and his hand touched a pile of small metal pieces that tinkled softly.

Mico clambered into the shaft and hunched over the objects. One by one he held them up to examine them in the half-light.

There were fragments of scrap metal, bits of tin cans, but each piece had been carefully fashioned into a very particular shape. One shard of metal had been bent into a hook, another into a point, a third into a jagged star; and all of them were dangerously sharp.

Weapons.

No longer content to throw stones or use sticks, the Resistance were using Human debris and Human ideas to create new ways of killing.

Mico shuddered as he realized that whoever the Resistance were, they seemed determined to take the battle between the monkey Troops to a new, and bloodier, level.

29

THUGS WITH SMOKE

"We need to strike back!" urged Stoneball. "Show the monkeys of this City who's in charge!"

Mico emerged from the cold damp of the Undercroft to find the patrols whipping themselves up into a vengeful mood.

"Let's not overreact here," he said firmly.

But Stoneball glared at him. "Tell that to my scars," he sneered, pointing to the wounds on his face that had only just healed after the ambush in the alley.

"We turfed some Rhesus scum out of the bus garage this morning," said Breri. "We should head to Temple Gardens and do to them what they did to our trooper!"

A guttural roar erupted from the patrols – they wanted blood.

"You're overstepping your orders!" Mico shouted above the angry hooting.

"I thought we were supposed to make our *own* orders," Breri mocked.

"Rhesus blood for Langur blood!" declared Stoneball.

"Yes! Rhesus blood for Langur blood!" thundered Breri and Sweto, and in a few moments both patrols had taken up the chant:

"RHESUS BLOOD FOR LANGUR BLOOD!!!"

Mico racked his brains; somehow he had to delay the patrols long enough to allow the refugees to reach safety.

He pulled Breri aside. "Call them off!"

"Why?"

"It's part of Lord Tyrell's plan," Mico lied, hoping mention of the Supreme Leader would carry enough weight. "He wants the Monkey-God shrines to be Rhesus ghettos."

Breri just shrugged. "The only good Rhesus is a dead Rhesus. If there's fewer alive at sunset than at dawn, I don't think Lord Tyrell's going to complain."

"If you take the battle to Temple Gardens, you'll be defying his orders!" warned Mico.

"Temple Gardens is exactly where we *should* strike!" Stoneball declared, stepping between the brothers. "That's where they harbour the Resistance. We have to go there and root them out!"

The ferocious roar of support sent a shiver down Mico's back – images of thugs with smoke rampaging through the Gardens flashed through his mind. In a last-ditch attempt to avert violence, he reached out for any argument he could find. "What about Bandha?" he said to Breri. "What would she think if she saw you murdering refugees as they ran?"

Breri glared at his brother through narrowed eyes, hurt at the suddenly personal attack. "What would Hister say if she thought you lacked the courage for battle?" he retorted.

The two monkeys squared up to each other, years of tension and rivalry between them now boiling over; Mico would have loved nothing more than to fight it out, but he knew the important thing was warning the Rhesus before it was too late.

"Do what you want, Breri. But don't look for my support when Tyrell calls you to account." And with that he scampered away.

The moment he was out of sight, Mico veered left, scrambled up an ivy-covered wall, swung across a series of window ledges and ended up on the shambolic rooftops. In the distance he could see the top of the giant Hanuman statue poking above the chimneys. No time to waste.

He had never run so fast or so precariously in his life: sliding across washing lines, clinging to gutters and drainpipes, leaping over the gaps between buildings.

Halfway there he glanced down and saw the Rhesus refugees trudging towards Temple Gardens.

"RUN!" Mico yelled down at them. "The patrols are coming!"

The refugees looked up at Mico timorously and drew back into the shadows. Why should they believe him? He was one of the hated Langur. For a moment he thought about dropping down to street level to persuade them, but there just wasn't time.

On he ran, pounding across roof tiles as hot as oven plates, leaping blindly into the topmost branches of trees, until finally he dropped onto Hanuman's head and looked down on the hordes of Rhesus monkeys lounging in the sun, utterly oblivious to the approaching danger.

"They're coming!" Mico yelled at the top of his voice.

No one took the slightest notice. They were all too preoccupied with life in the bustling Gardens.

Twitcher ... he had to find Twitcher.

Scrambling down the trees, Mico found him drinking from the ornamental fountain at the base of the statue.

"The patrols are coming!" he gasped. "You have to defend yourselves!"

Twitcher could see from the fear in Mico's eyes that this was serious. "How many?"

"Two patrols. And they're pumped for violence."

Mico glanced around the Gardens – those on the grass should be safe in numbers, but there were dozens of monkeys scattered across the trees and rooftops that could easily be picked off.

"Get every monkey into the Gardens! Young ones near the middle!" Mico snapped at Twitcher. "And where's Papina?!"

A look of alarm flashed across Twitcher's face. "The markets ... she's gone to steal biscuits." He pointed in the very direction from which the patrols were coming.

Dread welled up in Mico's guts. He had to warn Papina, but there were two markets close by – she could be at either, and with every moment the patrols thundered closer.

Mico leapt, grabbed on to the tail of Hanuman, scrambled up the statue then dived across into one of the surrounding trees; swinging from branch to branch, he finally made it to the rooftops, where he hurried along a narrow balustrade until he could look down onto the Hawkers' Market. Straining his eyes, he tried to pick out Papina.

Nothing.

He scampered over the roof and peered down into Anarkali Market. There were so many people milling around, but as ever the Humans were utterly oblivious to the life and death struggle of the animals that surrounded them.

There! He caught a glimpse of her perched on the canopy of a stall.

"Papina!" he yelled, but she couldn't hear him above the noise of the market. Mico glanced up the street and his blood ran cold as he saw Breri and his band of thugs burst out of an alley, heading this way.

"PAPINA!" he yelled again, but still it was no use. In a few heartbeats it would be too late.

Mico's eyes desperately scanned the rooftops, and lit on the cables running across the street. Reaching up, he grabbed one and yanked it hard. A few tugs later and the copper tore from the insulators, leaving Mico with a wire rope that stretched to the far roofs.

He didn't dare calculate the risks; recklessness was now the only option. Gripping the wire with all his might, he launched himself into the air ... and fell, plummeting towards the market stalls below, until suddenly his arms jerked upwards and pain seared through his shoulders. His fingers slipped; desperately he tightened his grip as the cable rope swung him along the street.

"PAPINA!" he yelled as he flew towards her.

She looked up just long enough to be astonished, then he smacked into her, wrapping his legs around her body as he went, plucking her clean off the market stall.

They hurtled through the air for a few moments until the cable reached the end of its arc and Mico let go, sending them crashing into a pile of plant pots on a nearby balcony.

Stunned and bruised, Papina leapt to her feet and disentangled herself. "Are you trying to kill me?!"

But Mico clamped his hands over her mouth. His eyes directed her gaze to the street level just feet below them, where the rampaging Langur patrols were surging through the market en route to Temple Gardens. He had saved her with moments to spare.

Suddenly a fist slammed into the window, startling Mico and Papina, who leapt back. A woman's face, smooth and fat, loomed up at the glass, gesticulating and screaming at the monkeys, shooing them away. Mico grabbed Papina's hand and pulled her along as he scrambled up the drainpipes.

They arrived next to the chimneys to hear a chorus of alarm shrieks from Temple Gardens. Looking down, they saw that Twitcher had gathered all the Rhesus around the base of the Hanuman statue. They were packed closely together, the females and infants huddled near the middle, the adult males forming a protective line around the outside.

As Stoneball and Breri thundered into the Gardens with their patrols, the Rhesus monkeys on the outer line backed away, bending and distorting the heaving mass behind them.

"SCUM!" yelled Breri as he grabbed the smoke pot and started swinging it round his head, lunging at the Rhesus line, forcing them back further.

Not having a smoke pot, Stoneball's patrol picked up trash from the gutters and started hurling it into the Rhesus throng. The more disgusting the debris, the more the Langur shrieked with joy.

Determined to claim at least one scalp, Breri swung the smoke pot lower, forcing the Rhesus to crouch down. Faster and faster he twirled it, driving the monkeys down onto the cobbles grovelling before him.

Until with a sickening clatter the smoke pot smacked into a Rhesus skull. There was a shriek and the crowd heaved backwards, leaving a concussed monkey lying in the road.

Breri let the smoke pot swing to a stop. As he strode towards his prostrate victim, an anxious silence gripped every monkey in the Gardens. Breri looked down at the Rhesus bleeding on the cobbles, and was suddenly unsure what to do next.

Acutely aware that all eyes were on him, Breri decided that everyone should know who was in charge. Snorting with derision, he flicked the lid off the smoke pot and callously tipped the smouldering ashes over the Rhesus monkey.

The scream tore across Temple Gardens, agony echoing off the surrounding buildings. Breri watched calmly as the poor victim writhed in pain, screeching desperately, until finally he passed out.

Stoneball strode next to Breri and looked down at the Rhesus splayed on the ground. Then he patted Breri on the back and, in a matter-of-fact tone, said, "Rhesus blood for Langur blood."

Breri nodded. "Exactly."

Then they calmly turned their backs on the Gardens and led the patrols away.

Until now Temple Gardens had been a safe haven, but with this attack, every Rhesus knew that a line had been crossed.

Perched high up on the statue, Papina and Mico surveyed the shocked scene in silence. In the past this had been their special place, but now a cold tension bristled between them.

"Why have you stayed away?" demanded Papina.

"I've been busy … Langur politics," he answered lamely.

"And?" said Papina, sensing that there was something else.

Mico drew a breath. "I had to take a mate," he said as gently as he could.

The silence between them thickened. He tried to reach his hand out but Papina recoiled.

"Listen to me—" he began.

"No."

"I didn't have a choice."

"NO! I don't want to hear!" Papina turned to hurry away but Mico grabbed her arm.

"Let me go!" she howled.

"You have to listen to me! Tyrell gave her to me."

Papina tossed her head contemptuously.

"I couldn't refuse!"

"What's her name?"

"Why does it matter?"

"Tell me!"

"Papina, don't do this—"

"TELL ME!"

"Hister. Her name's Hister."

It was as if Papina could read everything just from the name; she seemed to know how young and desirable Hister was. Mico could see the hurt break across her face.

"Then go to her," Papina said and leapt from the statue into the overhanging tree, desperate to get away.

"I don't want her!" said Mico, chasing up into the tree canopy behind her.

"Leave me alone! I'm sick of your lies!"

She leapt down onto the next branch, then launched into mid-air to switch trees; but Mico wouldn't give up. Swinging the opposite way round the tree, he leapt once, twice, through the air, then scrambled round to head her off.

"Listen to me," he began, but she turned away, angrily flicking her tail into his face.

Mico grabbed her shoulders and spun her round. "I've only ever wanted to be with you, Papina. You have to believe me, or it'll have all been for nothing."

Unable to find the words, she raised her fists and started to pummel him, but he caught her hands and held them tightly, absorbing her punches until the rage was spent and she slumped down.

Mico drew her close, reassuring her, until eventually Papina put her arms around him.

Slowly, silently, high up in the tree canopy, in the heady dusk air, it became a lovers' embrace. There was now no space between them.

It brought such a feeling of completeness to Mico, and at the same time it made everything impossibly complicated.

Now he was caught between two mates: Hister, who adored him and who was such an important part of his façade of respectable Langur life; and Papina, the monkey who had been a guiding beacon to him since he was young. Mico didn't know how it would ever be possible to reconcile these two worlds.

He tried to marshal his thoughts.

The Resistance. That was the most pressing issue. They were the force driving a wedge between the two Troops, ramping up the violence. He had to identify the Resistance and stop them.

Taking Papina by the hand, Mico led her out of the square and up onto the rooftops where he had hidden three small metal blades that he'd recovered from the Undercroft.

"Have you seen these before?" he asked.

Papina turned the shiny blades over in her hands. "Are they Human?"

Mico shook his head. "Resistance. We cornered them but they slipped away. But those—" he pointed to the small, vicious weapons—"those are our biggest clue. Have you seen monkeys making things like that?"

Papina shook her head and ran a finger gently along one of the blades. "Must be difficult to make."

"Have you seen monkeys with cuts on their hands?"

Papina thought for a moment, then shook her head again.

"What about Twitcher?" Mico finally asked, giving voice to his deepest suspicions.

"I'm not sure."

"Twitcher knows more than he's telling. I want you to keep a close eye on him. The Resistance must be scouring the dumps for metal. See where he goes, who he meets. But be careful."

"Are you going back to *her*?" Papina said quietly.

"I have to. But it won't always be this way, I promise."

He tried to make it sound as if he knew how everything could be resolved, but he fooled neither Papina nor himself.

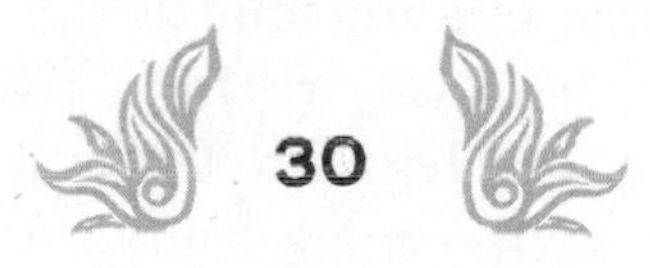

30

BARBARY

Mico didn't go straight home; he had a hunch he wanted to follow up. He suspected the enemy would be keen to recover their weapons from the hideout at the railway station, and as it had now been searched it was doubtful the Langur would return in a hurry. To Mico's mind this made the Undercroft the *most* likely place to find the Resistance.

Now was his chance to find out who they really were.

He made quick progress through the evening streets bustling with Humans buying food for their supper. Arriving back at the station, he decided against using the doors to the Undercroft – if the Resistance were holed up in there he didn't want to confront them head-on. Not yet.

Instead he clambered onto the station roof and found the chimney that led all the way down. Craning his head into the darkness of the shaft, Mico listened. As his ears filtered out the background noise of the City, he could just make out the low, gruff murmur of monkeys talking.

They were down there all right.

Stealthily, Mico clambered into the shaft and started to edge down, but the going was tricky. Soot had caked the chimney walls and he knew that if he dislodged any it would fall into the opening below, alerting the Resistance. It made progress painfully slow, but little by little he slid deeper and deeper, and the voices became steadily louder.

Pausing a short distance from the bottom, Mico jammed his arms and legs into the wall to anchor himself. He could hear the chink and rattle of metal being worked – they must be making more weapons, beating the tin with stones, perhaps.

Every now and then he heard a swell of malevolent laughter, but the fragments of muffled conversation drifting up the shaft were even more chilling. Mico heard talk of "rewards"; of plans to "increase the body count", and spread "a reign of terror".

This was not the language of resistance that Mico had expected. Where was the camaraderie of heroes fighting against the odds? Where was the talk of freedom? All Mico heard was the language of professional violence, as hard and cold as granite.

"We're three short," accused a gruff voice.

"Check again," replied another, testily.

The weapons – they were talking about the missing weapons.

There was a shuffling sound and Mico realized to his horror that one of them was coming back to check the hiding place in the base of the shaft.

Suddenly a monkey's arm appeared in the opening, just below Mico's feet. Mico held his breath, his muscles froze. The slightest noise would give him away.

He rolled his eyeballs down and saw a monkey's arm at full stretch, hand groping in the gloom, trying to find the weapons.

"Nothing," the fighter grumbled, but as he turned, a shaft of light fell on his face ... and with a shock Mico realized this wasn't a Rhesus monkey at all.

The bony brow that gave the impression of a permanent scowl, the dark brown fur and, most unnerving of all, the complete lack of a tail ... this was a Barbary Ape.

A wave of nausea swept over Mico. Barbaries were the stuff of dark legends. Fearless, violent monkeys, whose love of anarchy had earned them the nickname "The Wild Ones", they would roam in packs, stealing, biting, intimidating, sometimes for food, sometimes just for their own amusement.

When faced with stubborn opposition, the Barbaries' favourite tactic was to herd together and charge at full speed, trampling underfoot anything or anyone in their path. According to the stories Mico had heard, they came from far-off lands, where they had terrorized Humans.

They were fanatical.

They were beyond reason.

And now they were here.

Worry was turning into panic.

Papina had been searching for her mother all evening, but no one had seen Willow since the Langur patrols' rampage, and deep down she knew something was very wrong; her mother would never just go off without saying anything.

There was one place she hadn't searched yet, but it was a few streets from Temple Gardens, so Papina asked Twitcher to come with her.

"How often does your mother come here?" said Twitcher, as Papina led him up a rusting fire escape.

"Every day. It's her special place."

"She's kept this one quiet."

"She doesn't want everyone joining in," Papina said, flashing Twitcher a look warning him not to go spreading the word.

Twitcher shook his head. "I just hope her secret's not got her into trouble."

"It's the one thing she misses most of all from the Cemetery," Papina said, feeling she had to defend her mother's judgement. "No matter what the day brings, if she can relax in a bath and watch the clouds go by, she can cope."

At the top of the ladder they scrambled over the parapet and across the roof, picking their way through a jumble of pipes and fans, until they came to a large zinc water tank.

And then the sickly fear gripped Papina.

Ominous signs were everywhere – huge puddles of water were splashed across the roof as if there'd been a ferocious struggle; a clump of fur was caught on the corner of an air-conditioning unit; most sinister of all, smears of blood ran down the side of the metal tank.

Papina felt herself buckle. She reached a hand out to steady herself and Twitcher grabbed her.

"She's a strong monkey," he said, trying to sound hopeful. "We have to keep looking."

Papina nodded. She didn't want to accept what the evidence was screaming at her; she wanted everything to be just as it was yesterday. But deep down, she feared the worst news of all.

Hister had been waiting up half the night, worried. She knew Mico's work was secret and she was never sure when he would be home, but this time no one seemed to have any idea where he'd gone. He'd told Breri that he was heading back to the Cemetery, but that was in the afternoon, and now the moon was high.

So Hister waited, quietly fretting in the entrance to their home, until finally she saw Mico's familiar outline moving through the shadows towards her. She hurried over and clasped him tightly.

"I thought something had happened!"

"I'm fine. It's just work." He always tried to keep Hister's feelings at arm's length, reminding himself that theirs was a partnership of convenience, but her concern was so genuine he felt he owed her a better explanation.

"The Resistance are a tougher enemy than we'd imagined."

"I was so frightened," she said as she ushered him into their home. "I thought something terrible had happened, Mico." And she rested her head lovingly on his.

Her warmth triggered a heavy pang of guilt in him, and tonight it was quickly followed by another emotion: the desire to protect her.

Hister's trusting innocence wouldn't stand a chance against the Barbary darkness that was now invading the City. With chilling clarity, Mico imagined how pitiless a full-scale Barbary onslaught would be. Everyone was now in grave danger. Somehow, he had to stop them. But who could he turn to for help?

Mico's first instinct had been to go to Lord Tyrell and tell him everything; if the Barbaries were here to conquer the City, Langur and Rhesus should bury their differences and join forces to defend themselves.

But there was a terrible complication: Tyrell hated the Rhesus and had made sure the grisly details of Resistance atrocities were known to all Langurs; fighting the Resistance was a key reason for Tyrell's popularity – it was what made him the Protector of the Troop. But if it was now revealed that the Rhesus were *not* behind the attacks, that all along it was Barbary Apes, then Tyrell would be humiliated. The Langur would see that his judgement was fatally flawed, that the bile and hatred he had vented on the Rhesus was totally misplaced.

A humiliated Leader would not last long and, faced with downfall, who knew how ruthless Tyrell could become?

The only logical step for Tyrell would be to suppress the truth about the Barbaries, and to silence anyone who contradicted him.

Which meant that if Mico spoke out, he would put himself in mortal danger.

Mico sat quietly, Hister's arms wrapped around him, while his mind wrestled with the impossible choice.

And then came the knock on the door.

31

EXTRACTION

The Cadet who brought the message didn't know any details, just that there had been a Resistance attack directly on Langur homes.

For a dreadful moment, Mico imagined that somehow the Barbaries had followed him back from the Undercroft, that *he* was responsible for this raid.

"Are they still here?"

"No, sir. It was in the Eastern Province," the Cadet reassured him. "General Pogo has it under control."

Escorted by an Elite patrol, Mico hurried across the City in the cold dawn light; when he arrived at the Eastern Province, it was immediately obvious where the Resistance had struck – some creepers had been slung from an overhanging tree, allowing them to scale the high walls.

"Their target was the Larder," said General Pogo as he led Mico through the gates and pointed to a low stone building that the Langur used to store food for those monkeys who were too old to forage for themselves.

Something about this didn't make sense to Mico. "Why take the risk of scaling the wall? There's easier food to be had all over the City."

Pogo rolled his eye wearily. "They want to hurt us in any way they can. There'll never be peace until the Rhesus problem is sorted."

Mico nodded silently, but the burden of his secret was painfully heavy. He scrutinized General Pogo, wondering if he dared risk telling him about the Barbaries. At least then there would be two of them to deal with Tyrell's anger.

When suddenly the General pointed to some shrubs. "They left one behind."

Mico spun round. "You've captured one of the Resistance?"

"You could say that." Pogo strode to a shady area at the base of the wall.

Mico followed, his heart pounding – this would change everything. If Pogo had discovered a Barbary corpse, then the truth about the Resistance would be there for all to see, whether Tyrell liked it or not.

"Over there," said the General, pointing to the body of a monkey splayed in the undergrowth.

Immediately Mico saw it wasn't a Barbary; even though it was face down in the dirt, the tail was clearly visible. As he got closer, disappointment turned to dread. This was the body of a Rhesus monkey, a female, and, worse still, he recognized the flecks of colour in the fur.

Mico felt his mouth go dry. Desperately trying to control his emotions, he bent down, stretched out a hand – the body was cold. He took a deep breath and rolled it over.

A wave of nausea swept through Mico; he wanted to howl with anguish, but he couldn't, he mustn't. Pogo was watching – he had to react the way a Colonel would, with cool disdain for the enemy.

But this wasn't his enemy.

It was Willow who lay cold and dead, tangled in the undergrowth.

* * *

Papina staggered backwards and slumped down, struggling to take in the enormity of the news.

Mico stood there, utterly helpless, not knowing what he could say to console her. It was only after her breathing steadied that Papina's head sunk into her hands and her grief echoed through the trees.

Immediately Fig and Rowna pushed their way across Temple Gardens to be at Papina's side and enveloped her in their arms, trying to absorb her pain.

Rowna looked at Mico accusingly, blaming him for everything, but there was still kindness in Fig's eyes. "Thank you for telling us the truth," she whispered. "It was brave of you."

And gently they led Papina away.

Mico watched her with a heavy heart, remembering the promise he had once made to protect her. If he was going to honour that, Willow's death must not be in vain.

Quickly Mico made his way back across the Gardens to where the Elders usually sat. Knowing the truth about the Resistance at least meant that he could now trust Twitcher, and that could mean a valuable ally.

"I know what's going on," Mico said, dropping down between the stone pillars.

Twitcher squared up to him angrily. "Why should I believe anything a Langur says?"

"We haven't always seen eye to eye," said Mico appeasingly, "but we have to put that behind us."

"Forget it!"

"A Troop of Barbary Apes is hiding in the City."

The words struck dread into Twitcher. "Barbaries?" he whispered, hoping he'd misheard.

"They *are* the Resistance. But every time they attack, they make it look like Rhesus work. I think they killed Willow and left her body to stir up Langur hatred."

"No, it doesn't make sense—"

"I've seen them. I've heard them."

"You've talked to a Barbary and lived?"

"What I don't know, is *why* they're doing this, why they want to start an all-out monkey war."

Twitcher shook his head. "I don't understand."

"You don't have to understand. You just have to help. I need a handful of your fiercest monkeys."

"Why? What are you going to do?"

"Kidnap a Barbary Ape."

They had no military training, but they were strong and fearless. Mico could tell that much from the way Twitcher and his Rhesus volunteers sped through the shadows of the backstreets – not hesitant and nervous, but aggressive, ready to defend themselves. They knew their Troop was in trouble and they relished the chance to strike back.

Mico led them to a door canopy on the opposite side of the street from the Undercroft. If the Barbaries always moved as a pack, his young fighters didn't stand a chance, but Mico had a hunch that the Apes often moved around the City in ones and twos to avoid attracting attention.

So they waited silently, watching the moon creep higher in the sky, until finally their patience was rewarded – Twitcher spotted a lone Barbary lolloping quietly in the shadows, moving down the street towards them. The Ape was obviously an expert at covert operations, instinctively picking a path that would keep him hidden from view – but a path that would take him right underneath the canopy.

"On my signal, we drop down and take him," Mico whispered to Twitcher, who relayed the command to the others.

They watched as the Barbary got closer ... closer ... then Mico flicked his tail and they all leapt, landing on the Ape in a chaotic tangle of arms and legs.

Immediately the Barbary heaved his bodyweight left then right, trying to throw off his attackers. Mico and the Rhesus gripped ferociously on to his torso, shocked by the immense strength of his muscles under their fingers. There was no going back now – they had to subdue the Barbary or die.

The Ape lurched forwards, sending two Rhesus smashing to the ground.

"Get his legs!" yelled Mico, and the monkeys grabbed the Barbary's knees, trying to pull them apart and force him to the ground, but his limbs were like steel.

Twitcher made a desperate lunge for the Barbary's eyes but was met with a thundering head-butt that sent him flying into the wall, blood pouring from his smashed nose.

The Ape drew a breath and pursed his lips – he was about to howl for reinforcements. Desperately Mico launched at the Barbary's head and grabbed a lip, yanking down painfully on the soft flesh, clawing the Ape's mouth, forcing him to lower his head or have his lip ripped off.

Mico clamped his arms around the Barbary's snout and squeezed with all his might. Great angry snorts came from the Barbary's nose, but it was now impossible for him to cry out.

"The vines!" yelled Mico. "Use the vines!"

Twitcher shook his head, trying to clear his senses and sent a spray of blood splattering in an arc across the wall.

"Up there!" Mico pointed to the canopy, and finally the message got through. Twitcher hauled himself up and threw down a coil of vines. Mico and the others immediately tried to wrap them around the Barbary like a rope, but the Ape flexed his muscles and snapped the vines clean in two.

The Rhesus had never seen anything like it.

"Coconut him!" Mico shouted as a desperate last resort. "NOW!"

The fiercest Rhesus grabbed hold of a large coconut they'd hidden, and lofted it high above his head. He looked down at the Barbary and had just taken aim when suddenly the Ape spun his burning eyes on the Rhesus with such malevolence that the Rhesus froze.

"DO IT NOW!" screamed Mico. "OR WE'RE DEAD!"

The Rhesus closed his eyes and brought the coconut smashing down on the Barbary's skull.

The Ape started writhing, enraged and in pain.

"AGAIN!" screamed Mico.

Trembling, the Rhesus raised his arms and struck again, sending a sickening crack echoing round the street.

The Barbary stopped struggling, his eyes swam as they tried to focus, then he heaved a huge sigh and collapsed into the dirt, unconscious.

For a moment Mico and the Rhesus volunteers just stood there, breathless.

"Well, that's one way to open a coconut," said Twitcher, pointing to the trail of sticky fluid trickling across the street. The grim joke snapped them all to their senses.

Working with frantic speed, they bound the Barbary with the remaining vines, then dragged him away through the dark backstreets.

32

UGLY TRUTH

The Barbary awoke to pitch black and a searing headache.

He tried to stand up, but it was no good – he'd been tied to a pillar.

Everything was a blur of confusion.

How had he got here?

He struggled to piece together the jumble of memory fragments. He'd been walking down the street ... there had been shouting and screaming ... a fight ... a gang attacked him ... then suddenly everything went black.

Not much to go on.

The Barbary blinked, trying to force his eyes to adjust to the gloom.

His nose drew in the strange medley of smells – stagnant water, dirty drains, old smoke ... and a Langur monkey.

Suddenly he remembered that smell. It was the same Langur who had attacked him.

"What are Barbary Apes doing in the City?" Mico's voice echoed in the gloom of the deserted rooms where the Langur practised street fighting.

He stepped out of the shadows carrying an iron bar and glared at the Ape. "Answer me!"

The Barbary looked Mico up and down, then with a derisive snort said, "You're making a big mistake."

Mico felt anger rising in his gut – the Barbary was laughing at him. No fear, no respect.

"Untie these vines and run along. Before I get mad," the Ape said contemptuously.

The arrogance tipped Mico into rage – he raised the iron bar and brought it smashing down on the Barbary's torso.

"I am not an infant!" he yelled. "I am a Langur Colonel! And I want answers!"

He smacked the iron bar down again, venting all his frustration.

The battle-hardened Ape grunted as he absorbed the pain. He shook his body and dug in for the long, painful haul of interrogation.

"Have to do better than that," he muttered.

Mico could feel fury boiling inside him, but he had to control it. Information, he wanted information, and he couldn't get it if the Ape was unconscious, or dead.

"What are Barbaries doing in our City?"

"*Your* City?" the Ape scoffed.

Mico thrust his face close to the prisoner. "Are you going to invade?"

Silence.

"I can't hear you."

Silence.

Mico jammed the end of the bar into the Barbary's foot. "Tell me!"

The Barbary grunted, fighting the pain.

"Is there going to be an invasion?"

Mico pushed harder, feeling the bones creak under the metal. "Because you need to think again. This City is not for the taking."

Suddenly the Barbary let out an almighty roar,

startling Mico, jolting him backwards. The Ape chuckled, amused at how easy it was to unsettle his interrogator.

Humiliation cut into Mico; his plans were unravelling and it was all because of the Barbaries. He lashed out with the iron bar, thudding into the Ape's chest, knocking his breath away.

"Why are you stirring up war between the monkey Troops?"

He swung again, the bar cracked across the Ape's knuckles.

"Why are you framing the Rhesus?"

He smashed down on the Barbary's toes.

"Tell me! Or you don't leave here alive." Mico said the words with a coldness so ugly, it was as if death itself had spoken.

For the first time doubt flickered across the Barbary's face; he had pushed this monkey to the brink.

"One more time," the Ape warned, "let me go. Maybe you'll live to tell the tale. Maybe."

Enough. Mico would take no more defiance. He raised the iron bar and channelled all his rage into it; he felt powerful, unstoppable; he held the Barbary's life in his hands, and he braced himself to bring the bar smashing down on the Ape's skull, to finish this once and for all—

When suddenly there was a noise outside. Mico spun round as a monkey appeared in the doorway, silhouetted.

"Well done," the shadow said drily.

Mico squinted, trying to identify him.

"You've got to the heart of the matter," the shadow continued. Then it stepped into the room, and Mico saw that it was Lord Tyrell.

"Made of strong stuff, aren't they?" Tyrell said. He opened the palm of his hand to reveal a small metal blade, just like the ones Mico had found in the Undercroft.

Tyrell swung across the room and thrust the blade against the Barbary's throat. "Frighteningly strong."

Mico braced himself for the Ape's blood to spurt across the floor when, strangely, Tyrell stretched his arm behind the Ape, and with one swipe cut through the vines that tied him to the pillar.

Panic tore through Mico. "*They* are the enemy!" he cried. "The Resistance is a gang of Barbaries!"

Tyrell just smiled. "I know."

Mico looked on, astonished, as the Barbary stood up, rubbed his bruised body, then turned respectfully to Tyrell.

"You want me to silence him?" the Ape asked, casting a sideways glance at Mico.

Tyrell laughed. "Silence him? No, no. He is one of our finest monkeys!"

The Barbary grunted, disappointed but obedient.

"I appreciate the thought, however," added Tyrell. "As I appreciate the heroic effort you've made tonight." He patted the Ape like a pet. "You'll be handsomely rewarded."

Pacified by the promise, the Barbary turned and paced out of the room.

Mico looked at Tyrell, stunned. "You – you know him?"

"I *own* him," said Tyrell with a smile. "Him and all his gang."

The iron bar slipped from Mico's grip and clattered to the floor. Everything suddenly felt unreal, as if the ground was melting under his feet.

"If we weren't on the same side I'd be quite worried about you," Tyrell said with a knowing smile. "You have penetrated the deepest secret of the Langur Troop."

Mico stared at his Leader, frightened and confused. "Tell me everything. The truth."

"The truth is sometimes ugly."

"Tell me!"

Tyrell knew he had to be patient. Mico was understandably in some shock.

"As we know, many seasons ago the Rhesus murdered a Human leader, which is why the Humans turned to us to restore order." Tyrell nodded pensively. "Well, that's not quite how it happened. You see, there was no murder."

Mico stared at Tyrell in disbelief.

"Oh, the Rhesus were wild, for sure. But they didn't kill anyone. The Human leader tripped and fell from his balcony. He panicked. It was a simple accident. But that's not how the Humans saw it. They saw malice and were afraid.

"So Gospodar led us into battle and we punished the Rhesus. But in all the euphoria, *I* was the only monkey to see the fragility of our victory. Because *I* understood that the Langur were only needed as long as the Rhesus were dangerous. Once the Humans felt safe, they would reject us again. So I seized the moment. Covertly, I ..." Tyrell paused to find just the right words, "I engineered another incident, to make it look as if the Rhesus were waging war on the people of the City. Again the Humans encouraged us to deal with the problem. And so it went on. Every time we vanquished the Rhesus, the Humans gave us more food, better lands."

A broad smile broke across Tyrell's face. "Do you know the funniest part? Gospodar took all the credit, but even he didn't know that it was *me* who was controlling the whole situation."

Tyrell cradled Mico's face in his hands and looked at him earnestly. "You are only the second monkey to know the truth."

"So ... so our entire history is built on a lie?"

Tyrell bridled at the choice of words. "Our history is built on an idea," he corrected. "And not only our history, but our future as well. The Bonnets didn't kidnap a Human – there never was a baby." Tyrell said it with such twisted pride. "But the *idea* of the baby won us the Eastern Province."

"The Bonnet Macaques ... they were wiped out." Mico couldn't hide the disgust in his voice.

"That was unfortunate," Tyrell agreed. "Unfortunate, but necessary. There can only be one top monkey, and that is us."

Mico's mind flashed back to the battle of the Summerhouse and all its bloodshed. "So we're murderers ... the entire Langur Troop?"

Tyrell was annoyed; he had been expecting admiration not moral judgement. "Mico, you have to understand how power works," he said edgily. "Power is like a deadly snake – if you don't have your hands tightly round its neck, it'll destroy you."

Mico tried to back away, but Tyrell grabbed him. "You don't know what it means to be downtrodden! What it means to sleep in a slum or beg for rotten scraps of food!" The emotion quivered in his voice; he drew a breath, trying to regain his composure.

"And that's good. Really. No Langur should have to endure that humiliation. But if you had, you would know that a little deception is a small price to pay for what we have now."

"And what about him?" Mico pointed to the pillar where the Ape had been tied. "He's not in the past."

"It's all part of my bigger plan. You see, there never was a Rhesus Resistance," acknowledged Tyrell. "They're too cowardly to attack us. They should have fought back. I *needed* them to fight back – that's why I went to such lengths to dump their bodies at the scenes of the attacks."

Tyrell stepped closer to Mico, drawing him in. "The entire Langur Troop looks to us for leadership in these difficult times. You and me."

Mico scrutinized Tyrell, desperately trying to come to terms with how deep the conspiracy ran. "But when this is all over, the Barbaries won't just walk away. They're killers."

"The Barbaries will follow me anywhere," replied Tyrell with utter conviction. "I am worshipped in a way Gospodar could only dream about. There is nothing I cannot do."

"What more do you *want* to do?" Mico asked fearfully.

Tyrell studied Mico's eyes; he could see the doubt lurking there and he needed to dispel it – Mico was too intelligent to lose.

"I'm sorry I deceived you, Mico. I'm sorry you had to learn the truth like this. But now there are no secrets between us. I need to know that you are still with me."

It was a dangerous moment. The truth Mico had stumbled on was devastatingly powerful. If the Langur knew how they had been deceived and manipulated, how their entire history was built on lies, the Troop would collapse into anarchy.

Everything was at stake now; everything hung in the balance.

With frightening clarity, Mico realized that unless he convinced Tyrell of his loyalty, he would never leave this room alive. For all he knew, Barbaries were waiting outside the room right now, ready to deal with him swiftly should he become an obstacle.

Right and wrong would have to wait. Mico had to survive the next few moments.

So, with great solemnity, Mico prostrated himself on the floor with his arms spread wide and his nose in the dirt. "Forgive me for being unsure, Lord Tyrell. There's so much to understand. It's an honour to serve you ... to be part of the world you've so brilliantly constructed."

Mico waited in silence to see if his lie would be swallowed. All he wanted was to get away from Tyrell, to find a place where he could think through the chaos in his mind.

He felt Tyrell's hands grip his shoulders and lift him up. "You'll serve by my side, Mico, not at my feet. I couldn't have done this without you. Your brilliant mind, stuffed so full of ideas, has made all this possible."

The Supreme Leader of the Langur Troop, Overlord and Protector of the Provinces held Mico tightly in his arms, convinced of the undying loyalty of his faithful Colonel.

But inwardly Mico shuddered.

33

BREAKING POINT

Silence.

More than anything that was what Mico needed. Silence in which to try and untangle the twisted mess of his life. But he had forgotten that today was Empire Day, the traditional celebration of the Langur conquest of the Eastern Province, a day about as far from silence as you could get.

He arrived home to find Hister setting out piles of fruit and dates, cleaning the rooms with a bundle of grass and laying new palm leaves on the floor. As soon as she saw him, she hurried over. "You look tired, Mico. Why not get some sleep before everyone arrives?"

Hister was always so concerned for him, but they both knew there was no time to rest; their families would be arriving shortly in a noisy rush. Mico would just have to grit his teeth and get through this.

Breri and Bandha were the first to turn up, followed by Trumble and Kima carrying yet more food. Hister had three younger sisters, who arrived screeching and cavorting with delight as their parents struggled to control them. In no time Mico's home was transformed into an energetic whirl of wrestling and chasing. While the youngsters ran riot, the males talked about Troop politics and the females congregated by the piles of food to share gossip.

The conversations swirled round Mico like warm currents of air on a summer evening. He should have taken such comfort from them, been nourished by their familiarity, but all he could feel was an intense loneliness. He was adrift in the heart of his own family. They seemed to occupy a different reality, an uncomplicated, unquestioning reality where everything meant what it said.

A snatch of conversation drifted past him – Breri was holding forth, broadcasting his half-baked thoughts. "Every animal has its place – it's what makes the City work. Lord Tyrell's our Leader – that's his place. I'm an Elite – that's my place. But the Rhesus, they don't know where they belong."

Trumble nodded, drawn in by Breri's catchy phrases.

"First they take on the Humans," Breri continued. "Then they wage war on us. Someone has to deal with them, and right now we're the only ones with the guts."

What a fool, thought Mico. As usual, his brother went for the easiest answer. Never mind that it was ill considered, it justified Breri's whole approach to life: follow the strongest voice, because asking questions was too much like hard work.

There was a sudden flurry of excitement outside. Hister put her head round the door to see what was going on, then gave a laugh of delight. She came back into the room followed by some young Cadets who were carrying two large baskets between them.

"For Colonel Mico's family, with the compliments of Lord Tyrell," the Cadets announced as they put down baskets stuffed full with honeycombs, the rarest fruits, and stolen chocolate, all garnished with handfuls of sugar cubes.

A delighted cheer erupted and the monkeys vied to congratulate Mico. Trumble and Kima were bursting with pride that their son had achieved such status, Hister clung to him possessively and Breri gloated while greedily eyeing the food.

Mico was the only one who wasn't impressed; he alone knew his life was a sham, that he was an utter failure.

For all his power, he was impotent – if he exposed the truth about Tyrell's regime, he would shatter Langur society; if he perpetuated the lie, he would be propping up the tyrant.

Worse still was the guilty knowledge stabbing his heart that this was as much *his* regime as Tyrell's. He had helped him grab the reins of power; he had manipulated public opinion and created a weapon of terror. Mico had set out to achieve peace, but had ended up escalating the war.

He had been a fool, and he had been fooled. And a pile of dead bodies was the terrible price of his mistake.

Mico shuddered as he remembered the slaughtered Bonnets: Papina's mother, plucked from her bath and butchered; and even Lord Gospodar's agony-racked body on the floor of the Great Vault. Having boasted about using poisoned kiwis to vanquish rival Cadets, Tyrell wouldn't have hesitated to use similar means to remove Gospodar.

As Mico's family feasted on the delicacies, a feverish heat suddenly gripped his body; it was as if the air inside was too heavy to breathe. Excusing himself, he slipped away from the celebration.

Mico cut a lonely figure standing on the roof of his tomb, struggling for breath. He looked at his trembling hands and saw the Intelligence Division tattoo on his palm.

Once it had been a badge of office, a symbol that gave him power and influence; now it was a mark of guilt, indelible.

He felt his balance failing and he slumped down, paralysis tearing through his body. A wave of fear engulfed him as he realized he must be dying, his body finally breaking under the strain.

And then a moment of hope. Perhaps death would atone for his crimes, absolve him of guilt.

The panic subsided, replaced by calm resignation. He fell backwards and let the peace overwhelm him. No more fighting, no more struggle; the grey haze of resignation numbed everything as it took control of Mico's little body.

He saw a single cloud, white against the deep blue sky, drifting past high above, utterly indifferent to the fate of monkeys below.

Then Mico closed his eyes and fell into darkness.

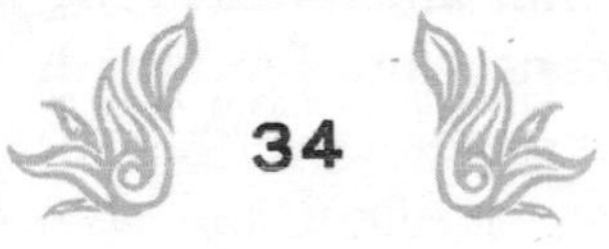

34

DENIAL

No one wanted to come near him. The Langur had a fear of sickness, especially one as strange as this, and they stayed away.

Only Hister stuck by Mico. As he lay motionless and silent on the floor of their sleeping chamber, she watched over him, gently bathing his body with water.

At dawn, Tyrell arrived – he'd only just been told the news, and he scrutinized Mico closely.

"Has he spoken?"

"No, my Lord," replied Hister.

"Did he say anything ... strange, before he collapsed?"

"Strange?"

"Unusual. About things in the past, maybe?"

Hister shook her head, not sure what he was driving at.

Tyrell put a hand on Mico's shoulder and shook him. "Mico. It's me. Speak to me."

No reply, just the steady rhythm of breathing.

The inexplicable worried Tyrell; it turned his mind to dark thoughts and made uneasy connections. Now he was starting to wonder if it was coincidence that Mico had fallen ill just after being told secret truths about the Langur.

Deciding that he needed to keep a close eye on the situation, Tyrell arranged for Mico to be taken to a special room in the Great Vault. Overlooking the long pool, it echoed peacefully to the sound of gently running water. Here Hister sat with him day and night, patiently dripping milk and honey into his mouth, lovingly placing clean palm leaves under him.

And there Mico lay, silent, still, oblivious to the world. It was as if some inner power had taken hold, forcing Mico to surrender, so that it could heal him.

But it would take time.

On the other side of the City, another monkey's patience was running out; and as it did, her heart cracked.

Papina perched on top of the Hanuman statue, looking out across the bustling streets. She had sat here so many times with Mico. This was where they'd laughed and teased, argued and loved. Now all that seemed a lifetime ago.

Mico had sworn he would avenge Willow's murder, but that was a full moon ago, and nothing had been heard of him since. He'd vanished.

It made Papina feel cursed; sooner or later everything she loved was snatched away – her childhood home, her parents, and now Mico. She had waited so patiently for him, but the silence could only mean bad news: either he had abandoned her, or he was dead.

She looked down at the Rhesus thronging in the square. There was no shortage of eligible males who had an eye for her, but she couldn't face the pain of entanglement. She had to close her heart, let no monkey, no home, no friendship get so close that it made her vulnerable.

From now on her solitude would be her strength.

Tyrell sat brooding in the Summer-house Tower. He had trusted Mico like a son, shared all the deepest secrets of power with him, yet now he had withdrawn to a strange, unreachable place.

With each passing day that Mico remained unconscious, the Lord Ruler became more anxious, and whenever Tyrell felt anxious, he tightened his control; it was a reflex reaction.

So he set to work.

Attacks by the "Resistance" intensified, whipping up the climate of fear, and kidnappings became so commonplace that civilian monkeys were no longer allowed out into the City. Gone were the days of innocent raiding parties hitting the markets; now only military patrols ventured beyond the safety of Langur walls.

To avoid malnourishment, Tyrell ordered the Elites to bring back enough food for the whole Troop; this was then handed out through official centres. The entire business of gathering and distributing food now came directly under Tyrell's command.

Most were grateful that action was being taken by the Leadership to keep everyone safe, and although some older monkeys resented the curtailment of their freedom to roam, no one objected too vehemently. After all, who was going to speak out against a regime that provided all the food?

And with everyone but the military now confined inside the walls, the Langur became totally reliant on official reports for news. Which meant Tyrell controlled the flow of information as well.

Hidden away in the middle of the Great Vault, Mico's body patiently carried on the painstaking task of healing itself, until finally his mind started to re-emerge.

At first it was just for a few moments, long enough

to hear snatches of conversation ... someone asking questions. Was he feeling better? Did he need anything?

Still too weak to respond, Mico grasped on to whatever words he could before lapsing back into oblivion, like a drowning monkey being sucked down by the currents.

Gradually his periods of awareness grew longer, a sense of the continuity of time returned, and as he started to regain the ability to talk, friends and family felt bold enough to visit.

The first to come were his parents who were unflagging in their care: Kima brought food and healing herbs, while Trumble helped Mico regain his co-ordination by playing "Catch the Orange". Mico was humbled by their patient tenderness.

The biggest revelation, though, was Hister. Mico had always taken her for granted, thinking of her as a trophy, but coping with illness had brought out hidden qualities in her.

When he thought of all she had done for him, Mico's heart filled with a turbulent mix of emotions – gratitude, guilt, and perhaps even love.

Desperate to avoid facing the lie at the centre of his life, Mico focussed his mind entirely on healing. Helped by his family, he pushed his frail body to reclaim a little more with each passing day.

There was one visitor, however, who was determined to punch through to the heart of the matter.

"They told me you were on the mend," Tyrell said as he strode into Mico's room one morning. "But I didn't want to be too hasty."

He placed two ripe kiwis on the floor as a gift.

"I'm honoured to see you," Mico replied politely, trying to hide his unease.

"Good to have you back with us. You gave me quite a fright."

"I'm sorry ... I don't know what happened," Mico ventured, but the words sounded hollow in his mouth.

"The pressures of Leadership are not for everyone," Tyrell said, looking at Mico intently.

"You think I'm weak."

Tyrell shrugged. "I wonder if there's something about the Langur stock that is inherently weak."

Mico couldn't believe what he was hearing. In public Tyrell had always spoken eloquently about Langur supremacy; yet here he was talking about weakness.

"Don't get me wrong," Tyrell added sharply. "I love the Langur. But no one can see the faults of a Troop more clearly than its Leader." He paused as a smile played across his lips.

"The Barbaries, on the other hand, they have a strength deep in their hearts. A brutal strength. And their only need is to unleash that. Don't you agree, Mico? The Barbaries are everything we should aspire to be."

Tyrell let the question sit like a heavy presence in the room.

This was the moment when Mico should offer his unequivocal support, but he remained silent, because the claws of guilt were tearing at his throat; silent because his heart had already decided that he could no longer be complicit in all the lies.

"Do you understand what I'm asking, Mico?" said Tyrell darkly.

Mico turned away. "Forgive me, Lord Tyrell, but I feel so tired. I need to sleep."

Tyrell looked at him in silence, unblinking, as if seeing Mico for the first time. "I'm sorry to hear that. Truly sorry."

Then he turned and was gone.

The encounter left Tyrell feeling deeply uneasy.

As he strode out of the Great Vault, his bodyguards fell into place around him, ushering him towards the Cemetery gates.

There could be no excuses. Mico was well enough to understand what he was saying, so why hadn't he voiced his support?

Much as Tyrell admired Mico's intelligence, it was clear that for the time being he couldn't be relied on.

Maybe Tyrell just needed to be patient; maybe in time things would get back to normal.

Or maybe that was just wishful thinking.

Either way, to protect his own position, Tyrell needed to take bold action.

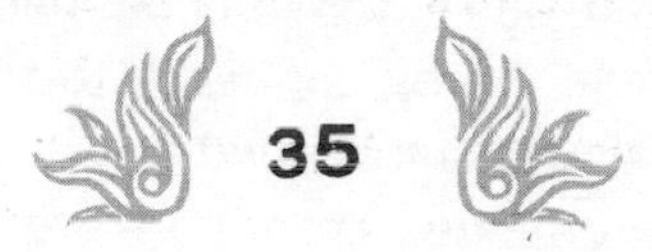

35

OUT OF THE SHADOWS

Trumble and Kima had to wait longer in the ration queue than usual, but it was worth it. A generous portion of figs had been added to the regular staple of soft fruits, so everyone was in good spirits.

Then, just as they started to make their way home, a murmur of excitement ran through the crowd. Heads turned and they saw Breri approaching, clearing a path; he was leading a small group of Elites and in their midst was Lord Tyrell.

The Supreme Leader exchanged pleasantries and patted young monkeys on the head. It all looked casual and impromptu, but nothing Tyrell did was ever truly spontaneous. The Elites made a space by the food distribution platform and the Leader climbed up to address the crowd.

"I trust we're keeping you well fed," Tyrell said with a smile, which earned an enthusiastic cheer.

"However, I'd like us to pause for a moment to pay tribute to our fighters who make all this possible. They are the ones who brave the dangers of the streets to collect this food."

The crowd thumped the ground solemnly in a show of support.

"Most of you have loved ones serving, and I know you worry about their safety. But let me tell you, each and every one of them is a son to me too. Which is why I understand that there are only so many sacrifices we can ask our brave young monkeys to make. So it is to keep *them* safe that I have forged a new alliance."

Anticipation crackled through the crowd. What alliance? Had Tyrell made peace with the Rhesus? Was this the end of the war?

"The Barbary Apes have come to serve and protect the Langur Troop," Tyrell announced calmly.

There was a moment of confusion. Kima looked at Trumble, her brow furrowed. "Did he say Barbaries?"

Trumble shook his head. "It's impossible—"

But all speculation was abruptly cut short as the huge metal gates creaked open and a column of Barbary warriors strode into the Cemetery.

Stunned disbelief gripped the Langur. This couldn't be happening.

"It's all right, my monkeys," Tyrell reassured them, as the Barbaries lined up before him. "Stay calm."

He studied the crowd, saw fear and incomprehension; that was good, it kept them off balance. What he didn't want was panic, so he jumped down, walked up to the lead Barbary and embraced him like an old comrade.

The crowd could hardly believe their eyes.

"Those terrifying stories you've heard about the Barbaries," Tyrell smiled, "they're all true. But now they are on *our* side!" He paced down the Barbary line. "They've sworn to help us fight the Resistance!"

Members of the Intelligence Division strategically placed in the crowd started to voice their approval.

"Under their leader, Hummingbird, the Barbaries will spearhead the next phase of our expansion," Tyrell went on. "And as they're risking their lives for us, it's up to us to extend our best hospitality. The Barbary fighters will live among us as privileged guests."

The carefully placed monkeys thumped the ground in appreciation, and gradually acceptance started to spread through the crowd; after all, if there was one thing the Langur understood it was how to honour courage.

The practicalities, however, were more far-reaching than anyone had imagined.

The best living quarters were immediately requisitioned for the Barbaries, and a generous food allowance was created for them by skimming portions off every Langur's meal.

Two days later, Tyrell changed the composition of his personal guard. Traditionally, a handful of select Elites served as the Lord Ruler's bodyguards, but suddenly Tyrell was striding out surrounded by a shield of Barbary Apes, advertising to the world that *they* were now the most trusted faction.

Castro and Rani, who had been loyal henchmen for so long, foolishly dared to object. Waylaying Tyrell as he entered the Summer-house Tower, they warned him that this would stir up resentment in Langur ranks.

Tyrell listened and nodded thoughtfully. "Thank you for your advice. I'll consider it," he replied politely.

That evening, Castro and Rani were transferred from Intelligence and put on front-line duties, patrolling the most dangerous areas of the City. A few days later news filtered back that they were missing in action, presumed kidnapped.

It was a blunt lesson to any monkey who was thinking of objecting, because in Tyrell's mind, dissent was weakness. He didn't want inquisitive monkeys; he wanted an obedient mass.

With this in mind, Tyrell created the idea of "Swarm Activities". He ordained that every morning the entire Troop had to gather for a communal workout. Ostensibly this was to improve levels of fitness, and to get the whole population living up to the ideal of physical perfection epitomized by the army. But its real purpose was to get everyone moving and thinking in unison.

Likewise with "Drumming Days", where all civilian monkeys had to form a line around the perimeter wall of the Cemetery. Tyrell would stand by the gates next to a large empty barrel and, with great ceremony, pound a single note on the drum. Immediately the next monkey in line had to thump the ground and grunt, followed by the next monkey, and the next, so that the sound rippled around the Cemetery. When it returned to Tyrell, he would bang the drum again to keep the wave going.

Each monkey, totally absorbed in the hypnotic rhythm, had to look to his neighbour for his cue; the longer it went on, the more their individuality was smothered, as they became just a tiny part of the bigger, swirling movement.

And at the centre of it all stood Tyrell, towering above every aspect of Langur life.

36

PURGE

It was the middle of the night when they came for Trumble.

An iron grip around his throat forced his eyes to snap open. He saw three menacing figures looming over him. Instinctively Trumble's arms flailed up, trying to grab his attackers, but he was no match for the Barbaries, who hauled him to his feet and yanked his hands behind his back.

"What is this?!" Trumble yelled.

Kima woke with a start, but before she could even sit up, the Barbaries grabbed her and slammed her against the wall. "Go back to sleep," hissed a voice.

"Leave us alone!" Kima begged, but Trumble caught her eye.

"Do as he says," he urged, then turning to his attackers, "Who ordered this?"

The Barbaries didn't even bother to answer, and before he could say another word Trumble was bundled out into the muggy night.

"Where are you taking me?" he asked, trying to sound more conciliatory. "Please, at least tell me that."

Silence.

As the brutish arms pushed him down the path towards the main gates, Trumble glimpsed other furtive groups moving through the shadows. Then a sack was pulled over his head, plunging him into darkness. But he had seen enough to know that he wasn't the only monkey arrested that night.

Far from it.

All across the Cemetery and the Eastern Province, Barbary hit squads were bursting into monkeys' homes, hauling away anyone that might pose a threat. Retired Elites who questioned military strategy, mothers who complained about the size of food rations, infants who were cheeky in class: all gone.

The sack was yanked off Trumble's head and he found he was in a gloomy, damp room that smelled of old rope. He tried to spin round but was immediately kicked in the back and slammed to the floor, his face grinding into the dirt.

Even so, Trumble recognized the place – it was the labyrinth of derelict buildings that had been used for street combat training. As he strained his ears he could hear the sounds of other prisoners.

Some shouted, some sobbed, some screamed in pain. As for the ones who remained silent, Trumble hoped it was because, like him, they had nothing to fear since they'd done nothing wrong. He didn't realize it was because they were already lying dead in pools of their own blood.

He heard a familiar rattle, then suddenly his Counting Stones were scattered across the floor. Angry at seeing his precious Stones treated with such disrespect, Trumble tried to move, but the hands holding him tightened their grip.

And then a face loomed into view. It was Hummingbird.

What had he done that the most senior Barbary of all was taking charge of the interrogation?

"Explain," Hummingbird said in a voice so quiet it was almost a whisper.

"What do you mean?"

"Talk." And he thrust some Stones into Trumble's face.

"They're my Counting Stones," he answered. "For supplies. For organizing supplies to the army, and—"

"Tell me something I don't know," growled the Barbary.

"Well, it's complicated... There's a system..."

Hummingbird snorted with derision, turned his back and walked to the far side of the cell.

"Accusations have been made," he pronounced.

"Accusations?"

"Against you. We have witnesses." Hummingbird spoke with chilling certainty.

"What have they said?"

Silence.

"I've been a loyal servant to this Troop!" exclaimed Trumble. "I fought in the Elites, and now—"

"Now you're in trouble."

There was no give in Hummingbird.

"What have I done?!" Trumble couldn't hide the exasperation in his voice.

"You've kept the secret of these to yourself," Hummingbird replied, flicking some Stones across the floor with his foot. "That gives you power. Power to use against Lord Tyrell."

Trumble could barely believe his ears. "This is insane! *Who* has said these things about me? WHO?!"

Hummingbird crouched down and scrutinized Trumble, reading every line on his face.

And then, strangely, the Barbary smiled. A thin, grudging smile of satisfaction. He had got the answer he wanted: Trumble was loyal. If he'd been hiding a guilty secret he would have been more defensive, and eager to denounce someone else. But Trumble's indignation smacked of honesty.

"You need to *prove* your loyalty," Hummingbird said, gesturing to the Barbary guard to loosen his grip.

"What more can I do? I've served the Troop all my life," Trumble said, real hurt in his voice.

"Much more."

Hummingbird nodded to the guard, who started gathering up the Stones from the floor.

"Teach others," the Barbary commanded.

"But ... but it's complicated," stammered Trumble. "No one's ever wanted to know."

"We do now."

For a few moments Hummingbird crouched there, silent, menacing, then slowly he extended his hand.

Trumble was astonished – behind this simple gesture was acceptance and trust. He put his hand in Hummingbird's and felt the Ape's strength pull him to his feet.

"Barbaries learn fast."

With that, Hummingbird opened the cell door and Trumble was free.

Still in shock, he hurried down the corridor, desperate to get away from this place of shadows. He should have been burning with indignation, furious at his mistreatment; he should have gone straight back to the Cemetery and told everyone about the appalling behaviour of the Barbary thugs.

But he didn't.

Because Trumble felt grateful. Grateful to have been given his freedom back, to have a chance to prove his loyalty. Grateful not to be lying in a pool of his own blood.

From now on he would be quiet and dutiful; he would teach his counting method to the Barbaries; he would do exactly as he was told.

Whatever happened, he did not want to go back to that cell. Ever.

Even though he was isolated in his convalescent room, Mico heard about the purge. It shocked him to the core – if loyal monkeys like his father were not safe, Mico knew that his life in the Troop was now untenable. He needed to find a way out.

The problem was knowing who to trust in this new climate of fear.

An answer came from the most unlikely quarter, on the day smoke pots and vine ropes were banned. The official reason for the prohibition was that Gu-Nah's innovations were difficult to use, but in truth it was because they relied on the individual being in control. Now everything was about Central Command.

In desperation Gu-Nah went to Mico and begged him to intervene.

Mico gazed at his old Drill Instructor. Gu-Nah had a strong face, simple, loyal, battle-scarred, but already its strength was starting to be eaten by signs of age – white hairs flecked his fur; his athletic body was carrying too much weight; his eyes looked tired, as if they'd seen too much life. Yet for all his weariness, Gu-Nah was the only Langur who had the strength to speak his mind.

"You have to run," said Mico. "Go into hiding."

Gu-Nah hesitated, uncertain if his loyalty was being tested.

"But this is my home, Colonel. Everything I know is here. I can't just leave."

"Then you'll die here. Sooner than you think."

The words sent a cold chill through Gu-Nah's bones.

"Has he … has he given the order?" Gu-Nah asked fearfully.

Mico shook his head. "I don't know. But I can see why Lord Tyrell would want you dead. And that's reason enough to run. I've heard talk of railway sidings where the Troop once lived. Somewhere near a button factory?"

"I know them."

"No one will look for you there. Too many bad memories. Try and survive as a lone monkey … until the moment is right."

"What moment? What's going to change?" Gu-Nah asked, desperately. "How will running away help anything?"

Mico shook his head. "I don't know. All we can do is prepare for an uncertain future … and hope."

It was the pain that woke him, then he felt the warm stickiness and smelled the blood.

Mico looked at his hand, throbbing with pain, shocked to see lacerated skin and bits of torn flesh. Hauling himself up, he started licking the thick clot of blood away, and then with a jolt he understood. In his fevered sleep he had been clawing at his own flesh, trying to erase the Intelligence Division tattoo from his palm.

Staring at his bloody hand, Mico was now forced to confront his guilt.

In the lonely pre-dawn, he finally realized with dreadful clarity what a coward he'd been. All his attempts to bring about peace had just been a smokescreen obscuring his own fear. His craving for acceptance had been his biggest weakness.

Now Mico could see that Tyrell's corrupt will sucked the life out of everything it touched. Now he could see that conflict was the only solution. A conflict that would define who Mico was and what he stood for.

It wouldn't be easy, but he could no longer live a life of lies. Mico had to destroy what he had helped to create.

And his only chance of doing that was to get to the one monkey he knew he could trust with his life: Papina.

37

A SINGLE STEP

Making the decision changed everything.

Mico tensed his muscles and with a huge effort hauled himself up. He swayed unsteadily and reached out to hold the wall, standing on his own feet for the first time since his collapse.

He tried to force his legs to move, but immediately stumbled and fell.

Crawling out of his room on hands and knees, Mico dragged himself towards the gently gurgling waters that ran the length of the Great Vault. When he reached the pool's edge, he crouched, gazing into the dancing reflections of the moon in the water.

Slowly Mico rocked forward, and closing his eyes he plunged into the pool head first.

And sank.

The water was cold and gripped his body like a vice. He urged his limbs to kick, but it was as if he was paralysed.

Mico knew he would have to dig deeper, much deeper. How could he hope to challenge a tyrant if he couldn't even command his own body?

Tensing his lungs, he opened his mouth and screamed. A bubble of air burst from him as the water rushed in, and suddenly Mico's limbs twitched. At first they thrashed wildly, then finding their co-ordination, his feet slammed on the bottom of the pool and pushed. He shot up, breaking the surface and gasping in great lungfuls of air.

He hauled himself from the water and rolled over until he was gazing up at the moon, then he started to laugh.

It was the beginning of a remarkable recovery. Every day Mico set himself a new challenge to rebuild his wasted muscles. Each day he pushed further and harder, grinding on with an unbreakable will, relishing the feeling of strength returning to his mind and body.

But outside the seclusion of the Great Vault, Tyrell's regime was also flexing its muscles.

Determined to stamp his identity on Langur life, Tyrell scoured the Cemetery, studying the strange Human markings on the gravestones, until he came across one that particularly fascinated him.

The way it simultaneously pointed in two directions resonated with Tyrell's cunning mind, and from that moment on it became *his* symbol – the Twopoint.

He ordered a team of monkeys to carve the Twopoint above the entrance to the Great Vault, the Cadet School, the food stores and the Summer-house. Then they set to work on the stone pillars at the entrance to both the Cemetery and the Eastern Province.

Soon the Elites were carving the symbol above the doors of their living quarters and before long any monkey who wanted to make a public display of loyalty carved Twopoints on the outside of their homes.

It spread across the Langur Empire, until the innocent symbol had been thoroughly corrupted by Tyrell's dark purpose.

Stealthily Mico left his room and made his way down the length of the pool. That morning he'd seen Hummingbird, General Pogo and other senior advisors enter the Great Vault, heading for Tyrell's inner sanctum. Even though the sun was now at its highest, the monkeys still hadn't emerged. Which meant something was being plotted.

When he got to the entrance, Mico hesitated. A strip of green marble was inlaid across the floor – on this side of it was the quiet sanctuary of his convalescence, on the other were the corridors of power. Mico ran his fingers over the cool marble line, the border between the two worlds.

He closed his eyes, trying to find his old confidence. Once, he had been a monkey who roamed the City, knew his way through the crumbling backstreets and over the patchwork of roofs... He had to be that monkey again.

Snapping his eyes open, Mico forced himself to step over the threshold.

* * *

The Council Chamber was being guarded by two Elites, who were surprised to see Mico.

"Glad you're better, Colonel," said the senior guard.

"Nice to be back," Mico said. But as he made for the door leading to the Chamber, the senior guard stepped in front of him.

"Lord Tyrell is in private session, sir."

"Nothing is private to me. I have authority in all areas," Mico said, finding his old voice.

The two guards exchanged an uncomfortable glance. "Perhaps Lord Tyrell could come and see you once he's finished?"

"Perhaps not," replied Mico. And with an uncompromising smile, he pushed past the guards and entered.

The discussion inside immediately stopped.

Mico saw Tyrell sitting at the head of the meeting, next to him was Hummingbird, then came General Pogo. None of the other faces in the room were familiar.

For a moment there was a dreadful silence. Then Tyrell snapped to his senses.

"Mico! How good to see you," he declared and scampered over. "This monkey has been one of the guiding lights of the Troop!" Tyrell said like a proud parent. "Our business can wait a moment."

The monkeys all started chatting among themselves, while Tyrell inspected Mico.

"They told me you were getting stronger, but this is remarkable."

"There's so much going on, how could I languish in a sick room?" said Mico, probing for information.

Tyrell hesitated.

"Mico ... it's precisely *because* things are moving so fast that you need to be completely recovered before stepping back into the fray."

"But I *am* better, my Lord. And I want to play my part."

"Your seat is by my side. You know that," Tyrell said, gently steering Mico back towards the door. "But I can't put your health at risk by burdening you with the pressures of leadership so soon."

"I'm much stronger now—"

"When I saw you, lying collapsed on the floor, drained and exhausted..." Tyrell shook his head sadly. "I beg you, look after yourself. And think of Hister." He chuckled suggestively. "Maybe now is the time the two of you should start providing the Troop with more of those brilliant minds."

So that was how it stood.

Mico knew that something of huge importance was being discussed here, but he was not to be a part of it; he was now shut out of the higher echelons of power.

Mico looked over at the huddle of anonymous monkeys. You could almost smell the fear and paranoia as their eyes darted this way and that, constantly assessing where the balance of power lay. It was vital that Mico didn't arouse their suspicion, so he smiled dutifully and bowed his head. "You're right, my Lord. I'm sorry. In my eagerness to serve—"

"Don't apologize, Mico. Your loyalty does you proud."

With that, Tyrell patted Mico on the back and ushered him out of the room.

38

DURGA PUJA

It was just as the moon emerged from behind Hanuman's stone head that Papina woke from an uneasy dream. For days now she had found it impossible to sleep properly – normal life in the City had been turned on its head because the Humans were in the throes of a religious festival.

Countless shrines adorned with gaudy statues and blazing candles had sprung up like mushrooms along the main thoroughfares; rooftops were decked with lights, so that from dusk till dawn the City became a glittering reflection of the star-studded sky; street musicians jostled on every corner, each banging and blasting louder than the next.

Temple Gardens didn't have any of the shrines, but the festival made the Rhesus' lives difficult in other ways: all the street markets had temporarily relocated, making the day-to-day business of pilfering food much harder, and the incessant noise of chanting and fireworks surrounded them and seemed to drag on all night.

What made it worse for Papina was the other monkeys had quickly adapted to the clamour, and her insomnia was aggravated by their contented snores and grunts. Unable to lie still any longer, she decided to go for a wander, and clambered all the way up to the top of the Hanuman statue. But as she gazed out across the noisy skyline, the memories assailed her. She had tried so hard to forget what she couldn't control, to close her heart to Mico, but these long, lonely nights always let the past back in.

Then strangely, just as Papina was thinking about the Langur, she glimpsed one, moving across the rooftops. Her eyes scoured the darkness ... there it was again, the sweep of a long tail past the cold whiteness of the moon.

Papina tensed – for a few moments she wondered if Mico had finally returned, but in this light it was impossible to be sure. She watched as the Langur leaned over the edge of the roof and signalled to someone in the street below. Papina's eyes followed...

Shadows ... lots of shadows, teeming through the backstreets.

Shadows which were coalescing into thick lines, blocking off the streets.

Papina spun round – the same sinister movement was building in all the streets around the Gardens, encircling them. She felt fear in her mouth, a bitter, all too familiar taste.

A rogue firework exploded, and in the bloom of decaying light, Papina glimpsed the entire Langur army bearing down on Temple Gardens, led by a terrifying horde of Barbary Apes.

She screamed at the top of her voice, but none of the sleeping Rhesus so much as stirred.

Urgently she scrambled down the statue and dropped into the sleeping throng.

"GET UP! GET UP!"

Finally they started to wake, confused and irritated.

"LANGUR! They've come for us!"

Too late. Suddenly a ghastly, deathlike roar echoed through the streets. It froze the marrow in Papina's bones. She spun round and saw the Langur army charge.

Mayhem erupted. The Gardens became a heaving mass of Rhesus running for their lives; but in whatever direction they fled, they found Barbaries bearing down on them, herding the Rhesus into as small an area as possible.

An enraged Elder charged at the Barbary line, desperately trying to break free, but the Barbaries slashed their blades mercilessly, drawing crimson lines across his face. The Elder staggered backwards, collapsed, and was trampled underfoot by the Langur troops surging forward.

Recoiling from the blades, the Rhesus crushed each other further. Hordes of monkeys were now jammed together with no way out.

Desperately Papina tried to wriggle free, but her arms were pinned to her sides. She could feel the heat of the crush, smell fear on the breath of faces pushed into hers.

Suddenly she heard a flurry of orders shouted down the Langur line, then miraculously a squad of attacking troops fell back, creating a break in the line.

Freedom.

The Rhesus rushed for the gap, pouring out of the Gardens. They hurtled down the street away from the Barbaries, and for a few glorious moments it felt like escape...

Until they saw that they were running into the sheer wall of a tea warehouse that cut across the street.

A trap.

Papina spun round, tried to run back, warn the others, but it was too late. More and more monkeys were rushing towards her.

As the cul-de-sac began to fill, the monkeys desperately began to clamber on top of one another, fighting to keep their heads above the crush, terrified of being trampled.

Papina leapt onto a side wall and managed to scramble up a solitary drainpipe. Then she saw the true horror of the Barbary tactics – a massive Langur line was re-forming across the end of the street, an impregnable barrier of brute force.

"ADVANCE!" The word bounced off the surrounding buildings, galvanizing the hordes of Langur.

And the massacre began.

Papina could only watch in horror as the Langur front line raised their clubs, and with primal pleasure brought them crashing down on Rhesus skulls. The Rhesus fell, crumpling to the ground, their bodies twitching, as the Langur troops stepped over them and raised their clubs to strike again.

Hanging from the drainpipe, Papina was deafened by the screams and howls that rent the air, as monkeys struggling in vain to retreat, jammed harder into the throng.

"Please! Take him!" Papina heard the desperate cry and saw a young mother lifting her infant towards her.

Papina swung down, dangling off the pipe with one hand and managed to snatch the youngster. She threw it on her back and could feel its whole body trembling.

"Don't let go!"

The young monkey dug its nails into Papina's fur and whimpered helplessly.

Seeing the rescue, more Rhesus leapt for the drain-pipe, but it was too flimsy to hold their weight. The screws ripped from the wall and the bottom section buckled away, forcing Papina to scramble higher.

Now she could only watch, powerless as the Rhesus were annihilated. The fear on the faces beneath her blurred into one frantic image of despair.

"PAPINA!" A scream rang out. She glimpsed Fig a little way off in the throng, desperately holding up her two infants by the scruff of their necks.

"Pass them over!" Papina screamed back. And somehow, in the midst of all the pandemonium, monkeys who knew they were about to die tried to preserve life, any life.

They grabbed the baby monkeys and started to pass them over the heads of the crowd, hand to hand like a bundle of stolen fruit.

Fig howled with relief as she watched her precious young roll away from her, across the heaving bodies.

And then the first one dropped out of sight into the writhing mass.

"NO!!!"

But Fig's alarm spread more confusion – the second infant peered into the darkness searching for his brother, slipped from the hands holding him and vanished.

Fig tore at the monkeys around her, trying to get past, but in the mayhem it was hopeless – everyone was now scrambling on top of one another, limbs clawing to reach an impossible freedom.

And all the time the pitiless Langur line advanced, possessed by brutal bloodlust. The air was filled with murderous grunts; the troops relished the power in their hands.

Suddenly one of the Barbary Commanders noticed Papina clinging to the drainpipe. She saw him shout orders to a squad of Barbaries who lingered in reserve, and moments later rocks thundered into the wall around her.

The infant on her back started screeching hysterically. Papina realized there was nothing more she could do here. She had to escape, save this one life clinging to her while she still had a chance. Clawing at the wobbling pipe, she shimmied up to the roof and scrambled away.

People. That was all she could think.

Head towards people – the Langur wouldn't kill in front of Humans. So Papina headed towards the fireworks being let off in the centre of the City, her heart pounding, her mind overwhelmed, letting her instincts take over.

Eventually she found herself on a low rooftop overlooking a shrine where revellers were enjoying some impromptu street dancing.

The very last thing Papina wanted right now was to be around the drunken laughter of Humans. She felt numb, as if someone had scooped out her insides. But for now this was probably the safest place in the City.

That the whole massacre was carried out to the distant echoes of music was an irony not lost on Tyrell.

"Where were the Humans when the Rhesus needed them most?" he said to Hummingbird as he looked down at the body-strewn street. "They were busy worshipping their Gods."

Hummingbird just nodded. He was a monkey of action, not fancy words. He had been commanded to take the Gardens and eliminate the Rhesus, and he'd done it with brutal efficiency. Now he and his troops were looking forward to the rewards that would be lavished on them.

There was, however, one last bit of dirty work.

"And the bodies?" Tyrell asked.

"Leave them for the rats," replied Hummingbird.

Tyrell shook his head. "Too slow. And too messy." He waved his hands with disgust at the mass of twisted corpses. "We can't risk the Humans seeing this. Dispose of the evidence."

Tyrell turned and started to stride away, surrounded by advisors, when suddenly he winced – something sharp had stabbed his foot. He looked down and saw some coloured pieces on the ground.

"What's that?"

One of his advisors obligingly scooped up the bits and handed them to Tyrell – they were the remains of a carved object that must have been trampled underfoot during the operation.

Curious, Tyrell pieced the fragments together, until he could make out three Rhesus monkeys, one covering its eyes, one its ears, and the third its mouth.

"Pathetic," he scoffed, and with irritated contempt dropped the broken carving into the gutter.

Hummingbird watched Tyrell go. There was no fight, no battle the Barbaries would shy away from, but taking away the bodies? His warriors could not be seen to demean themselves with that kind of work, so he delegated the job to General Pogo, then took his troops back to the Cemetery to bathe.

Through the night Pogo organized Langur patrols to carry away Rhesus bodies. One by one they were scattered in ditches and dumps across the City, so that for weeks to come, bewildered Humans would find decomposing monkeys in bins, stuffed down sewage pipes, hidden in derelict buildings.

* * *

As the sun crept above the City skyline, a few more Rhesus survivors emerged. Seeing Papina on the rooftop gave them the courage to scamper from the shadows and huddle next to her. Some she knew; most were strangers – before the massacre, Temple Gardens had become so overcrowded it was impossible to know all the faces.

Each survivor had a tale to tell about the night's horror – some had been out scavenging and, returning to find the attack in full frenzy, fled for their lives; others had hidden under dead bodies and waited until the massacre was over before scrambling into nearby buildings.

But some wished they hadn't survived – like Fig and Twitcher. When Papina saw them she ran over and hugged them tightly.

They just crouched, silent and unresponsive. No words could begin to express the pain of their grief – both their precious infants had been killed. Fig and Twitcher stood in a place of total darkness; they had survived with nothing to live for.

Papina had always regretted the fact that she wasn't a mother, but at least today it meant that she didn't have to suffer the harrowing pain that came with maternal love. Now her loneliness was a source of strength, and the other monkeys sensed it too. Instinctively they gathered round, waiting for her to lead them.

As the Humans finally ran out of energy and staggered home to their beds, Papina knew they couldn't stay on the roof any longer – it was too exposed and still too close to the Langur.

As gently as she could, Papina organized the survivors; there were about twenty altogether – she had to assume the rest of the Troop were dead. With broken hearts, the desperate band of refugees followed her down from the roof and away through the streets.

Where were they going? She didn't know. In this new world, where could a Rhesus go to live in peace?

One thing was certain, never again would she trust a Langur. Never. The horrors of the night had hardened her anger into hatred.

Once she had trusted Mico, shared his dream for a City that wasn't riven with fighting.

No more.

If Mico was alive, he should have warned them.

And if he was dead, then there was nothing good left in the Langur world. Nothing.

39

RALLY

Rumours of the massacre swirled feverishly around the Cemetery, as returning soldiers talked excitedly about a "permanent solution" to the Rhesus problem.

There had been no official announcement, that wasn't how Tyrell played things; instead, all the monkeys were summoned to a sunset rally where a "great victory" would be proclaimed.

But Mico couldn't wait until sunset – he had to know now.

He arrived breathless at his parents' home, only to find Breri already there. Kima and Bandha were fluttering around him making a great fuss of the returning war hero, while Trumble hung off his eldest son's every word.

Breri glanced up and gave Mico an imperious smile.

"So good to see you," he said, extending his arms, inviting Mico to embrace him as if he was the head of the family.

"What happened?" asked Mico impatiently. "Were you there?"

The atmosphere in the room suddenly bristled.

"Is it true? Was there a massacre?"

The females looked down, reluctant to get involved.

Breri looked searchingly at Mico. For so long his younger brother had been the star of the Troop, commanding all the respect. But he had fallen and been marginalized, while Breri had risen to command key battles that would change Langur fortunes for ever.

So Breri just smiled cryptically, enjoying the moment, and pronounced, "There is only one monkey now."

Kima and Bandha thought it was an assertion of Breri's rank within the family – he was now the dominant male. But Mico and Trumble knew it meant something quite different: the Rhesus monkeys had been annihilated.

Mico slumped down onto his haunches. Images of all the innocent monkeys at Temple Gardens raced through his mind, but more than anything, he thought of Papina. Had she survived the night? When she needed him most, Mico had not been there to protect her. He had failed her again; he had been weak at the very moment he should have been strong. The claws of remorse dug deep into his guts.

"How shall we celebrate?" asked Kima brightly, trying to move things on.

But Breri was studying his brother's reactions. "You don't seem pleased."

Mico was sick of hiding his true feelings; he wanted to howl his disgust, to condemn the barbarity. He looked over to his father, desperate for someone to share his outrage, but Trumble avoided his gaze.

It was pathetic. Mico had grown up thinking of his father as such a tower of strength, but now he was just a crumbling ruin. And if Trumble was broken, who else was there in the Langur Troop with the courage to make a stand?

"I think I'd better leave," Mico said quietly, and hurried away as fast as he could.

* * *

There was little comfort to be had elsewhere.

Mico wandered, dazed, through the Cemetery walkways, eavesdropping on conversations, but no one seemed in the least disturbed by the rumours of massacre. No one was appalled because no one else was appalled. Conformity had eaten away courage.

Then just as he made his way back from one of the food stations, Mico was startled by a voice from the shadows.

"So it's true."

Mico looked up. A monkey he didn't recognize was sitting in the trees, nonchalantly picking his teeth.

"You're really not pleased."

"Who are you?" Mico asked, trying to peer into the gloom.

"No one."

A shudder ran down Mico's back. "I don't know what you're talking about," he said, trying to sound innocent.

"Is that so?" The stranger dropped down, looked long and hard at Mico's face, then scurried off towards the Great Vault.

One of Tyrell's strengths was his ability to harden his heart. Through an act of sheer will, he could become like granite, impervious to all sentiment. When word came to him that Mico was now openly hostile to official policy, Tyrell knew exactly what to do. With ruthless speed he summoned Hummingbird and issued orders for Mico's immediate assassination.

Even the Barbary, with his battle-tempered soul, was momentarily taken aback. Hummingbird knew how much Mico had once meant to Tyrell; to see all that affection revoked with the cursory flick of a tail made him question whether any monkey could be safe in Tyrell's world.

From the roof of his home Mico heard the buzz of anticipation as the crowds gathered for the victory rally. He knew that his presence was expected, but the thought of joining the cheering throng made him feel sick.

Hister sat next to him, silently grooming him. She knew his worries occupied a different world to hers, but she also knew that talking would solve nothing, so she comforted him in the only way she understood – with the gentle touch of grooming fingers.

Finally she tickled his ear. "Time to move, dreamy head. Or we'll miss the speech."

Mico nodded, but didn't stir; so, giggling, Hister grabbed his tail and pulled him playfully from the roof. Mico tumbled over and landed on her; he gazed into her pretty face, marvelling at how she managed to remain so untroubled by all that was going on around her.

"Catch me if you can!" she declared, and wriggling free, scampered off towards the Great Vault.

By the time they arrived at the rally, the entire Troop had massed and the crowd was chanting itself into a frenzy.

"Lan-gur! Lan-gur! Lan-gurrrrr!" echoed round the Cemetery walls, followed by "Ty-rell! Ty-rell! TY-RELL!"

Hister laughed as she felt the power of the crowd, but a cold shudder ran down Mico's back – it was terrifying to see monkeys abandon all reason and give themselves to hysteria.

The chanting grew louder and louder, refusing to fade, until with perfect timing Tyrell climbed onto the podium.

He raised his arms, basking in the adulation, then modestly pointed to General Pogo and Hummingbird, acknowledging their role in the historic day. This simple act of mock-humility entranced the mob, turning their adulation into love.

Somewhere in all this euphoria, Tyrell looked down … and caught Mico's eye. It was only for a fleeting moment, but it was long enough – in the tyrant's cold eyes Mico glimpsed farewell.

Mico spun round, scanning the faces of the crowd jostling around him … and saw a lone Barbary lurking near by, his dark eyes locked with a deadly resolve. The Barbary didn't care about speeches; he was only interested in Mico.

His prey.

Mico grabbed Hister and pulled her through the crowd, desperate to get away. But every time he glanced over his shoulder, he saw the assassin following. Fighting back was impossible; escape was his only chance.

With no time to explain to Hister, all Mico could do was hug her tightly as they reached the edge of the crowd. "I have to leave you now."

The words hit Hister like a physical force. "No—"

"Forgive me—"

"No! Mico! Don't go!"

"It's safer this way."

She grabbed hold of his arm, refusing to let go. "I've done everything for you. Everything! You can't abandon me!"

The look of pain and rejection in her eyes tore Mico's heart, but he knew she wouldn't survive the hardships of exile.

He put his hands on her face and looked into her eyes, trying to make her understand that everything they knew was turning inside out.

"I'm sorry, Hister. I never wanted to hurt you." But it was no use; every word drove the knife deeper. Desperate to put an end to the pain he was inflicting, Mico turned and ran.

Numb with shock, her world shattered; Hister swayed back and forth. Suddenly a shadow slipped out of the crowd. She turned and saw a lone Barbary, his eyes searching the shadows. He looked at Hister, and the coldness of his gaze made her recoil. But the Barbary hadn't come for her. Not just yet.

He snorted, then swept past her.

If Mico was to survive the night, he needed to confuse the Barbary assassin, buy some precious time. Dodging from shadow to shadow, he ran to the Great Vault, but instead of returning to his old sick room, he took one of the corridors that led to the far side, then double backed until he arrived at the long pool. Mico drew a deep breath, then stealthily slipped into the water.

He looked up through the ripples, waiting for the assassin to appear. As Mico's lungs tightened a twinge of panic fluttered down his back, but he couldn't come up for air now; he had to wait...

Still nothing moved up there.

As air seeped from his lungs, a lightness came over Mico, the pain cut deep into his chest, and just as he was about to open his mouth and breathe in the water, he saw movement above.

He froze, watching as the hulking form of the Barbary assassin ran down the side of the pool and kicked open the door to Mico's room...

Empty.

The assassin spun round, glared left and right;

he knew Mico was hiding somewhere in the Great Vault. Determined to draw blood, the Barbary stalked back to the entrance to start a systematic search.

As soon as it was clear Mico burst to the surface, gasping. With the air came clarity.

And fear.

No time to waste.

Mico scrambled up the Vault wall, dropped down into the feeder stream, and waded along it until he was standing by the water inlet at the bottom of the perimeter wall.

He turned and took one last look at the Cemetery. He could hear the frenzied chanting of the Troop, the sound of ignorance and violence.

Mico drew a breath, then slipped underwater, and was gone.

PART THREE

MONKEY WARS

They enslave their children's children
who make compromise with sin.

JAMES RUSSELL LOWELL,
"THE PRESENT CRISIS"

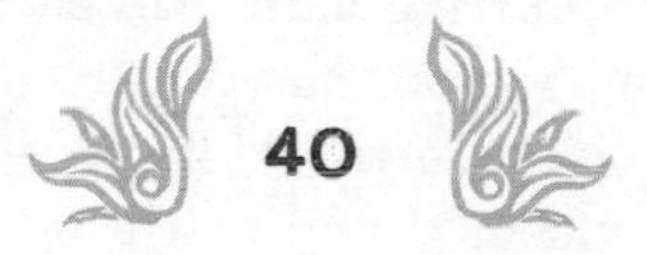

40

GOING TO GROUND

Returning empty-handed was not an option.

Having failed to kill Mico, the assassin knew that his own position was now gravely compromised. In an attempt to shield himself from the worst of Tyrell's rage, the Barbary hastily gathered some reinforcements and stormed Mico's home, dragging the grieving Hister off to the interrogation cells.

She didn't put up any resistance. Her world had already fallen to pieces, and the physical pain inflicted by fists and sticks made no difference now.

Having Hister under arrest, though, made a big difference to the assassin. He stood anxiously in the Summerhouse next to Hummingbird, who explained the situation to Tyrell.

"If she knows anything, she'll talk."

"Even if she *was* involved, Hister couldn't have acted alone. She's nothing more than a pretty bauble." Tyrell's paranoid mind quickly wove a web of intrigue from this single strand. "There must have been others helping Mico escape. Others who knew of our intentions..."

Hummingbird hesitated. If he agreed, he would inflame Tyrell's paranoia; if he disagreed, he risked a furious outburst. So he just reiterated, "I'll make her talk."

"Press her hard."

Hummingbird nodded, darkly amused at the way the more palatable "pressing hard" had become an integral part of the regime's vocabulary.

"For what it's worth, I think Mico's finished," Hummingbird added, trying to close the whole issue down. "He's run for his life."

"For what it's worth," Tyrell replied with thinly veiled scorn, "I think whoever has even the slightest sympathy for Mico must be rooted out and dealt with. No dissent will be tolerated. None. Is that clear?"

Hummingbird lowered his head respectfully. "Perfectly."

With a sweep of his hand, Tyrell dismissed the Barbaries and swung over to the window of the Tower, where he sat, stroking his tail thoughtfully.

Of all the monkeys in the City, Mico was the only one who Tyrell feared. He tried to tell himself that he was being irrational, that Mico was insignificant. Why should the Supreme Leader of the Langur Troop, Overlord and Protector of the Provinces, be afraid of a refugee who had never even fought with the Elites?

Intelligence. That was why.

Mico was the only monkey who could think on Tyrell's level. He might be an exile, but he was too clever for that to be the last anyone heard of him. Tyrell would never know peace until Mico's severed head was brought back to the Cemetery.

But as the Barbary assassin had failed, who could now be trusted with the task?

In the days after the massacre, Papina led her shattered Troop of monkeys away from the City.

They walked and climbed and scrambled.

They made their way past long lines of shanty huts, too crowded with seething humanity to afford any space; past the quiet, affluent houses of the suburbs which would not tolerate a Troop of monkeys ... until finally they came to a sprawling steelworks.

The survivors crouched outside the chain-link fence, looking at the mess of huge, ugly buildings which grew around each other without any obvious logic; tangles of smoke-belching pipes burst from the roofs at random, and everything was coated with a grimy blackness that matched the mood of the monkeys.

Food would be hard to come by here as there were no markets to pilfer. On the other hand that would keep rival animals away, and as long as the monkeys could avoid the Human factory workers and dodge the trucks that rolled in and out, they should be safe.

After some cautious exploration they found a disused water tower and clambered inside – it was dark and damp, but it was out of sight. For the time being, it would have to be home.

The survivors huddled together. Exhausted as she was, Papina only slept fitfully; she found it impossible to silence the urgent questions swirling around her mind.

But as she tossed and turned, she realized that she wasn't the only one who couldn't sleep – crouched in the darkness, Fig was rocking back and forth as if in a trance.

It was frightening to see her like this; Fig had withdrawn to some remote place deep inside herself. Watching her muttering incoherently, Papina realized that the murder of Fig's infants had smashed a hole in the centre of her heart with the force of a Monsoon flood, leaving her with nothing but twisted wreckage.

Papina knew there was nothing anyone could do to ease that unimaginable pain; she just had to hope that as the days passed, time would heal the wounds.

The next morning they set to work.

Determined to get the monkeys re-engaged with the business of living, Papina divided the survivors into groups and set them tasks. Some carried out a reconnaissance of the steelworks, others tracked down food supplies, while she looked after drawing up a rota of lookouts.

Tentatively, Papina approached Fig and asked her to organize a safe area where the youngsters could play.

Fig ignored her. She just huddled silently in the shadows, untouched by anything around her.

Even Twitcher didn't know how to get through to her. All his confidence had been shattered by the massacre. He was now so hesitant and unsure it was hard to believe he'd once swaggered through the City with urbane charm.

The survivors weren't just outcasts; they were now lost from themselves.

Mico had to assume that a massive hunt was already in full heat, which meant his best hope was to stick to the maze of narrow backstreets where there were plenty of dark doorways and crumbling basements to scurry into for hiding.

But these streets had their own problems – large, aggressive rats stalked the alleys, scavenging for food, and where there were rats, snakes were never far behind. So it was with ears bristling and eyes flashing nervously in all directions that Mico ran, not stopping to rest, relentlessly darting from shadow to shadow, putting distance between himself and the Cemetery.

At least he had a plan, and that focussed his thinking.

The City was criss-crossed with railway lines, but having always had the run of the streets, Mico had never learned his way around the tracks, so when he stumbled across the first set of steel lines he had no idea which way to follow them. He would have to do this the hard way.

He ran along the railway track until he came to a signal gantry, then clambered up the tower and waited. It wasn't long before he heard the heavy metal creak of a shunting engine groaning closer; Mico braced himself, then as the engine trundled underneath, he leapt on top. But as soon as he landed, he started to slide off.

His hand reached out for something to cling on to and found a pipe, but it was searingly hot and immediately his palm started to blister.

Forced to let go, he slid further along the roof, tumbled down onto the tender and finally slammed to a halt.

Mico gripped his hand as the pain throbbed through it. He couldn't even let the agony out with a howl for fear of alerting the engine driver; all he could do was lie there, willing the pain to subside.

Eventually the engine arrived at a massive railway junction where tracks from all over the City converged, and as it passed under another signal gantry, Mico leapt off and found a perch next to a red light.

His curious eyes took in the scene – trains of all shapes and sizes were being shunted relentlessly back and forth. It seemed so random, and yet the more he looked, the more he saw a pattern: the small shunting engines would pick up carriages and push them off into the darkness, then re-emerge with a different load.

It gave Mico an idea: he could ride each of these engines in turn until he found what he was looking for, knowing that if he had no luck in one direction he could always come back to this junction and try a different line.

It was a long, fascinating process – the City he thought he knew so well looked totally different from the top of a moving train. The geography seemed quite alien, and areas that by road felt far apart suddenly connected in surprising ways. But train-surfing was also dangerous. Several times Mico slipped or was jolted from his perch and nearly ended up under the thundering wheels. Then again, that was why monkeys kept away from trains, and right now other monkeys were the biggest danger Mico faced.

Finally his perseverance was rewarded – he found himself trundling through some sidings that were surrounded by hulking brick warehouses, and on one of the roofs stood a huge disc with holes in it – a button. This was the clue he'd been looking for.

As the train slowed to go over some points, Mico leapt from the roof onto a pile of coal, which crumbled under his feet in a black avalanche.

Directly opposite the button warehouse was a large, half-derelict engine shed. He would start searching there and work his way methodically through all the buildings around the yard.

As he drew closer, Mico saw that the shed was in a bad way – window frames were twisted at ugly angles, fragments of glass clung to the putty like decayed teeth; planks of wood, tired from the effort of hanging on, had dropped from the walls, and half the corrugated metal roof panels had been torn off by the Monsoon storms.

Mico stared at the shafts of moonlight punching down into the gloom like pillars in a great temple.

And then he heard it – the gentle sigh of something falling through the air.

He glanced up – something was bearing down on him. His muscles tensed as he tried to jerk backwards, but it was too late; suddenly the thing was all over him, tangling his arms and legs.

For a heart-stopping moment Mico thought he had been caught by a snake, but as his hands lashed out he felt something dry and fibrous.

Rope. He was caught in a net.

The weight of a body slammed down on his back and two monkey hands clamped around his throat. Mico rolled forward, clawing at the fingers, trying to prise them away, but they were impossibly strong. Suddenly two knees drove into his shoulders, forcing his face into the oily grime of the shed floor.

Panic trembled through Mico's body.

Mico had to cry out, make a last desperate appeal, but he only had enough breath in his lungs for one word. One word to save his life.

Summoning all his willpower, he managed to gasp into the darkness, "Spy!"

The attacker paused, trying to work out what it meant. Was it an accusation? Or a warning?

The hands grabbed his shoulders and spun him over. Mico blinked as he tried to make out the face in the darkness. It was a monkey, but covered in stripes of black oil and soot to camouflage his features.

And then Mico saw a flash of white teeth as his assailant spoke.

"Mico?"

The voice; he knew that voice.

"Gu-Nah?"

Anger flashed in Gu-Nah's eyes. "I knew they'd send an assassin." He clamped his hands back round Mico's throat. "I didn't think it'd be *you*."

"Wait!"

Gu-Nah's thumbs pressed on Mico's voice box. "One squeeze, and you're dead!"

"I'm on the run too!"

Gu-Nah looked around suspiciously, his eyes searching the shadows, wondering if this was all a trap.

"I swear!" gasped Mico. "Tyrell's my enemy. He always was!"

Gu-Nah studied Mico's face, considered his words, then with one swift movement he pulled the net clear. Mico staggered to his feet and wiped the dirt from his mouth.

The two monkeys looked at each other like strangers in the moonlight. Gu-Nah saw a monkey who had once been in the highest echelon of the Langur Troop now reduced to a frightened refugee. Quite a change.

But not as big as the change Mico saw: only a couple of moons ago Gu-Nah had just been a tired old soldier. Not any more. The Gu-Nah who stood before him had a wild, raw danger pumping through his veins.

"What happened to you?" Mico asked apprehensively.

Gu-Nah's eyes danced in the darkness. "Freedom."

41

TREASON

Lesser rulers would have gone to great lengths to keep Mico's disappearance quiet, nervous that the defection of such a senior monkey would reflect badly on them. But Tyrell understood that by sharing his sense of betrayal, he could win the sympathy of the Troop.

Which is why, a few days later, a special group of Langur monkeys emerged from the Great Vault with a mission to spread the news of Mico's defection far and wide. Hand-picked by Tyrell, these impressionable young monkeys formed the newly created Twopoint Brigade. They worked the rooftops and the lounging trees, persuading mothers who gossiped at the food stations, and youths who played in the banyan groves.

Everywhere they went the message they pushed was the same: *Mico is a traitor! He's stolen all our secrets – how we defend ourselves, where we keep our food. As we speak he's inciting other traitors to spy on us. A neighbour behaving strangely? A friend questioning military strategy? These could be warning signs. Better to report them to the Twopoints and be safe than keep quiet and help traitors.*

On the roof and branch the propaganda created a wave of gratitude that Tyrell's strong leadership was protecting his monkeys.

In Mico's family, though, the reactions were very different.

Trumble and Kima were devastated. Nearly losing their son to illness had been bad enough, but now to have him branded a traitor...

They knew Mico with a deep, instinctive knowledge, like a familiar scent, and they refused to believe the accusations were true.

Breri looked at his parents with a dispassionate eye, and judged that they were showing far too much concern for an enemy of the Troop, so one evening he cornered his father in the small space under their home.

"You shouldn't feel sympathy for Mico."

Trumble looked up with grief in his eyes. "He's my son—"

"He's a traitor."

"But he's still my son!"

Breri shrugged. "More's the pity."

"What happened to you?" Trumble asked, unable to hide his dismay. "When did you become so cold?"

"I worked hard to prove myself," Breri snapped as the back of his neck prickled with anger. "*I* wasn't plucked out of obscurity and handed everything on a palm leaf! I had to struggle every step of the way, and now Mico's put all that in jeopardy. Now I'm the brother of a traitor!"

For the first time Trumble saw the utter selfishness of his eldest son. There was no right or wrong for Breri; there was just the simple calculation: how would it be of benefit to Breri?

As if unable to look at the ugliness of his own creation, Trumble turned away and muttered, "Get out of my sight."

* * *

Anger lashed Breri's heart as he thundered through the shady alleys of the Cemetery. He wanted to hurt his father the way he was hurting, and he knew exactly how to do it.

In a short while, Breri found himself standing outside the ominous Black Vault that the Twopoint Brigade had taken for its headquarters. He looked up at the official symbol carved above the door – they would teach Trumble about loyalty.

But something made Breri hesitate.

A fleeting memory danced into his mind: when he was a young monkey, he had fallen from the branches of a gum tree. Trumble had picked him up, put him on his back and ran all the way across the City to get him home, where Kima sat with him day and night. Whenever Breri opened his eyes, she was there. It was as if his mother never slept or ate, as if he was the only thing in the world that mattered to her.

Breri shook himself, casting off the memory. *Forget the past,* he told himself. *The past is dead and gone. There is only the future.* He had to do the right thing, which meant putting the needs of the Troop above all personal sentiment. That was the truly courageous thing. Troop first, family second.

And having convinced himself, Breri stepped into the Twopoint Brigade's headquarters.

Whereas before the Barbaries had turned up like thieves in the night, this time they swarmed into Trumble's home in broad daylight, determined to make it a public spectacle.

Kima closed her eyes and let herself be dragged into the dusty sunlight, but Trumble still clung to some notion of justice.

"We've been through this!" he exclaimed. "Ask Hummingbird! I've taught him about the Stones!"

The Barbaries just kicked Trumble to the ground.

"This isn't about your silly Stones, Trumble." The voice was quiet, cold.

Trumble craned his neck and saw a Langur standing over him. "And it's nothing to do with Hummingbird," the Langur added. "It's Twopoint business now."

Trumble tried to make out the Twopoint Commander's face against the blue sky – there was something familiar about him.

"You're ... you're one of Breri's friends. You played together as youngsters."

"And you're the father of a traitor," the Commander said ominously.

So that was why they'd come.

The Twopoint Commander nodded to the Barbaries, who bundled Trumble and Kima away, marching them slowly along the paths, giving the monkeys who peered out from the shadows plenty of time to see the shame of traitors.

They kept marching, out of the Cemetery, through the Langur-controlled streets until they came to the gates of the Eastern Province. The prisoners were taken across the Great Lawn, down the narrow steps that led to a cellar under the Summer-house Tower, where they were thrown into a dark, damp room.

The door was slammed shut behind them. This time there was no interrogation.

Trumble and Kima had been shut away from the sunlight to be forgotten.

Far above, Tyrell was standing at the window of his room; beside him was Breri. They had watched the arrest in silence, and only when he heard the heavy clang of the metal door did Tyrell turn to Breri and see the grave expression on his face.

"Not having second thoughts?"

Breri quickly pulled himself together. "No, my Lord."

"You made a difficult choice. But you made the right one."

"Thank you, Lord Tyrell."

"Not every monkey would've had the courage to denounce his own parents."

Breri hesitated. There were so many conflicting emotions rampaging through his heart, when all he wanted was certainty.

He looked at Tyrell and with heartfelt sincerity replied, "It wasn't an easy decision, my Lord."

Seeing the enormity of the step Breri had taken, Tyrell opened his arms and embraced him. "Think of *me* as your father now. We are a Troop first and individuals second."

As the ruler's arms held him tightly, Breri felt a huge sense of relief. All he had to do was follow Tyrell unquestioningly, do as the Leader ordered, and everything would be all right.

"There is nothing greater than loyalty," Tyrell reassured him. "It is the fabric of the Troop."

Gently he led Breri over to the massive, carved map of the City that dominated one wall of the room.

"Do you think your brother's out there somewhere? Or has he fled the City altogether?"

Breri looked at the tangle of lines, struggling to understand the visual abstraction.

"You've known him since he was born. Watched him grow up, played with him, fought with him. If Mico could go anywhere, where would he run for safety?"

Tyrell plucked a selection of the juiciest fruits from his own personal supply and laid them down in front of Breri.

"Sit. Eat. Think."

And Breri did exactly as he was told.

42

FRACTURE LINES

Mico woke with a start as a furious whistle split his eardrums. He leapt to his feet in utter confusion. For a few moments he was totally disorientated; his mind rushed to catch up with his body.

Then someone behind him chuckled, "Welcome to my world."

Mico spun round and saw Gu-Nah tucking into a pile of freshly pilfered fruit.

"The express trains all do that. You'll get used to it," Gu-Nah said and tossed an orange across the hide.

Mico went to catch it, but he wasn't awake enough and the orange dropped through a gap in the rafters. There was a soft *splat* as it exploded on the floor far below, reminding Mico exactly where he was.

Gu-Nah sighed. "Concentrate."

He tossed another orange – this time Mico caught it and sank his teeth into the flesh. As he sucked hungrily on the juice, Mico studied Gu-Nah, and saw that his wild fur wasn't the result of neglect; it had been carefully cultivated.

"Not keen on the crazy look?" said Gu-Nah.

"It's a bit ... extreme."

"It has to be. A lone monkey is vulnerable. Rabid dogs, hungry rats – they all want to have a pop. But enemies back away from madness. It's too unpredictable."

"So, the crazier you look, the safer you are?"

Without warning Gu-Nah lunged at Mico, baring his teeth. Startled, Mico tumbled backwards, slipped off the rafter and plummeted.

In an instant, Gu-Nah swung down and his iron grip clamped around Mico's tail, hauling him painfully back to safety.

"See? Unpredictable," the old soldier chuckled darkly.

Mico wasn't amused. "You could at least have made the place a bit safer," he said looking at the chaotic jumble of rusting metal sheets wedged between the rafters.

"The secret is all in the gaps. From below, it looks like junk." Gu-Nah thrust his head between two planks. "But all the while you can keep an eye on the approaches."

Mico peered out between the roof sheets – the view certainly was impressive.

"And the gaps let in tell-tale sounds," Gu-Nah explained. "It's a warning system ... the slightest change in water dripping from a gutter, or the sound of falling coals—"

"So that's how you knew I was coming!"

Gu-Nah gave a wry smile. "The trick to seeing the future is to study the present more closely than your enemy."

Mico was impressed and daunted as he realized how much he had to learn about survival outside a Troop.

He would need to learn fast.

In the Map Room at the top of the Tower the hunt for Mico was gearing up, with Sweto newly appointed to lead the mission. This devious Langur had held a grudge against Mico ever since they'd clashed in the Undercroft, and he longed for the chance to settle the score.

For an entire night, Tyrell had kept Breri in the Map Room, remembering every hiding place Mico had used when playing as an infant, every neighbourhood he'd mentioned in casual conversation.

As he listened to Breri reel off the targets (honey farm, bins behind the pastry shop, burnt-out tamarind tree...) Tyrell realized that in all the time he'd known Mico, he had never had those private conversations that offer glimpses into a monkey's soul. It was as if Mico had been holding back all along, and the thought filled Tyrell with an angry dread.

Never again would he make the mistake of trusting another monkey with so much power.

Perched on the guttering, looking down on the shunting yards, Mico was amazed to see how busy the tracks were. Last night there had just been the odd train passing through, but this morning there was a rattling confusion of engines shunting back and forth with long lines of carriages in tow.

"So..." He turned to Gu-Nah. "What now?"

"Chocolate," Gu-Nah replied, tossing over a pilfered bar. But Mico wasn't going to be distracted so easily.

"You know what I mean." He gestured to the derelict engine shed. "Is this it? Just living wild?"

"What would you rather do? Overthrow Tyrell's Empire?" Gu-Nah chuckled at the absurdity of the idea, but when he looked up he saw that Mico wasn't smiling.

"Oh no," said Gu-Nah. "I'm just pretending to be mad. You really *are* mad if you think—"

"We know all his secrets."

"He's got a whole army!"

"We know their tactics."

"He's got the Barbaries—"

"We know their weaknesses."

"This is the monkey who massacred the Rhesus!"

"And we're going to let him get away with that?!"

Mico and Gu-Nah glared at each other testily.

"How can two outcasts take on a whole empire? Tyrell is indestructible," Gu-Nah said firmly, trying to finish the argument once and for all.

"Powerful, yes. Indestructible, no." Mico handed the chocolate back as a peace offering. "In their strength is their fatal weakness."

"They don't have a weakness."

"Tyrell controls everything," Mico went on. "All decisions have to come from him. That makes the Langur inflexible. You said it yourself, but your ideas about fighting were never going to catch on because they flew in the face of Tyrell's need for control."

"What's gone is gone." Gu-Nah shrugged. "We missed our chance."

"But what if we trained *other* monkeys? If we had just a small troop, highly trained in your new fighting skills..." Mico picked up a coconut and tapped it. "It looks so strong, doesn't it? But if you know how to attack it..." And with a swift hand, Mico slammed the coconut on a roof girder, striking it at just the right angle so that it split in two.

Gu-Nah looked at the shell, then reached out and took the half with the sweet milk. "No point wasting it."

"If we strike at Tyrell in a new way," Mico said quietly, "we can send a fracture line through his whole Empire."

Gu-Nah gulped down the coconut milk. He was certainly tempted – although his experiment in the new form of fighting had been cut short, he had glimpsed its power. If the enemy had to wait for information to travel up and down a chain of command, maybe, just maybe, a small, highly trained force really could win, even if they were massively outnumbered.

The more Gu-Nah thought about it, the more it intrigued him. He felt the old urge of combat start to stir.

"Did you know some of the Rhesus survived?" he said finally.

Mico stared at him in disbelief. "Survived? Are you sure?"

"Oh yes."

"How many? Where? Do you know how to find them?" The questions spilled from Mico's mouth as he dared to hope that Papina may still be alive.

Gu-Nah passed the chocolate back to Mico. "Eat well. We've got a long journey ahead."

It was sunset by the time Sweto and his Elites arrived at the railway sidings. They had spent all day searching bolt-holes across the City and turned up nothing, but Sweto had high hopes for the engine shed; hiding here – a place most monkeys did not dare visit – was just the sort of devious move he would expect from a traitor.

The hit squad hurried across the tracks, then Sweto peered through a crack in the engine shed walls, searching for clues that might give away the enemy's position.

His eyes darted to all the possible hiding places: abandoned offices – too obvious; inspection pits – too damp; gantries – too visible; the tangle of roof girders ... maybe.

Using hand signals, he directed his troops inside, and with deadly speed they flitted up the walls like shadows. As they crawled into the roof space, converging on the ramshackle shelter, Sweto picked up the musky scent of Langur ... and then the first solid clue: bits of orange peel.

His heart raced. Only a monkey would leave this kind of food debris up here, but how careless of Mico not to cover his tracks.

Sweto's prey was within grasping distance. They were moments away from a kill.

Slowly, silently, the Elites closed in, tightening the noose, converging on the hide... Sweto reached out, grabbed hold of one of the planks of wood, then yanked it aside ...

To find nothing.

The traitor had already fled.

43

INNER STRENGTH

Papina checked the colour of the sunlight dappling through the holes in the water tank, and could see it was time to bring the youngsters in.

With one deft move, she swung up the rickety iron ladder and emerged onto the top of the tank. The young monkeys were squealing with delight as they played among the tangle of steel debris that had built up around the water tower. Earlier they'd found a large, rusty spring and had spent the whole day balancing a plank of wood on it to make an improvised trampoline.

Papina looked on thoughtfully as the monkeys yelped with delight, never seeming to tire of launching themselves onto the plank and being hurled off in random directions. It seemed so long since she'd been like them, when life was just a series of joyful games, so rather than call them in straight away, she sat and watched.

These youngsters hadn't forgotten the horror of the massacre or the pain of losing their families, but somehow that didn't stop them living for the moment and laughing with open-hearted enthusiasm.

When did that change? Papina wondered. When did the accumulated weight of memory reach the tipping point where you could no longer pick yourself up again?

Perhaps that was what it really meant to get old; not just a stiffening of the legs and failing of the eyesight, but a hardening of your innermost being, so that when you fell, you didn't bounce, you started to chip ... until the day came when you shattered.

Soon sunset gave way to twilight and Papina scampered to round up the young monkeys, fending off the barrage of protests by allowing them to bring the spring inside so that it wouldn't go missing in the night. She smiled at their jumble of voices, all gabbling over one another about how they would build a bigger, better, bouncier device the next morning.

Then something made her hang back.

Her ears pricked up, scanning the familiar sounds of the industrial yard. She turned. Through the dim light she saw two figures making their way towards her.

Two monkeys.

A moment of panic pulsed through Papina as she recognized the distinctive shape of the Langur. So this was where it was all going to end, in a derelict water tower on the forgotten edges of the City – they had finally been hunted down.

Papina opened her mouth to screech the alarm, then hesitated. The Langur would never attack with just two monkeys. And if they were spies they wouldn't have given their presence away.

She peered more closely...

And then her heart seemed to stop.

Walking towards her out of the gloom was Mico. He looked older, frailer, but it was him.

Her vision swam, the strength drained from her legs and Papina crumpled to the ground.

* * *

She was aware of coming round and finding herself being carried somewhere in Mico's arms. She struggled to break free, but Mico held her tightly, as if he would never let go.

Then darkness again.

A long and dreamless sleep, as if her mind had shut down.

When Papina woke the sun was already burning hot in the sky. She blinked, looked for the others, then heard a voice, gentle, familiar ... a voice she hadn't heard for a long time.

"They're playing outside."

She turned and saw Mico crouched a little way away. So many thoughts tumbled through Papina's mind, tripping one another up in the race for expression. There were so many things she wanted to scream at him – her rage at being abandoned, her pain that his promise of love and protection had been broken.

But the words wouldn't come. Looking into Mico's eyes, she understood that he had also been on a long, dark journey.

"They betrayed me too," Mico said quietly. "I had no idea of the cunning I was up against. But in whatever time is left for me, I've sworn to bring Tyrell down."

Papina could hear the remorse in his voice, but she said nothing. She felt so numb from all that had happened she didn't even trust her own reactions.

"Give me another chance, Papina. Maybe I can do something to build a better life. If not for us, then for those young monkeys playing outside."

Papina didn't stir. What the survivors needed more than anything else was help, inspiration, leadership; but could she trust this Langur that had let her down so badly before?

Slowly Mico edged closer until he was sitting next to her. He could feel the warmth of her body, hear her small delicate breaths. Tentatively he raised his hand and placed it gently on her head.

She didn't move away, but she didn't move closer.

With the enlarged Empire now secure, General Pogo found himself increasingly involved with Internal Security. He didn't particularly like the work; he was an old-fashioned soldier, temperamentally more suited to open warfare than mind games and subterfuge, but Tyrell had promised him that this would be his last posting before a well-earned retirement, when he could expect to be kept in comfort for the rest of his life.

So Pogo applied himself to the task with his usual diligence, organizing the Twopoint Brigade, establishing secret internment cells in every province, and training specialist interrogators to make wayward Langurs see the error of their ways.

Despite his best efforts, though, Pogo had been unable to persuade three particular prisoners to co-operate and, as a last resort, he'd asked Tyrell to personally intervene.

Leaving his Barbary bodyguards upstairs, the Lord Ruler approached the internment rooms. He hated coming down here – the grim hopelessness of the place was too stark a reminder of the ugly foundations of his power – but now and then these things had to be done.

As the cell door swung open the fetid smell hit him, turning his stomach in a nauseous convulsion. Tyrell steeled himself, then entered the darkness.

Crouched on the floor, dirty and unkempt, were Trumble, Kima and Hister. Their eyes were sunken and vacant, their bodies thin; smears of blood streaked the walls and floor.

Tyrell shook his head dolefully. "They're such monsters, those Twopoints."

Kima and Hister didn't stir; Trumble looked up bitterly, aware that Tyrell was trying to fool them into trusting him.

"I've tried to rein them in but ..." Tyrell gave a sympathetic sigh, "their loyalty to me is too fierce to restrain." He looked around the pitiful cell. "The fact is, I could stop all this today."

Trick or not, Trumble knew they had nothing to lose by begging. "We'd be most grateful if you would help us, Lord Tyrell."

"It's the very least I'd do for loyal subjects," declared Tyrell. "But how do I know you *are* loyal?"

"I've served the Langur all my life. I've shed blood for this Troop. What more can I do?"

"Denounce your son."

It was a brutally simple answer.

"Make a public declaration of Mico's guilt. Disown him, swear not just your allegiance to me, but your determination to see Mico hunted down."

Trumble looked away, trying to hide the pain on his face, but Tyrell had one last twist of the knife. He leaned close and whispered, "When Mico is executed for his crimes, not only will you watch, but you will be the first to applaud."

Trumble hung his head low, then in a voice broken with emotion replied, "I can't do that."

"You have to," Tyrell insisted.

"I can't."

"There's no other way. You must accept the reality of the new world."

Trumble glanced over to Kima, but she just stared at the ground. The last time he'd been imprisoned Trumble had co-operated, accepted the power of the Barbaries and spent many days teaching them about the Counting Stones, yet still it hadn't saved him. He wasn't going to make the same mistake again.

Trumble reached out and held Kima's hand. "Kill us now. Have done with it."

Not the answer Tyrell wanted to hear, but one he had expected. Old monkeys had so little to live for they became hard to manage. So Tyrell turned his gaze on Hister, who had been trying to remain unnoticed in the shadows of the cell.

"And what about you?" he asked softly, almost tenderly. "Surely you're too young ... too pretty to languish down here in the darkness?"

Trumble looked at Hister, expecting her to follow his defiant lead, to remain loyal to Mico, but she avoided his gaze and whispered her reply.

"Yes."

Tyrell nodded. "Yes to what, exactly?"

"Give me my freedom. I'll denounce Mico."

Trumble couldn't believe his ears. Even Kima raised her head and glared at Hister.

"I devoted my life to him, and he abandoned me." The anger trembled in Hister's voice.

"And he will be punished for it," Tyrell pronounced. Bending down, he gently helped Hister to her feet. "You are free."

He guided her to the door, then turned to Kima and Trumble. "You see? That's how easy it is."

As the bodyguards led Hister away, General Pogo and Tyrell paused in the blanket of humidity that cloaked the Summer-house gardens.

"Do you want Trumble disposed of, my Lord?" asked the General.

"No, no. He's far too useful to kill."

Pogo nodded to Hister. "But you're not really going to give her another chance?"

"Of course. I gave her my word," replied Tyrell.

"With all due respect, my Lord, how can we ever trust her?"

"Her spirit is broken. I have rescued her. Hister feels nothing but gratitude towards me. That's how you bend monkeys to your will, General. How you make a Troop of conformists."

They treated Hister with kindness; they fed her and cleaned her, they coached her in the art of denunciation, and then they left her alone to rest.

It was the one thing she didn't do.

All night the pretty young monkey wrestled with her conscience, struggling to summon the courage to defy the Leader. By dawn she had found it. Not through any grand philosophy, but through a tiny pulse that was beating in her womb.

Even though she had been abandonned, Hister had to live for her unborn baby. She could not raise an infant in a world where its father had been branded a traitor, a world where it would live in constant fear.

New life deserved better.

When the guards came for her in the morning, Hister was gone.

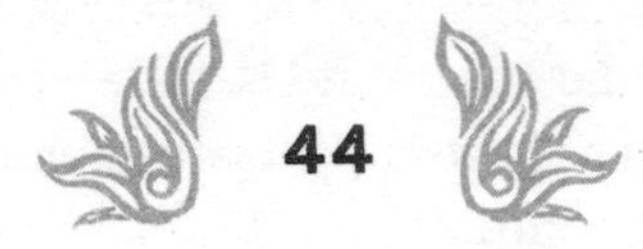

44

BEGIN AGAIN

"How?" Papina demanded. "A few refugees against a whole army? You've spent too much time in that engine shed."

Gu-Nah smiled; he liked this outspoken monkey. If they had all been like her maybe the Rhesus would never have been conquered in the first place.

"How?" he replied. "Simple: by not fighting on his terms."

Papina shook her head. "The only way we're going to survive is by not fighting at all. We have to hide, rebuild our numbers."

"And that's it?!" Mico exclaimed. "That's your answer? Spend the rest of your days skulking in the Slums?"

He'd thought Papina would leap at the chance to fight back, but she shook her head stubbornly.

"My monkeys have seen enough suffering to last a lifetime. They need peace."

Mico gestured at the ugly industrial sprawl. "You call *this* peace?"

"For now."

"A broken Troop, frightened of its own shadow?"

"Typical Langur!" Papina growled. "You don't think anyone's strong unless they're swinging a weapon."

"Sometimes that's the only way—"

"And sometimes strength is just about surviving! We did that. And we're not going to throw it away."

Gu-Nah hurriedly stepped between them.

"Papina," he said with quiet authority, "I'm a fighting monkey; I don't think deeply. But I know one thing for sure: you won't be safe until Tyrell is dead."

His words hung in the air, simple, forceful.

Papina looked out across the yard at the young Rhesus monkeys who were finding new games to play with their salvaged spring. All she wanted was to do the right thing for them.

Seeing how torn she was, Mico crouched next to her, trying to rekindle their old intimacy. "What's the point of surviving if you live in fear?" he whispered.

Papina looked at him, searching his eyes for the young monkey she'd fallen in love with, the monkey she'd trusted with her life. "All you've given me is fancy words. How could it possibly work?"

Gu-Nah smiled. "By getting up early. Dawn tomorrow."

"Even the infants?"

"Especially the infants."

Trying to appear eager for their first lesson, the Rhesus had lined up in neat rows as Gu-Nah and Mico approached. The monkeys were just doing what they thought soldiers did, but when Gu-Nah stood in front of them he shook his head. "That's exactly how we're *not* going to win this war."

The Rhesus exchanged nervous glances.

"Now gather round," Gu-Nah said casually. "For the next few moons we're going to do nothing but play games. The way I see it, if you want to fight different you have to think different; and to think different you need to grow up all over again, which means learning to play all over again."

But it was play with a difference...

Wrestling became an exercise in the inequality of power. Gu-Nah organized the monkeys into pairs, adult against adult, youngster against youngster, and made them wrestle each other for control of a square marked in the dirt.

At first everything was evenly matched and very few fights had a clear conclusion. Then Gu-Nah secretly told half the monkeys to change their tactics – instead of simply wrestling, they were to focus all their energy on attacking one part of their opponent's body.

The monkeys were puzzled, but they tried it anyway.

Twitcher was matched against a Rhesus male called Cadby. That morning they had wrestled each other to exhaustion without either getting pushed out of the square. Now, though, Cadby decided to focus all his effort on Twitcher's left arm.

"Attack!" shouted Gu-Nah and, as the two monkeys threw themselves at each other, Cadby dived for Twitcher's arm and yanked it towards the ground. Twitcher tried to prise him off but it was no use; Cadby just focussed more of his energy on the arm, leaping up and locking both his legs around it.

Twitcher paused, utterly confused about how to counter the attack. As he hesitated Cadby swung round, pulled Twitcher off balance and sent them both tumbling to the ground. Still Cadby didn't let go – he leapt to his feet and dragged Twitcher across the dirt by his arm. Trying to relieve the searing pain, Twitcher scrambled after Cadby and was promptly bundled out of the square.

The monkeys were astonished at the bizarre but brilliantly effective technique.

"You get the point," said Gu-Nah, stepping into the square. "Two matched forces will just keep slugging it out.

But *winning* is what fighting is about. Whatever forces you have, focus them where the enemy is least expecting it and you create confusion. You throw them off balance. You win."

Gu-Nah looked along the line of monkeys. "Any youngsters want to try it?"

"Me!" exclaimed Joop, a particularly enthusiastic youngster.

"Good. Who else?" said Gu-Nah, looking at the other young monkeys.

"No, I want to try it on Cadby!"

The monkeys all laughed – Joop was half the size of Cadby and obviously didn't stand a chance.

Gu-Nah just gave a wry smile. "Even better." And he ushered Joop into the square.

The monkeys murmured nervously.

Joop looked up at Cadby with a solemn face. "Don't go easy on me."

Cadby smiled indulgently. "As if."

"Attack!" barked Gu-Nah.

Cadby thrust forward to grab Joop by the shoulders – his plan was to lift the young monkey clean off his feet and toss him out of the square. That should get a laugh. But he'd forgotten that the whole point of the exercise was about upsetting plans.

Cadby lunged and Joop flung himself to the ground, avoiding his grasp. Then as Cadby swung back round, Joop hurled himself towards the bigger monkey's left leg. The speed and force took Cadby completely by surprise; he didn't even have time to tense his muscles; his leg was just snatched away and he tumbled into the dirt.

The watching monkeys gasped in surprise; a few started to laugh. Anger pricked Cadby – he'd show this little upstart who was the better fighter.

But immediately Joop struck again, grabbing the bigger monkey's ears and twisting his head, forcing Cadby's body to follow ... and roll right out of the square.

The spectators burst into spontaneous ground-thumping, delighted at the triumph of the underdog.

With the battle over, Joop switched back from warrior to polite little monkey, helping Cadby to his feet and asking, "Are you all right?" as if the attack had been nothing to do with him.

Gu-Nah immediately set everyone to work practising the technique. Young wrestled old, females wrestled males – there was no hierarchy.

There were more upsets in the days that followed, as each new game turned some preconception or other on its head.

For "Command or Control", Gu-Nah split the group into adults against infants and gave them an objective: to build a bridge across the storm gully that ran behind the steelworks. This was no easy task – the concrete ditch was as wide as a small road, and full to the brim with swirling water.

Gu-Nah organized the adults along traditional Troop lines. Twitcher was put in charge of the operation and had to direct operations from the water tower. Strict military discipline was to be maintained at all times.

The youngsters, on the other hand, were given no leader. Instead, Gu-Nah told them that they were each personally responsible for successfully bridging the gully. It was as if they had all been made leaders.

A well-organized hierarchy of adults against an anarchic band of infants all vying with one another? It should have been obvious who would win.

While the youngsters dispersed in random directions, all doing their own thing, Twitcher issued a long stream of carefully considered orders, sending out some monkeys to look for materials, ordering others to find a good crossing point.

As the sun reached its highest point, Twitcher was still looking at designs drawn in the sand, while the rival team had amassed a huge pile of materials at the side of the storm gully and was starting to experiment with various constructions.

Cadby reported back that the youngsters were in the lead, but Twitcher wasn't worried. "No point being the fastest if your bridge collapses," he chuckled, convinced that good organization would win the day.

But by sunset the young monkeys put the final piece of their bridge in place and successfully crossed the gully. The race was over, and the adults hadn't even finished their foundations.

Twitcher was stunned. All the adult monkeys were. They stared, incredulous, at the euphoric infants dancing back and forth across their bridge. It was the weirdest bridge any of them had seen, a kind of pontoon, floating on old tyres and secured to the bank at either end with bits of cable ... but it worked, and that was what mattered.

"What just happened?" demanded Gu-Nah.

"We won! We won!"

"But *why* did you win?" insisted Gu-Nah.

The youngsters quietened down; they had no idea why.

"One word: freedom." Gu-Nah let the word hang in the air for a moment. "The young monkeys were free to try anything they wanted; the adults could only follow orders."

"So it's *my* fault," said Twitcher fractiously. "For giving the wrong orders."

"It's not the orders you gave; it's the fact that you had to give them at all," Mico intervened diplomatically. "You had to work with a hierarchy. It gave you control, but it lost you time. The youngsters just collected whatever looked interesting. A lot of it was junk – they didn't care; they collected it anyway. But when they started *playing* with their pile of junk, that's when their ideas started coming. Because they didn't need to worry about following orders, some of those ideas were crazy."

Mico pointed to a rubber tyre under the middle of the bridge. "They wouldn't have thought of using a floating support if they hadn't just happened to have collected a tyre."

"I saw a pile of tyres as well, behind the small warehouse," protested Cadby, trying to save face for the adults.

"Then why didn't you collect some?" asked Gu-Nah.

"I sent word to ask for permission."

"And?"

"The order came back: *We're building a bridge, not a boat. Leave them.*"

Gu-Nah nodded. "You followed orders, like a good soldier."

Mico put a reassuring hand on Twitcher's shoulder. "And you tried to keep everyone focussed on the mission: bridge not boat. Just like a good commander." He spun round and looked at the group of adults. "No one did the wrong thing. The point is, you lost because you didn't have the freedom to win."

Gu-Nah swung across the ground and made a dramatic leap onto the bridge, which bobbed under his weight. "And it's the same for the Langur. When we attack Tyrell's Empire, we need to do what the youngsters did with this bridge. Move fast, react quickly, strike while his army is waiting for orders. We'll make mistakes," he grabbed the bridge and shook it. "Their first three attempts collapsed, but they fixed the problem fast because they didn't have to wait for orders. Winning a battle isn't always about making the right decision. No, sir. Sometimes it's about making the quickest decision."

Mico looked along the line of monkeys, wondering whether they'd understood. He saw a mixture of confusion and doubt, then he caught Papina's eye. She was smiling; she had grasped exactly what he and Gu-Nah were saying. And if Papina was on board, sooner or later, the others would get it too.

Papina had every reason to smile – each new exercise changed the way she saw the world and, for the first time in many moons, she no longer felt like a victim.

The exercise she loved most of all was the one they started and ended each day with – the "Zigzag". All the monkeys would gather in a circle and link arms, then on Gu-Nah's signal, every other monkey would lean inwards, while all the others leaned out. If every monkey kept calm and trusted it worked beautifully: your weight was taken by your neighbour's and everyone just hung peacefully, defying gravity.

Papina always tried to make sure she was next to Mico for the Zigzag. Looping her arms tightly through his, holding him, yet at the same time being held by him, that feeling of mutual reliance ... it reminded her of the simple trust they had enjoyed when they were younger, stealing illicit meetings in the moonlight.

And after all the heartache, it felt good to trust again.

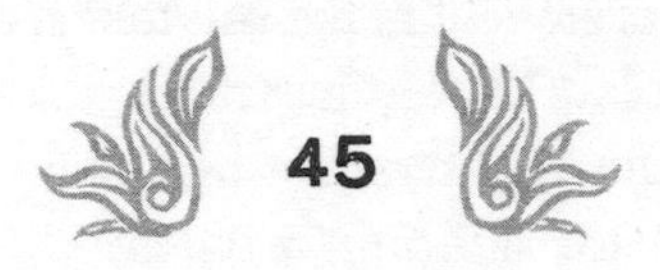

45

SUPREMACY

Hister's disappearance ramped up Tyrell's paranoia. He was convinced that Mico had somehow plucked her from the heart of the Cemetery just to taunt him.

It rammed home the urgency of capturing Mico; as long as the traitor lived, there was a fatal flaw in the Lord Ruler's strength.

Urgently he summoned Breri and Sweto to the Map Room at the top of the Summer-house Tower and demanded to know what they were going to do about the problem.

"Perhaps he's fled the City altogether, my Lord," suggested Breri.

"Perhaps," Tyrell said tetchily, but he wasn't convinced. The orange pip carelessly tossed away had a nasty habit of taking root where you least expected it.

"I'm doubling the monkeys at your disposal," he said, glaring at Sweto. "You are to pursue every lead, report every sighting, search every street."

"Don't worry, my Lord. We'll find him."

"That's what you said last time," snapped Tyrell. "Now go!" He gave an impatient flick of his tail, which sent Breri and Sweto scampering away.

The Lord Ruler sat alone in the middle of the room cradling his head in his hands, trying to ease the pain that gnawed at his mind. There was only one thing that gave him peace these days: his Great Plan. As long as he was thinking about that, he felt safe.

He swung across the room and stood in front of the carved map of the City, gently trailing his fingers across the tangle of streets. The Great Plan would give him total control of all this; it would be a world where nothing moved without his knowledge, a world where Tyrell could finally know happiness.

The ruling cadre gathered expectantly in a room overlooking the long pool. Rumours had been circulating for days about what Tyrell was going to announce, but one thing was certain; this meeting was of the highest importance as only a handful of the most senior monkeys had been invited.

General Pogo was there, his long record of unquestioning loyalty made sure of that; the Barbaries were represented by Hummingbird and his deputy, the wily Oatsack, which meant that whatever Tyrell had in mind was going to involve some heavy-duty fighting. Breri was surprised and delighted to be summoned, and realized that he was now reaping the rewards of turning in his own parents. The last monkey was Sweto, whose influence seemed to be growing by the day.

While they waited, attractive young female Langurs circulated, handing out unusual fruits.

Then suddenly the females withdrew, the delegates fell silent, and all eyes focussed on the door, waiting for their Leader to appear.

Tyrell paused outside, kindling the expectation. Then with a brusque, business-like flurry he bowled into the room.

"Fellow monkeys," he began, not bothering with small talk, "I had hoped this wouldn't be necessary. When news first reached my ears I refused to believe it. But I was wrong. I'm afraid we have to face the brutal truth: the traitor Mico is working with the Humans. Together they intend to attack us, smash the Langur Empire, murder those of us they can catch, banish those they cannot."

There was an audible gasp in the room.

Sweto and Breri were astonished that, despite all their work hunting Mico, they hadn't the slightest inkling of this plot. They gazed at Tyrell, wondering at his omniscience.

That was the beauty of a brilliant lie, thought Tyrell. It gave you power that was difficult to challenge, because there were no facts to dispute.

"I have to say," he went on with a bitter smile, "Mico's plan is a good one."

Again the monkeys were thrown off balance, expecting Tyrell to rail against his enemy, not praise him.

"The fact is, no other animal would dare attack us. The Rhesus tried it and we wiped them from the face of the City. But Humans ... they are the only creatures left who are arrogant enough to turn on us.

"I don't have to tell you how dangerous Humans are. We're surrounded by proof of their ingenuity – the huge buildings, the thundering trains, the animals they slaughter to satisfy their hunger. If all that energy was turned against us..."

Tyrell looked at each monkey in turn, seeing the fear as they imagined the carnage.

"So what can we do to protect ourselves?" Tyrell mused ominously. "We strike *first*."

Astonishment in the room. Had they misheard their Leader?

"In battle, the first strike defines the conflict." Tyrell rose and started to pace around the monkeys.

"Close your eyes and imagine what this City would look like if it was cleansed of Humans. No cars or buses to run over our young; no cacophony of noise day and night; no Human filth to encourage the rats. Why should we be forced to live in the cracks and shadows when Humans occupy the grandest buildings with the finest views?"

By now there was real indignation in Tyrell's voice. "The Humans have ruled this City for long enough. We monkeys are more agile, we have sharper teeth, we can climb higher, run faster, and ... we have tails! *We* should be the rulers of this City. This is our destiny, and you..." His gaze passed over the monkeys. "You are the generation chosen to fulfil it."

A feeling of soaring ambition galvanized the room as the thought of ruling the entire City took hold, tempting the monkeys to reach far beyond their grasp.

Breri was hypnotized by the power of the vision; this was why he had sworn undying loyalty to Tyrell, to be a part of greatness. Bursting with pride, Breri raised his fists and brought them thumping down on the floor. Once, twice, and immediately Sweto joined in, thundering his unquestioning support.

Not wanting to be outdone by Langur loyalty, Oatsack declared, "This is our destiny!" and joined in with the thump of approval.

Only Hummingbird hesitated.

When he imagined the City without Humans, he saw barren markets and the empty ruins of shops; he saw a world where the fountains would run dry, where there would be no one to drive away the snakes. Surely a City without Humans was no place for monkeys.

But when he saw the others thumping their support, Hummingbird knew he had to go along with it. For now.

He hadn't wavered for long, but it was enough to alert General Pogo, because in truth, Pogo too was gravely worried. He hadn't been so foolish as to give any outward sign of doubt; in fact, he had applauded more enthusiastically than the others.

After the meeting, though, as the monkeys all went their separate ways, the General allowed himself to think freely. And then he understood exactly what made him feel so uneasy: wasn't the foundation of all Langur power the fact that they *protected* Humans from the violence of monkeys? Which surely meant that what Tyrell was now proposing was the quickest way to self-destruction.

For the first time, Pogo realized that the Lord Ruler had moved beyond visionary leadership into madness. But who was going to tell him?

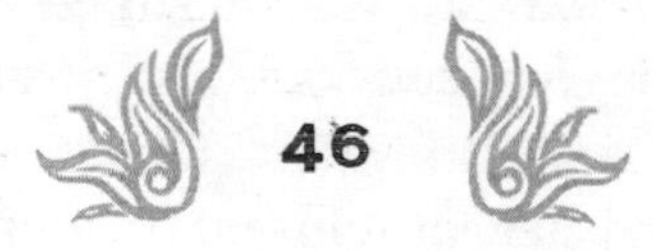

46

WARRIORS

In the days after the massacre, one thought had come to dominate Fig's life: how was she going to end it?

Since the murder of her infants Fig had neither hope nor purpose. Her heart beat, her blood flowed, her nerves tingled, but deep in her spirit, where it really mattered, there was no pulse.

So while the other monkeys were hard at work, Fig sat quietly brooding on top of the water tower, trying to will her life away.

She watched the monkeys set out every morning full of nervous excitement and return each evening exhausted and challenged. At first it just deepened her despair to see others so engaged with life. And yet, the more Fig watched, the more she saw a bond grow between the survivors. In the youngsters' excited banter, she could hear the thrill of minds being opened.

Day by day, as Fig saw hope nudge out fear, she felt something quicken in her own heart. But it wasn't hope.

Papina was sitting alone by a puddle under the water tower when she felt the gentle touch on her back. She turned round and saw Fig crouched quietly.

"What's wrong?"

Fig shook her head. "I just came to groom you."

Papina couldn't hide her astonishment – all those

moons of silence broken by such a mundane comment.

Fig started to back away. "I'm sorry—"

"No!" Papina reached out and grabbed her arm. "Please ... that would be nice." She smiled, turned her back and rippled her shoulders, inviting grooming fingers to get to work. "Dig away."

Fig shuffled closer, reached out her hands ... and hesitated. She had been locked inside her own grief for so long she felt like a prisoner staggering out into the light, unsure of her footing.

"There's a flea in there that's been giving me trouble all day," Papina said, trying to make it easier. "Feels like a juicy one."

Fig gave a wan smile. "How funny." And her fingers started to comb through Papina's fur.

For a while neither said anything. There was no need to rush; grooming was all about sharing a space. Then just as Fig started on Papina's scalp, she said quietly, "I want to do my bit ... in the fight."

Papina wanted to shout with joy, but wisely she decided to play it cool. "Well, we need all the help we can get. What were you thinking? Medical duties?"

Fig stopped grooming. She stepped in front of Papina, looking at her with burning eyes.

"There's a black rage inside me. I have to do something with it or it'll destroy me. I need revenge."

Papina could hardly believe this was Fig speaking, gentle, compassionate Fig, who never wanted to offend anyone.

"I'm sorry it's taken so long," whispered Fig, as if any hint of weakness now had to be treated like a shameful secret.

"There's nothing to apologize for," replied Papina. "Nothing." And she opened her arms and hugged her.

* * *

Mico was nearly asleep when Papina dropped silently into the gloom of the water tower and lay next to him. She stroked the back of his head, observing the grooves her fingers carved in his fur. Mico felt a tingle of pleasure run down his spine.

"Everything all right?" he whispered.

"How did you know we wouldn't tear you to pieces?"

"What?"

"When you walked back into our lives? How did you know we wouldn't turn on you?"

Mico shrugged. "If that's really what the world had come to, then I'd be better off out of it."

Papina put her arms around Mico's torso. "Fig's come back to us."

Mico turned to face her, his eyes wide with surprise. "She wants to fight?"

Papina smiled. "We're *all* warriors now."

Fig's return lifted the whole Troop, and inspired Gu-Nah and Mico to move their training to a whole new level.

As infants, all monkeys were taught to stay well away from the tangle of power lines that ran across the City's rooftops, where deadly electricity fizzed and crackled.

"And that is precisely the point," said Mico to the Troop. "Because no one else goes there, we must."

"I thought the idea was to kill Tyrell, not ourselves," said Twitcher testily; having seen Fig turn back to life, he didn't want to lose her through recklessness.

"There's wires ... and there's wires," said Gu-Nah cryptically. "While you've been enjoying your beauty sleep, we've been getting up early to find out the facts."

"You see, there are two types of wires up there," continued Mico. "One is deadly; the other harmless. They're all tangled up, but if we can learn to spot the difference, we'll be able to use the wires to get right into the heart of Tyrell's Empire. All Langur stay away from the overhead lines, even the Elites. And if they ever followed us up there, they'd soon touch the wrong wires—"

"And BOOM!" added Gu-Nah with dark relish.

"You'll have to relearn what it means to swing all over again," said Mico. "You're going to need accuracy, vision and balance beyond anything you ever thought possible. You're going to need the guts to swing fast, high above the streets, with your fingers brushing past death time and again. Succeed at that, and you'll achieve what no monkey has ever achieved: control of the air."

Rafa put her hand up tentatively. "If no one's done it before, how did *you* learn?"

Gu-Nah smiled. "We haven't. Not yet."

They rose at dawn each day to start their research, memorizing the different wire networks above the City. As the morning wore on and the Langur patrols ramped up, the Rhesus retreated to the safety of the steelworks, where Gu-Nah had built a special training course on the ground around the water tower, laying out a network of branches and interweaving them with some coloured piping he'd found on a dump. The idea was to run across the carpet of branches while touching only the piping.

At first it seemed impossible; no monkey was that agile. But as the days passed they started to get the hang of it.

The trick was decisiveness – see the options, make your choice, then leap. As you got faster you had to speed up your thinking, until eventually you could surrender to the momentum, completely trusting your instincts, forgetting that one wrong footfall meant death.

Once the monkeys had mastered the ground exercise, Gu-Nah moved it up into the trees. They would trek out to a small, neglected park where he had marked the trees with the dye from crushed flowers, indicating which branches were "safe", and which "deadly".

Here the Rhesus spent day after day practising high-speed swinging. The painful drop was the price of thinking too slowly.

As Mico and Gu-Nah watched the monkeys become sharper and bolder, they thought of another use for these new skills: tram-surfing.

A network of trams rattled right through the Langur Empire. Fed via pantographs that skimmed along a power grid, the sparking electricity kept monkeys well away. But if they had the guts to negotiate the power lines and the skill to judge how to leap onto a moving tram, this would be a brilliant way to move around the City.

Practise. As always, that was Gu-Nah's prescription. It was just a question of putting in the hard work.

They started by leaping off road bridges onto trucks that passed underneath. From trucks they moved to smaller targets to improve their accuracy, like cars.

Gradually, and with many bruises, they started to master this new art. Training was not all about derring-do, though. The Rhesus were peaceful monkeys by nature, and Mico worried that when the fighting actually started, when things got ugly and messy and painful, his troops would lose their resolve. To harden their determination, he created the "Outsider Ordeal".

The whole group was set a simple task: prepare a feast to mark the new moon. But secretly, they were also instructed to shun one designated monkey. After much thought, Mico decided the victim would be Cadby.

Initially Cadby was puzzled why everyone ignored him, then when he realized this must be some kind of exercise he laughed it off.

The laughter didn't last long.

Before they were even halfway through, he had turned moody and resentful; then he started lashing out, assaulting other monkeys to try and get some attention, but still they didn't engage, they just turned their backs. It was as if Cadby didn't exist, as if he had vanished.

Frustrated and rejected, Cadby felt rage boiling up inside him; wanting to destroy what he couldn't be part of, he started stockpiling weapons – rusty barbed wire, broken glass, iron bars – as if he was planning a murderous rampage.

Mico looked on, alarmed. Even though all the monkeys could see how distressed Cadby was, none of them broke the rules, none of them protested that the exercise was too cruel. It was as if a sinister force had moved among them, binding them together, and the more ruthlessly they shunned Cadby, the more they seemed to bond.

That was when Mico stopped the Ordeal.

The moment he spoke to Cadby, the spell was broken. The young monkey snapped to his senses and looked at the weapons in dismay. Cadby had been shaken to his core – he had glimpsed a terrifying darkness.

Afterwards they all gathered in a circle as Cadby told them about the fear he had felt, the sense of utter worthlessness.

"And that's exactly what Tyrell has done to *us*," Mico said after Cadby had bared his soul. "He's turned us all into outsiders. He's built a world where we don't exist. Which is why we have to destroy him."

47

BLACK CLOUDS

Mico looked up at the sky, waiting for the Monsoon.

This was the most dangerous season for monkeys, when the rain pummelled down, wild and unpredictable, stinging like thorns; when food was hard to pilfer because market traders were driven from the streets; when storm gullies were monstrously transformed into raging torrents, hurtling unlucky monkeys to their deaths.

No monkey ventured out in the Monsoon unless it was essential, which was why Mico decided that it would be the perfect time to declare war on the Langur. It was the very last thing they would be expecting, and it was why the final section of Rhesus training was devoted to water war.

They began in Kolkata's famous Dancing Fountains. At dusk every evening, crowds of Human children trooped to the park for a surreal nightly show: dramatic music thundered through the loudspeakers, banks of coloured light burst into life as countless moving nozzles squirted torrents of water into the air in perfect sequence, painting fleeting pictures in the evening sky.

Swinging deftly along the telegraph wires, the Rhesus dropped down into the splash pools just before the show was about to start. They were not there to play or bathe, but to conquer their fear of water, to sit absolutely still as the sprays pounded them.

The opening sequence of the show was quite restrained – alternating pulses of water shot up into the air, and as the patterns dissolved into rain the monkeys were soaked just like in a regular storm. But as the show progressed the high-pressure jets spun into action, creating elaborate concentric swirls, turning the splash pools into a raging confusion of painful spray.

In the early days, this was the point when most of the monkeys dived out of the fountains. The water was just too fierce and frightening – it felt as if you were drowning.

Fig was the first to conquer her fear, standing frozen like a statue as the water battered her from all directions, absorbing the pain without complaint.

Seeing Fig's resolve, Papina refused to be outdone, and where the females led, the males had to follow. Cadby put on a brave face and endured it even though he clearly hated every moment. But the biggest turnaround was with Joop and Rafa. At first they were terrified and had to be dragged into the splash pools, but once they realized that they could still breathe even though water was firing at them from all directions, they relaxed and started to enjoy the sheer anarchy of the experience.

As the Troop's water confidence grew, Mico and Gu-Nah moved on to the Hooghly River.

It was a huge step – the murky water of the great river was a world apart from the Dancing Fountains. Here they were confronted by frighteningly fast currents that whipped branches and debris past with unrelenting energy.

"The trick is to remember that the currents may be strong, but they'll pull you right across the City with very little effort. They're your friends," said Mico. "And who doesn't want to have strong friends?"

They started by rummaging among the flotsam in the mud and experimenting to see what floated, what sank, and which bits of debris were big enough to keep a monkey above the water.

Clasping these improvised floats, they launched themselves into the Hooghly. Under no circumstances were they to paddle or swim; they had to let their floats do the work while they concentrated on feeling the river, steering by changing the position of their legs.

With practice, fear turned into excitement – surrendering to a massive force, while using ingenuity to surf it, gave the monkeys a huge thrill. Within days, they were riding the river for the entire length of the curve that arced all the way from the Howrah Station Jetty to the Botanical Gardens.

It meant the Rhesus had mastery of land, air and water. Now all they had to do was watch the sky and wait for the rains to come.

Tyrell barely looked at the sky these days – the Monsoon didn't concern him. In fact, the routine business of ruling his empire no longer held the fascination it once did. Tyrell was now absorbed by only one thing: the Great Plan.

This was his bid for immortality; driving Humans out of their own City would mean that never again would Humans *anywhere* treat monkeys as inferior.

No effort was spared in visualizing the Great Plan. Sweto and Brerl, now the most trusted of Tyrell's inner circle, worked tirelessly in the rooms at the top of the Summer-house Tower. Under the Lord Ruler's direction, they re-carved the wall map, flattening some areas, shaping new ones, creating a bold three-dimensional impression of what the City would look like after the Great Expulsion.

What made Tyrell happy, though, made Hummingbird uneasy. When the Barbary had once asked *how* the Humans were to be driven out, Tyrell flew into a rage, accusing him of disloyalty, implying that to harbour such doubts bordered on treason.

So everyone stopped asking. But Hummingbird could see disaster looming, which is why one evening he secretly gathered all his troops on the canopy above the stage of Kolkata's open-air theatre.

"We are Barbaries," he declared. "We fight for hire. That's why we came. And Tyrell rewarded us well. But Tyrell has lost his mind."

An uncomfortable murmur ran through the troops – such blunt speaking nearly always heralded a bitter fight.

"His lust to fight the Humans has blinded him. We must abandon Tyrell before his world collapses. Or we'll be dragged down with him."

Disappointed silence. So it was all over. The Barbaries would have to move on, leave this life of ease and take their chances on the road once again.

Then just as they started to disperse, a lone voice spoke up; not the laconic voice of a typical Barbary, but a smoother, more articulate one.

"Perhaps there's another way of looking at this," said Oatsack.

"My decision is made," pronounced Hummingbird.

"But," Oatsack persisted, "surely the facts speak for themselves?" He stood up, determined to put his case. "We Barbaries have roamed far and wide, fought many battles for many leaders, but which of us has ever encountered a Troop as powerful as these Langur of Kolkata?"

Oatsack let the question hang in the air for a few moments, but no one had an answer.

"The fact is," he continued, "Tyrell has built the greatest empire known to monkeykind, and it is frankly inconceivable that it will collapse."

"Everything crumbles!" boomed Hummingbird, infuriated by Oatsack's oily rhetoric that mimicked the tricksy manner of the Langur. "Even things the Humans build crumble. Remember the temples we saw in the jungles? Reduced to rubble and ruin!"

"Tyrell's point exactly," persisted Oatsack. "If mere creepers can triumph over Humans, why can't monkeys?"

"I'll tell you why," said Hummingbird, his patience wearing dangerously thin. "Because most Langur don't want to fight Humans. They're too frightened to say it, but look into their eyes. A rift has opened between Tyrell and his Troop."

"Then *we* should step in and take the Langur from him," Oatsack retorted defiantly. "We can depose Tyrell and rule the Langur ourselves. We can keep the empire he's created and enjoy our privileges without having to uproot all over again."

He gazed at the troops, making his appeal directly to their indolence. "How far will we have to roam, how many battles will we have to fight before we find a life as good as the one we enjoy now?"

Tentative nods of agreement told Oatsack that his point had hit home. All eyes turned to Hummingbird for a response.

The leader drew himself up to his full height. "We are warriors who fight, not politicians who talk. Barbarics fight. It's served us well for generations. If Tyrell knew who he was, he wouldn't have dreamt up his Great Plan.

But he is doomed. And I tell you this: long after Tyrell has fallen, the Barbaries will still be a force that is feared and respected."

Hummingbird sat down with the gravitas of unshakeable conviction; his words had chimed with deep tribal memories, and in the silence the will of the Barbary troops swung behind him.

Only Oatsack didn't feel it. "Well, you're wrong!" he blurted out petulantly. "All of you! This is just the kind of primitive thinking that condemns us to a life of brutality!"

Hummingbird kept frighteningly calm. He stared Oatsack in the eye, and saw that this young monkey would always be trouble.

"That's not how the rest of us see it," Hummingbird said coldly.

It was Breri who made the gruesome discovery.

He had risen early to walk the perimeter wall, and saw a strange shape hanging from a branch of the lemon tree that marked the start of the Barbaries' quarters.

Breri strained his eyes in the dim light, trying to make out what the shape was, but couldn't place it. He swung through the canopy to get a closer look ... then froze in horror.

Hanging by its feet was the battered and bloody body of Oatsack. His face had been pummelled until it was barely recognizable; his body was twisted and broken, the fur matted with thick clots of blood, some of which still dripped lazily into the dust.

Desperate to raise the alarm, Breri stumbled past the lemon tree and into the Barbary compound ... only to find it deserted. The Apes had vanished in the night as if they'd never existed.

Fear gripped Breri's throat; he struggled to stop himself retching.

Get to Tyrell. Must get to Tyrell, tell him what's happened. Maybe the Lord Ruler already knew. Maybe he had sent the Barbaries on some secret mission.

But even as he thought it, Breri knew it wasn't true.

And then he felt a drop of rain patter down on his head.

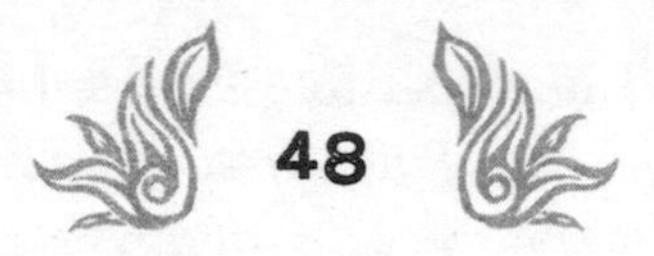

48

FIRST STRIKE

The Rhesus were perched on the water tower when the first drops of Monsoon rain landed like falling berries hitting the dust.

Finally the waiting was over.

They gazed up at the menacing sky in silence, wondering which of them would survive the coming days.

It took Joop's agitated cry to tear everyone's eyes from the storm clouds, but as Mico watched the young monkey scurry across the steelworks yard his stomach tightened. Joop had been on lookout duty on the Synagogue tower and wasn't due to return until the middle of the day – if he'd abandoned his post, something must be wrong.

"The Barbaries..." Joop gasped when he got within earshot. "The Barbaries have *gone*!"

"Gone?" exclaimed Mico.

Joop started laughing as he scrambled up the ladder. "They moved out of the Cemetery at dawn. All of them, the whole Troop. At first I thought they were on a mission, so I followed. But they headed out of the City and just kept going!"

Mico and Gu-Nah looked at each other, hardly daring to believe it could be true.

"I don't trust it," Twitcher said with a frown. "They're setting a trap."

"I swear! It was the whole Troop. Even their young," Joop retorted.

"Barbaries never mobilize as a whole Troop," said Gu-Nah. "They prefer small strike squads."

"I saw it with my own eyes," said Joop. "They were heading into the sunrise, pacing themselves for a long journey. I tell you, they've gone!"

Mico looked at his troops; a fleeting smile passed across his face. "Then let's go to war."

By noon the whole sky had turned black, as clouds tumbled over each other in the race to deluge the City. Not long after, the winds arrived, great battering-rams driving through the streets, forcing those with homes to flee inside, and those who lived in the shanty towns to pray their flimsy dwellings wouldn't blow away.

Cars put on their lights, confusing the street dogs, who howled plaintively; children dangled excitedly out of windows.

Finally the deluge was unleashed with merciless ferocity, pouring off roofs in glistening sheets, overwhelming gutters, surging through every twisting street and alley, soaking rich and poor alike.

At first, life in the City ground to a halt. People laughed and drank and celebrated the watery bombardment, but by the following morning the novelty had worn off; life had to get back to normal, rain or no rain...

And the same applied to the Langur.

Because Tyrell used food to underpin political control, he needed a plentiful supply regardless of the season.

To help keep the Langur storehouses full, he had instigated daily raids on the trucks that got stuck in the traffic jams gridlocking the City every morning.

Langur Elites would hide in the shadows, waiting until the traffic ground to a halt; then a scout would hurry down the line of trucks smelling for the juiciest produce, steal a sample and take it back to his Commanding Officer. If the C.O. deemed the food good enough, the squad would swing into action, pilfering and ferrying as much as they could to a temporary store until they were chased away by the drivers.

The system worked well – by targeting a different approach road each day, the Langur made sure that no individual truck was hit so often that it provoked a violent backlash; and by using a makeshift store they ensured that even if a mission was cut short, they would still return with some supplies. That was the crucial thing – if you wanted to have a future in the Langur, never return empty-handed.

It was precisely because these raids had become such an important part of Tyrell's regime that Mico made them the target of his first strike.

Scampering across the glistening rooftops, Joop and Jola made their way to the synagogue in the centre of the City and clambered up the maintenance rungs until they were at the weathervane on top of the spire; from here they had a commanding view over the streets. They had brought with them a set of religious masks stolen from a street market a few days earlier; these were to be their signal flags, each mask representing a different approach road.

As soon as the traffic started to snarl up, Joop spotted a Langur squad moving towards Central Avenue – that meant Ganesh. Jola hung the elephant's head mask from the weathervane and, across the City in his temporary command post, Mico saw it.

"Central Avenue!" he shouted, and swooped down onto the roof of a ring-road tram, quickly followed by Twitcher, Fig and three of the strongest young Rhesus. Speed was everything; it was vital they got into position before the Langur started their raid.

Mico's team leapt off at the end of Madan Street; Gu-Nah, Papina, Cadby and the others who were riding the following tram stayed on for a few more streets. They knew that when the Central Avenue gridlock was targeted, the Langur used a derelict bakery as their temporary store; Gu-Nah's team was to surround this bakery.

The Monsoon floods had made traffic congestion even worse than usual, and many truck drivers had given up all hope of moving anywhere before lunch. Bunkered down in their cabs with newspapers and cigarettes, they paid little attention to their loads, which made the monkeys' job a little less dangerous.

Mico's team worked their way down the line of trucks, trying to decide which ones would be carrying delicacies that would be irresistible to the Langur palate. Twitcher suggested a load of walnuts, but Mico shook his head. "If you could steal anything, would you choose nuts?"

"We have to decide soon!" urged Twitcher. Further up the line he could already see two Langur scouts approaching the traffic jam.

"It has to be just right," said Mico, "or there's no point."

Holding their nerve, the Rhesus moved to the next truck ... and the next ... until suddenly Fig froze. She breathed in deeply, savouring the smell. "Peaches. A whole truck of them."

"Now *that* is irresistible," Mico said with a broad smile.

The monkeys scampered up the sides of the truck, slid under the tarpaulin and hid between the crates of fruit.

It should have all be so routine for the Langur – dive under the tarpaulin, smash the crates, grab some peaches and ferry them away.

But then a primal scream tore out of the darkness.

The Langur scout spun round and saw a flash of teeth. A split second later they plunged into his neck and he felt the sticky warmth of blood on his fur.

The others heard the grotesque gurgle from his punctured throat, reeled back, and were suddenly overwhelmed by Rhesus fighters dropping down on them, smashing into their chests, twisting their necks.

The Langurs' training kicked in immediately. They fought back, lashing out with fists, tearing into whatever flesh they could reach with claws and teeth.

Trapped in the spaces between the fruit crates, it was an ugly fight, a raw, brutal battle for survival.

In the mayhem, hidden from daylight, Fig unleashed her rage, pouncing on one of the Langur troopers, battering his limbs and clawing at his face, venting her black hatred on his flesh like a monkey possessed. He collapsed under her relentless blows, but Fig didn't stop. She hammered her fists down on his broken body, beating every last drop of life from him. Even when the bottom of the truck was slippery with blood, still she kept destroying until the pain in her own heart had emptied.

It was Twitcher who reached out and grabbed her. "Enough. That's enough."

Fig caught her breath, then gazed dispassionately at her ghastly handiwork. She looked up at the others and blinked.

"What next?"

* * *

At the disused bakery the Langur Squad Commander was busy organizing the pilfered supplies. So far this morning, they'd grabbed some sugared sweets, a sackful of cakes and some cartons of orange juice. They'd need far more if they were to impress High Command, but the morning was young, the line of trucks long, and hopes for a bumper haul were high.

Until one of his troopers ran into the bakery, breathless and frightened.

"They're dead!"

The Commander stared at the trooper in astonishment. It had been a while since he'd seen terror on a Langur face; usually it was on the faces of their victims.

"Something attacked them!"

"Show me," growled the Commander.

They splashed through the mud of the rain-soaked streets, back down the gridlock of trucks, until the trooper stopped at the entrance to a dark alley.

"In there, sir," he said fearfully.

The Commander strode into the alley ... and stopped dead as he saw the broken bodies of three of his troopers, the blood pouring from their wounds, mixing with the rain that swirled down from the gutters.

Shock. Then confusion.

"How?"

The trooper pointed fearfully to the peach truck. "Something in there killed them. Some ... monster."

The Commander hesitated. What could have cut his monkeys down with such ruthless force? Part of him wanted to retreat – whatever was in that truck clearly had ferocious power. But his orders were to steal a day's worth of food, and if he returned without it he would be harshly punished. Circumstances may have changed but his orders hadn't.

The Commander had no choice but to gather his entire squad, both the pilfering monkeys and the ones at the bakery and marshal them into a ring surrounding the peach truck.

"GO!" he ordered, and in one co-ordinated move, his troops scrambled up the sides and dived under the tarpaulin, swooping in from all directions so that whatever was inside had no chance of escape.

The Langur surged through the darkness, banging crates with their fists, driving their sticks into the gaps, ransacking every hiding place...

And found nothing.

No monster. No enemy. Nothing.

Keep moving, keep changing the parameters of battle – that was the key for Mico's monkeys.

No sooner had they dumped the Langur bodies than they scurried away, letting the heavy rain cover their tracks and wash away their scent. Then double backing through the sidestreets, they linked up with Gu-Nah and Papina's team.

With the bakery now unguarded, the Rhesus formed a chain to whisk the food away to a distant rooftop, where they enjoyed a celebratory feast.

Day one of the war, and first blood had gone to them.

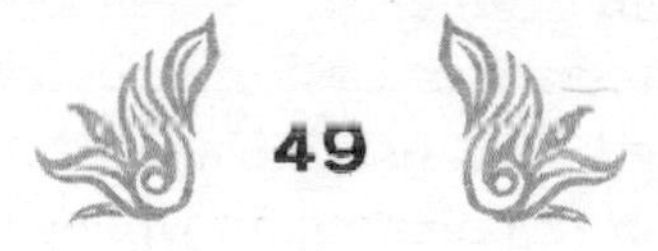

49

STRIKE TWO

Shock punched through the Langur Troop.

The Squad Commander was disciplined for incompetence, and the whole attack made to look as if it was his fault. It had to be, as the only alternative was to admit that someone out there could mount a lethal strike against the Langur. Which was unthinkable.

Secretly, however, Tyrell was reeling.

It had been a bad time for the Lord Ruler – the shock of the Barbary desertion had hit him hard, and it took all his wily cunning to make out that it was actually part of his strategy. Langur Commanders were hastily promoted to fill the gaps, and extra food was distributed to reassure everyone that all was well.

But Tyrell was tormented day and night by one question: Why had his trusted Barbaries abandoned him?

As if struggling with that wasn't bad enough, now Tyrell had to deal with a direct attack on his troops. It wasn't the loss of food or the death of the monkeys that worried him; it was that someone had dared to raise a defiant fist against him. Worse still, the attack had been executed in such a mysterious way that none of those involved had any idea who was responsible.

Determined to get a grip, Tyrell threw force and rhetoric at the problem.

"Whoever has provoked us will find they have woken a vengeful monster!" Tyrell boomed. "We are the greatest Troop monkeykind has ever known. We have the strength to crush anyone who opposes us. In future, every food snatch squad will be protected by *six* guard patrols!"

Which was exactly the response Mico wanted; the more reinforcements, the better, because the Rhesus had no intention of hitting the same target twice. Unpredictability was one of their key weapons.

They waited until there was a particularly intense deluge, then leapt onto a set of trams heading downtown to the old Cemetery.

Lying flat on the slippery tram roofs, they looked down on the streets speeding by and could see that, despite the atrocious weather, Langur patrols had been stepped up all over the City. Tyrell was obviously rattled.

Once at the Cemetery, the monkeys divided into three units under the commands of Mico, Gu-Nah and Papina, as their inside knowledge would be crucial to the mission's success.

With all the flooding, the drinking pool had turned into a churning drain, channelling a fast flow of water under the wall.

"Ready?" Mico asked.

Silent nods as they steeled their nerves. But Mico could sense something wasn't right. He studied their eyes: Fig met his gaze with unblinking determination; the younger monkeys were tense and excited, eager to get started; but Papina looked down briefly.

"What's wrong?" he asked quietly.

Papina hesitated. "How many do we have to kill?"

So that was it – the bloodshed had got to her. The attack on the food snatch squad had been brilliantly effective, but the sight of the twisted, smashed bodies had sat heavily on her conscience. And now they were going to kill again.

"We've only just begun," said Fig, cold as steel.

"I know," Papina whispered.

Mico looked at the two monkeys thoughtfully. Despite all that she had lost, Papina still had compassion.

The problem was, right now, compassion had to be smothered.

"Remember, it was Tyrell who waged war on you," Mico said, addressing them all. "Tyrell who drove you from your homes, who herded you into an alley and slaughtered you in cold blood. But he didn't act alone. Ordinary Langurs helped him, cheered him, struck the blows on his behalf. They didn't have to follow orders; they could've chosen resistance."

He pointed at the Cemetery. "Every monkey inside those walls has chosen to stay, chosen to accept what's going on, which makes them all guilty. Even my own family." As Mico's words sank in, he saw Papina's expression change, her resolution harden.

"We didn't start this," he said grimly, "but we are going to finish it. We have to finish it."

He looked at Papina, stretched out his hand and stroked her head gently. "Now do you see?"

Papina nodded.

"Then GO!"

One by one the monkeys jumped into the swirling pool and let themselves be sucked through the water flume. They bobbed up on the other side of the wall, and were carried along the torrent inside the Cemetery, grabbing hold of roots sticking out of the banks to steer themselves.

Everything seemed eerily deserted – the Langurs were all huddled inside their homes, sheltering from the rain which fell heavily on the tombstones and made huge, muddy puddles of the paths.

Silently, swiftly, the Rhesus floated undetected towards their target: the Great Vault.

They arrived at the back wall and, with the help of some wild ivy, scrambled up. Looking across the court-yard and the pool, Mico could see that little had changed since he was last there. All the security effort was con-centrated on the main doors; once inside, the Vault was a quiet sanctuary.

Not for much longer.

Gu-Nah's squad was to target the guards at the main entrance, while Mico had to lead his team deep inside, where senior Langurs carried on the day-to-day business of running the Troop.

Papina's squad was charged with securing the pool area, as this was the vital escape route, so splitting into twos they swept down the rooms, searching for the enemy.

Twitcher kicked open the door to the first cubicle and Papina dived in, heart pumping, ready for the kill, only to find it empty.

He slammed open the next door. Again Papina rushed in, nerves jangling ... again, nothing.

A strangled cry from the opposite side of the pool made her spin round – she saw Cadby yanking down on the neck of a Twopoint guard, who crumpled to the ground.

Cadby swayed, shocked by his own actions. For a

moment it seemed as if he was going to be engulfed by a wave of remorse.

"Cadby!" Papina's voice was hard, uncompromising. Cadby blinked, looked up, caught her eye. She pointed to the pool, reminding him of the plan. Cadby shook himself, then picked the dead guard up and tossed him into the water.

At the entrance to the Great Vault, Gu-Nah's squad took out three guards with brutal efficiency, then dragged the bodies back to the pool, leaving blood-red stripes criss-crossing the stone floor.

Mico led his team deep into the Vault interior, where they heard voices echoing in the stone chambers. Closer and closer they crept, peering round doorways, until they saw three senior Langurs chatting over some papaya fruit.

Mico thought he recognized one of them and for a moment struggled to place him. Then he checked himself – no point remembering.

With well-practised discipline, Mico's squad burst into the room – the Langurs barely had time to understand what was happening before they were beaten to death.

The attack hadn't lasted long, but as Mico gazed at the pool, swirling red with blood, he knew it had changed the monkey world for ever. This pool, the ultimate symbol of Langur power, was now defiled with the bodies of dead guards. With a guilty pride, he saw that there was a dark brilliance in the savagery of this symbol.

"RHESUS!!!" a screech from outside the Vault walls. One of the Langur guards must have escaped.

Immediately the Rhesus started scrambling up the walls, then they launched into the tree canopy and climbed for their lives.

Down below, Twopoint guards splashed through the mud and launched themselves into the lower branches, determined to catch the terrorists.

But a treetop battle wasn't in the Rhesus' plans – they swung through the branches until they were within leaping distance of the power lines that fizzed dangerously in the rain. After a moment's pause to check which cable was which, they leapt onto the grid and scattered across the wires.

As the senior Twopoint guard watched the attackers melt away, he saw his own career vanish with them; in a last desperate attempt to salvage something from the debacle, he commanded the guards, "FOLLOW ME!"

He launched towards the power lines, reaching out and gripping the wires tightly with hands and feet.

Not so difficult, he thought.

They were the last words that flashed across his mind before thousands of volts put an end to everything.

As word of the attack spread through the Cemetery, incredulous Langurs emerged from their homes, looked up into the rain and saw panicked guards hurrying nervously around the tree canopy ... and the dead Twopoint hanging in the power lines.

It was a grotesque image of failure. Far from being wiped out, their old enemy had returned to strike a blow at the very heart of their Empire. And if the Rhesus could attack the Great Vault in broad daylight, then nowhere was safe.

Tyrell was quick to visit the scene. Flanked by Breri, Sweto and General Pogo, he strode through the Cemetery with a grim countenance.

It wasn't just the audacity of the attack that worried Tyrell, nor was it the fact that it was another distraction from the Great Plan. What really worried him were the expressions on the faces of ordinary Langurs as he inspected the scene. In the shocked silence he knew that something had shifted; whereas before the monkeys would look at him as the Supreme Dispenser of Power, now Tyrell saw doubt in their eyes.

Decisive action was taken: the Vault guard was doubled, a new perimeter patrol was established to police the Cemetery wall day and night, and the families of the victims were generously compensated with food and relocated to the Eastern Province.

Tyrell gave a series of speeches reassuring his Troop that security was a top priority, that every Langur life was precious, and that no attack on the Cemetery would ever again succeed.

General Pogo stood on the podium listening dutifully to the rhetoric, but he had already understood the truth – extra security was useless because the Rhesus had no intention of striking at the Cemetery again.

And so it proved.

In the days that followed, Mico's monkeys pulled off a series of brilliant attacks on different targets using ever-changing tactics, each one catching the Langur unawares.

In their wildest dreams, they couldn't have hoped for a better start to the war.

Yet, despite this, Mico was worried. Only now did he understand the true scale of the challenge facing them. So one stormy evening, he and Gu-Nah called their troops together to thrash the problem out.

"I think we've proved that we can fight as well as any Langur," Mico said with a wry smile that was greeted with self-assured laughter.

"But winning a battle is very different to winning a war," he went on in a more pensive mood. "We could go on as we are, chipping away at Tyrell's Empire, but where would that get us?"

The monkeys looked at him, puzzled. Their entire fighting philosophy was based on the idea that the huge imbalance of power was their friend. Now Mico seemed to be having doubts.

"Surely, the more we attack, the more the Langur will lose confidence in Tyrell?" said Twitcher.

Papina agreed. "If we keep up the pressure, they'll overthrow him for us."

But Mico had already thought further than this. "In theory that's what'll happen; but in practice, how long will it take?"

"Depends how hard we hit them," said Fig coldly.

"When the Monsoon passes, we'll lose a crucial advantage. Will Tyrell have fallen by then?" insisted Mico.

Silence from the monkeys. Pinpointing a specific moment in time suddenly made the task seem more daunting.

"And remember," Mico continued, "the longer the war goes on, the more the balance of power shifts in *their* favour. At some point we'll sustain casualties, deaths even. But deaths mean nothing to the Langur – they have a massive army to draw on."

"So what are you suggesting?" asked Papina.

"I wish I knew," Mico confessed. "But unless we want to spend the rest of our lives fighting, we need to find a way of delivering a decisive blow. A shock that'll stop the heart of the Langur."

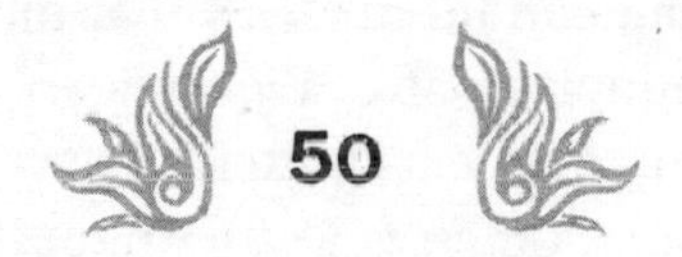

50

OBEDIENCE

Tyrell may have been Lord High Commander, Supreme Leader of the Langur Troop, Overlord and Protector of the Provinces, General of the Twopoint Brigade and Beacon of the Future, but he was powerless to stop the Rhesus attacks. No matter what the Langur military did, the terrorists always found new targets and new tactics.

Eyewitness reports had built up a picture of the enemy, and Tyrell now knew the bitter truth: the Rhesus forces were being led by the traitors Mico and Gu-Nah. It added a new layer of rancour to the war.

Worse than the hurt of betrayal was another feeling, one that Tyrell hadn't experienced since he was a young monkey: the feeling of being a helpless victim. He had done everything he could to wipe the Rhesus from the face of the City and still they persisted.

The strain started to show on his face. His eyes looked sunken and tired; his brow knitted with a permanent frown; his shoulders, no longer arrogant and proud, began to sag forward.

Tyrell was made of stubborn stuff, though, and the more he was pushed into a corner, the harder he fought back. With grim determination, he convened a Council of War and ordered them to create a new strategy to defeat the insurgents.

"It's simple: our army is in shock," explained General Pogo, a blunt but candid analysis that only the old war-horse could get away with. "We've been conquerors for so long, our troops have forgotten what it means to fight. I mean *really* fight, to the death, with tooth and claw."

"When you say 'troops', do you include their Commanders?" asked Tyrell pointedly.

But Pogo was beyond these kind of political games – this was war and he knew what he was talking about.

"The Rhesus are now ruthless and hungry, hard as steel, while our fighting forces are flabby. But every defeat we suffer makes us stronger, more battle-hardened. Lord Tyrell, I really believe that the longer this war goes on, the more the balance will shift in our favour."

Tyrell swirled the analysis round his mind. What exactly was the General proposing? Do nothing and wait until the enemy started to tire. Easy to say, but Tyrell knew that with every defeat his own authority weakened.

Mind you, Tyrell reflected, perhaps that was the General's devious strategy. Perhaps Pogo saw *himself* as the next ruler of the Langur. Yes, that made sense. Offer advice that sounded loyal, but was in fact designed to topple the Leadership.

The Lord Ruler was not going to be fooled so easily. He had built his Empire through single-minded determination – it was *his* vision, *his* political manoeuvring, *his* will that had achieved all this. He should trust his instincts, and right now they were urging him to seize the reins of battle.

He stood up, trying his best to exude confidence. "From this moment on, all battlefield decisions will be taken by me. Breri, set up a command chain so that my exact orders are conveyed to the troops, day and night."

"Very good, my Lord." Breri bowed humbly, dazzled by the prospect of yet another sphere of operations being put under his control.

"This is the turning point," pronounced Tyrell to the Council of War. "I am personally taking responsibility for the campaign and, as history has shown, the more I take control of a situation, the better the outcome."

With a cursory nod, Tyrell turned and started to sweep from the room, when a lone voice dared to speak up.

"With all due respect, my Lord..."

Tyrell spun round, and met the gaze of General Pogo.

"Forgive me, Lord Tyrell," the General went on, getting the deference out of the way early, "but I fear that will only play into the enemy's hands."

"You doubt my military competence?"

"We're dealing with something quite different here. Gu-Nah is putting his unorthodox fighting methods into practice."

"Well," said Tyrell, "I proved him wrong once. I'll just have to do it again. A little more forcefully, this time." Which garnered some sycophantic laughter from Breri and Sweto.

"We've seen how the Rhesus operate in battle, my Lord. Their success is based on speed of reaction," persisted the General, gaining confidence as he moved on to military strategy. "If we're going to win this war, we have to be as fast and fluid as the enemy."

Tyrell glared icily at him. "So I am wrong?"

"Central command of the battlefield is the opposite of what we need, my Lord."

The silence was so tense the air almost crackled.

The Lord Ruler felt his mind swim as rage took hold; he could hear the blood pumping through his temples.

"YOU!!!" he screamed at Pogo with terrifying

malevolence. "If you had done your job we wouldn't even be in this war! DEAD! I wanted them all dead! Was that so much to ask? But you couldn't even do that!"

Tyrell loomed menacingly towards him. "You are to blame for all this! YOU! And now *you* dare to question *my* judgement?"

He reached out and grabbed hold of the fur on Pogo's neck, shaking him. "Why did you let Mico live? What are you plotting with him?! Are *you* a traitor too?" And with the terrifying energy of rage he slammed Pogo to the floor.

"You are NOTHING! Nothing but a weak and incompetent soldier who dreams of things he doesn't have the courage to grasp! You will apologize to me, Pogo!" Tyrell stood over the General, trembling with anger. "APOLOGIZE!!!"

Silence.

Pogo was shocked to the core. In all the time he'd known Tyrell, he had never seen him like this.

"APOLOGIZE!"

The General felt indignation churning in the pit of his stomach. *Apologize for what?* he thought.

It was Tyrell who had brought about this bloody war. *He* had failed to appreciate Gu-Nah's military brilliance; *he* had personally taken charge of the hunt for Mico and failed; *he* had created the monster they were now fighting.

But that was not how Tyrell remembered it.

Pogo knew that if he so much as raised a finger to protest, he would be finished. He would disappear like countless others.

Survival, that was what mattered. Survival at any cost; that was how the world worked. Pride, honour, truth counted for nothing if you were dead. For so many years Pogo's cynicism had justified his compliance, and now he needed something of substance to hold on to, it eluded him.

So the great General, a monkey who had always fought with such dazzling physical courage, bowed his head in utter humiliation and said quietly, "I'm sorry if I have offended you, my Lord. I was only trying to serve."

Which was exactly what Tyrell wanted to hear.

He bent down, extended his hand to help Pogo to his feet, then embraced him like an old friend.

The feeling on the street was not so deferential. Much as the Langur command tried to restrict the flow of information, Footsoldiers kept talking, and the long series of military defeats had not passed unnoticed.

The official line was that Langur forces had won the last two battles; that some Rhesus terrorists were dead, with others now in captivity ... though no one had actually seen the prisoners with their own eyes.

Tyrell's spies reported back nervously some of the strange ideas starting to take root. Some monkeys believed that the Barbaries were going to return to save the Langur; others believed that nothing could save them because the Rhesus had developed special powers, like invisibility, and even the capacity to fly.

All this wild speculation damaged Tyrell. How could he hope to wage war on the Humans when he couldn't even deal with a few outcast monkeys?

His response was ruthless: he ordered Sweto and the Twopoint Brigade to clamp down on unpatriotic thinking. No mercy was to be shown to monkeys who spread malicious rumours at a time when everyone should be pulling together for the war effort.

The Twopoints were obedient and diligent; beating, torturing, imprisoning, silencing. But even their cruel hands couldn't stop the rumours from spreading.

51

THE DREAM

In the disused water tower at the steelworks, Papina had been waking up night after night, plagued by the same dream.

It always started so pleasurably, scrambling through a tree canopy in the brilliant sunlight, relishing the freedom, the clean air, the glowing green of the sunlit leaves. But as she ran, the branches would start to get thinner and thinner, until impossibly, she was somehow running on twigs ... and the moment she saw this, Papina would fall, plunging down and down, the air rushing through her fur, branches flailing painfully past her hands, until finally she would grasp a hanging vine and swing into the tree.

And then the moment of horror as she realized it wasn't a vine she was holding, but the tail of a massive snake. She'd turn to run, but the snake was always quicker, whipping round to engulf her.

Papina opened her mouth to scream but nothing would come out, her lungs were empty as the huge snake crushed her body ... and then the sickening click of the monster's jaws unhingeing—

Papina woke with a start, trembling. She sat bolt upright in the darkness and fearfully checked the shadows between the sleeping monkeys to make sure that no snake had slithered in. Reassured, she clambered up the ladder and stood on the roof, breathing in the sticky night air, trying to calm down.

Always the same dream, and she always woke at the same point. At first she put it down to old memories raked up by the stress of battle; then another idea occurred to her: perhaps there was a reason for the dreams, perhaps her mind wasn't tormenting her, but was trying to tell her something.

As she sat on top of the water tower, letting the sweat from her nightmare ease away, Papina tried to think how a vision of her own death could possibly help the war.

As thoughts collided in an unexpected way, slowly the notion came to her: the problem of the unbeatable could be solved by conquering the unthinkable.

The idea was so perfect it sent a physical jolt through Papina's body. Unable to contain her excitement, she swung down into the tank and shook Mico, who woke with a start.

"What's wrong?!" He sat up and went to cradle her in his arms.

"I know how to beat the Langur," she burbled excitedly. "I've seen it in my sleep!"

Mico took her hand to guide her to the ladder. "You need some fresh air."

"No, listen to me!" she insisted. "The killer blow ... I know what it is."

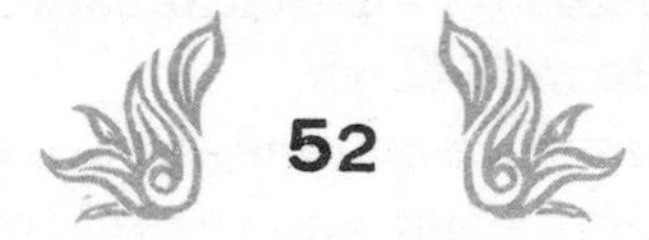

52

TO CATCH A NIGHTMARE

The monkeys were often tetchy first thing in the morning, so Mico thought it best to wait until they'd all had breakfast before calling the meeting. Only then did they gather in the shade under the water tower.

"Papina's got an idea," he said, trying to sound nonchalant. "We all know she's not prone to flights of fancy, so you should listen to her with ... an open mind." He gave a wry smile. "It's a bold plan. It may even be an insane plan, but *I* think it's brilliant."

He looked expectantly to Papina, who immediately felt the intensity of all the monkeys gazing at her. What had seemed like a good idea in the middle of the night suddenly felt ridiculous in the harsh light of morning, but it was too late to back down now.

"There's a snake, a huge snake – a python – that lives under the trash mountain in the Slums." Papina saw the monkeys shuffle uneasily just at the mention of the word "python".

"When we first escaped from the Cemetery, this snake killed one of our females. Swallowed her whole. And it would've got me if it hadn't been for the quick thinking of my mother."

Papina hesitated. Suddenly she remembered what it meant to be loved by a mother, and like an ache deep in her heart, she felt a longing for peace. That was why they needed this plan, she reminded herself, forcing her thoughts back on track.

"If we want to win this war, we need to capture that snake. We need to take it into the heart of Langur territory and release it, so that it can kill Tyrell and all his henchmen." Papina sat down. "That's my plan."

Her calm, matter-of-fact delivery was utterly at odds with the astonishing conceit of the plan; it left the monkeys frozen with incredulity.

"Exactly," said Mico. "Just hearing the plan has shocked you into silence. Imagine how you'd feel if you'd witnessed it ... watched as your leader was devoured by a giant snake."

Mico gazed into the anxious faces. "This is about striking a blow so terrifying the enemy won't understand how mere monkeys could've achieved it."

"It's also suicidal," pointed out Cadby.

Joop and the other young monkeys laughed, relieved that someone had objected to the madness.

"I don't want to disappear down a python's gullet," agreed Twitcher. "Dying in battle's one thing, but a snake..." He shuddered at the thought.

"Fear is the point," replied Mico. "By conquering our own fears, we'll terrify the Langur all the more."

"But it's impossible!" exclaimed Cadby. "We can't catch a python – it'll kill us!"

"Look at the victories we've already pulled off," countered Mico. "Not so long ago you'd have said those were impossible too. How could a small band of refugees take on the Langur Empire? But we trained; we used our brains; we found a way. It's the same now. We know the objective ... all we have to do is think of a plan."

The monkeys exchanged anxious glances. This was so far outside their normal thinking they found it hard to make any kind of rational decision.

It was left to young Jola to break the deadlock. She turned to Gu-Nah and asked with disarming frankness, "Can it be done?"

The old warrior scratched his head thoughtfully. "Can it be done? I don't know. But if we *could* find a way... " A mischievous grin spread across his face.

So they talked.

They talked through the oppressive heat of midday, and through the torrential rain that deluged the City in the afternoon.

And as they talked, the python became less a terrifying monster and more a strategic problem. With the fear removed, the monkeys were able to roll the problem around their heads, experimenting with different approaches, treating the whole thing as a game.

Until gradually a plan started to emerge. A plan that was strong and bold, that held its shape no matter how hard it was prodded and pulled, a plan that stood a fighting chance of achieving the impossible.

Two days later, everything was in place. As Mico led his Rhesus fighters downtown on the roof of a tram, he'd never felt more proud.

Or more apprehensive. This time there was no margin for error.

As the tram pulled into the terminus, they jumped from the roof and scampered into the sidestreets, where they gathered round Fig protectively.

"Is there anything else you need?" Papina asked gently.

Fig shook her head.

"I'm sorry you have to face it on your own."

"Don't be sorry," replied Fig. "It's how it needs to be."

The monkeys fell silent.

"Well ..." Mico said, looking up at the sky, "we'd better get on with it."

Fig nodded. "Good luck."

"I think you need it more than us," he replied.

"We'll see."

Then Fig put her arms around Twitcher and held him tightly, for a few moments rekindling memories of happiness they'd once known.

"Live for me," she whispered.

Twitcher nodded silently, clinging to her fur, desperate to prolong the moment. But too soon, she let go.

"Goodbye," Fig said gently, then she turned and headed off on her lonely mission without even a backwards glance.

"Well, well," said Sweto with a malicious smile. "This really is our lucky day." He pointed across the bustling street; the Langur troopers with him looked over and were stunned to see a couple of Rhesus monkeys lazing in the sunshine.

Sweto knew that if he returned with enemy corpses he would be handsomely rewarded, but *live* captives who could be tortured and interrogated would secure his place as Tyrell's favourite.

The problem was, three against two didn't give them much advantage. In situations like this the protocol was clear: keep the enemy in sight and call for reinforcements.

But Sweto was too ambitious for protocol.

"Let's get them ... NOW!" he roared, and led his troopers charging across the street.

Which was exactly what Twitcher and Cadby wanted. Immediately they turned and bolted into a side alley, scampering as fast as they could. But the Langurs were faster, and as Twitcher and Cadby raced towards a fire escape at the far end of the alley, they heard Langur feet thundering through the puddles behind them, gaining ground with every heartbeat.

Cadby glanced over his shoulder, saw the angry faces and sharp incisors, saw the excitement of violence in the Langurs' eyes.

"Don't look!" roared Twitcher. "RUN!"

It jolted Cadby to his senses and he re-focussed on the fire escape, trying to ignore the pain splitting his lungs, the heaviness pulling at his legs.

Ten paces, five ... he had just reached out to grab the ladder when suddenly Rafa and Joop leapt down from a first-floor window, locked eyes with the pursuing Langurs and ran.

For a few confusing moments Sweto didn't know what to do. The two Rhesus they'd been chasing were tiring, but once up the ladder they'd have the run of the rooftops, where their size and lightness would give them the edge. The new Rhesus may be fresher but they were down here, and when it came to it one Rhesus scalp was as good as another.

"THEM!" Sweto commanded, and he charged along the alley after Rafa and Joop.

As the Langurs hurtled through the maze of backstreets their nostrils flared with bloodlust, their judgement clouded and they forgot about everything but the kill ... so, when they emerged into the dump and saw two monkeys standing on a mound of trash, they assumed these were the ones they'd been chasing. In their frenzy they scampered over the garbage hills, creating an avalanche of plastic.

Only when they were halfway across did Sweto realize that the Rhesus weren't trying to escape; they just stood there defiantly. He blinked in the hard morning light, looked closer, and saw that these were different monkeys – one Rhesus, and one Langur.

Could this really be the traitor Mico? Could Sweto now return with the greatest prize of all to offer Lord Tyrell?

But as quickly as hope raised its head, reality whistled past and cut it off at the neck – Sweto watched, open-mouthed, as two ropes dropped down, allowing Mico and the Rhesus to escape by scrambling up to some overhead cables.

Yet strangely, the monkeys didn't scamper along the wires and disappear; they just clung there, looking down, enthralled.

Sweto glanced around the dump, wondering what could be so interesting ... and then he heard the sound of movement close by.

The rubbish was stirring.

Sweto's spine tingled with fear, but it was already too late. In an almighty explosion of debris the monstrous python burst into the light and loomed over the monkeys.

The Langurs staggered backwards ... straight into the waiting coils of the snake's grotesquely long body. It happened so terrifyingly fast Sweto didn't even have time to put his thoughts in order.

A sudden jerk of the python's body and the monkeys were being dragged down towards the mysterious subterranean world under the trash.

They clawed at the rubbish, desperately trying to pull themselves back to the surface, but their efforts were pathetic against the strength of the mighty reptile.

As the garbage closed around him, Sweto looked up at the sky one last time; he glimpsed Mico, perched on the overhead wire, a look of triumph on his face, before a last violent tug dragged the Langur down into the darkness for ever.

"Now for the *really* tricky bit," said Mico.

He looked across to the roof team, Twitcher and Cadby, who signalled that everything was ready; Gu-Nah, who was going to do the drop, was already sliding out to take his place on the overhead wire; the remaining Rhesus lined the surrounding rooftops ready to intervene if the plan went wrong, although what they could possibly do against an angry python was anyone's guess.

With an almighty heave, Twitcher and Cadby started dragging a huge, rusty air-conditioning unit until it was teetering on the very edge of the roof, then they gave it a final kick and sent it tumbling down the side of the building.

The unit hit the trash and shock waves rippled through the garbage in all directions. There was no way the python hadn't felt the impact.

The monkeys waited fearfully for a reaction.

Nothing happened.

Mico dangled from the rope just above the surface, his eyes scouring the trash, braced for the slightest movement. Above him on the telephone wire, Gu-Nah held his breath; Papina watched from the roofline, wondering what could be taking so long.

Then they saw it.

Not a dramatic surge of power, but an irritable heave, as the python surfaced and looked around. Having just swallowed the first monkey, all it wanted was to digest in peace.

Mico screeched to attract its attention. The snake craned its head round and saw the lone monkey swinging from a rope just above the trash.

The python wavered, as if tempted to ignore this irritating creature.

Quickly Mico stretched out, picked up some tin cans and started hurling them at the snake.

That did the trick.

The python opened its mouth, stretching grotesquely wide then, with a heave of its gullet, started to regurgitate its meal. Covered in nauseous slime, Sweto's lifeless body gradually emerged from the python's mouth, feet first, limbs bunched together. As it disgorged, the python rolled onto its side to relieve the discomfort, until finally the monkey's head slid out, an eerily peaceful expression on its face.

Now the trouble could begin.

The snake dived under the surface.

Moments later its head shot vertically upwards, jaws fully dislocated, hurtling straight towards Mico, who scrambled up the rope in a desperate attempt to escape.

This was Gu-Nah's moment. He looked down into the python's mouth and stretched out his hand. The snake loomed closer and closer; Gu-Nah aimed ... and finally let the ball of hemlock root drop ... straight into the python's gullet.

Shocked at the unexpected morsel, the snake snapped its jaws shut and swallowed, disappointed not to be swallowing a monkey. Furious with frustration, and now at the limit of its reach, the python could only slump back onto the garbage, thrashing its body angrily.

Gu-Nah watched anxiously, looking for signs that the drug was taking effect. He had guessed that the same quantity of hemlock needed to kill three monkeys would put the huge snake to sleep, but it was just a guess.

The monkeys all watched with bated breath ... and then they saw the confusion kick in. The python swayed, looked left and right, its eyes struggling to focus. It shook its head, trying to clear its mind, but that just made everything worse.

"All right – let's take him for a walk!" Mico shouted, and immediately the Rhesus leapt down onto the trash and started running towards the rain-swollen storm gully.

The python craned its head round, but its drug-addled mind couldn't concentrate – all it could see was a confusion of running monkeys.

Attack. It had to attack. That was the only form of defence it knew. The python marshalled its will and slithered through the garbage in pursuit.

As the Rhesus converged on the storm gully, they scrambled onto two rafts they'd lashed together from discarded tyres, and pushed off into the angry waters.

Moments later they heard a splash – Mico turned and saw the python slide into the gully in pursuit.

"It's coming!" yelled Mico. "Hold tight!"

Desperately, the monkeys tried to keep the rafts in the fastest currents, steering with their hands, kicking away from the brick walls with their feet.

Whipping its huge body through the water, the python surged after them. Closing in with every thrash of its tail, it raised its head out of the water to strike, only to see the rafts veer off down a side gully.

Every attempt cost the python precious energy, which made the next strike even more difficult.

Mico could see the snake's strokes get weaker and weaker as the hemlock pumped around its body, until finally, too exhausted to carry on swimming, the python rolled to the side of the storm gully and let the currents wash it up onto the bank.

"PULL OVER!" Mico yelled.

Twitcher and Gu-Nah grabbed on to some overhanging branches while Papina and the others furiously paddled to the bank. Further downstream, the second raft saw them clamber ashore and swerved their raft so that it rammed to a stop against the pillar of a bridge, giving them a chance to scramble onto dry land.

The monkeys stood on the gully edge, soaking wet and trembling.

"Is it close enough?" Papina asked.

Gu-Nah peered through a gap in the buildings and glimpsed a section of the Cemetery wall a little way up the hill. "We can manage that."

"But only if the snake's really out," said Twitcher, looking anxiously at the motionless python sprawled over the gully bank upstream.

"One way to find out," said Mico, and he started edging towards the python.

Closer and closer he crept, his eyes locked on the snake, ready to bolt at the slightest movement ... until he was standing right next to the grotesquely small head with its cruel expression. He reached out and prodded the creature. Nothing.

He leaned closer, until he could smell the freshly killed meat on its breath ... in ... out... It was still breathing.

Mico beckoned urgently to the others, who immediately scrambled along the storm gully carrying a large muslin sack they'd stolen from a fruit warehouse the night before.

"Quick!" he urged. "We don't know how long we've got!"

And they all started coiling the python into the sack. It was unbelievably heavy, each armful a dead weight, and it took far longer than they'd planned.

They tied up the sack and slumped down to rest, but Mico knew there was no time.

"Up! UP!" he yelled. "Come on! We've got to get there before it comes round!"

And with weary legs, the monkeys started dragging the sack through the final few streets to the Cemetery, desperately hoping that the effects of the hemlock wouldn't wear off too soon.

53

END OF DAYS

It fell to Breri to deliver the ominous news that Sweto and his troopers had vanished. Tyrell didn't even try to hide his alarm – he slumped onto his haunches, cradling his head in his hands. He knew Sweto was too smart to get himself killed, but what if he'd been captured? What if the Rhesus were holding him hostage?

Tyrell's brow furrowed; he would not have his hand forced by a bunch of savages. If the enemy thought they could trade Sweto's life for some military advantage they were wrong. Everyone was disposable. Tyrell would just have to pluck another bright monkey from the Langur ranks and train him up. He'd done it before; he could do it again.

Suddenly he heard noises in the stairwell outside – General Pogo entered, breathless and animated.

"My Lord, we've captured one!" he exclaimed, as two Elites dragged a Rhesus monkey into the room and threw her to the floor. She was battered and bruised; it was clear the guards had already dispensed some street justice.

"She was in the bushes outside the perimeter wall."

"On her own?" demanded Tyrell.

"She was digging a hole, trying to tunnel under the wall. She had food – she was well prepared. She'll have information. But she's stubborn."

Tyrell strode over to the Rhesus and looked down at her small, defenceless body.

"I don't like stubborn," he said softly, then he reached out and yanked her head up. "Do you hear me?"

Fig looked back at him with fearless eyes.

Finally she was face to face with the monkey who had destroyed everything she loved.

"I've nothing to say," Fig said quietly.

Tyrell gave a curt laugh. "Trust me, everyone talks in the end."

This time the torture was personal.

Tyrell didn't indulge in the physical violence himself; he didn't have to – that was left to the brutes of the recently established Special Interrogation Unit. They had a formidable array of techniques, from the basic beatings and lacerations to the removal of teeth and claws. The really high-level practitioners had developed a whole set of water-related techniques that simulated the horror of drowning.

Pain, however, was not always enough. The braver the monkey, the greater the risk that pain would harden their defiance; these monkeys would rather die than be broken. But a dead monkey could tell no tales, and information was invariably what Tyrell craved. So he developed his own unique torture technique: mental violence.

Tyrell's trick was to make everything unpredictable. Sometimes he would present himself as the bringer of pain, ordering brutal beatings; at other times he would pose as the victim's friend, stopping the torture to offer respite with water or soothing herbs. As soon as the victim thought they understood the rules, he would change them, then change them again; until the victim could conceive of no authority except Tyrell's, no reality outside the dark room in which they were held.

No monkey was strong enough to withstand this destruction of their identity.

Except Fig.

She had been forged by something much crueller. The pain tearing through her body at the hands of the Langur torturers became penance – every blow, every drop of blood somehow eased the agonizing pressure of her own guilt.

Soon it would all be over. Finally she would know peace again.

But not quite yet.

"Enough." Her voice croaked as she spat some blood onto the floor.

A warm glow of satisfaction welled up in Tyrell's heart; no monkey had the strength to defy him. He nodded to the torturers, who withdrew to the shadows at the edge of the room, then he crouched down next to Fig's beaten body and gently stroked her head like an indulgent father.

"Speak."

"Kidnap ..." rasped Fig, "kidnap you."

This was hardly a surprise. As the entire Langur Empire looked to Tyrell for leadership, it was only logical to try and seize him.

"Ambitious. But impossible with my security."

"Informant," Fig coughed the word out.

Tyrell glared down at her.

"Informant," she rasped again. "We know ... your movements ... hiding places."

Tyrell felt his confidence start to ebb away. He lashed out, grabbed Fig and hauled her up.

"Who?!" he demanded.

Fig couldn't help smiling – seeing fear grip Tyrell was so rewarding.

"WHO?!" he screamed, infuriated. "WHO IS BETRAYING ME?!"

But Fig just shook her head weakly. "Don't know... Mico knew. Only Mico."

That name again, coming back to haunt him.

Mico, Mico, Mico.

Like a swarm of insects eating away at his mind.

Mico, Mico, Mico.

Pulling him to pieces, devouring him alive.

"NO!" Tyrell roared, as uncontrollable rage convulsed him. He watched as his own hands grabbed Fig's head and smashed it down on the floor, venting his fear and frustration on the contemptible monkey.

But once was not enough. His hands had a will of their own, and they brought her head smashing down again ... and again ... until Tyrell felt a warm trickle of blood ooze over his fingers.

Only then did he stop, breathless, drained of all emotion.

"Interrogation over," he said quietly.

This was why it was right to be paranoid, because you really couldn't trust anyone. Tyrell had long suspected there was a traitor in his ranks. What else could explain the string of military victories the Rhesus had enjoyed?

Whoever it was, he would root them out and punish them without mercy. But right now the important thing was to out-manoeuvre them.

As the plan was kidnap, Tyrell had to assume that the informant had told the Rhesus where he was supposed to be on that day – meeting with his Council of War in the Summer-house. Which meant that Tyrell's best stategy was to give the impression that nothing had changed, that his routine was carrying on as normal, while secretly ordering General Pogo to re-deploy the army to the Eastern Province, where they could set a trap to catch Mico and his Rhesus insurgents as they made their kidnap attempt.

To complete the deception Tyrell made a big show of going to his rooms at the top of the Summer-house; but covertly he doubled back and, with a handful of his most trusted Twopoint guards, made his way across the City to the Cemetery. There Tyrell withdrew to the innermost sanctum of the Great Vault, and positioned his body-guards at all the entrances.

Finally he was starting to understand how to defeat the Rhesus. They never struck the same target twice – and now Tyrell would use their tactic for his own ends. The Great Vault had already been attacked once, making it the safest place to hide. All he had to do was wait for word from the Summer-house that Mico's forces had walked into the trap.

After an exhausting trudge dragging the snake-sack behind them, the Rhesus arrived at the spot where the spring bubbled under the Cemetery wall. Mico, Twitcher and Joop went through first, diving down into the brown stench, groping their way to the hole and hauling themselves up inside the Cemetery.

Mico's eyes darted everywhere, looking for guards and patrols, but all was quiet.

"She did it!" He put a reassuring hand on Twitcher's shoulder. "Fig's thrown them all the wrong way."

Twitcher gave a thin smile; the Langur may have taken the bait, but what would they do to Fig when they found out they'd been tricked?

In the street outside, Gu-Nah, Papina and the others plunged the snake-sack into the water and forced it through the hole. Moments later, the whole attack squad was inside the Cemetery walls, but the sack was now twitching restlessly – the shock of the cold water had started to revive the python. They had to hurry.

With the civilian Langurs sheltering from the downpour in their homes, the squad made swift and silent progress to the Great Vault, where they attached vines to the snake-sack and hauled it up and over the roof, dropping it down into the seclusion of the Vault.

Papina, Gu-Nah and Cadby sprinted on ahead to eliminate Tyrell's bodyguards, while Mico, Twitcher and the others started to drag the writhing sack towards Tyrell's inner sanctum. With every heartbeat the python recovered its strength and tensed its huge muscles, trying to rip its way out.

Tyrell sat hunched up, deep in thought, trying to work out the identity of the informant. Despite his anger at having to root out another traitor, he couldn't suppress a tingle of excitement, because the chance for total victory was finally within his grasp. If Pogo and Breri could slaughter the Rhesus in the Eastern Province, the Monkey Wars would be over.

Finally Tyrell would know the peace of absolute power, all monkeys would look up to him in awe, his authority would be—

The door flew open with a *crack*.

Tyrell spun round, and was aghast – standing in the doorway were Mico and Gu-Nah, the two monkeys he feared and hated above all others.

"Guards!" yelled Tyrell. "Guards!!!"

"Dead," said Mico calmly. "All gone. There was no informant. Your army is in the wrong place. There's no one here to save you now."

Tyrell felt the pounding in his head return.

He had to defend himself, fight back. Desperately he marshalled his thoughts. Divide the enemy. Plant seeds of doubt, set one against the other.

Tyrell shook himself and cast a withering look at Mico and Gu-Nah.

"A broken old soldier and a deceitful coward," he scoffed. "Do you really think a couple of weak and ragged outcasts can challenge the greatest empire in monkeykind?"

"I'll tell you about strength," Mico replied. "About Fig, who volunteered to face your torturers."

Slowly he advanced on Tyrell, each footstep driving home his words. "She is a monkey who has been robbed of everything, but who has the strength to turn despair into a will as hard as stone."

Tyrell cocked his head defiantly. "If she's that strong, why is she dead?"

The words hit Mico and Gu-Nah like a blow. Listening outside the room, Twitcher slumped to the floor and let out a soft howl of grief. Papina put her arms round him, desperately trying to offer some solace.

"Oh, you didn't think she'd actually survived?" said Tyrell, amused that, even when backed into a corner, he could shatter hopes. "I dealt with her myself."

Mico steeled his nerves. Painful as Fig's death was, they had to see this through, or her death would be in vain.

"There's no greater strength than self-sacrifice," he said, eyes locked on Tyrell. "Search as long as you like, you'll never find that kind of courage in your Langur."

Tyrell sneered and turned away but Mico grabbed him, forcing him to listen. "That's why we will win."

The tyrant wriggled angrily, pushing Mico away. "Order, hierarchy, discipline, obedience!" Tyrell snapped. "That's what strength is. That's what builds a great empire—"

"Which is rotten from top to bottom!"

"And what would you have? A bunch of outcasts scrabbling in the dirt for a few berries? Is that your vision for the future?"

"All you've created is a monster that crushes monkeys to your will," retorted Mico. "There's no freedom in your world. Everything is about serving you."

"You should have stayed in the belly of the beast. Then it could have been about serving *you* as well," said Tyrell.

For a brief moment he remembered the dream he'd once had of ruling with Mico at his side, the two of them like brothers, sharing everything. How the hurt of Mico's betrayal still rankled.

"Your 'heroic fight' is nothing but envy," Tyrell declared with contempt.

"There's nothing heroic about my fight," Mico said, with the guilt of a confession. "It's not envy, but shame that torments me. Shame that I helped you grab power by treading on the necks of others."

"My world works," Tyrell said, his patience wearing thin with all this moralizing. "My monkeys are safe. They have food in their mouths."

"At what cost?"

"There's always a cost. Just as there's always a will in command. And my will is to see you and your rabble destroyed."

Mico shook his head slowly. "Not this time."

He signalled to Papina and Twitcher, who dragged the writhing sack into the room.

Tyrell looked at it, puzzled, trying to work out what was heaving so violently inside. Then he heard the sound of cotton tearing as the seams started to split.

And he glimpsed scales. Snake scales.

Fear seized Tyrell as he understood the size and anger of the creature that was bursting out of the sack. He looked up and saw Mico, Papina and Gu-Nah backing away, leaving him to face the monster alone.

"Kill me, and someone else will rise up to take my place!" Tyrell shouted, his voice wavering with fear. "You can't change the nature of monkeys – they are born to be led! Monkeys are followers! It's what they do! It's what keeps them safe!"

Mico took one last look at the raging tyrant as the python's head finally tore out of the sack. It spun round, trying to shake off the confusion of the hemlock, but nothing made sense. It had no conception of where it was or what had happened. Overwhelmed by confusion, the python could only do one thing – attack.

Mico slammed the door shut. Moments later a terrible scream reverberated from inside the room.

"NO!!!"

It was pure, primal fear.

The door shook on its hinges.

Mico and Gu-Nah gripped the handle tightly, desperate to contain the snake.

And then a scratching sound – fingernails clawing against the wood, desperate to escape.

Mico clamped his eyes shut, trying to hold his nerve. The scratching speeded up, frantic, terrified, then a strangled gasp ... then silence.

Mico and Gu-Nah strained their ears at the door – they heard the heavy, sinister *swoosh* of the python's body moving across the stone floor, but nothing else.

"It's done," whispered Gu-Nah.

Still Mico gripped the door handle, refusing to let go, his knuckles white. Gently, Gu-Nah prised his hands away, then opened the door a crack.

They peered into the room and saw the python's jaws wrapped around Tyrell's body, its gullet distending obscenely as it swallowed the tyrant whole.

The monkey who had unleashed such terror and cruelty on the City was now reduced to nothing more than a lump of meat. One final suck and his feet vanished for ever.

"At last…" Mico whispered.

"Ssh!" Gu-Nah held his finger to his lips, urging Mico to be quiet, but it was too late. The python whipped its head round, saw Mico and Gu-Nah and lunged towards them.

The monkeys stumbled backwards and ran through the Vault, back towards the main entrance, with the writhing snake in furious pursuit.

"NOW!" screamed Gu-Nah to Cadby, who hauled open the Vault doors, unleashing the python on the Cemetery and all its inhabitants.

54

CARNAGE

The Twopoint guards shivering in the rain didn't know what to do. Alarmed by the strange sounds from inside the Vault, they had sent word to the Eastern Province for reinforcements, but that would take time ... and as the Vault doors swung open they realized that time was the one thing they didn't have.

As the senior guard peered into the Vault, the python's head thundered out of the gloom and blasted into his chest.

He staggered backwards, but with terrifying speed a loop of muscle whipped around him. The last thing he saw was the cold eyes of death bearing down on him as the snake's mouth yawned wide, clamped on to his head and flicked him sideways.

The python swung left and right, its furious cold gaze surveying the walled Cemetery, tongue flashing in and out, picking up the scent of dozens of monkeys near by.

As the snake surged into the mass of tombs, Mico, Papina, Gu-Nah and Twitcher scrambled into the tree canopy and took up positions on the overhead wires. Even from here they could feel the shock wave of fear bowling across the Cemetery.

The python moved with terrifying speed, its sheer size giving the impression that it was everywhere at once. While its head thrust into one tomb, savaging the cowering occupants, its body coiled round those from another tomb, crushing them as they tried to run; the tail thrashed through the air like a demented limb, groping for anything it could catch, and its unblinking eyes searched every shadow and hiding place.

Utterly beyond reason, the python had gone into enraged frenzy, killing anything that moved, offering no second chance.

General Pogo and Breri heard the terrified hysteria when they were still a few streets away. Birds screeched frantic alarm calls as they circled the treetops. Stray dogs in nearby alleys took up the call. Even the rats hurried away.

Pogo's troops heaved on the gates and entered the Cemetery. There were no monkeys anywhere. The Rhesus terrorists must be hiding.

Silently, the General deployed his troops: Breri would take a team of Elites around the base of the perimeter wall to outflank the enemy, while Pogo would lead the main thrust straight down the Central Pathway.

They pushed into the Cemetery, senses bristling, eyes scanning the undergrowth for the slightest movement. The only place they weren't looking was behind them.

Cadby, Joop and Jola sprang down from a tree and swung the massive gates shut, as more Rhesus emerged from under the wheels of a cart and rolled it across, barricading the gates shut.

The troops at the back of the Langur column saw they had been shut in, but obedience had been drilled into them so thoroughly they didn't dare act without orders. All they could do was send word back up the ranks; by the time General Pogo knew what had happened it was too late – the Langur army was trapped.

"SNAKE!" One of the Elites pointed to the diagonal path where scales could be seen slithering past the gaps between the tombs.

"THERE IT IS!" cried another trooper, pointing in the opposite direction.

Instinctively the Elites huddled together, not knowing which way to run.

Then a dark shadow fell over them. They looked up and saw the python's huge body rearing up in front of them, furious and unrelenting.

The snake slammed its body down on the terrified column of monkeys, crushing and scattering without pity.

Some made it to the trees, but as they clambered up the branches they met the fists of Rhesus fighters dropping down on them with savage ferocity, biting and clawing until the Langurs lost their grip and tumbled through the air, smacking onto the hard ground.

Seeing the ferocity of the attack, Breri cut accross towards the main path. "The General's in trouble!" he shouted.

But when he turned to urge his troops on, he saw them scatter in a terrified disarray. The python had smashed all military discipline; it was every monkey for himself now.

In utter bewilderment, Breri looked up at the overhead wires, and saw Mico perched with his band of Rhesus followers. For a moment the two brothers locked eyes. Breri blinked, hoping that despite everything, his brother would show him some way to escape the carnage. But Mico didn't flinch.

A horrified scream rent the air, jolting Breri to his senses. He looked across, saw the python encircling the remains of Pogo's team, and he quickly darted in the opposite direction, searching for refuge.

Pogo and the python finally came eye to eye in the shadow of the Great Vault. As the snake closed in, its huge body cutting off any chance of escape, Pogo realized with a heavy heart that all he had to show for a life of loyalty and obedience was this moment, staring down the gullet of death.

In those last few seconds, the General finally understood that he should have been fighting a different battle all along, that strength and power were two different things.

But it was too late now.

He closed his eyes and waited for the end to come – he had lived long enough.

Mico and his fighters looked down on the carnage like spectators at some grim performance.

The unflagging cruelty of the python was mesmerizing – each new kill was swept onto a gruesome pile of monkey corpses outside the Great Vault. Some it would eat later; most would rot. This wasn't about food – it was about annihilation. The python had decided that the Cemetery would be its new home, and it would hunt and destroy anything that moved inside the walls.

Kill after kill, the Rhesus watched in silence; they had waited a long time for this moment; they were owed this hour of reckoning.

As word of the massacre spread through the City, civilian Langurs from the Eastern Province hurried to the

Cemetery ... but they didn't join the fight. They could see that their entire army was being crushed into oblivion.

More frightening than the snake itself was the knowledge that somehow Mico and the Rhesus had brought a great python under their control and unleashed it on the Lord Ruler.

When Mico finally looked up from the carnage, he saw a mass of petrified Langur faces gazing at him from the surrounding rooftops ... swarms of them, and not one who dared to raise a fist against his small band of conquering warriors.

55

PEACE...

The door creaked open and daylight penetrated the darkness. At first nothing; no movement, no sound, just the rancid stench of imprisonment.

Mico peered into the gloom, clinging to the hope that in these last few cells he would be spared the worst horrors of the tyranny. As his eyes scoured the darkness, he heard a faint gasp.

"Mico..." The voices were so weak they were barely audible, but it was enough to know they were still alive.

"It's safe now," Mico said gently.

He knew he mustn't rush them; they had to emerge slowly from the depths of captivity. He stepped away from the door and listened to the feet shuffling closer. Then slowly, eyes squinting, two monkeys crawled into the light of freedom.

Mico felt the strength drain from his body as he looked at the degraded figures of his parents. He drew his arms around Trumble and Kima, and held them tightly. It was a far cry from the triumphant liberation Mico had always imagined.

For an age they just crouched there, huddled in silence, terrified that if they spoke it would shatter this dream.

Only when he was sitting in the warm sunlight of the Great Lawn was Trumble finally able to thank his son.

His voice thick with emotion, he reached his hand up to touch Mico's face.

"You came back for us ... when everyone else had given up."

"Of course I came back."

Mico hesitated, looked down, then finally found the courage to ask, "And Hister?"

Trumble knew the very least he owed his son was the truth. "She gave up."

"She's dead?" whispered Mico, the guilt rising in his gut.

Trumble shook his head. "She gave up on *you*. She collaborated."

"Where is she now?"

But Trumble just shook his head. "We heard nothing in the darkness of the cell. Nothing."

Mico hadn't seen Hister in the fighting, nor in the crowds that lined the paths of the Eastern Province as the conquering Rhesus had marched in. She had vanished. Now he would never know what had become of her; it was another regret marring his triumph.

But there were no regrets for most of the Rhesus, who relished their total victory.

Victory, though, gave them a whole new problem: what to do with all the conquered monkeys?

"Vengeance," said Twitcher uncompromisingly, his voice resonating in the Summer-house, where the Rhesus had gathered for a debate about the future. "Before anything else, the guilty must be punished." He had hoped for a rousing cheer of support, but it didn't come. A few Rhesus nodded their agreement, but to most his dark tone was at odds with the sense of relief that the war was over.

"Surely we had our vengeance when we defeated their army," said Mico.

"Easy for you to say," snapped Twitcher. "You didn't lose everything." He looked around the room, his eyes challenging anyone to question his right to hate the Langur. "Papina, your parents were murdered by them. You must understand?"

She nodded sympathetically. "No one's suffered more than you ... but Fig knew what she was doing."

"Then we should honour that and take our vengeance."

"Tyrell is dead, his regime destroyed," said Mico emphatically.

"But it wasn't just Tyrell," retorted Twitcher. "You said it yourself – they *all* knew what was going on. Every single Langur took food from Tyrell, sent their young to join his army, cheered his victories. They were all collaborators; now they have to answer for it."

"How?" asked Papina with disarming simplicity. "With another massacre? Is that really what Fig died for?"

"I didn't fight just to forgive!" cried Twitcher.

"We fought so that truth could prevail," said Mico. "And it will. Each and every Langur needs to confess their role in Tyrell's regime, acknowledge they were wrong—"

"Talking!" Twitcher spat the word out with contempt. "Is that it? Just talking!"

"He held them in his sway!" Mico insisted. "You can't imagine what it was like to be caught up in that rush of power."

"*You* broke free. *They* didn't." Twitcher pointed out of the window indignantly. "Which is why they're guilty."

Papina looked anxiously from Mico to Twitcher. Now that the pressures of battle were lifted, the cracks of old rivalries were opening up again. "I share your anger," she said, trying to ease the tension, "but I don't think it's going to help."

She swung over to one of the windows and looked pensively out across the lawns where groups of Langurs were huddled together. "Look at them. It's like they've woken from a dream. A nightmare. Monkeys question – it's what we do. We question and we test; we break and we discover. It's messy, but it's what makes us what we are. Tyrell made them forget that."

Papina turned back to the Rhesus. "If we storm out there and punish, kill, exile, their instincts will be to fight back. But if we give them the space to see what they've done, to understand how they betrayed themselves..." She looked at Twitcher. "To win the war we needed to believe that all Langurs were guilty, but to win the peace we need to believe that most of them are innocent."

She sat down, letting her words do their work, and one by one the monkeys started to tap the ground with their fists. Tentatively the support grew until the room reverberated with the sound of thumping.

There were notable exceptions – Twitcher sat immobile and silent; Cadby crossed his arms defiantly, refusing to join in the applause; young Joop also sat in silence – he too felt that the war would not be finished until more Langur blood had been shed.

For now, though, the dissenters would have to remain silent. The majority of Rhesus favoured reconciliation, so that became the new policy.

The argument had rattled Mico. There was so much to sort out – food supplies, living quarters, security, education – all of which depended on Rhesus and Langur living together peacefully.

"Can this really work?" he asked Papina as they walked across the Great Lawn.

"Whatever we do, it has to be better than Tyrell's cruelty," she said calmly.

"We may just have replaced order with chaos."

"Stop!" Papina looked at him, her eyes dancing with conviction. "Don't talk like that. Now we can dare to hope – and that's progress."

"You can't eat hope," said Mico.

Papina laughed. "You'd be surprised how long it can keep you going."

As a surprise, she had prepared Tyrell's old room at the top of the Summer-house Tower for the two of them and, without another word, she took Mico by the hand and led him there.

It was beautiful, dressed with fruits and flowers, scented with spices, the floor covered with fresh palm leaves.

As Mico and Papina lay together that afternoon, the rest of the world faded away ... there was nothing but the two of them.

Mico woke with a start. He could tell from the background noise of the City that it was the dead of night, but for the first time in many moons he didn't feel tired.

Gently he disentangled himself from Papina's embrace, took a refreshing drink from the water bowl, and gazed at the carved map on the wall where Tyrell had laid out his vision of the City without Humans. Now that the regime was toppled, you could see the map for what it really was – a deluded work of insanity.

How could anyone ever have taken it seriously? But they had. The entire Langur Troop followed Tyrell way beyond the realms of reason.

Just to reassure himself that the City remained unmolested, Mico walked to the window to breathe in the sticky night air.

A mist hung above the rooftops diffusing the lights and bathing everything in a surreal glow. It was strange to look across the skyline and not fear what was out there, to enjoy the view without planning an escape route. Peace would take some getting used to.

Then just as he turned back, Mico saw a movement down on the Lawns. He peered into the gloom ... and gradually his eyes started to make out figures sitting silently under the night sky. The more he stared, the more monkeys he saw ... family after family ... the whole Troop of Langur monkeys had gathered and were all staring up at him, as if in a trance.

"What are you waiting for?" Mico called down to them. His question was met with silence, as if none of them dared speak.

"Tell me!" Mico called out, now starting to feel a little unnerved. "What are you waiting for?"

And then an anonymous voice from deep in the crowd replied, "You. We're waiting for you."

The crowd of monkeys all murmured their agreement.

Mico was puzzled. His eyes ran across their faces, the masses of white eyes blinking up at him.

Then a cold shiver ran down his spine, as Mico realized that all these monkeys, silent and obedient, were waiting to be led.

As he stared at the passive faces, he saw that they wanted to be told what to think, how to think, when to think. They wanted to be told right from wrong. They wanted to be given a set of rules carved in stone that they could meekly follow.

Nausea rose from the pit of Mico's stomach as he sensed the utter futility of his victory. He had brought a tyrant down, only to find that at the deepest level, the Langur didn't want freedom at all.

The corruption wasn't just Tyrell or his henchmen; it was the weakness in the monkeys' own hearts.

The tyrant's dying words rang, painful and shrill, in Mico's ears: *Kill me, and someone else will rise up to take my place...*

"No. NO. NO!" He staggered back from the window, gripped by panic.

"Mico!"

He spun round and saw Papina standing in the gloom.

"What's wrong?" she said, clasping him. She could feel him trembling, as if he had a fever. "Talk to me!"

"It's not over. It'll never be over," he whispered.

"Shhh. Calm down," she said, stroking his brow. "Everything's going to be fine."

He looked up at her, his face creased with a terrible sadness, and shook his head. "Tyrell was right: monkeys are born to be led."

He slumped down in shame.

Gently, firmly, Papina put her hands around him, lifted him up and looked into his eyes. "You're wrong, Mico. You have to be."

"They don't want freedom—"

"How can they want what they've never had?" she insisted. "Freedom is the thing to live and die for. It was strong enough to bring down a tyrant." She cradled his face lovingly in her hands. "Trust me, once the Langur taste freedom, they'll never want to lose it."

Mico put his arms around Papina and held her tightly, hoping from the depths of his soul that she was right.

* * *

There was one Langur who held his nerve as the python stalked the Cemetery – Breri.

Hiding under a tombstone, he waited until nightfall when the snake was so gorged it could barely move, then he scrambled up an old vine, vaulted over the wall and scampered off into the labyrinth of backstreets.

If he'd been wise, Breri would have chosen to disappear and live out his life as a lone exile. But there was anger burning inside him now, anger that his brother had destroyed a great empire and stolen his life.

Breri refused to accept that everything was lost. He would not take the outrage of this massacre meekly. He would be avenged on Mico and all his accomplices.

Maybe, by some miracle, other Langurs had survived. And maybe they shared his rage...

A few streets away, a young female Langur sat huddled in the shadows of a derelict statue of some long-forgotten colonial leader. In her arms was a newborn infant, a male who looked just like his father.

Hister had been betrayed by everyone. All she had now was this baby monkey, and she gazed at him with pure, untainted love. She didn't know what the future held for him. But as she looked into his big round eyes, innocent of all the troubles that had condemned him to be an outcast, Hister vowed that her son would not grow up scavenging in the Slums.

But she also knew she could do nothing on her own. She needed to find like-minded souls to help her.

Mico sensed the change just after dawn. The air had suddenly become dry and crisp; all the heaviness had gone.

The Monsoon was finally over.

He looked out of the window. A brilliant blue sky arched over the City; there wasn't a cloud in sight. It was as if they'd all fled in the night.

Mico smiled to himself. Maybe this time the rain clouds had gone for ever.

Maybe there would be no more storms and floods.

Maybe.

THE END